HE COMPLETES ME

(2ND EDITION)

Not even his mother's funeral can convince self-proclaimed party boy Zach Johnson to tone down his snark or think about settling down. He is who he is, and he refuses to change for anyone. When straight-laced, compassionate Aaron Paulson claims he's falling for him, Zach is certain Aaron sees him as another project, one more lost soul for the idealistic Aaron to save. But Zach doesn't need to be fixed and he refuses to be with someone who sees him as broken.

Patience is one of Aaron's many virtues. He has waited years for a man who can share his heart and complete his life and he insists Zach is the one. Pride, fear, and old hurts wither in the wake of Aaron's adoring loyalty, and as Zach reevaluates his perceptions of love and family, he finds himself tempted to believe in the impossible: a happily-ever-after.

Word Count: 94,711

COPYRIGHT

REVIEWS

Home Again by Cardeno C.: The level of connection, the pace of the story and the characters is truly amazing.

— Redz World Reviews

Just What the Truth Is by Cardeno C.: An incredible story that is charming, loving, witty, humorous, touching and moving. I would recommend this to everyone who wants a story that leaves you with a happy warm heart, a smile on your face and a sheen of tears in your eyes. Get this book, a bottle of wine and curl up on your sofa and enjoy a brilliant story.

— MM Good Book Reviews

Love at First Sight by Cardeno C.: This is a beautiful story for anyone who believes in love at first sight. Jonathan is a wonderful character who, with his childlike outlook, opens up to the true beauty of the world for the reader. ... This is one truly memorable story!

— Fallen Angel Reviews

The One Who Saves Me by Cardeno C.: This author has a way of making every story unique, sexy, loving, emotional, and just plain wonderful. 'The One

Who Saves Me' centers around a deep and abiding friendship that begins to change and the issues that can arise. ... I'm running out of words to express how very much I love this author's work.

— *Rainbow Book Reviews*

Walk With Me by Cardeno C.: I have really enjoyed this entire series and this book was a perfect addition. Eli and Seth will quickly grab your hearts as they take you on their journey that spans over a decade.... It was the perfect completion of their friendship and the start of their love affair. It was also the perfect way to end our stay in Emile City.

— *Prism Book Alliance*

Where He Ends and I Begin by Cardeno C.: Where He Ends and I Begin is a heartwarming, sexy, sensual story. Cardeno C. writes with poise and passion, tenderness and love.

— *TLA Gay*

DEDICATION

Thank you to the kind readers who encouraged me to publish my work.
I wouldn't have had the courage to do this without your support.
And to Jayden Brooks, who has Aaron's heart and
Zach's perseverance. Thank you for everything.

CHAPTER ONE

"COME ON, Zach. This is going a little overboard, even for you."

My friend, Luke, sat on a closed toilet lid, watching me apply eyeliner. I held the pencil back and looked over at him.

"What? I am who I am. I'm not going to change for them. I told them that when I left, and there's no fucking way I'm going to change now."

Luke sighed and put his head in his hands, elbows resting on his knees.

"I know, Zach. I'm not telling you to change. I'd never do that. But this isn't a club opening, it's a funeral." He paused, looked me up and down, and then repeated himself with more emphasis. "It's your *mother's* funeral."

I shrugged and finished my eyeliner. He was right, of course. The look I was going for here wasn't just a *little* overboard—a skin-tight, pink tank top and white pants that weren't any looser. I'd also gotten my brown hair frosted for the occasion. Frankly, I didn't like it. I preferred the natural color. But I knew it would help complete the picture.

I was driven out of my family for being gay, and I was going to make damn sure they didn't think they had succeeded in causing me to question myself or to hate who I was. I was going to walk in there confident and proud— and as gay-looking as I could possibly make myself. That way, there could be no question in their minds that I was living my life on my terms. And that I wasn't ashamed, even if they were.

Luke gave up on talking to me about my appearance, realizing it was a hopeless cause. We had been friends since high school, and he knew me pretty well. I'd moved away after graduation and then stayed away. There was nothing for me back here. My family had pretty much disowned me when they found out I was gay, and I hadn't had a lot of friends growing up. I stayed in touch with Luke and a couple of other people that mattered in my life, and that was good enough.

"So, I'm sorry that you can't stay here but with Chris and me both living in this six hundred square foot studio, there isn't any room for guests. Next time you're in town, I'm sure we'll be in a bigger place, and then you can crash with us as long as you want."

I finished applying the eyeliner, put some slightly shiny gloss on my lips and grooming clay in my hair, and then turned back to Luke. From the look on his face, I could tell he didn't approve. But he was done trying to talk some sense into me. Smart guy.

"Don't worry about it. I should stay with Dean anyway. When he called to tell me our mother had died and begged me to come to her funeral, I told him that I'd see what I could do. Of course that meant thanks, but no thanks. But then he pulled out the nephew card and reminded me that I haven't met his kids. Since I plan on leaving tomorrow, staying at his place is about the only way I can spend any time with them."

I picked up my toiletry bag, walked out of the bathroom and over to Luke's couch, where I'd put my duffel when we walked in. He had picked me up at the airport and agreed to let me change at his place before dropping me off at my brother's house, where I'd be joining the rest of his family for the drive over to the mortuary. After I put the toiletry bag away, I turned to Luke.

"Not that I know shit about kids anyway, but Dean was practically crying on the phone, asking me to come and telling me they have plenty of room to put me up. I'm actually surprised he doesn't mind exposing his faggot brother to his children, because, as you know, all gay men are pedophiles."

Luke cringed.

"Jesus, Zach. Did he actually say that to you?"

I thought back to my conversations with Dean over the years. There hadn't been many, so it didn't take long to go through the catalog in my mind. I shrugged.

"Well, no. Not directly. But I heard variations of that theme from my stepfather, my mother, her parents, etc., etc., etc." I waved my hand as I spoke. "Dean was out of the house by then, so he didn't have the chance to jump on the bandwagon." I picked up my bag and opened the door. "But if I'm really fucking lucky, maybe he'll get his two cents in tonight. I think he at least has the manners to wait until after the funeral. Come on. We need to get going. I can't wait for the fun to start!"

I walked down the stairs and tried to calm my nerves. I was quiet on the drive over, reminding myself in my head that I was a grown man. They didn't control my life, and there was nothing that they could do to hurt me, not anymore. The last part wasn't completely true, of course, but I kept repeating it to myself anyway. I'd been telling myself that same thing for years.

"All right, Zach. We're here. How's that for door-to-door service?"

I looked up at the pretty Tudor-style house. There were flowers planted in window boxes and pots, a green lawn, toys on the front porch, and a white picket fence. I felt like I'd arrived at a Norman Rockwell painting.

That was typical of my brother. Mister Perfect. He was a jock and a good student in high school. Then he went off to college, got his doctorate in English, married a pretty blond cheerleader-type, had three kids, and moved back to teach at the local college.

I knew all of this from the e-mails Dean had sent over the years, and from the very brief, very sporadic telephone calls. I had a rule where I forced myself to return at least ten percent of his calls. Seriously, what the fuck did we have to say to each other? The ten percent was painful enough.

Dean was six years older than me, and it wasn't all that long after he moved away that my family wrote me off. Oh, they let me stay in the house, fed me, clothed me. Basically did what they were legally obligated to do, along with some shit that was definitely not legal. But I wouldn't let myself think about that, not anymore.

"Thanks for the ride, Luke. I'm glad I got to see you." I opened the door and stepped out of the car. "I'm sorry I didn't get a chance to meet Chris. He sounds great, and I'm happy you met someone."

I didn't mean that. I didn't believe in relationships. Fuck buddies, yes. But open relationships never worked, and monogamy was not a natural life as far as I was concerned. Why limit yourself to one guy? Variety was the spice of life, after all.

"Well, you can meet him next time you're here."

I raised my eyebrows at him in a look that clearly said that was never going to happen. Not because I didn't want to meet Chris, but because I was never fucking coming back. I actually considered asking him to drive me to the airport right then, but my brother's door flew open, and he came running out to greet me.

"Zach! I'm so glad you're here. Thank you for coming." He took me into his arms and hugged me tightly. "Where are your bags? I'll carry them in for you."

I pointed to the bag on the backseat.

He furrowed his brows. "That...that's it? Just the one bag?"

I could hear the disappointment in his voice. What was that about? Did he expect me to bring a bunch of gifts for his kids? I wasn't even sure how old they were. Actually, I stood there trying to remember their names.

Dean picked up the bag, slung it over his shoulder, and held his hand out to Luke. "Luke, right? I'm Dean Johnson, Zach's brother. Thanks for getting him from the airport. I offered to pick him up but—"

"No problem, Dean. It's nice to meet you. Call me later, Zach."

And with that, my friend drove away and left me at the gates of hell, deceptively decorated to look like a Martha Stewart magazine.

CHAPTER TWO

"KIMBERLY IS excited to finally meet you, Zach." Dean put his arm over my shoulder and walked me to the door. "So are the boys. Simon has been telling all his friends at school that his Uncle Zach is coming to see him."

Yeah, right. Like the kid gave a shit about me coming. Or, for that matter, like the kid even knew who I was. Oh well. At least now I remembered that the oldest one was named Simon. We walked into the house, and I was greeted by an overly enthusiastic blond fireball. I think she practically wrapped her legs around me as she hugged me. On the plus side, she was so short that I actually felt tall for the first time in my life.

My brother was almost six feet tall, like my dad was. But I got the genes from my mother's side of the family, so I barely cleared five and a half feet. I was also thin, which added to the whole "little guy" picture. I spent a good bit of time swimming and running, so I had defined muscles. And I ate constantly, but I couldn't seem to put on any bulk.

"Kim, I'm going to put Zach's bag in his room. Do you want to see if he wants a drink before we head out?"

She nodded and turned to me with a smile, taking

my hand in hers and leading me to the kitchen. "What can I get you, Zach? We have regular soda, diet soda, iced tea, juice, and milk. Or would you rather change first?"

I immediately dropped her hand and stiffened.

"Why would I change? Is there a problem with my clothes?"

Okay, my reaction and the rude tone weren't fair. I didn't know Kimberly, and she seemed perfectly nice, if a bit too peppy. Still, I was all geared up for a fight. And I wasn't going to back down.

Her face flushed, the red color creeping up her cheeks. "Oh! No, of course there's nothing wrong with your clothes. I, ummm, I... What did you say you wanted to drink?"

I was about to ask for a diet soda, but then we walked into the kitchen, and I felt like all the air left my body, and my mouth went dry. There, sitting at the kitchen table, was a man who literally took my breath away. Dirty blond hair. Warm blue eyes. Broad shoulders. Muscular chest. I couldn't tell how tall he was, because he was sitting with a baby in his lap while feeding another baby in a highchair.

Just when I was about to get myself under control and regain the power of speech and the ability to breathe, he stood and I froze. He was probably a little taller than my brother. The broad shoulders and defined chest led down to a flat stomach, narrow hips, and long legs. And as he shifted the baby onto his hip, his arm pushed against his chinos, tightening them and showing what looked to be a nice-sized cock.

"You must be the famous Zach. It's great to finally meet you. I'm Aaron."

He held his free hand out to me, looked down into my eyes, and spoke with a voice that was deep, smooth, and warm. As if this trip wasn't going to be difficult enough, now I had to try to keep my dick from getting hard in my too-tight white pants.

Awww, shit! I didn't do straight guys. Well, obviously, I didn't "do" straight guys. What I meant was, I didn't go after straight guys or even fantasize about straight guys. It was stupid and self-defeating. I couldn't tell you how many friends I'd mocked over the years for their ridiculous straight-boy crushes.

Aaron was sort of grinning at me with a funny look in his eyes. Suddenly I realized that I'd taken his hand, but instead of shaking it, I was holding it in-between both of my hands and running my thumb over the top.

I dropped his hand like it was made of fire and my face flushed with heat. What the fuck was wrong with me? I'd never had anything close to a reaction like that to any other guy. And I had to start in my brother's *Leave It to Beaver* kitchen with one of his jock buddies? Fabulous. Well, at least he wasn't kicking my ass.

I still hadn't managed to put two words together when Kimberly came back with a regular soda in one hand and a diet soda in the other. I reached for the diet, opened it, and chugged it down, hoping that somehow caffeine would calm my nerves. Yeah, right. Seriously, what the fuck was wrong with me?

My brother came back into the kitchen, looking a

little stressed. "Okay, guys, let's get going. Aaron, thanks for watching the boys. Simon is still down for his nap, but he should be up soon. He might be hungry, so…"

Kimberly put her hand on Dean's arm. "Are you telling *Aaron* how to take care of Simon?" She laughed and turned to me. "Aaron spends as much time with our boys as your brother." Then Kimberly kissed Aaron. "Thanks, sweetie. I need to freshen my makeup, and then we're going to leave. I know you have plans tonight. What time do we need to be back?"

Aaron smiled back at her. "I'll be fine, Kimmy. You come back whenever things are done. Don't hurry. You know I love being with the boys. And I can always skip the meeting tonight. It's not a big deal."

She nodded and walked away.

"Ready to go, Zach?" my brother asked.

I think I managed to nod. I wasn't sure, though, because it took all of my energy to pull my eyes away from Aaron. He helped by walking toward the door where my brother stood. He took his one empty hand, the other still holding my nephew, and wrapped it around the back of Dean's neck and looked him in the eyes.

"Are you okay, man? I know this has to be hard." His voice was low, and there was real concern in his eyes.

Dean nodded and gave Aaron a tight hug. "I'm good, Aaron. I need to get through this, and then things will calm down."

They both started laughing at that point, and then Aaron rubbed Dean's arm as he responded. "You've been saying a variation of that for the past couple of years. Let's hope it's true this time."

I'd never seen straight guys relate to each other that way. It was affectionate and warm. I was pretty sure Aaron was the cause. There was something about him that exuded kindness and comfort. I had an uncharacteristic desire to press up against him, not for sex—that would be typical for me—but for the warmth and safety that I intuitively knew he could give me.

My brother left the kitchen, and I was trailing behind him when I heard Aaron's deep voice again. "It was nice *talking* with you, Zach."

I blushed when I realized that the entire time we were in the kitchen, I hadn't managed to say a single word. He laughed and patted my back. The laugh wasn't mocking; it was friendly and familiar, and it gave me goose bumps.

CHAPTER THREE

I THOUGHT about Aaron throughout most of the funeral: his eyes, the sound of his voice, his body, the warmth that somehow poured out of him. Those thoughts comforted me through most of the afternoon.

Not one family member spoke to me, which wasn't a surprise. And Dean stayed glued to my side, which was a surprise. It was getting more and more difficult for me to stay there, surrounded by people who I once thought loved me—that was, until they found out who I really was. Then, just when things were wrapping up and I was feeling pretty proud of having made it through that nightmare, Dean stepped away to talk with some people I didn't recognize.

Within a few seconds, my uncle walked up and glared at me as he hissed in a quiet voice, "You have some nerve showing up here, Zach. You were an embarrassment to your mother, and you're a disgrace to this family. No one wants you here. Are you too stupid to realize that?"

I'd prepared myself for big speeches and bravado if they talked down to me. I was going to laugh in their faces or tell them off. But when the time came, I couldn't say a thing. Instead, I froze and stood there, trying to hold back the tears that I could feel forming in my eyes. My uncle opened his mouth to say something else, but then he looked over my shoulder, stopped, and walked away. Suddenly, Dean was at my side with his hand on my back.

"Is everything okay, Zach?"

No, everything wasn't fucking okay. Why in the hell had he made me come back here? I didn't need that shit. I had my own life, and these people weren't a part of it. They were history, and that was where they needed to stay.

"I'm fucking dandy. Can we get the hell out of here now?"

I stormed away from the mortuary and over to Dean's car. The doors were locked, so I couldn't get in. But I stood by the door and waited, my arms crossed over my chest and a scowl decorating my face. After a few minutes, Dean and Kimberly walked out, their faces looking strained. Dean unlocked the car, and we all got in. I didn't think any of us said a word during the drive back to their house.

When Dean pulled up in his driveway, I opened my door and stepped out before the car had even come to a complete stop. I picked up my phone and dialed Luke's number as I walked into the house. As soon as he answered, I started talking.

"I need to get drunk and get laid. Come get me. We're going out."

I ended the call and looked up to see Aaron standing in front of me and Kimberly and Dean a bit behind me and to my side. Okay, well that was probably too loud and a little TMI for this crowd, but whatever. After an awkward silence, Dean walked up to me and spoke quietly.

"I, umm, well, we were hoping for us all to have a family dinner together tonight. Aaron can't join us, but Simon has been looking forward to getting to know you, and even though Chad and Ryan are still so small, I know that they'd love to spend time with their uncle."

Since when did my brother's buddy become part of the family? Well, he was there more than me, so I guess I didn't have much room to talk. Chad and Ryan, those must be the babies. Okay, now I knew all the names. I still wasn't sticking around.

"Yeah, listen, Dean, I'm going to go out. This isn't my scene, you know? I know it's like straight guy paradise around here, but I need to get some cock."

Kimberly's mouth dropped open at that point. Dean looked at me, clearly not knowing what to say. And Aaron...well, Aaron gazed into my eyes with an expression that somehow looked concerned, yet understanding. Damn, that boy had great eyes. And his hair looked so soft I wanted to run my fingers through it. Jesus! I needed to get a grip.

"Dean, where's my bag? I need to get ready."

I was looking at Aaron as I spoke, because I couldn't seem to find a way not to stare at the guy whenever he was in the room. I was past being embarrassed by it at that point, and I'd moved on to being disgusted with myself. It was hormones, I told myself; he was simply the only un-related adult male in the house. And he was incredibly gorgeous. Damn! No, not the last reason.

"I'll show him the room, Dean. It's this way, Zach."

Aaron put his arm, strong and warm, around me and directed me down the hallway. I was pressing myself too closely against him, but I couldn't force my body to pull away. We walked down the hallway, and Aaron opened the door at the end. I thought he'd walk back to my brother, but instead, he followed me into the room, closed the door, and sat on the bed.

"Do you want to talk about it?"

Normally, I would've made a flippant remark, pretending nothing was wrong, or been outwardly hostile. But he was looking into my eyes, no, he was looking *through* my eyes. I had the sense he could see me, really see me. That should sound frightening, but it wasn't. It felt good. And, suddenly, the words started tumbling out.

"They hate me. I mean, they really hate me. I've never done anything to them. I haven't even seen or spoken to them in ten years. And they're my family. They're supposed to love me, right? But they don't. They never have, and they never will. The dumb fucking thing is, I still let this shit hurt me. I thought I was past all of this."

You know, how sometimes when you're hurt or upset, you're able to hold it together until someone is nice to you, and then you lose it? Well, that was what happened. Aaron didn't even say anything. He just gazed at me in a way that no one else ever had. I wasn't sure what to make of it. It seemed so intimate, so...loving. And the next thing I knew, I was bawling, and Aaron's arms were around me. I wasn't sure how long I stayed wrapped in Aaron's arms, crying my eyes out, but I managed to fall asleep.

When I woke, we were both lying on the bed. I was on top of Aaron, with my face on his chest. His shirt was damp from my tears and smudged with my eyeliner. He was rubbing my back with one hand and stroking my hair with the other. I felt safe. For what I was pretty sure was the first time in my life, I felt safe. And that scared the ever-living shit out of me.

I shot up off his body and jumped off the bed.

"I'm sorry. I, ummm, I…"

I didn't know how to finish my sentence or even what I was planning to say. And then I heard the doorbell.

"That's Luke. I have to go. Thanks."

I was out of there before Aaron could respond. I practically ran out to the living room and to the front door. I had one foot out before Dean managed to make it into the entryway.

He started pleading with me. "Zach. Zach, please wait a second."

But I couldn't wait. I couldn't stay in that house any longer. It wasn't even about the funeral anymore or my family. It was about Aaron. I couldn't be around the guy. He did something to me, something wonderful and meaningful. For the first time in my life, I wanted a guy in a way that wasn't sexual. Well, I wanted that, too, but it wasn't *only* sexual. And because I couldn't seem to catch a single fucking break, that guy had to be my brother's straight friend.

I ran out the door and pulled Luke toward his car.

"Slow down, Zach. Where's the damn fire?"

There was a guy in the driver's seat. I figured that was Chris, so I got in the back, leaving shotgun for Luke. Then I put on my best smile and used my most upbeat voice.

"All right, boys, are you ready to party?"

Chris drove us to a gay bar they liked. We got drinks at the bar and sat down at a table. A couple of hours and a couple of drinks later, I still wasn't in the mood to troll. I sat across from Luke and Chris, who were sickeningly lovey-dovey, and had my own nauseating thoughts about Aaron. How warm his body had felt against mine, how much I enjoyed having his arms around me, what it would be like to wake up like that every morning. I actually disgusted myself so much that throwing up wasn't out of the question.

When did I become this pathetic, sappy schmuck who obsessed about unavailable straight guys? Hell, when did I become a guy who obsessed about anybody? That wasn't me. I was, well, for lack of a better word, a big fucking slut. Sorry, folks, that was how it was. I slept around, and I wasn't ashamed of it. No, that wasn't accurate. There wasn't any sleeping involved. There was just sex. Lots of sex. Mostly blowjobs, although there was fucking, too, usually on the receiving end.

I'd never had any trouble finding willing partners. I wasn't a bad-looking guy, I stayed in shape, and I was easy. What wasn't to like, right? But there I sat, in a bar full of available men, and all I could do was think about the one who wasn't available. And to make matters worse, not all of my thoughts were dirty. I actually found myself thinking of how nice he was to me, how caring he was to my brother, how sweet he was to my nephews. And then, when I thought I couldn't get any more pathetic, I actually saw him on the other side of the bar.

I thought back to how much I'd been drinking. I was sure that I'd only had two martinis. That was nothing for me. I didn't weigh much, but I'd been able to build up a decent alcohol tolerance over the years. I'd had lots of practice. So, it couldn't be the gin making me see things.

I rubbed my eyes, but he was still there. What was this shit? Had my brother sent his lackey to follow me? I didn't care how hot the guy was, that pissed me off.

"Excuse me, guys. I see someone I know."

I got up and walked across the bar until I was standing behind Aaron. Then I tapped him on the shoulder, ready to wail into him. But when he turned around, I lost my resolve. He looked so surprised and so...happy to see me.

"Zach! You're here."

Then he hugged me. Tightly. And for a long time. I pushed him away when I started getting hard and, as a result, embarrassed. Damn it! Why should I be embarrassed?

"What are you doing here, Aaron? Did my brother send you to follow me?"

He looked confused.

"What? No, of course not."

He was a good actor. I'd give him that.

"Umm, hmmm. So what are you doing here?"

He smiled that warm, caring smile and threw in

just a bit of mischief. I'd never met anyone with such an expressive smile.

"Well, I'm here for a drink. It's a bar."

Then he held up his glass.

"No shit. What I mean is, if my brother didn't send you, what's Mister Straight-jock-boy doing in a gay bar? You have looked around and noticed that there are no women here, right? And that half of these guys are all over each other. No, don't tell me. You just happened to wander in here off the street by mistake, and I just happened to be here with my friends."

Aaron looked truly shocked, and then he started laughing.

"Wait, am I the Mister Straight-jock-boy in your rant? You...you think I'm straight?"

What? I stood there, processing this latest turn of events. I have great gaydar. It was how I'd always been able to stay away from straight boys and how I found it unbelievably easy to find the next guy to suck or fuck. This guy was definitely straight.

"Save it, Aaron. We know. We can tell when other guys are gay. So what are you doing here?"

He was no longer laughing, but his eyes still twinkled a bit.

"We? And who is the 'we' that you're describing? You might want to tell 'we' that he's off this time. I'm gay. Completely gay. As in, not straight. But the jock-boy part is true, so I guess you're not totally off."

Okay, two could play at this game. I leaned back against the bar and crossed my arms.

"Prove it."

Aaron laughed.

"How do you want me to prove it, Zach? I left my membership card at home, and I forgot the secret handshake."

I took his arm and started pulling him toward the bathroom.

"Let's go, tough guy."

"Where are we going?"

"Somewhere a little more private."

Thankfully, that bar wasn't very big, and it had separate bathrooms. I opened the door to one, pulled a surprised-looking Aaron in behind me, and locked the door.

"What now, Zach?"

I started unbuttoning and unzipping my pants.

"Now you prove it, gay boy."

His eyes suddenly lost their sparkle, and he looked sad. I almost felt sorry for him. He was probably just doing a favor for my brother by following me around, and when he got caught, he used the first excuse that came to mind. I decided I wouldn't give him a hard time when he bolted for the door.

But he didn't try to leave. He raised his hand and softly stroked my cheek.

"Not like this, Zach. Please, not like this. Our first time together shouldn't be in the bathroom of a bar."

His voice was, once again, loving, and he gazed into my eyes, making me feel the warmth he exuded. And I realized that I'd somehow developed feelings for this guy. Deep feelings. In the course of one day, I felt more for him than I did for any other person in my life. My entire body tingled, I had goose bumps, and I was holding back tears.

How dare he fuck around with my emotions that way? Talking about a first time, like there would be other times. This might be some joke for him, a story he could go back and tell my brother about how he talked his way out of the bar by playing on my feelings. But to me, it was real. It was the most real thing I'd ever felt.

"That's what I thought. You're playing some game with me," I told him in a quiet voice as I reached for the door.

"No." He put his hand on the door, so that I couldn't open it. "I'm not playing a game with you, Zach."

I turned back to him, and he moved his hand off the door and cupped the back of my head, pulling me toward him as he bent his head down to me. I stiffened.

"I don't kiss."

He didn't move away, but he stopped and looked at me.

"What?"

"I don't kiss."

"Zach, you pulled me in here and opened your pants. Unless I'm missing something, you're asking me to put your dick in my mouth. But a kiss is off limits?"

Well, when he put it that way, it did sound silly. But the thing was, kisses were intimate. Blow jobs were, well, they were blow jobs. They were a way to get off that usually felt better than my hand. At least if the guy had a decent technique. It wasn't like I was the only one who felt that way. Most guys didn't even try to kiss me when we fucked. And those that tried didn't question me when I turned away or said no.

"Yeah, that's what I'm saying."

Aaron pressed me back against the door and put a hand on each side of my face.

"You've watched too many silly shows or movies. I'm going to kiss you, Zach. On the mouth. And then I'll give you your proof."

As he slowly moved his face down toward mine, I realized that I wanted that kiss. I wanted to feel his lips against me. With Aaron, I wanted the intimacy that I'd always carefully avoided.

His lips pressed on mine, warm, soft, and gentle. He mouthed my lower lip between both of his as he stroked my face with his thumbs. I sighed and relaxed against him. Then his tongue caressed my lower lip, my upper lip, and eventually ran in the crease of my lips, seeking entry. I opened my mouth to him, and his tongue was in me, licking my tongue, exploring my mouth. I instinctively sucked on his tongue, and that made me moan. All too soon, he pulled his mouth back, looked into my glazed eyes, and dropped to his knees.

CHAPTER FOUR

AARON KNEELED in front of me. My pants were still open, so all he had to do was pull them down. I was going commando, so my painfully hard cock slapped up on my stomach when it was released from my pants.

Aaron groaned. He stroked my balls lightly with his fingers, covered them with his hand, and caressed them. Then he moved his fingers up my shaft, petting my skin. I felt like I could come just from that, just from the feeling of Aaron's fingertips on my cock.

I looked down at that beautiful man and saw the way he was gazing at me, with desire, with hunger. And I knew it wasn't a trick. He really was gay. And he really did want me.

Without breaking eye contact, he reached his tongue out and ran it from the base of my cock to the top. He swirled it around the crown and then took the top into his mouth, sucking on it while he rolled my balls in his hand.

Seeing Aaron's mouth wrapped around my cock was incredibly arousing. I put my head back against the door and moaned as I kept looking at him. Then he changed his technique, and instead of just the crown, he pushed his mouth down to my pubes and held my entire cock in his mouth and throat.

Holy shit! He was no amateur. This was definitely not the first time he'd had a cock in his mouth and throat. He was good, very good. It wasn't long before I was thrusting gently into him. He was humming with my cock in his throat as he pulled my sac gently down and swallowed, sending waves of pleasure over my cock head.

"Aaron. Aaron, I'm...ungh...I'm there. Aaron!"

I tried to warn him so he could back off, but he didn't. Instead he sucked harder and bobbed his head up and down.

"Aaaaaaaarrrroooon!"

I shouted his name as I came. He took the first couple of shots in his throat. Then he pulled back and took the rest on his tongue, moaning and making an "*mmmmm*" sound as he tasted me.

I was gasping as I recovered from what was the best blow job of my life, when Aaron stood. I grasped the front of his shirt and pulled him down to me, cupping my hand on the back of his head. When he was low enough, I pressed my mouth against his. This time, it was my tongue demanding entry, wanting to taste his mouth. After a couple of minutes, we pulled apart, both of us needing to catch our breath.

"Wow, Aaron. That was...that was..."

He kissed my cheek and nuzzled my neck.

"Yeah, it was." Then he sighed. "What now?"

I reached my hand down and rubbed it over the front of his pants. He must have adjusted himself, because his dick was pressed up against his stomach, and from the feel of it, tucked under the waistband of his briefs. Shit, it felt huge. I'd say well over eight inches, and a nice thickness around.

Now, you might be wondering how I could tell this while the man was still dressed, but when you've had as much practice as I've had, you get good at dick measurements.

I was making my way toward his zipper when he covered my hand with his.

"That's not what I meant, Zach. What I meant was, what now between us?"

I squeezed his cock through his pants.

"This is what's now between us. My turn."

He took my hand in-between his, laced our fingers together, and brought it to his mouth, kissing the back of my hand.

"No, Zach. I gave you your proof, but that's the last time we do this in a public toilet. I don't want to be some trick to you. We're more than that, much more. Can't you feel it?"

Those words normally would've made me get the hell out of there. Not that I had occasion to have guys ask for more all that often. Unless by "more" we were counting another round in bed. I didn't exactly exude the I'm-looking-for-a-relationship vibe, and those types of guys had never held any interest for me. I'd always been the guy looking to get fucked, not the guy looking for dinner and a movie.

But with Aaron...I did want more. I could *feel* it. It

scared me, terrified me. But I couldn't walk away from it. I couldn't walk away from him.

"Yes, I can feel it."

My voice shook. I moved our joined hands toward my mouth and kissed his hand. And then, a knock on the door interrupted our moment.

"I need to take a piss. Are you about done in there?"

Aaron laughed.

"Well, that sure is a mood killer. We better get out of here."

He squatted and pulled my pants up, tucking my equipment in. I decided to finish the job.

"These pants are pretty tight and your hand right there isn't exactly making things go down. I don't want my dick to get caught in the zipper."

He grinned.

"Okay. I don't want to hurt your dick. I have plans for it later."

I managed to zip up around my hardening member, and we walked out of the bathroom. Aaron took my hand in his.

"So, do you think your friends would mind if I took you home?" His voice was hesitant and wishful. He really did want more than a blow job. And surprisingly, so did I. My silence must have discouraged him. "You...you left so quickly that Dean didn't have the chance to give you a key, and they go to bed early."

"No." His whole face dropped when he heard that response. "I mean no, my friends won't mind. They weren't planning on going out tonight anyway. I dragged them here. You can take me home."

That brought the smile back, all the way to his eyes. Like I said, Aaron had a very expressive face.

"Great! Hey, when was the last time you had anything to eat? You didn't eat at Kim and Dean's, and they told me that there wasn't any food at the funeral. I know this place doesn't serve anything. You must be hungry."

He was right. I hadn't eaten anything all day except a protein drink before the flight and few bags of pretzels in the air. That wasn't like me at all. I was a big eater. I guess the stress of the day distracted me.

"Yeah, I am hungry. What do you have in mind?"

"There's a great place not far from here. Cool atmosphere, good food, and they're open late. Can I take you to dinner?"

He looked at his watch.

"A really, really late dinner."

"That works for me. I could eat just about anything right now. I'll go tell my friends."

He was beaming.

"Okay. I need to tell my friends that I'm leaving, too. They're probably wondering what happened to me. I'll meet you by the door."

He turned and walked toward one end of the bar as I walked toward the other. As I said my goodbyes to Luke and Chris, I realized that when I saw Aaron earlier, he was by himself, ordering a drink. He wasn't with any friends. That struck me as odd, but I forgot about it when I saw his happy face waiting for me by the door.

"Let's go eat."

He took my hand again as we walked out of the bar, and he didn't let go until we got to his car. The restaurant was a short drive away. I noticed there were several other gay bars in the area, a Metropolitan Community Church, and a few other businesses with rainbow symbols on their doors.

We parked and got out of the car. Aaron put his arm around me, and I pressed up against him, enjoying his warmth. When we walked into the restaurant, I saw several other same-sex couples and groups of people who were clearly "family."

I hadn't grown up in that area and, as a kid, I hadn't ventured far out of my own neighborhood. I wondered whether this gay-friendly part of town had always been there. In my mind, all of Emile City was as homophobic as my family. But that obviously wasn't true. It still wasn't West Hollywood, but I felt comfortable here.

Aaron and I sat down and ordered our dinner—burger and fries for me, a pasta dish, hold the red peppers, for him. I had another martini, and he ordered soda water.

"Soda water? Don't you want a real drink?"

He reached across the table and took my hand again. I noticed he was a very tactile guy, always wanting physical contact.

"I don't drink."

"What do you mean you don't drink? Not ever?"

He gave me a little smile and shrugged.

"Nope. Never have. It's not my thing. I never acquired a taste for it, and I don't like how it makes me feel. I guess I'm a bit of a control freak."

Hmmm. I thought about whether I had any friends who didn't drink. I couldn't come up with a single name. I had friends who should probably stop drinking, but none who were sober. In fact, most of us were pretty lit most of the time.

Our food came and went, and Aaron and I stayed at the table and talked. The conversation flowed smoothly about lots of different topics:

Books—

I told him *The Outsiders* was one of my favorites. I had an old tattered copy that was held together by clear packing tape. It was one of those books I liked to reread every year. I almost felt like I knew the characters.

He was reading *Degrees of Retribution*, a more current novel by Dennis Milholland. A thriller with gay characters.

Work—

Aaron was a veterinarian and, as it turned out, so was my sister-in-law, Kimberly. They had gone to school together. Dean had probably mentioned his wife's occupation at some point in an e-mail, but I rarely read what he wrote. I mostly skimmed and then deleted. Sometimes I just deleted. I'd always tried to put distance between myself and my childhood. And Dean was part of that childhood.

I told Aaron about the restaurant where I worked. I'd gone to cooking school in LA and had been working in restaurants in some form or another since I moved there at age eighteen. My dream was to open my own place one day, nothing big or fancy, just a small place with a cool vibe and good food.

Hobbies—

Aaron told me that he loved art. He wasn't an artist himself, but he appreciated other people's work. Apparently, there were lots of small galleries in the area that supported local artists, and one night a month, they stayed open late, and the streets filled with people walking around, supporting the local art scene. Aaron said that he never missed those events.

He also liked theater, but not the big productions that came through town. He told me about a local theater that produced unusual shows, the kinds of things most other places wouldn't dare touch. Often times, but not always, they featured gay characters. He had season tickets that included about eight plays every year. Other than that, it seemed, Aaron didn't go out much. He did, however, spend a lot of time volunteering for a gay rights organization and watching my nephews, so my brother and Kim could have what he called an "adult night out."

I told him I liked music. The indie music scene in LA was great, and my friends and I often went to bars to hear new bands. I also loved to paint. As I was talking to Aaron, I realized I hadn't painted much lately. Between work and bar/bed hopping, I hadn't had time. I decided not to tell him that, realizing how pathetic and empty it sounded. And I wondered why I hadn't realized it until then.

Friends—

Aaron told me that he had moved into town a little over a year earlier. Other than his work at the veterinary clinic and volunteer work, which sounded like it took a shitload of time, he spent his free hours with my brother's family. He said with all of that, he hadn't had time to make other friends.

I had a big circle of friends in LA, and I told Aaron about them, a few funny stories, a little background. Most of my friends were gay men, about my age. And most of the things we did together involved bars or house parties. I didn't have any friends with kids. I didn't even have many friends in couples.

Whenever someone in our crowd got into a relationship, they sort of dropped out of the scene. The truth was, the things we did weren't compatible with monogamy. When my friends got together, we were all usually wasted in short order. It didn't take long after that for people to get naked and start fucking around or, at a minimum, flirting very heavily.

The one topic we steered clear of was family. I was still pretty raw from the funeral, and I think Aaron realized that.

I'd never enjoyed talking, just talking, with anyone so much. As different as we seemed, Aaron and I actually had a lot of similar interests, so the conversation never waned. And before we knew it, the restaurant was closing.

We walked to the car, holding hands. Aaron led me to the passenger door and kissed me softly before he opened the door for me. My chest tightened during that kiss. I sat down in my seat and tried to catch my breath, process what was happening to me. Aaron must have been thinking, too, because neither of us said anything on the drive to my brother's house. He did hold my hand, though, and I noticed him turning to look at me every couple of minutes.

When we pulled into my brother's driveway, Aaron turned off the car and walked me to the door. He put the key in the lock but didn't turn it. Instead, he pulled me up against him and bent his head down to mine. I was done telling him that I didn't kiss. There was nothing I wanted more than to feel his warm skin, his soft lips, his tongue dancing with mine.

So, we stood there, outside of my brother's perfect gingerbread house, kissing and rubbing each other's arms and backs. When we reluctantly pulled apart, Aaron spoke, his voice sounding husky.

"I want to spend more time alone with you, Zach. Can I take you to dinner tomorrow?"

I nodded. I'd have to change my flight, seeing as how I'd been planning on leaving the next morning or, more accurately, later that morning (it was already past one thirty a.m.). But if it meant spending time alone with Aaron, that was fine.

He smiled and hugged me tightly, whispering in my ear, "Thank you. Thanks for giving me a chance, Zach, for giving us a chance. I won't let you down."

And with those words, he unlocked the door, reached in after me and tapped a code on the alarm panel, kissed my cheek, and said good night.

CHAPTER FIVE

I MADE my way to the spare bedroom and flopped down on the bed, replaying the night in my head. Aaron was hot, crazy hot. But he was also interesting and kind. He took care of animals for a living, spent hours doing volunteer work, and talked about my nephews like they were his own kids. The guy was so perfect, he didn't seem real. No one was that selfless, that nice.

And even if he was real, what on earth would he want with me? Selfless and nice were not words that anyone would use to describe me. Shallow and self-absorbed, yeah. Promiscuous and fun, check. Maybe he didn't realize what kind of a guy I was. Once he did, there was little chance that he'd want to continue...doing whatever it was we were doing. Until then, though, I'd have some fun. I called the airline, changed my flight, and got ready for bed.

I had a restless night, tossing around the bed and never falling into a deep sleep. I kept thinking about Aaron. Beautiful, kind Aaron. I could never get a guy like him. I didn't deserve a guy like him. And it wouldn't take long for him to figure that out. Hell, maybe he'd already figured it out. Maybe he'd gone home that night and realized he had spent the evening with a slut who liked to get blow jobs in bathrooms.

By the time morning came, I was tired, anxious, and inexplicably angry with Aaron for leading me to believe that he could ever want anything other than sex from a guy like me. No one had ever wanted anything but a fuck from me, and that wasn't going to change with Mister Wonderful.

I took a shower, brushed my teeth, and reached into my bag for the only clean clothes I'd packed—an old pair of jeans and a T-shirt from a delivery company with the words "Receiving Department" on the front. That shirt gave me and my friends a chuckle. I doubted my brother and his wife would get the joke.

I walked into the kitchen and smelled something burning. Kim stood at the stove wearing her pajamas. There were dirty bowls and spoons all over the counter. My brother sat at the table, feeding the two babies (Ryan and Chad—I actually managed to remember), and there was a little boy lying on the floor, coloring with crayons in an oversized coloring book. That must be Simon.

"Good morning, everyone."

I sort of grumbled out my greeting. Dean smiled at me.

"Hey, Zach! Are you hungry? Kim's making breakfast."

I looked over at the burnt concoction in the frying pan and wondered if it would be rude to ask for cereal. Simon popped his head up and got a huge smile on his face.

"Uncle Zach!"

He jumped up and ran toward me, hugging my legs. I stood there, dumbfounded. How did the kid know my name?

"You look just like your pictures. Daddy says that I'm going to look like you when I grow up. See, I have brown hair and brown eyes like you."

He furrowed his small eyebrows a little.

"Your hair looks browner in the pictures."

Then he turned to Dean.

"Uncle Zach is supposed to have brown hair like me, Daddy."

I looked at my nephew and realized he did look like me. A lot like me. My brother was blond with blue eyes. Kim had brown eyes, but she had platinum blond hair, probably aided by a good stylist. It wasn't just that, though. Simon had my same hairline, my thin eyebrows, my long lashes, and my slight frame. For some reason, I liked having this little person look like me. It meant as much to me as it seemed to mean to him.

I hunched down so Simon and I were eye-to-eye.

"I do have brown hair, Simon. I colored it before I came out here. But I like the brown much better. I'm going to let it grow back out, so that we can have the same hair again."

That seemed to make the kid happy because he jumped into my arms and hugged me. I felt a heart-tugging thing, and then he was gone.

"I'm coloring. I need to get more purple. I'm going to my room, and then I'll show you when I'm done."

I stood up, feeling oddly sentimental. Then the back door opened and my eyes locked with Aaron's.

"Good morning, everyone."

He was smiling and holding a grocery bag. He set the bag on the counter and walked up right behind Kimberly. She pressed back against him, and he hunched down and kissed her cheek. Then he looked down over her shoulder and into the frying pan.

"Kimmy, I'm not sure what you think you're making here, but it isn't working. Go get dressed, and I'll take care of breakfast. I brought bananas so I can make those pancakes you like so much. I have blueberries for Dean's pancakes. And I think you're out of chocolate chips, so I brought those too. That way I can make Simon those Mickey pancakes with the smiley face."

My brother laughed.

"What would we do without you, man? I was sitting here trying to choose between starvation and food poisoning."

Kimberly walked up to Dean and swatted his arm.

"Hey! At least I was trying to make breakfast."

I stood there, feeling like an outsider in what was supposed to be my family. They were all so familiar with each other, teasing and laughing together. Aaron knew what they liked to eat, and I didn't know anything about them.

And what was his deal with Kimberly? He was way too touchy-feely with her as far as I was concerned. It seemed like they were always hugging and kissing. And why didn't he kiss me? Last night, he hadn't been able to keep his hands off me, but now, I was what, persona non grata?

I felt angry and...jealous. But I had no right to be jealous. Not of his closeness to my family, not of anything. I had no claim on any of them.

As far as my family was concerned, I'd walked away over a decade earlier, and I'd made no effort to stay in touch. As for Aaron, well, it wasn't like I was his boyfriend. Ha! Like I could ever be anyone's boyfriend. That thought upset me more than I wanted to admit to myself.

"How was your meeting last night, Aaron? Were you able to make it on time?"

I'd forgotten Kimberly's comment before the funeral about Aaron having a meeting. I wondered if he would tell her that he hadn't gone to a meeting, and that the two of us had been out together. That was my opportunity to know how he felt, to know whether he'd changed his mind about us, so I looked over at him.

He hesitated and looked at me. I didn't say anything. Then he sighed and started picking up the bowls and spoons on the counter and moving them into the sink.

"The meeting was fine. I didn't miss much. No worries."

What in the fuck was that? The meeting was fine? There was no damn meeting! There was me and him, talking and laughing and kissing. I'd never had a night I enjoyed more, never felt a closer connection to another person, and, to him, it wasn't even worth mentioning? I was hurt and angry, trying to rein in my tears when Dean turned to me.

"What about you, Zach? Did you, ehm, have a nice time last night?"

I knew it was petty, but I wanted to get back at Aaron for his whole "last-night-didn't-mean-anything-to-me" game. So I shrugged and spoke nonchalantly.

"Well, I got drunk, and I got a blow job, so the night wasn't a total loss."

Kim had the same surprised look on her face as she'd had the night before when I'd said I needed cock. Dean seemed uncomfortable. I decided to push it further.

"What? Don't tell me you've never gotten a blow job in a bar?"

This was good. This was the real me. I wasn't good enough for them. I got that. But I wasn't going to apologize for who I was. Dean shook his head, without a sound.

"Yeah, well it's different with gay guys. We're not so uptight. A blow job isn't a big thing for us. Right, Aaron?"

I turned to Aaron and saw that he was frozen, the bowls in his hand hovering over the sink. There was a long stretch of silence before he answered.

"I...I don't know about that, Zach."

At first, I didn't understand his reaction. And then, all the pieces fell into place. He wasn't out. That was why he'd lied to Kim and Dean about having a meeting, instead of telling them he was going to a bar. It was also why I didn't see him with any friends at that bar—he was there by himself, probably cruising, even though he'd fed me that shit about not wanting to have a blow job in a bathroom.

Well, I wasn't going to out the guy, no matter how pissed I was. But I was pissed. So much so that I was shaking when I stormed out of my brother's kitchen, leaving him, his wife, and Aaron standing and staring at me in silence.

I didn't make it far, just into the living room where I sat on the couch and put my head in my hands. Why was I surprised? I knew it was all too good to be true. So, my brother had a cute closet-case friend who wanted a walk on the wild side. Why should I give a shit? It was just a blow job. Yeah, right. And Kurt Cobain was just a singer.

"What was that all about, Zach?"

I looked up into Aaron's blue eyes. The sadness there tore at me. But what did he expect? He was going to hide what happened between us, hide who he was from the people he claimed to be closest to, and *I* was the bad guy?

I shrugged.

"What do you mean?"

He sat down next to me.

"Don't give me that. You know exactly what I mean. 'I got drunk and got a blow job. A blow job isn't a big thing.' What is that?"

Why was he pretending? I knew he'd been trolling in that bar, just like me. Why act like it was anything more?

"It was just a blow job, Aaron."

I was surprised when the ever-calm Aaron raised his voice.

"That's baloney, Zach, and you know it! That was *just* a blow job like *Star Wars* was *just* a movie."

I laughed in spite of myself. It seemed like our brains worked in the same way, even if the guy did use words like "baloney." Who talked that way? And why did I find it cute and endearing? Damn, I had it bad for him. So, he was in the closet, was that such a big deal? Well yeah, it was. But I lo...liked him so much.

"Yeah, you're right. I didn't expect that in there," I said, pointing at the kitchen. "I didn't know you weren't out. With everything you said last night, I got the wrong idea. Sorry, Aaron. I guess I don't deal well with closet cases. But I understand. Well, sort of."

He took my hand and intertwined our fingers.

"So last night I was a straight jock-boy, and today I've been, what, downgraded to a closet case? That's not fair, and it isn't true."

"Oh, come on, Aaron. My brother and Kim are your closest friends, yet you can't tell them that we were together last night. You're so far in the damn closet that you probably had breakfast with the lion and the witch."

He sighed and dropped his head back on the couch.

"Is that what you think? Darn it, Zach! I haven't been able to stop thinking about you since you walked into Kimmy's kitchen yesterday. And I haven't felt this way about another man since...well, I haven't ever felt this way about another man. But you have to meet me at least partway here.

"Please, stop expecting the worst of me. I didn't say anything to Kim and Dean about last night because he's *your* brother, and I wasn't sure what *you'd* want to say. Do you need me to prove this one, too, Zach? Go ask your brother how we met. They're out of eggs and milk, so I'm going to the store."

And with that, Aaron got up and walked briskly into the kitchen. I sat on the couch, dumbfounded by his show of emotion, amused by his choice of words (Darn? How cute was that?), and a little ashamed of how quickly I seemed to jump to conclusions about him. My thoughts were interrupted by Dean.

"Zach? Do you want to tell me what's going on with Aaron? I've never seen him so upset. He walked into the kitchen and out the door without saying a word."

"He said you were out of eggs and milk. He went to the store."

Dean started tapping his foot, looking like an impatient dad.

"And?"

"Hey, Dean?"

My voice was quiet, and I thought he sensed the change in my tone. He sat next to me on the couch.

"Yeah?"

"How do you and Kim know Aaron?"

He seemed surprised by the new conversation, but he answered me.

"He was my roommate. For years, while I was finishing my doctorate. And he was in veterinary school with Kim. He's actually the one who introduced us. Why?"

I wasn't ready to answer his question because he still hadn't answered mine.

"So Kim met him at school. But how did you meet him? I mean, before he became your roommate?"

"At a PFLAG meeting."

Well, that was unexpected.

"PFLAG?"

"Yes, PFLAG. I have a gay brother, you know. And I wanted help reaching out to you, Zach. Nothing I ever did seemed to work. I went to a meeting and met Aaron. He was about to start school, and he was looking for a place to live. I had an extra room. And the rest, as they say, is history."

I hadn't ever realized my brother cared so much about our relationship. Actually, I hadn't ever realized that he cared at all. Back to Aaron, though. Being at a PFLAG meeting didn't prove he was out. After all, my brother was at that meeting, and he wasn't gay.

"What was Aaron doing at the meeting? Does he have a gay family member?"

"No. I mean, yeah, I think he has a gay cousin that he's close with. But he was at the meeting to talk with us. To tell us about his experience, about his family and how they supported him. And to answer our questions."

There was no way to take that other than that Aaron was out. But I still needed to ask.

"So, he's gay?"

My brother raised his eyebrows in surprise.

"Of course he's gay. What? You thought Aaron was straight?"

I couldn't understand that reaction. I mean, Aaron wasn't stereotypically gay. In other words, he wasn't anything like me.

"Well, yeah. At first I did. It's not like the guy is out waving the rainbow flag."

That, made Dean laugh. A lot. And for an annoyingly long period of time. Eventually, he wiped the tears from his eyes and continued chuckling.

"Actually, Zach, that's exactly what it's like." He walked over to the bookshelf and pulled out an album. Then he brought it back to the couch and flipped through the pages. I saw pictures of Dean and Kim, looking a little younger but mostly the same. And I saw Aaron with them at the beach, sitting next to Kim on a couch, outside of a tent with Dean. "Here we go."

Dean seemed to have found what he was looking for, so he put the album in my lap. I looked down and realized why he had been laughing. There was Aaron, standing on what looked like a street corner, waving a rainbow flag.

"What is this?"

"It was a protest. When that whole Prop 8 thing was going on in California, Aaron organized a protest at school. There were a few hundred people there. It got decent press. Aaron was interviewed by a couple of television stations and that picture ran on the front page of the college newspaper. He was heartbroken when Prop 8 passed. He's usually an upbeat guy, always finding the silver lining in bad situations. But when it passed, Aaron was down, really down." Dean looked up at me. "I'm sure you understand. You actually lived in California when that was going on, so you probably spent as much time fighting it as Aaron."

How could I respond to that? Yes, I lived in California. But, no, I hadn't spent any time fighting Prop 8. I was too busy having fun and getting laid.

Marriage wasn't something that mattered to me. As far as I was concerned, straight people could keep it, assuming they could make it work. But seeing that picture of Aaron, who didn't even live in California, who was busy going to school but still found the time to organize a protest and take interviews about our rights, well, I felt a little ashamed of myself at that moment.

I closed the album and rubbed my eyes with my palms.

"I'm such an asshole, Dean."

"Why are you saying that, Zach? And what's with the questions about Aaron? Is there something going on between you two?"

Now that was the million-dollar question. No, actually, it wasn't. It was an easy question.

"Yes, there is. I ran into him at the bar last night. You already heard about some of what went on, but we also had dinner together and spent hours talking."

I replayed my words in my head—hours talking. When had I ever spent time talking with a guy about anything, other than who was hot, where we could party, or how drunk one of us was the night before? It had been so long that I couldn't think of it. Or maybe that was because it had never happened.

How was it possible I had so many friends, yet I didn't know anything about them? I was starting to question my entire life, the same carefree life that I'd fucking loved two days prior. Dean's voice broke into my thoughts.

"I heard about some of what went on? What do you mean? Were you talking about Aaron when you said that you...that you, ehm, that you got a blow job?"

"Yes, I was talking about Aaron. But it wasn't just a blow job. We talked and got to know each other. There's something there. I don't know what it is, but there's something between us."

"You're saying that Aaron gave you a blow job?"

Oh, come on! Why was my brother fixated on this? Did his wife not put out? I was talking with him about something that mattered, and he was focused on sex. Wait, did I just think that something mattered more than sex? Who was I?

"Zach. I asked you a question. Did you say that you had sex with Aaron last night?"

"Yes, Dean. That's what I said. I also said a lot of other things, which you're oddly ignoring in favor of focusing on your friend with my dick in his mouth. Are you sure you're not gay?"

I was kidding, of course, but come on. What was with the blow job obsession?

"I heard what you said, Zach. But I've known Aaron for over five years, and I've *never* known him to have sex with anyone. I'm not even sure he's dated a guy in those five years. And it's not like he didn't have options. But, as far as I know, this is the first time he's had sex with anyone since...since before I knew him, since Michael."

"Michael?"

"His ex. I don't know much about him. They dated in high school and college, and then...you should be talking about this with Aaron. It's not my place to talk about his personal life. This took me by surprise, that's all."

Five years. He hadn't been with a guy in five years? Not possible. Dean didn't know about any of the guys because Aaron probably didn't tell him. No one had a five year dry spell, especially, not someone as good-looking as Aaron.

"Zach?"

"Yeah?"

"Don't hurt him, okay? I mean, I know you don't owe me anything, and I know it's not my place to ask. But Aaron, well, he saved us. Me, Kim, the boys—he's done so much for us, given up his whole life for us. I know he comes across as strong, and he is. But he also wears his heart on his sleeve. You've seen him with the boys. I'm sure you can tell how sensitive he is. And, please don't take this as an insult, Zach, because it isn't. But if you're only looking for sex, tell him upfront. Be honest with him. He deserves at least that much."

Where was the insult in that? Hell, I was always looking for sex and actively avoiding everything else. So Dean's comment should've been right on point. But it wasn't. Not this time. This time I wanted...what did I want?

Aaron and I didn't live in the same place. Literally and, it seemed, figuratively. I had no idea how to have any kind of relationship. I wasn't even sure I was capable of being a decent boyfriend or even a decent person. And Aaron didn't sound like a fling kind of guy.

So what did I want? And did it matter anyway? After the way I'd been treating him, it seemed unlikely that Aaron would want anything more to do with me.

CHAPTER SIX

I THOUGHT about the way I'd spoken about, and to Aaron, and I felt angry at myself. I put my head back on the couch and closed my eyes.

"Ugh! Dean, I've been such a big dick."

Instead of Dean responding, I heard Aaron's voice.

"Nah. You haven't. Besides, I'm a sucker for big dicks. Is that fact finally all cleared up for you?"

I laughed out loud at his comment and opened my eyes to see Aaron smiling. And I found that I'd missed his smile. That was what I wanted—Aaron's smile, Aaron's warmth, Aaron's kindness. I wanted Aaron.

I got up off the couch and walked over to him until we were practically touching. He gazed down into my eyes, still looking hesitant.

"Come down here, big guy."

That made his smile even broader and his eyes twinkle. He leaned down to me, and our lips met in what started as a gentle little kiss but ended with Aaron's hand on the back of my head and my arms wrapped around his neck, as our tongues danced.

I could feel Aaron's hard cock against my stomach, and I wondered if there was any possible way to get my brother's family out of the house, so that we could get naked, and I could get fucked. Then Aaron pulled away, looking sorry as hell that he had to do it. I sighed, knowing sex wasn't on the breakfast menu.

"So, did I hear you say something about pancakes? I'll help. I know my way around a kitchen."

"Thanks, Zach, but I have this. Simon would love to spend time with you."

He turned and walked back into the kitchen, then he looked over his shoulder and winked at me.

"You can take care of breakfast tomorrow."

I turned toward the bedrooms in search of my nephew. And I wasn't even surprised to realize that the idea of breakfast tomorrow sounded...good. I liked the idea of a tomorrow with Aaron.

ALTHOUGH CRAYONS and copy paper weren't usually my medium of choice, Simon and I were able to make some pretty great pictures together. When I walked into his room, he was sprawled on the floor, trying to figure out how to draw a butterfly. I joined him, and we worked together, making a whole spring garden drawing. It was fun talking with my nephew, listening to his funny comments, and teaching him how to do something I enjoyed. Before I knew it, Kim was standing in the doorway.

"Hi, boys. Are you ready to eat? Uncle Aaron made your favorite Mickey pancakes, Simon." Simon jumped up

and ran to his mom, cheering the whole way. I followed
him, smiling to myself at his enthusiasm. "First, let's go
potty and wash our hands. Come on, Simon."

Kim scooped Simon up and walked toward
the bathroom, and I went into the kitchen in search of
sustenance. When I stepped in and saw Aaron standing
at the counter, cutting up fruit, I completely forgot I was
hungry. He was whistling along with the song playing on
the radio and swinging his hips a bit from side to side.
His rhythm wasn't great and, from the sound of things, his
musical abilities weren't much better. But he looked so
happy and relaxed, and he was so fucking adorable, that
those shortcomings somehow added to his charm.

I walked up next to him and gave his hip a little
bump with my waist.

"Tell me where the knives are, and I'll help you
finish this up."

He looked down at me and the smile left his face,
replaced with a smoldering look. He set his knife down
and turned his body toward mine, put his hands on my
hips and turned me toward him, and then hunched down
and spoke into my ear.

"I'm not sure that I should be handling sharp objects
with you this close to me. I find you rather distracting,
you know?" He licked the skin at the nape of my neck
and behind my ear. "I've never had a physical reaction to
anyone like I do to you. Your skin tastes so good, Zach. It
makes me think of last night, of licking you, and sucking
you. I want that again. I want you in my mouth again. I
want to taste all of you."

My knees went weak, my heart raced, and I lost my breath. I whimpered against him, rubbed my erection against his leg, and heard him gasp.

"We need alone time, don't we? Otherwise, I'm not sure I'll be able to control myself much longer. And I could end up emotionally scarring Dean when I attack his little brother in the kitchen." I found myself considering whether the kitchen table could hold our weight, or if the counter would be better. Aaron laughed as he looked down at me, apparently able to read my thoughts. "My friend is having a birthday party tonight, and when I was running out on them last night, I promised I'd stop by. If you don't mind coming with me, we could go to dinner before the party, stop in for a little bit, and then have some alone time together."

I was focused on the alone time part of the evening's program.

"That sounds great."

I kissed him softly, amazed at how much I enjoyed those kisses, and wondering why I went my whole life avoiding something that made me feel so warm and connected. But then I realized those were the exact reasons I had avoided it. I wasn't going to let myself focus on my past at that moment, though. I was going to enjoy the breakfast Aaron had made and spend a nice Friday afternoon with my nephews and Kim. Amazingly, I wanted to get to know them. And, of course, it didn't hurt that Aaron had taken the day off, so I'd get to be with him all day too.

It was a great day. We didn't do much, mostly hung

around my brother's house, played with the kids, made lunch. Like I said, we didn't do much. But it was one of the best days I'd had in a long time. Probably one of the best I could remember, ever.

I was sitting around the living room, chatting with Dean, when Aaron asked if I was ready to go. Normally, I spend quite a bit of time getting ready to go out. But I'd planned on leaving after one night, so I hadn't packed any other clean clothes. Besides, it seemed that Aaron was going to stay in the jeans and T-shirt he was wearing. In the short time I'd known him, I realized Aaron was a very low-key guy, no muss, no fuss. And I found I liked that about him.

"Have fun tonight, guys. Hey, Uncle Aaron?"

Aaron looked at my brother. Dean pointed at the bottom of his T-shirt.

"It looks like you have some peaches, or maybe those are sweet potatoes, on your shirt."

Aaron looked down.

"Hmmm. I think those are sweet potatoes. Ryan can't get enough of them. We got through a jar and a half at lunch. I'll be right back, Zach. I'm going to wash this off in the sink."

And with that, he turned to the bathroom. I sat down next to Dean.

"You really do like him, don't you?" Dean asked.

Yes, I liked him. I really liked him. I more than liked him. I realized that, of course. But I was too scared to admit it to myself, and I surely wasn't going to say it out loud.

"Yeah, I do. He's not like anyone I've ever known. And he has this magnetic combination of being fucking hot and yet adorable at the same time."

Dean laughed at my answer. "Adorable? The guy has, what, at least seven inches and forty-five pounds on you, and you think he's adorable?"

I shrugged. There was a sweetness to Aaron, a sincerity, that I wasn't used to. I didn't know how else to describe it. "So are you going to give me the speech about not hurting him again?"

Dean looked into my eyes and patted my knee. "Nah. There's no point, anyway. It's too late. He's already fallen for you. I hope you realize what a great catch he is, Zach."

Aaron came back into the room with a big wet spot on the bottom of his shirt, where the baby food used to be.

"Ready to go?"

I looked down at his shirt.

"Do you need to change?"

"It'll dry. Besides, these guys have seen worse. There were many times when I showed up to our volunteer meetings with baby vomit on my shoulder or something. You can imagine how well that went over."

We walked to the car, and I wondered how much time Aaron spent with my brother's family. The way they made it sound, he was like a nanny or a third parent. And I'd been thinking about Dean's comment to me that Aaron saved them. What did that mean? We hadn't talked about family the previous night; I'd still been upset about the funeral. And I wasn't ready to say much that night either, so I decided to leave that topic alone.

I was also curious about Aaron's sexual history. What Dean had told me about Aaron's not being with any other guys the entire time he'd known him, seemed impossible. But, once again, I wasn't sure how to bring up his history without having to talk about mine. And I was pretty sure once he knew my history, he'd have second thoughts about wanting any kind of relationship with me. I could've told myself it didn't matter, that I wasn't into relationships, that this was just a fling with a hot guy for a few days. But who would I be kidding?

We chatted about work and movies on the drive to the restaurant. After we ordered, Aaron took my hand, something I was getting used to and enjoyed.

"Dean mentioned that he told you about Michael."

The ex. Another thing I'd been wondering about. Dean said they dated in high school and college, which is longer than most people I know have ever dated one person, especially at that age. But Dean didn't say why they ended things. I assumed it was the typical deal where people grow apart as they age.

"He didn't say much. Just that you dated when you were younger."

Aaron nodded. His eyes looked sad.

"Do you want me to tell you about him? I don't want to hide anything from you, Zach."

If not telling me details about a childhood boyfriend constituted hiding something, I was pretty sure Aaron would expect me to tell him about, at a minimum, guys who I'd been fucking around with over the past few years or the past few months or the past few weeks or the night before I left LA to come to the funeral. Not that there was any possible way for me to remember all of them. Fuck, I was a slut.

Aaron must have taken my silence as a desire for him to tell me about his ex, because he started talking again. His voice sad, quiet, and far away.

"We went to high school together. He was a year ahead of me, but it wasn't a big school, so everyone basically knew everyone else. Anyway, Michael came up to me one day and asked me out. I wasn't into him, but he was a nice guy, and there was something in his eyes that told me he was hurting. I could tell he needed to talk. So I agreed to go out with him, thinking we could be friends.

"Well, it turned out that he was hurting. He was sick. Very sick. He'd been diagnosed with leukemia, and they didn't know what his chances were. I think that's what gave him the courage to ask me out. He figured if he was facing death, then being gay wasn't the end of the world.

"I wanted to help him. His family was great, don't get me wrong, but he didn't have any close friends, and when you're going through treatments and all that, you need all the support you can get. So, I spent a lot of time with him, went with him to his appointments when his parents had to work, sat in his hospital room when he had to go in for an infection, that sort of thing. Before I realized it, I was his boyfriend. At least that's how he saw me. And I wasn't going to disagree. No matter what his parents said, Michael and I both knew he wasn't going to beat the cancer.

"He gave it his best, though. He made it through high school, and at one point they even thought he was going into remission. Unfortunately, that was pretty short-lived. When I graduated, I decided to go to a local college, so I could stay close to Michael. He needed my help more by that time, driving him to appointments that were a few hours away, keeping track of what he needed to do. Plus, he didn't want me to leave.

"I think Michael realized what we had was friendship more than anything else, but we were young and horny, and we both knew he didn't have much time left. So when he wanted to start fooling around, I agreed. It was hand jobs for the first couple of years. And then, sometime during my first year in college, he took a turn for the worse. After about a month of hell, in which Michael had more treatments than I ever remembered, making him sick almost every day, they decided to stop the meds and give his body time to recover.

"That's when I first gave him a blow job. I could tell he wanted it, but he wasn't going to ask. And I didn't mind. He was my friend, and he'd been hurting for so long. Besides, I wanted to know what it was like to have a dick in my mouth. He wanted to reciprocate, but he couldn't. I knew how nauseous and weak he was most of the time, and having my dick stuffed down his throat wasn't going to make that easier.

"He died when I was nineteen, and his family was a complete mess. I probably spent as much time with them over the next couple of years as I had with Michael.

I think his parents liked having me around because I reminded them of their son. Plus, they kind of checked out after Michael died, and he had two little sisters who were super-sweet. So I spent my free time there, helping with the girls, keeping his parents company.

"Thankfully, they got things together and healed a lot by the time I graduated, so I didn't feel too guilty when I left for veterinary school. I still see them when I go home. They've become like a second family to me."

Aaron held my hand between both of his the entire time he was talking, his eyes far away, like he was seeing the past, walking through it for me. When he finished, he took a deep breath, seeming relieved he'd gotten the story out. Then he looked at me expectantly.

I hadn't said a word. What could I say? I didn't know whether to admire him or feel sorry for him. Maybe both.

Trying to buy more time, I decided I'd ask him about the next guy. Whoever he was, the story couldn't be as confusing as a dying boyfriend who he didn't want to be with and yet stuck with for years.

"So, after Michael, what did you do?"

Aaron looked confused.

"What do you mean? I told you—I finished college and then went to vet school."

"No, I mean, as far as guys. Did you only play around or did you get into another relationship?"

"There haven't been any other guys. I don't know if it makes any sense, Zach, and I know it sounds cruel but—" He hesitated and looked at me before continuing.

"I was so lonely when I was with Michael."

He sighed and looked down at the table. "He was my friend, and I loved him, but I wasn't in love with him. And as I got a little older, I wanted to be in a real relationship, but I couldn't. Michael needed me. So after he was gone, the idea of playing around held no appeal for me. It seemed like more of the same emptiness. And I never fell in love with anyone, so I stuck with these guys." He held up both of his hands. "I was a pitcher for my high school baseball team, and the coach worked hard with me on being ambidextrous. Turns out, it came in handy off the field too."

I knew he was trying to lighten the mood, and his comment was funny. But I couldn't eke out even a chuckle. If I thought wrapping my mind around the dead boyfriend was going to be tough, thinking through Aaron's self-imposed celibacy, since the age of nineteen, was worse.

I'd never been one of those guys who fantasized about corrupting a virgin or some shit. I'd always preferred guys with experience. That way they could take control and make me feel good. And I knew I couldn't lie to Aaron about my history. I could get over his lack of experience. Hell, we could make our own experiences. But, he was like the virgin bride, holding out until he fell in love. He'd never be able to accept my past.

Aaron stood up. He brushed my hair back and looked into my eyes.

"I promised my friend, Micah, that I'd stop by his party. I'm sorry, Zach. I can see that you're upset about this. We can talk more about it after the party. I know it's a lot to take in, but I promise you, I'm not hung up on Michael. I don't usually tell people how I really felt about him. In fact, I've never told anyone. I wanted you to know, though, so you wouldn't think you had to compete with a ghost or something."

I nodded, only partially processing what he was saying, still thinking through our conversation. It wasn't until we'd arrived at his friend's house, parked the car, and walked up the steps that I realized something. Aaron said that in all the years since Michael died, he hadn't had sex with anyone because he hadn't fallen in love. But the previous night, at the bar, in the bathroom with me, he... Was Aaron saying he was in love with me?

That thought shook me up. It was too much, too fast. The next hour was sort of a blur for me. We were in his friend's house with lots of other guys. It was much tamer than the parties I was used to, but, thank God, there was vodka. I needed a drink to calm me down and help me relax. Aaron's story, and his implication that he was in love with me, were causing me to feel a whole bunch of things. Now, you might be thinking that I was honored or excited. And, I guess, in some ways I was. But the dominant feelings were anxiety and...disappointment.

Knowing about his past, seeing him with my brother's family...fuck, even listening to the words he used, it was clear to me that we couldn't be together. The reality was, I couldn't be the kind of boyfriend he wanted. That was, if I could be a boyfriend at all.

Over the past couple of days, I'd developed feelings for Aaron, deep feelings. I could see myself wanting to spend a lot of time with him. And I was attracted to him sexually. But, being realistic, I wasn't sure I could be monogamous or, frankly, whether that was what I even wanted. Not that any of that mattered, of course, because once he found out about my past, I knew he wouldn't be interested any longer.

Those were my thoughts as I wandered through the party, drinking continuously. Alcohol, combined with an emotional evening, and topped off by jealousy, could lead people to act in ways they normally wouldn't. I'd like to say that was what happened—that those factors combined in me, and that was why I did what I did next. But that would be bullshit. I did what I did next because that was who I was.

CHAPTER SEVEN

I WAS standing in the kitchen, finishing off a bottle of vodka, when I felt someone reach around my waist and grab my dick. That was usually the sign of a fun end to the evening, so I pressed back against the hard body.

"It's nice to see you too. Wait, I can't see you. Do you want to let go of my cock for a minute, so I can turn around?"

My voice was playful but my words were slurred because of all the alcohol.

I heard a laugh, and then the hold on my cock loosened. I turned around to see a guy a few inches taller than me. He was okay-looking. Nothing special, but not someone I'd throw out of bed, either.

"Hi, Zach. It's been a while. You're looking good."

I wondered how he knew my name. I looked at him closely, going back through my high school Rolodex, thinking if he was at that party, then I probably knew him from those days. But I couldn't place him.

"You don't remember my name, do you?" he asked.

Umm, yeah. That too. Not your name, not your face, not a fucking thing. I didn't say that, though. Before the guy could say anything, someone else walked into the kitchen.

"Hey, Robert. I was looking for you." The new guy put his arm around Robert—now I had a name, but still had no fucking clue who he was—and then they both looked at me. "Who's your friend?"

His tone was suggestive, and he was drunk. It was comforting to me. That whole scene was familiar. We were all drunk, and there was sexual innuendo in the air. I'd been there, done that, hell, I owned the fucking T-shirt. Speaking of T-shirts—

"Nice shirt. So, are you offering?"

New Guy was pointing at my shirt and using what I guessed was supposed to be a seductive tone, but he wasn't pulling it off. I looked down and realized that I was still wearing the "Receiving Department" shirt.

"This is Zach. The guy I was telling you about earlier. The one from LA."

My face must have shown my surprise because Robert started laughing.

"You have no fucking clue who I am, do you?"

I didn't say anything, and then New Guy joined in the laughter.

"Damn, Robert, I'd say you should be insulted. The guy sucked your dick, and he has no clue who you are. Not very memorable, are you?"

Robert pouted a little. It wasn't cute.

"Well, he didn't have any complaints that night. I'm staying here for the weekend, and I have a nice big bed. What do you say we head into my room, and I can give you a reminder, Zach?"

New Guy decided to get in on the action.

"I'll join you. Then I can find out if you're being aboveboard with that T-shirt."

I was going to laugh the whole thing off and walk away. Really, I was. But then I looked out through the door and saw Aaron talking with a few guys. They were all dressed conservatively, like professionals of one kind or another. And they seemed to know each other pretty well.

One of them was standing very close to Aaron, taking every opportunity to touch him, stroke his arm, laugh at whatever Aaron was saying. The guy was cute, and it was clear to me that he was into Aaron.

And, even though I'd already realized I would have no chance with Aaron once he knew about my past, I was jealous. Unreasonably jealous. Suddenly I didn't want to tell him about my past. I didn't want to see the look in his eyes change from loving to disgusted or, at a minimum, disappointed. No, I didn't want to tell him who I was. Instead, I decided, in that drunken, jealous state, that I'd be who I was, and he could see for himself. Then he could walk away, and I wouldn't have to face him.

I pushed myself off the table I'd been leaning against.

"Sounds good, boys. Give me a sec."

I walked just outside of the kitchen door and spoke to the first guy I saw.

"Hey, do you know Aaron Paulson?"

"Oh, sure. He's right over there."

He pointed over to Aaron, which caught Aaron's

attention. He looked at me and raised his eyebrows. I avoided his eyes.

"Would you please let him know that his friend, Zach, found another ride home? Thanks."

I didn't wait for an answer. Instead, I turned back to the kitchen, knowing Aaron's eyes were on me as I grabbed Robert's ass and whispered in his ear.

"Let's go to your room."

The three of us walked down a hallway in the opposite direction from the living room. We got to the bedroom and started shedding our clothes.

Now, I realize this is the part of the story where I'm supposed to describe a steamy three-way for you in explicit detail. But here's the thing, I'd have to do that from a memory that didn't happen that night. No, that night was probably the worst sexual experience of my life. And, considering the number of sexual experiences I'd had, well, that was really fucking saying something.

It wasn't Robert and New Guy's fault. They were drunk and horny, like I usually liked my guys. No, it was me. No matter how much I wanted to be into it, no matter how often I reminded myself over the next twenty minutes that this was hot, it was fun, it was sex—no matter how hard I tried not to think of Aaron, I couldn't stop thinking about him. And I couldn't get myself to relax and enjoy being with someone who wasn't him.

Being fucked while you were tense was not a good idea, as it turned out. New Guy lubed up his condom-covered cock. I saw that, but it wasn't enough. Not when I couldn't relax. So, by the time the whole thing was done,

I hadn't come—hell, I hadn't even gotten hard—but my ass was sore as hell, and my jaw didn't feel much better. Robert had the courtesy to pull out of my mouth before he came, but I could still taste his cock in my mouth, and it sickened me.

The three of us got dressed. Robert and New Guy were talking. I couldn't tell you what they said because I wasn't paying attention. I felt like shit physically, my mind was cloudy from the vodka, and most of all, I realized I'd just lost what would probably be the only chance I'd ever have to be in a real relationship with a guy who was smart, kind, interesting, and hot as fuck. A guy who, a few hours earlier, had all but told me he was in love with me.

"Robert, would you mind if I stayed here for a minute? I need to catch my breath."

He nodded and patted New Guy on the back as they walked out the door.

"See that? I went from not memorable to breathtaking. I'd say that's an improvement."

I sat on the bed and tried to think. What the fuck had I done? I'd been reckless many times in my life, and I wasn't a particularly considerate person, but I'd never been cruel. Not until that night. I realized, even in my drunken condition, that I'd crossed a line. And that, as a result, I'd likely hurt a person who had been nothing but good to me.

I couldn't call my brother to come pick me up. That would require an explanation of why I wasn't with Aaron. Not that I knew how I'd get into Dean's house without raising some questions. After all, I didn't have a key, but Aaron did, so if I rang the bell, it'd be pretty clear something had happened with Aaron. Shit.

I picked up my cell phone and called information for a cab. I figured by the time the driver got there, I'd have decided whether to go to Dean's or go to the airport and leave my shit behind.

"You don't need a cab, Zach. I'll take you wherever you want to go."

That was Aaron's voice. What was he still doing here? My head shot up so quickly it hurt. I saw Aaron, standing in the doorway, looking sad and tired. I was frozen, sitting on the bed, staring at him, not sure what to do. He had to know I'd been having sex with those two guys. So why hadn't he left? Or, at the very least, why wasn't he yelling at me?

But he hadn't left. And he wasn't yelling. Instead, he walked over to me, took my hands, and pulled me up.

"So, did you find what you were looking for, Zach?"

His eyes were peering into mine, as if he could get his answer by looking at me. The depth and intensity of that gaze were too much for me.

"I think I'm going to be sick."

Aaron quickly led me to the bathroom. I barely made it to the toilet before my stomach emptied its contents. When I was done, I stood up, and Aaron handed me a warm, wet washcloth. As I was wiping my mouth, he looked through the vanity drawers and then gave me an unopened toothbrush and a bottle of mouthwash. I was actually grateful for the taste of vomit, because it helped cover up the taste of Robert's dick. Though, I realized that was probably more in my mind than in my mouth. But cleaning all of those flavors out was what I needed.

I brushed furiously, my teeth, my gums, and my tongue. Then I sloshed the mouthwash in my mouth until my tongue was burning, and my sore jaw could take it no longer. I spit into the sink and felt grateful that I'd mostly burned the taste of Robert out of my mouth.

I stared at Aaron, confused by his presence and his caring attitude. Why was he still there? I'd walked into a room at his friend's house and fucked around with two guys while we were on a date, and he was standing in the other room. Logic dictated he should be hitting me, not taking care of me. And then he made my mind spin even further when he reached over and stroked my hair. I would've flinched, but he was moving so slowly I knew he wasn't going to hit me. Actually, I'd realized by then that Aaron would never hurt anybody.

He put his arm around me, recognizing I wasn't exactly steady on my feet. And to make matters worse, my ass was sore as hell, and I knew he could probably tell that from the way I was limping. But Aaron didn't say anything about it. In fact, he didn't say anything at all. He held onto me as he walked me down the hallway, back through the kitchen, and out the back door. When we got to his car, he opened my door and helped me get into my seat.

I was completely exhausted and the alcohol was taking effect, making me want to pass out. I must have closed my eyes for longer than I realized, because when I opened them, I saw Aaron opening the car door and getting back in. I looked out the window and noticed we were in front of a drug store. Aaron set a bag on the floor of the car and pulled out of the parking lot.

I fell asleep again, and the next thing I remembered was standing in a bathroom and leaning on Aaron as he took off my clothes. When I was naked, he turned toward the shower and pulled the curtain open. The water was already on. He helped me step into the shower, and I put my hand on the wall to keep myself steady. Then Aaron got in behind me.

I turned to look at him and immediately got hard. His body was incredible. His chest and stomach had no fat on them. Every muscle was defined. He had a small diamond of blond hair on his chest that trailed down, disappearing at his belly button, then reappearing to lead down to his cock.

Holy shit, his cock. It was perfect. The skin was a bit darker than the rest of Aaron's golden color. It was smooth, and it looked plump and long, even as it lay flaccid against his leg. His legs and arms were also covered in that soft, blond hair, and like his chest and stomach, the muscles were well-defined. I was pretty sure Aaron spent a lot of time running or swimming.

Damn it all, I was so fucking screwed. I couldn't get it up when I was in bed with two guys, but with Aaron, I had an instant erection even when I felt sick as shit.

Aaron picked up the shampoo bottle, poured some on his hands, and then started massaging my head. Standing next to each other that way, with him focusing on my head and both of our bodies exposed, made me realize even more the difference in our sizes. My eyes were lined up with his chest, and when he picked up the bar of soap and lathered up my body, it was like I was wrapped up in him.

His touch was soft. He washed my chest, my arms, my pits, my stomach, my dick and balls, and my legs. My dick pulsed when Aaron rubbed his slick, soap-covered hands on it. But he kept washing me. When he was done with my front, he turned me around and paid the same gentle attention to my back and legs. He also washed my ass. First the cheeks, and then his soapy fingers ran up my crack. I shuddered and moaned.

Even though I was more sore than I'd ever remembered being, I wanted him in me more than I'd ever wanted anyone else. So much so, in fact, that I found myself silently begging in my head for him to fuck me against the shower wall. I decided the pain would be worth it, and I didn't care that he didn't have a condom; I trusted him. How fucking stupid was that, right? I had *never* had sex without a condom. Not once. I may have been slutty, but I wasn't stupid.

Aaron turned me around so the water could wash off my soapy back. That put us face-to-face under the spray. I saw his eyes move down to my dick, which by that point was rock hard, pressed up against my stomach, and weeping. For some reason, I felt the need to explain myself to him.

"I didn't come back there, at your friend's house. And the way you were touching me...I'm sorry. I'm just so fucking attracted to you."

He didn't speak. Instead, he picked up the soap, lathered his hands, reached down to my dick, and started stroking me.

"Ohhh!"

I was surprised to feel him on me, and I instinctively thrust forward into his hand. He put his other hand behind me, on the small of my back, holding me steady. Then he continued to stroke me, with a firm but gentle grip, occasionally running his thumb over my crown.

It didn't take long for me to start feeling that familiar tingling. I rested my forehead on his chest and put my hands on him to keep myself upright. The water was running over us, washing the soap off my body, as Aaron's gentle but firm movement on my cock continued.

And then he spoke to me, his voice low and hoarse. One word, but it carried so much emotion, so much longing.

"Zach."

I gasped, thrust my hips, and clutched his skin in my hands as I exploded, shouting his name in response.

Damn it all, I had no idea how the guy could make me feel so good and come so hard with a hand job. I lifted my head off his chest and looked into his eyes. He took his hand off my cock and brought it to his mouth, licking off the cum that was dripping from it.

"Oh, shit, Aaron."

I was panting, staring at him, wanting...something. He still had one hand on the small of my back, and he used it to pull me even closer to him. Then he lowered his other hand from his mouth, put it behind my neck, hunched down, and pulled me up to meet his lips. I couldn't believe he'd still want to kiss me, knowing my mouth had probably been on at least one or possibly two other guys' dicks that night, and that I'd thrown up.

But he did kiss me. He licked my lips, entered my mouth with his tongue, and explored me completely. By the time he was done, I could taste only Aaron. The sickening thought of Robert's dick in my mouth was gone, and it had been replaced by the feeling of Aaron's lips, Aaron's tongue, Aaron's desire. And that was when I realized that was exactly what I'd needed.

I started running my hand down his chest, analyzing the feeling in my jaw and wondering whether I could blow him in my current condition or if I'd have to settle for stroking him off. I wanted to feel him in my mouth, but I wasn't sure. Then Aaron reached behind me and turned off the water. He pulled a towel from the rack and wrapped me in it, then stepped out of the shower, opened the vanity, and took out another towel that he used to dry himself off.

What the fuck? We weren't done. I started to step out of the shower to follow him and protest, but I'd forgotten about the soreness in my ass, and the sudden movement hurt, causing me to gasp and slip a bit. Aaron's hands were on me before I even realized what had happened.

"I'm sorry, Zach. I shouldn't have left you in there."

He put one arm around my shoulder, bent his knees, put another arm under my legs, and lifted me up.

"Wrap your arms around my neck. I'm taking you

to bed."

I was going to object, tell him I was perfectly capable of walking. But I enjoyed being in his arms, feeling his strength, so I wrapped my arms around him and rested my head on his shoulder.

When we got to the bed, Aaron bent down and used the hand under my legs to tug at the sheet. When he had it pulled away, he lowered me onto the bed.

"Turn over, Zach. I'm going to get the stuff from the drug store. I'll be right back."

So he wanted to fuck me? That was why he didn't let me get him off in the shower. Well, it'd hurt like hell in my current condition, but it was fine with me. It was more than fine. I wanted him so desperately that my cock hardened again in anticipation. And I was grateful he'd had the good sense to buy condoms.

My arms were folded on the bed, and I was resting my head on them with my eyes closed when Aaron came back into the room. He surprised me by turning on the overhead light and the table lamp by the bed. I looked at him and blinked my eyes.

"I'm sorry, Zach. I'll turn the light off soon. I need to be able to see."

What? There was enough light coming into the room from the open bathroom door to do what we were going to do. Whatever. Light, dark—I didn't care as long as I was getting Aaron inside me. I sighed and relaxed as I continued to watch him.

He scooted his naked body in between my spread legs and ran his big hand softly over my ass. Then he reached over for a pillow and tucked it under my hips, raising me. He bent his head down and spread my cheeks, gently prodding me with his fingers. I hadn't ever been touched like that. I was enjoying it, because I enjoyed all of Aaron's touches, but I couldn't figure out what he was doing.

Then he reached into the drug-store bag and pulled out a tube. It wasn't lube, it was a cream. He must have taken my surprised look as fear.

"Don't worry; I won't hurt you, Zach. I'll be careful. This will help. You're torn and this will make you feel better."

And with that, Aaron opened the tube and gently rubbed the cream onto my pucker and pushed in a little to get the cream spread around my internal sphincter. Then he closed the tube, scooted off the bed, and walked into the bathroom.

I was shocked and hadn't moved from the position I'd been in when I realized what Aaron was doing. What in the hell was that? Taking me home so he could have his turn with me was one thing. It made sense. But he stopped at a store to buy cream for me to help with pain from when I got fucked by *another* guy, and then he actually applied the cream. Who did that? I was shaken up by the whole experience.

CHAPTER EIGHT

I WAS lying on my stomach in the middle of the bed when Aaron came back from the bathroom. He was still completely naked and fucking breathtaking. He had turned off the overhead light and the table lamp. He ran his hand lightly down my back and then got into bed next to me.

The blanket was pooled down at the bottom of the bed. Aaron yanked it and covered us, then reached over to pull me closer. I scooted over and let him press my body against his. I rested my head on his shoulder and gazed into his eyes as his hand reached up and stroked my hair.

"You must be tired, babe. Go to sleep now."

I was tired. The day had been draining, both physically and emotionally. But I couldn't sleep. Thoughts of Aaron kept me awake. The way he spoke to me, the velvet warmth in his voice. And the way he treated me. No one had ever been so careful, so gentle, so kind to me. Aaron made me feel loved, truly loved.

My father died when I was eight, so I didn't remember him very well. But in my fuzzy memory, I remembered him telling me that he loved me. That was the only time anyone had said those words to me, and it was the only time I'd felt loved. Until Aaron. He hadn't quite said it, but he showed it with his actions, through his voice, in his gaze. And he implied it. But why?

He was a great-looking, successful guy. I'd already known he would've had no trouble finding a partner before I met his friends, and it had been confirmed by the way several guys had looked at him at the party that night. So, why me? I had an idea, but I didn't have time to explore it because I could feel Aaron shaking.

We were both on our sides, having moved around while we slept, with Aaron spooning behind me, his arm slung over my chest. I was half-asleep when I felt his body shaking and heard him sniffling. He must have thought I was completely asleep, because he spoke quietly to himself as he clutched me and pulled me tighter against him.

"Please let me love you, Zach. Please just let me love you."

I could hear the longing and the pain in his voice, and it touched me in a way I couldn't recognize, a way I didn't know I was capable of feeling.

"Please, Zach, please. Let me love you."

I turned over onto my other side, so we were chest to chest. I could see surprise in his wet eyes, but he didn't move his arm, so he was still holding me.

"I...I'm sorry. I didn't mean to wake you."

"You didn't wake me, Aaron."

Those were the only words I spoke to him. There was nothing more for us to say that night. I knew the next morning I'd have to talk with him. But at that moment, lying in his bed, sharing his warmth and his strength, I wanted to give in to my feelings. I wanted to know what it would be like to share a bed with Aaron, what it would be like to have a lover and not just a fuck buddy.

So I stroked his cheek with my hand and felt my heart skip a beat when he pressed his face into the touch and whimpered. Then I leaned in to share one of those kisses to which I'd become addicted. As soon as my mouth neared his, Aaron pulled my body against his and pressed his lips to mine, his tongue sweeping in between my lips and into my mouth. I hadn't expected that level of passion and my dick immediately hardened to capacity in reaction. I raised my other hand to Aaron's face so that I was cupping both of his cheeks and held him close as we kissed.

We lay there for several minutes, pressed together, kissing passionately. By that point, I was so turned on I could feel the moisture at the tip of my dick. I started thrusting gently against Aaron, pressing against his cock. Aaron groaned and rolled me onto my back, lying on top of me. Then he cupped my cheeks in his hands so we were both holding onto each other's faces, and we came together again, kissing and licking. Aaron continued the thrusts, and I met him, pressing up against him.

Our movements had gone from slow to fast and constant. We were both panting for air but we couldn't stop kissing. Aaron was moaning deeply, and I was whimpering from the feel of his hard body pressing me down and covering me completely as we thrust against each other.

"Oh, Aaron. Ungh. I'm close."

I was able to get out the breathless warning, and it succeeded in making Aaron thrust harder and faster. I don't know which one of us came first, but within minutes, the room was filled with both our voices, moaning and shouting, and then our stomachs and chests were coated in our joined cum.

Throughout that, our hands never left each other's faces and our mouths didn't separate. We were moaning into each other, shouting as we were pressed together. And even as I tried to catch my breath, I held him against me.

"Oh my God, Aaron. I've never... I've never..."

I couldn't finish my sentence. I needed to feel his tongue in my mouth again. I needed to taste him. So I pushed my mouth up to his. He met me and took my lower lip between his, darting his tongue out to lick me as he continued to hold my face and stroke my cheeks. Then he mumbled softly, "I know, Zach. I know."

I buried my face against his neck and held him tight. He returned the hug with equal pressure. After a few minutes, he started to pull back.

"Let me get a washcloth to wipe you off, babe."

I spoke without thinking.

"No, I don't mind. Please stay with me. Don't leave me, Aaron."

He looked intently into my eyes.

"I won't leave you, Zach."

I relaxed against him and closed my eyes, feeling secure in his warm embrace.

As I was drifting off to sleep, he whispered into my ear, "I love you."

And in that moment, I allowed myself to believe him and to enjoy how those words made me feel. Even though I knew that, in the light of day, I'd have to walk away, and it would all end.

Morning came all too soon. I woke up in Aaron's arms, with his warm blue eyes gazing at me. As much as I hated to do it, I knew the time had come to say goodbye.

"Aaron..."

I swallowed and tried to push myself forward. I knew I had to end it. But the look in his eyes held me, and I couldn't, I couldn't walk away completely.

"I don't know if I can do this. I need time, Aaron. I need to go back to LA so I can think."

He didn't say anything, but there was understanding in his eyes.

"I know. Let's get dressed, and I'll take you back to Dean's. When's your flight?"

The previous morning, I'd pushed the flight back one day. So I was scheduled to leave at noon that day. I glanced at the clock.

"In a few hours."

"Okay. That gives us time to take a quick shower, and you can hang out with your family before I take you to the airport."

Whatever I was expecting, it wasn't that. He was calm and didn't seem surprised by my decision. But he continued to treat me and speak to me as if nothing had changed. That familiarity Aaron had with me, that way of behaving as if we were a couple, despite the fact we'd essentially just met, none of that changed when I told him I'd be leaving.

We cleaned up, got dressed, and drove to Dean's. When we walked into the kitchen, Dean and Kim were both smiling broadly. Their joy at seeing Aaron and me together was palpable.

"Hi, guys," Kim squealed as she bounced up to Aaron and practically jumped into his arms.

Dean patted Aaron's shoulder.

"Thank goodness you're here. Aaron, the gutter on the side of the house came loose again. Can you give me a hand?"

Dean didn't wait for an answer. He simply turned toward the back door, assuming Aaron would follow. I stood there wondering whether handyman was in his job description as well. Was there anything Aaron didn't do for Dean's family?

"Sure thing, Dean."

Aaron leaned down and kissed my cheek, then he followed Dean out. Obviously, he wasn't getting the picture. I sighed.

"So, things seem great between you and Aaron. I'm so happy, Zach. This is wonderful!"

I couldn't handle Kim's cheeriness that early in the morning. Especially without any coffee in my system and with the sadness I had about leaving Aaron. For some reason, no matter what I said, or how big of an asshole I was, the guy stuck around and didn't get angry. Actually, I understood the reason, and it was exactly why I was leaving.

"I'm going back to LA, Kim. I don't think things will work out between me and Aaron."

"What? Why?"

She looked incredulous. I opened my mouth to answer her, but I couldn't do that without talking about Michael and the things Aaron told me he hadn't shared with anyone else. So I asked a question I was fairly sure would lead me to the same place.

"Dean told me that Aaron saved your lives. What did he mean?"

Kim was taken off guard by the question, and color rose to her cheeks as she looked down at the ground. She seemed embarrassed or ashamed. But then she raised her head and met my eyes.

"I don't like to talk about this, Zach. It was a dark time in my life. But I want you to know because I can see how Aaron feels about you. And you need to know how wonderful he is, Zach. If you realize that, I know you'll make sure things work out between the two of you."

I sat down at the kitchen table and gave her the space to tell the story in her words.

"I got pregnant with Simon right after we got married. Dean and I both wanted a big family, so I thought getting started right away was a good idea. I'd just finished vet school, but we hadn't moved yet because Dean was doing some work at the university. It was all like a dream. I had a wonderful husband, good friends, and an easy pregnancy. Everything was perfect. But that all changed when Simon was born.

"I didn't know what was wrong with me, but I couldn't stop worrying. My whole body hurt. I couldn't sleep. I couldn't concentrate. Nothing Dean did was right. And I couldn't take care of Simon. My goodness, I couldn't even take care of myself. To make a long story short, Zach, I was suffering from postpartum depression.

"We had a hard time getting it under control. I went to see doctors and therapists, etc., etc. But while I was...sick, Dean and Simon struggled. So Aaron stepped in. Literally.

"We were living in Dean's two bedroom condo. Aaron had been his roommate before we got married, but he moved out right before the wedding. We turned his old room into a nursery as soon as we found out we were pregnant. But after Simon came, when I couldn't get myself under control, Aaron moved back in.

"He put a twin bed next to Simon's crib, and he lived with us for a full year. He was still in school at the time. Aaron and Dean managed to arrange their schedules so I was never alone. And that's how it went. Aaron left to go to class. But, other than that, he spent every moment at the house. He cooked, he cleaned, he took care of Simon. And he never once complained or tried to make me feel guilty. He'd tell me how much he loved Simon, how lucky he was to get to spend so much time with us."

Kim paused a bit, caught her breath, and looked like she was holding back tears.

"Well, eventually I got better, and Dean and I decided it would be best to move back here. He had a great job lined up, and we could start fresh. When we got here,

I was looking for a job at a veterinary clinic, and I came across a practice that was for sale. The owner was moving out of town, but he had a great office and a lot of existing clients. Anyway, I thought it made more sense to buy his clinic and work for myself than to go to work for another vet in town. I realize, now, how naïve I was. Dean realized it then, but he didn't say anything because it was what I wanted, and he was still walking on eggshells around me, not wanting me to fall back into darkness again.

"This story is rambling on, Zach, so I'll skip past some of it and tell you that I was woefully unprepared to own the clinic. I knew nothing about business, nothing. So I managed to mess things up pretty well. I mean, not completely, but it was heading in that direction. And, by the time Dean noticed and stepped in, I'd done enough damage that the business was no longer worth what we owed, so we couldn't sell. And, as if that wasn't bad enough, I messed up with my pills."

Her voice lowered for the last part, so it was almost a whisper. Then she stopped talking and looked at me in an odd way. I thought maybe she needed me to say something, so she'd know I was listening.

"You had an issue with your medication? For the depression?"

She shook her head.

"No, not that. My, ehm, birth control pills. I wasn't taking any other medication, though I probably should've been. So, I got pregnant. The twins weren't planned, Zach. And, frankly, the timing couldn't have been worse. I tried to keep it together, to improve things at the clinic. Dean and I both hoped that somehow we could put things back on track and sell it before the twins came. We were terrified of what would happen if I had the same issues I'd had after Simon was born, and we knew I couldn't possibly manage the babies and work, not in that condition.

"But, as hard as I tried, I was big and hormonal, and I had done too much damage already, so we couldn't sell the clinic, and my C-section was coming up. I didn't know what we were going to do. Dean was stressed, which made me feel guiltier. The whole thing was a nightmare, Zach. I can't tell you how awful it was.

"And then, one Sunday morning, there was a knock on the door, and we opened it to find Aaron on the steps with all his belongings packed in suitcases, sitting on the ground. After Dean and I had moved away, Aaron had had a lot more free time, and he was in his last year at school. So, along with his volunteer work, he started working at a very well-regarded animal hospital. They provided care to domestic pets and also to animals from the zoo.

"I'll skip the details, but believe me, it was a prestigious clinic and a great job for a student. They liked Aaron so much that they offered him a position after graduation. Two years on staff and then he could become a partner. He gave it up, Zach. He walked away from an offer anyone else at our school would've jumped at. And he did it to come and move into our guest room.

"And that's where he stayed, until last month. He lived here, helped with all three boys, helped with the house, and he saved the business. I've still been trying to help, but I'm only able to treat a small percentage of the animals. All of the rest of it, the other animals and the actual business management, that's been Aaron. And, in that short time, he has not only managed to undo the damage I caused, but when we had the clinic appraised a few weeks ago, we heard it was worth twenty percent more than what we'd paid.

"So you see, Zach? He's a wonderful person. He's brilliant. He's kind. He's selfless. And, I'm not even going to pretend here, he's gorgeous. I'm telling you, Zach, I love your brother dearly, but if Aaron were willing to be with me, I'd do it in a heartbeat, even if it meant no sex for the rest of my life because...well, you know."

"If no sex were part of the deal, I'd go for Aaron myself."

Dean's voice startled me. We hadn't heard him come back inside. Surprisingly, he wasn't upset to hear his wife say she'd be willing to leave him for his best friend. And, because I know tones and body language don't come across in writing, I'll tell you that he didn't seem to be kidding when he said he'd do the same thing.

"So, what's with the sales job on Aaron, Kim? From the look on Aaron's face, and the way he was talking about Zach outside just now, it seems to me that these guys are already in...into each other."

Kim didn't say anything, but she glared at me. I sighed.

CHAPTER NINE

"I'M LEAVING, Dean. My flight is in a couple of hours."

"Oh. I guess that makes sense. You hadn't planned on staying long, so you probably didn't make arrangements with work. Are you coming back next weekend?"

I could tell from his anxious tone that he already knew the answer to that question.

"No, Dean, I'm not coming back."

I intentionally left out the next-weekend part of his question. I wanted things to be clear. Kim was almost shaking at this point, but she still hadn't said a word. She glared at Dean. And turned a disturbing shade of red.

"Oh...ummm...but you stayed with Aaron last night and, ehm...I...I guess this is none of my business."

I could see he was upset and that he was holding back because he didn't want to make me mad. It was his business, though. I was his brother, after all.

I know, I know. That was a surprising thought, coming from me, right? I'd never been Mister Family Values. But the past few days with Dean had made me realize I'd been wrong to group him in with the rest of my hateful family as a cause for my miserable childhood. And I also understood, for the first time, that he actually cared about me and wanted us to have a relationship.

So I was about to explain the situation, but then Kim slammed her hand on the table and pushed her chair back with such force that it hit the floor. Who knew little Miss Cheerleader had so much anger? Dean and I both stared at her.

"That's it! I know he's your brother, Dean. I know he's the only family you have. At least the only family that matters, and that you want. But this is too much! Aaron is our family too. He has always been there for us, whenever we've needed anything. And what Zach is doing is going to break his heart. You know that as well as I do, Dean! He has *never* brought a guy over. He doesn't even date, Dean. You do realize that, don't you?"

Then she turned her angry face toward me.

"You act like life is a big party. Like it's all about fun and games. Like you can come here for the weekend, have a fling, and then leave as if it doesn't mean anything. But you're a smart guy, Zach. I can see that. And, even if you weren't, I know Dean warned you about hurting Aaron. So you have to know how he feels about you, how much he has emotionally invested in this thing between you, and how much you're going to hurt him. How dare you come into our home and take advantage of our friend. He trusted you. We trusted you. And you used him."

She put her hands down on the table, looking as though she was trying to catch her breath. Then she continued, but she was no longer shouting.

"You know what? I can't do this. I'm going to go to Mary's for a while. Dean, I'll be back in time for dinner."

And with that, she went to the door, picked up

her purse and keys, and walked out, slamming the door behind her. Dean and I sat in stunned silence.

You might think I was angry about Kim's outburst, but I wasn't. First, it was nice to know she cared so much about Aaron. Also, I liked people who spoke their mind. And last, but not least, I knew she was wrong. I hadn't used Aaron. And my leaving wouldn't hurt him, not really. It was the best thing for him.

"I'm sorry, Zach. She isn't usually like that, but Aaron has done so much for her, for us…"

I put my hand on his.

"I know, Dean. I understand, and I'm not mad."

He looked surprised.

"You know? She…she told you?"

I nodded. I didn't even bother asking how he knew Aaron hadn't been the one who told me. We both knew he wouldn't.

"Jesus, Zach. I don't understand. I get that things growing up were hard, and you didn't have great role models for healthy relationships. And I know a lot of it was my fault, that I should've been there for you. But, trust me, Aaron can give you that. He's loyal and patient. He'll stand by you, Zach. I know I'm not gay but what more could you possibly want in a guy?"

I looked at my brother closely.

"I'm not broken, Dean. I don't need to be saved."

"What? I didn't say you were broken."

"No, I know you didn't. But that's what he thinks. I can see how great he is, Dean. I'm not blind. And I know I'd be lucky as hell to have him. But what he sees in me…

that's not why I want someone to want me. And, believe me, I'm not what he actually wants. He just can't stop himself."

Dean was looking at me with his mouth hanging open. I could tell he had no idea what I was talking about. But that was the only way I knew how to explain it. And frankly, if I sat there much longer talking about walking away from Aaron, I probably would've broken down and cried.

"I need to get going, or I'll miss my flight. I'm going to go spend a little bit of time with the boys, and then I'll grab my bag and head out."

I walked to Dean's guest room and sat on the bed. I'd been in town three days, but it seemed like an eternity. I didn't feel like the same person anymore. I told myself I was tired from the emotions of being in my home town, of my mother's dying, of seeing my family. And that once I got back to LA, things would return to normal.

You're not buying it? Well, neither did I. Telling myself something and believing it weren't exactly the same thing.

After coloring again with Simon, and lying on the floor with Chad and Ryan crawling all over me, I realized it was probably time to go. I stood up and noticed Aaron leaning against the door, watching me. He was a little sweaty from whatever project Dean had him doing, and my dick jumped to attention. Fucking hell, the guy was breathtaking.

"You look good like that, Zach. With kids crawling all over you."

My stomach clenched. I think the panic on my face must have been obvious, because Aaron laughed.

"Don't worry, babe. I'm not making any suggestions."

I laughed nervously, relieved he was kidding around. I picked Ryan up and Aaron picked Chad up. Simon trailed behind us as we walked toward the kitchen. Just before we walked in, Aaron put his hand on my shoulder.

"Yet."

It took me a moment to understand that he was continuing his previous sentence. But when I did, the panic came back, and I froze. Aaron started laughing again.

"Man, are you ever easy!"

Oh, yeah? Two could play at this game.

"Yes, I am. But I always use condoms, so I haven't gotten knocked up so far."

Aaron blushed a little and joined my laughter. We walked into the kitchen to see a somber Dean sitting at the table. He looked back and forth between our laughing faces.

"Ummm, are you ready to go, Zach?"

"I'm taking him to the airport, Dean."

Aaron set Chad down in one highchair, then reached for Ryan. I handed him over, and Aaron buckled him into the other highchair. Aaron looked down at me while he spoke to Dean.

"I want every minute possible with my guy before he leaves." He kissed my cheek, then walked over to the door where my bag was sitting, picked it up, and walked out. "I'll get this in the car while you say goodbye."

Dean was staring down at the table when Aaron walked out. But when the door closed, he looked up at me. His voice sounded tired as he spoke.

"So you haven't told him?"

How could I explain that I'd not only told Aaron that I wasn't ready for a relationship, but that I'd also shown him firsthand by having sex with two guys while he was a few rooms away?

"I told him, Dean. I did. He...he just isn't hearing it." I put my hand on his shoulder. "Don't worry. Once I'm gone, he'll be back to normal."

Dean shook his head at me, but he didn't say anything else about it.

"I'm glad you came, Zach. I've missed you. I hope we can stay in better touch."

I hugged Dean and Simon, kissed the twins on their heads, and walked out to the car. The ride to the airport didn't take long. Aaron pointed out stores, restaurants, and museums as we drove. The town had completely changed during the past decade.

As we pulled up to the airport, my heart felt heavy with the realization that I would likely never see Aaron again. Everything was so comfortable between us, so right. I could talk to him about things I'd never been able to share with another person. We could joke with each other and laugh together. We liked similar movies and books. And he turned me on like no other. I learned all of that in three days, and now I was walking away. It was the right thing to do, but that didn't make it any easier.

I'd been lost in thought, so I didn't realize we were parked at the curb outside the departing flights doors. When I came back to reality, I looked at Aaron. He was gazing at me with understanding in his eyes. I wondered what it was he thought he understood. Was it me?

"Will you please call me when you get home, Zach?"

I didn't want to lie to him. I couldn't lie to him. So, I didn't answer.

"Okay. Then, I'll call you." His voice was husky as he spoke. He moved his hand toward my face and ran his finger along my jawline, over to my chin, and then softly across both of my lips.

The intensity of that moment made my heart race so fast it felt like it was going to beat itself right out of my chest. I wanted, no, I needed to kiss Aaron. It was taking all my effort to hold myself back, but when Aaron slipped his hand behind my head and pulled me toward him, I broke.

I crawled over to his seat and straddled his lap. The steering wheel poked my back, but I didn't care. I plunged my mouth against his, and then we were a blur of mouths and tongues connecting. By the time we separated for air, both of us were out of breath, our hair was disheveled, and our lips were swollen.

I reluctantly returned to my seat, picked up my bag, and sighed heavily as I opened the door. I turned to look at Aaron one last time, trying to engrave his face into my mind so I'd have a happy memory to go to when things looked down.

"I love you, Zach. Take all the time you need. I'll be

here when you figure it out."

Just like that. No pretenses. No posturing. No ultimatums. It almost made me believe him.

I closed the door and turned away so he wouldn't see the wetness in my eyes. I couldn't let him know how much I wished his words were true. I didn't want him to feel guilty when he realized he didn't want to be with me after all.

THE FLIGHT was on time. There was an unusually low amount of traffic on the freeway, and the weather in LA was sunny and beautiful. So why was I so sad to be back? I'd been in my apartment for less than an hour when my phone rang. I took it out of my pocket and saw Aaron's name flashing on the screen.

"Hey."

"Hey, yourself. How was your flight?"

His voice made shivers run down my back. I decided talking to him on the phone wouldn't hurt. Besides, I wasn't ready to say goodbye, yet. So I sank down on one end of the couch and put my feet up at the other, getting comfortable. Our conversation was light. We talked about movies, friends, our jobs. The one thing we didn't talk about was "us."

Maybe we can be friends, I thought to myself. We clicked so well together. There was no reason why I couldn't be Aaron's friend.

Three hours later the battery on my phone was dying, my stomach was growling, and Aaron needed to go to Dean's house, no doubt to help unclog a toilet or some shit. We said our goodbyes, and as I was about to end the call, Aaron added, "I'll call you tomorrow, babe. I love you."

Just friends? Yeah, right. And if you believe that, I have a bridge to sell you.

The next day, I went into work and then met my friends after. It was a big group, and everyone was pretty toasted and loud, so they didn't notice that I hadn't said much. And they didn't say anything when I went back to my apartment, alone.

Aaron had called me while I was out. I'd answered but let him know we couldn't talk. I was pretty down about that missed opportunity and was surprised to realize I would rather have been sitting in my apartment talking to Aaron than having been out with my friends. I'd gotten back to my place, gone through my nightly routine, stripped, and crawled into bed when my phone rang again. It was Aaron.

"Hi." I wondered if he could hear the smile in my voice.

"Hi. I'm sorry for calling again. I missed you, so I thought I'd take the chance that you were done for the night. It doesn't sound as loud in the background. Does that mean you're home, or am I still interrupting your time with your friends?"

He missed me. My chest tightened, and my smile grew bigger.

"You weren't interrupting when you called earlier, Aaron. It was just too loud for me to be able to talk. And, yes, I'm in my apartment and in bed now."

"Oh, yeah? Me too. So, tell me about your day."

So, I did. I told him about a new waitress at work who couldn't seem to keep her orders straight. She managed to deliver a cold turkey sandwich and fries to a customer who'd ordered a hot chicken sandwich with a side salad. Luckily, she has a big chest and a flirty personality and the customer was a middle-aged straight guy. By the time she was done apologizing, he actually thanked her for giving him the wrong order, saying he preferred it to what he'd actually ordered. Aaron laughed and said having good staff was the most important part of running a business.

Aaron told me about his day. He had a full schedule of animals to see, and he also had to handle the books, personnel matters, and ordering of supplies for the clinic. And when he was done with all that, he'd gone to Dean's house to say goodnight to the boys and to give Kim and Dean time to go out by themselves for a drink.

There wasn't any anger or resentment in his voice, but there wasn't joy either. Aaron sounded lonely, and I wondered whether that was true, or whether I was projecting my own feelings.

We couldn't talk as long that night as we had the previous day, because he had to be up early for work the next morning. So we said our goodbyes, and Aaron told me he loved me. Instead of the tension I expected those words to give me, I felt...happy and fulfilled. I drifted off to sleep with thoughts of his warm blue eyes and magical smile dancing in my head.

And that was how life went for the next few months. Nothing had changed—I still had the same job, saw the same friends, worked out at the same time—but everything was different. Every part of my day had an overlay of Aaron: What would he do in this situation? I'll have to tell him this story; he'll get a kick out of it. This reminds me of the time he...

And every night he'd call me.

Sometimes, we only had time to talk for fifteen minutes, and sometimes it was five hours. But it was always comfortable. There was never any pressure. He didn't bring up our relationship status. He didn't ask me about other guys, and he always told me he loved me.

And, in case you're wondering, there were no other guys. I hadn't been with anyone since I got back to LA. There were offers, plenty of offers. But I wasn't interested. I actually didn't even want to be interested. There wasn't anything for me in that life anymore. My friends noticed and mostly made jokes about the change in my behavior.

So that was how things were going in my life, and I was starting to think about whether it made sense. What was the point in trying to live my old life, trying to stay away from Aaron, when it was clear we both wanted to be with each other? Shit, I'd spent more time talking with him on the phone than I'd spent talking with everyone else I'd ever known combined.

But I still wasn't completely sure about my

relationship with Aaron. I didn't know if I could give him what he needed, which was essentially a lifetime commitment. Politically, Aaron was a very liberal person, and he was open-minded and never judgmental of other people. But in his own life, he was very conservative. He wasn't looking for a fling or even a boyfriend. He was looking for a life partner. I spent endless hours contemplating whether I was capable of being that partner, whether monogamy was in my makeup.

And I still wasn't convinced I was the one he wanted. All those hours talking and getting to know each other had quenched some of my fears, and his constant proclamations of love had chipped away at my doubts. But I still worried that the part of his nature that wanted to take care of people, to heal them, was the root of his attraction to me, so that, much like his relationship with Michael, he wasn't in love with me, but instead, he saw a wounded boy who needed healing. And that, as a result, he would ultimately have the same loneliness and emptiness with me that he'd had with Michael.

One good thing that came out of our nightly calls was that I was able to tell Aaron about my sexual history. About all the guys. Of course, I couldn't remember all of them. But I told him that too.

It was hard to get a handle on someone's feelings and reactions over the phone, because I couldn't see facial expressions or body language. But I'd gotten to know Aaron's voice well by then, and I didn't sense any change in him when he found out I'd been with so many guys. He didn't even seem surprised by it. But he didn't ask for details, and I didn't volunteer.

For the most part, I hadn't been into anything too crazy. But group sex wasn't terribly unusual in my life, and there had been some guys who were into toys, role playing, or water sports. I wasn't ashamed of my past, but I didn't think Aaron would want to hear that level of detail, and I wasn't sure he would understand. Truth be told, I wasn't completely sure I understood it myself. I'd changed so much in those few months that I could no longer relate to the "me" I'd been.

And I didn't miss it—the sex with all those guys. Well, for the most part, I didn't miss it. Through the calls with Aaron, I received warmth and companionship. And I could meet most of my physical needs by stroking myself off, which I did at least twice a day. The one thing I did miss was being fucked.

I lost my virginity when I was sixteen, and since that time, I hadn't gone without it for more than a few weeks. As mid-November approached, I realized it had been more than four months since I'd been fucked. The last time was the completely unsatisfying experience with New Guy from Aaron's friend's party.

I'm a very sexual guy, in case you hadn't noticed, and I don't have any hang-ups. I'll try anything, and I enjoy everything. But having a cock deep inside me, stretching me, massaging my prostate, well, that is more than enjoyment. It's something I crave and need. And going that long without it makes me a little crazy.

CHAPTER TEN

IT HAD been a hectic day at work. The head chef had a family emergency, so he couldn't make it in. That meant I had to cover the dinner hour alone. By the time I got back to my place, it was late, and I was tired and stressed. To me, that didn't translate into going to sleep or watching television. No, instead, I'd found the best way to relax was to get off. So when Aaron called me, I decided to try something new.

"What are you wearing?"

He laughed.

"Well, hello to you too. Is that a new way to answer the phone?"

"It can be. Let's see how it goes this time. So, what are you wearing?"

I'd lowered my voice and used a seductive tone. I could hear Aaron's breath quicken through the phone.

"I'm in bed. And I don't like wearing clothes when I sleep so I'm not wearing anything. What about you, Zach? What are you wearing?"

"I just got in, so I'm wearing my jeans and T-shirt."

"Take them off."

I set the phone down and stripped to my briefs.

Then I picked the phone up and walked into my bedroom.

"They're off."

"Are you naked?"

"No, not yet. I'm wearing black briefs. And I'm running my hand down the front of them, feeling my dick trying to press its way out." Aaron moaned. "Do you want me to take them off, Aaron?"

"Yes."

I could barely hear him, his voice was breaking up.

"Tell me what else you want."

"Oh, Jesus, Zach. I want to make you come. I've wanted to make you come since the first time I laid eyes on you. And the few times we were together weren't enough. I need to hear you moan. I want to make you feel good. With my hand, with my mouth, anything, Zach, anything so I can hear those noises you make. I dream about those noises you made when we were together."

I hadn't expected him to react that way, to exhibit that kind of need. And I was swept away in it. My dick was hard and pulsing. I stroked it with one hand, rubbing the wetness at the tip into the skin. I must have whimpered or made some other noise Aaron enjoyed, because he groaned.

"Are you touching yourself, Zach?"

"Yes. But I've got my eyes closed, and I'm imagining it's your hand on me. I need more, Aaron. Can you give me more?"

"Ungh," he moaned. "I'll give you anything. Tell me what you need. I'm close, Zach. I'm so close. When I hear you finish, we can go over the edge together. Tell me what you need."

"I need you inside me. That's what I want. That's how I want you to make me come."

I was panting as I spoke, the speed of my hand increasing.

"Use your finger. Zach, I want you to put the phone against your shoulder so I can hear you. Then suck your finger until it's good and wet. And push it in. Don't stop stroking, though."

I did what he said. When I sucked on my finger, I moaned and slurped, so he could hear me. I heard him groan in response. Then I reached down between my legs, found my opening, and circled it.

"Ohhhh. Fuck, that feels good. It's been so long."

I pressed in, burying my finger inside myself, and that pushed me over the edge. My dick pulsed and shot ropes of cum on my chin, chest, and stomach. I moaned and shouted. And I could hear Aaron joining me from his own bed.

Once we both caught our breath, Aaron spoke.

"I haven't wanted to push, Zach. But I need to see you. I miss you. What are you doing for Thanksgiving? Do you have time off?"

I reached for my discarded briefs and wiped off my chest and hand.

"Well, I celebrate with my friends on the Tuesday before. We've done it for years. We usually get together at one of the guy's houses and have dinner with our chosen family. That way, those who still celebrate with their families can do both. The restaurant stays open Thursday night. We have a special menu, and we get booked up early with people who don't want to cook. I've always worked that night because I don't have other family."

Aaron was quiet for a few seconds.

"I can come see you. I'll wait until you're off work. We're closing the clinic that whole weekend because of the holiday. I was going to go home to see my parents for a couple of days but...I'm sorry. I don't want to push you."

"I can be there Saturday."

His voice changed completely when I said that. He sounded joyful.

"Really?"

"Yes, really. I'm scheduled for Thanksgiving and Friday. But other than that, I can get away. And I miss you, too, Aaron. You're not being pushy. I'm glad you want to see me."

I surprised myself with those words. With how easily they came out. There I was, sharing feelings. Who knew I had it in me?

"That's great. I was going to fly out on Wednesday to see my family, stay for dinner on Thursday, and fly back Friday morning. We have an event for the civil rights group I volunteer with that night. But afterward, the weekend is completely empty."

I thought about a weekend alone with Aaron. I had no intention of leaving the bedroom. Well, maybe we could shower, but only together. We'd order a pizza or something if we needed sustenance.

"Don't make any plans, then. I want you all to myself."

He laughed.

"That won't be a problem. I don't like to share."

THE NEXT couple of weeks dragged by. The holidays were a busy time of year. The restaurant was packed constantly, so I was working overtime. Everyone I knew seemed to be throwing a party. So time should've flown by, but facing another day without Aaron made that day drag. He still called me every night. And we had many more of those "what are you wearing" conversations. But as much as I enjoyed our talks and the phone sex (really, I did—who would've guessed?), I didn't want the distance anymore. I didn't want to be away from him.

We still had a lot to resolve. I needed to understand what it was he actually saw in me. Whether his attraction was born of some deep-seated obligation to fix all the broken people, or whether he was actually attracted to *me*. And I was still uncertain about whether I could give him what I knew he needed—whether I could actually commit myself to one guy for any period of time, let alone forever.

But what I'd realized during the previous several months was that I wanted to work on those issues, and find answers to those questions. There was something between us, something heavy, something strong, something right. I knew I would never be able to return to my old life without giving that something a chance.

Frankly, I wasn't sure I'd be able to return to my old life at all.

When I went online to make my flight reservations, I realized there was no reason for me to wait until Saturday morning. I had the afternoon shift on Friday. If I packed the night before and left my bag in the car, I'd be able to make it to the airport in time to take a flight that would land in Emile City in the early evening. That would give me one more night in Aaron's bed. I swear I literally shivered in anticipation. Go ahead, laugh at me. I don't give a fuck.

After I made the flight reservation, I called Dean to let him know I'd be coming into town. Yeah, yeah. I know I said Aaron and I would be in bed naked all weekend, but Dean would be upset if I didn't come to see my nephews. And, truth be told, I wanted to see the little guys and my brother.

Since I'd returned from Dean's house, I'd been much better about keeping in touch. I actually answered the phone when he called, didn't look for an excuse to hang up right away, and read all of his e-mails. For the first time in my life, I realized that I hadn't ever known my brother.

I was twelve when he graduated from high school and moved away. That was plenty old enough to know someone, when you were living under the same roof. But I couldn't remember anything about Dean from those days—not a funny story or a fight. I had a vague memory of a golden boy with a smile. It was almost as if Dean was a picture or a character in a book, but not someone I ever actually knew. So, those calls and e-mails weren't only an opportunity to reconnect, they were the first formation of our relationship. And, for me, the first time I felt like I had family other than the faded memories of my father.

Aaron had told me he had an event with the gay rights organization he was involved with on Friday evening. I knew he'd skip it to come pick me up at the airport if he knew I'd decided to come in on Friday instead of Saturday morning. But I didn't want him to do that. So I decided to surprise him and asked Dean to pick me up.

"Sure, Zach, can do. I'm surprised Aaron is willing to give up that privilege, though."

"He doesn't know. He thinks I'm not getting in until Saturday. And I know he has that thing Friday, so I figure if you pick me up, he won't have to miss it."

"So, you're expecting me not to tell him you're coming in, like, twelve hours earlier than expected?"

"Yeah, Dean. I know it's a sacrifice. Jesus, man, it's not like I'm asking you to keep a bad secret from him. It's a surprise."

"Ha, ha, Zach. I know that but I can't tell Kim because there's no way she'll keep it from him. Aaron can read her like an open book, and she'll be all giggly and excited about this."

I rolled my eyes at his internal struggle over a fucking airport pickup.

"So, don't tell Kim."

"We're supposed to be at that event with Aaron. We donate to the organization, and it's like a thank-you thing. Plus, Aaron planned it, so we want to support him.

We even got another sitter. I guess I can tell Kim I have to be a little late, and I'll meet her there."

They *even* got another sitter? Didn't it strike Dean as *even* a little odd to say that sentence? As if it was such a big thing to find someone other than Aaron to watch his kids. Maybe they could use that same approach to find someone other than Aaron to do their household repairs and cook their meals. I found myself wondering if he mowed their lawn and pulled their weeds.

"I'm glad we got that all worked out, Dean. Call me later, if you need help figuring out how to put your pants on and can't reach Aaron. Spoiler alert—try one leg at a time."

I kid you not, when Dean picked me up at the airport, he was all excited about how he'd been able to evade suspicion about our "surprise" and how Kim asked him blah, blah, blah, and he said blah, blah, blah. If you actually want me to fill in the blanks on this hopelessly boring information, you must be out of your fucking mind, and you clearly overestimate my capacity to give a shit about that sort of thing.

The event was being held on the roof of a small, locally owned hotel in EC West, the neighborhood where Aaron and I had run into each other at the bar and then eaten dinner. The place had a cool vibe and I, once again, noticed how comfortable I felt in this clearly gay-friendly part of town. Dean wandered off to find Kim as soon as we got there, and I looked around for Aaron.

The place wasn't very big, so it didn't take long for me to spot him standing with a small group of guys. They were all smiling and talking, but Aaron looked disengaged. He was staring down into his glass and tapping it with his finger. I was behind the group, and there was a potted tree between us, so they didn't see me approaching.

"Earth to Aaron. Where are you tonight?"

"Oh, sorry, Frank. I'm a little distracted."

Another voice joined in laughing.

"Aaron is daydreaming about his boyfriend. He's coming to visit tomorrow. I didn't get to see Mister Wonderful that night after our meeting. You took off without introducing him. Will we get to meet him this weekend? Maybe you can bring him to brunch on Sunday. We've been wanting to have you join us for that weekly ritual."

"Oh, umm, I...I think we have plans. Sorry, Tim."

More laughter, from several guys this time.

"Ummm, hmmm. Plans. Is that what we're calling it now?"

Yet another voice.

"I'm just grateful you found someone, Aaron. I knew the situation was getting dire when I saw the guy you brought to Micah's party. Jesus! What were you thinking there?"

I stood, frozen behind the potted tree, feeling a little guilty for eavesdropping but wanting to hear the conversation. The guy who made the comment about me was laughing, but Aaron spoke over him. His voice was angry.

"What are you talking about, Roy?"

"Don't tell me you don't remember. Micah's

birthday party? You brought that guy who was really..."

"He was 'really' what, Roy?" Aaron asked.

Someone else cut in. It wasn't Tim, and it wasn't Roy. Maybe it was the first guy, Frank. His voice sounded tense.

"Shut up, Roy."

"What? What did I say?" Complete silence. And then Roy again. "Don't tell me that's your boyfriend. Really?"

"Yes, really. Zach's a great guy, and I'm lucky to have him. What is your problem, Roy? You didn't even meet him when we were at Micah's."

"I didn't meet him because he was too busy getting drunk. Not that I wanted to meet him anyway. Why would you want to be with someone who is so...so...obvious?"

Aaron's voice was raised and angry.

"Obvious? What, like obviously gay? Is that what you mean, Roy?"

"Yes, that's what I mean. Come on, don't act like it isn't true. You could spot that guy a mile away."

"Roy, he *is* gay. I'm gay. *You're* gay!"

"That doesn't mean we have to advertise it, Aaron, and you know it. You don't dress like that, carry yourself like that. No one would know you were gay if you didn't tell them. Whatever, if that's what you're into. I like my guys to be *men*, that's all. I don't understand why you'd want to be with someone who acts like such a—"

"I see. So, it's okay to be gay. We just can't be too gay. Is that it, Roy?" Aaron's voice was shaking with anger, and I could tell he was struggling to maintain control. "As long as no one can tell, it's fine? That's pathetic! Zach is who he is. He isn't afraid to show it. He isn't ashamed of being gay. Instead of insulting him, you should be admiring his strength. You need to reexamine what it means to be a man, Roy, because there's no pride in being able to hide. As far as I'm concerned, it proves you aren't half the man he is."

He thought I was strong? In my mind, Aaron saw me as someone who needed healing. Not as a strong man. It was the reason I'd tried to break things off with him. And it was a big reason why I wasn't sure things could work out between us. I'd assumed he would feel trapped with yet another boyfriend out of obligation, rather than desire. My assumptions were cracking under the weight of Aaron's words. Oh, and PS, his angry out-lash in defense of me really turned me on.

My mind snapped to attention when I noticed Aaron stalking off from the group. I walked toward him. When his eyes met mine, I watched the expression on his face change from cloudy to hungry. My heart skipped a beat, and I froze.

I'd been smiling, wanting him to know I was excited to see him. But seeing the raw desire etched across his face, my smile faded, and I swallowed—hard. Holy fuck, folks, the sound you just heard was my cock doing everything in its power to break its way out of my fucking pants.

CHAPTER ELEVEN

AARON COVERED the space between us in a few short strides. He didn't say anything, and he didn't look away from me. When he was standing right in front of me, he put one hand on each of my cheeks, hunched down, and covered my mouth with his.

"Zach."

He sighed into my mouth as his light kisses turned to licks, his tongue seeking entry. I opened my mouth to let him in, and he moaned and pushed his tongue into me, devouring my mouth. I whimpered as I sucked on his tongue, feeling him dart it in and out of my mouth, reminding me of how much I wished his dick was doing the same thing to my ass. As if I needed a reminder of that longing. I was already hard and aching.

My whimpers were getting a little too loud, but I'd lost control over my body. Aaron eventually broke our kiss, wrapped his arm around me, and navigated us to the elevator. As soon as the door closed, he had me pressed against the wall, his mouth ravishing mine as his hands seemed to touch every part of my body.

I didn't remember ever being that excited, especially with all my clothes on. I felt like I was going to explode, right there in the elevator. I managed to push out a few words.

"Aaron... Oh, fuck, Aaron. If you...don't...stop... Ugh! I'll come... Aaron..."

He pulled his head back and looked into my eyes, his torso still pressed against mine. I could feel the hard planes of his body, his thick cock pushing through our clothes onto my stomach. His breath came out in short puffs. With his eyes looking deeply into mine and the elevator making its final descent in what had to be the longest couple of minutes of all time, Aaron's husky voice spoke into my mouth.

"Do it, Zach."

And then his tongue was back in my mouth, doing that darting thing. His hands were everywhere, and my grasp on reality slipped. His last words, and the possessive tone in his voice as he said them, pushed me over the edge.

"Come for me, Zach."

His mouth was back on mine, swallowing my moans as my body released. I was pressed up against the elevator wall, my knees weak, my lungs not able to get enough air, and my brain not registering what the hell had just happened to me.

Aaron wrapped his arms tight around me and practically carried me to his car. He opened my door and buckled me up. Then he pushed my hair off my forehead and kissed me softly.

"I like your hair like this. You're so beautiful."

My hair was back to its natural brown, and I was

wearing it a little longer than usual. Aaron ran his fingers through it and sighed. Then he closed the car door and walked around to the driver's side, got into his seat, and started the engine.

It wasn't until we had pulled out of the parking lot that I had the capacity to speak. But I didn't know what to say. I would say I felt like a teenager, coming in my pants, but that had never happened to me as a teenager or otherwise. I'd never experienced that kind of unbridled desire. So, I stared at his profile as he drove through town.

"Aaron?"

He reached his hand over to me and rested it on my thigh, giving it a light squeeze. Then, he spoke in a low voice.

"I've never been like this. I'm so crazy about you that I felt like I was going out of my mind when you were gone. But that was nothing compared to what happened when I saw you standing on that rooftop. Nothing else mattered at that moment."

He turned his head to me and continued speaking.

"I *had* to touch you, to taste you, to hear you, to make you feel good. I don't know how to explain it. I don't know what to say, Zach."

So he felt the same way. Whatever we had between us, I believed more and more that it was mutual. I picked his hand up off my thigh and brought it to my mouth, kissing his palm and then the back of his hand.

"How about we start with 'hello' and then we can go from there? A traditional follow-up is 'I'm glad you're here' or 'it's nice to see you'." Aaron laughed and the mood lightened. "Although, I must say 'come for me' could easily become a new fan favorite."

I waggled my eyebrows at him.

It didn't take much longer for us to get to his apartment. I hadn't eaten dinner so my stomach growled.

"I'm sorry, babe. You must be so hungry after your flight. I promise to feed you. I just thought you'd want to clean up after that, ehm, elevator ride."

My briefs were wet and the cold cum was drying on my skin, making me feel itchy.

"Yeah. A shower sounds pretty good right now."

We walked into Aaron's apartment, and I looked around. I hadn't paid attention to the place last time I was there. It was clean, but sparse and sterile. White walls, apartment-issue brown carpet, a brown sofa, and no pictures or art.

"There's shampoo and soap in the shower. I'll bring you a towel."

There was a hallway off the living room with two doors. I opened one door and walked into Aaron's bedroom. I'd slept there the night of Aaron's friend's party, but I hadn't looked around. The bedroom was as plain as the living room—the same white walls and brown carpet, a large mattress and boxspring resting on a metal frame in the corner, a single nightstand, and a dresser with a few framed pictures on it.

I walked over to the dresser and looked at the pictures as I stripped off my clothes. One picture was of a man and woman in their fifties with their arms around each other. The woman also had an arm around a pretty, younger version of herself. The man had an arm around Aaron, who was wearing a graduation gown. And on Aaron's other side was a slightly smaller, heavier, older-looking version of Aaron. I knew those must be Aaron's parents and siblings.

Then there was a picture of Kim and Dean sitting on their living room couch. Simon was on Dean's lap and two wrapped bundles of baby were in Kim's arms. The last picture was of two dark-haired girls wearing formal dresses, with corsages on their wrists. I guessed those were Michael's sisters on prom night.

I was standing there, looking at Aaron's three families. My clothes were gathered in a pile by my feet. I picked them up and glanced around the room, hoping to see a laundry basket. That was when I noticed one last picture frame. It was on Aaron's nightstand. I walked over, sat on the bed, and picked it up. It was a picture of me. I was wearing the jeans and T-shirt I'd brought on my last trip, and laughing.

I remembered that moment. We were at Dean's house, and I was laughing at a story Aaron was telling. I didn't know anyone had snapped a picture.

"That's my favorite one. You look so happy."

Aaron was walking through the doorway, holding a folded towel. I stood up, and he gasped. I looked up at his face and saw him staring at my ass, and then running his eyes up and down over my body. His blue eyes darkened, and he sounded breathless when he spoke.

"Oh, Zach. You better get into the shower."

I turned and walked toward him. His eyes darted

over my chest and stomach, then rested on my cock, which had hardened in reaction to the clear desire I saw on his face.

"You like what you see, Aaron?" I asked, my voice husky.

He nodded, swallowed, and licked his lips. I kept walking until I was right in front of him. Then I stood up on the balls of my feet and whispered into his ear, "I'm glad you like how I look. I'm all yours, though. You don't have to settle for looking. You can do anything you want with me."

Aaron groaned and wrapped his arms around me, settling them on my ass. I moaned and put my hands behind his head, pulling him down to my lips. It didn't take long for our tongues to find each other again. But I needed to taste more than Aaron's tongue. I fumbled with his belt and then the buttons on his jeans. Once I had them opened, I broke our kiss and pushed Aaron's jeans and briefs down to his ankles.

His cock was as beautiful as I remembered—smooth with a rich golden color. His balls were just as smooth, and they hung low. I bent down and lapped his cock head, taking the moisture into my mouth. Aaron's hands were running through my hair, and he was moaning softly.

"Yes...oh, yes."

He'd been hard and worked up when we were making out in the elevator, and I wasn't sure his cock had ever softened. I imagined he was probably aching and past ready for a release, so I decided not to draw this out. Instead I licked and sucked, bobbed and swallowed, and took him down into my throat. It wasn't long before Aaron was moaning my name and pouring himself into my mouth. I pulled back a little so the last few shots would land on my tongue, and I could taste him.

When he was done, I licked him clean, straightened up, and nuzzled his neck while he caught his breath.

"Thank you, babe."

I laughed against his skin and considered complimenting his mom on the good job she did teaching him manners. Then, I decided bringing up his mom, at that moment, was probably a little weird.

"No, thank *you*. That was the best appetizer I've ever had."

He stroked my hair and then tickled my chest and stomach lightly until he reached my cock. I considered getting him into bed and skipping dinner entirely, but I was hungry and I needed a shower. It had been a long day at work, followed by a flight, followed by the elevator ride. You get the picture.

"Later," I said as I stopped the trajectory of his hand. "I'm going to go shower now."

He let go of my cock and sighed.

"You go ahead and shower. Once my legs start working again, I'll walk into the kitchen and make us some dinner."

I picked the towel up off the floor, where it had dropped when I'd taken Aaron into my mouth. I could've bent at the knees instead of the waist, but doing the latter put my ass up in the air in Aaron's direct line of sight. He growled.

"Go now. I swear I can't be responsible for my actions if you keep teasing me like this."

I straightened up and walked into the bathroom, knowing his eyes were on me.

"It's only teasing if I'm not willing to act on it. And, believe me, I'm willing."

The shower didn't take long. As I stood in the tub, drying myself off, I heard Aaron's phone ring. Yes, his apartment was that small. If you're reading this and thinking, "I thought veterinarians made good money," then you're reading my mind.

Anyway, I walked out of the bathroom using the door that didn't lead to the bedroom, and found myself in the hallway facing the living room and entryway. Aaron stood in the attached kitchen, stirring something on the stove with one hand and holding his phone with the other.

"I mean it, Kimmy, I'm sorry. It was my fault. I, ummm, I thought Zach would be hungry after his flight, so we left. I didn't think about finding you and Dean to say goodbye."

A pause when Aaron was likely listening to Kim.

"Oh, right. I should've thought about all of us having dinner together." Pause. "Yes, I have heard that hotel has a great restaurant. I'm sorry." Pause. "I know you have the sitter. It was inconsiderate of me. I'm sorry." Pause. "You want us to meet you there now? But—"

Okay, that was it. I marched into the kitchen with the towel wrapped around my waist and took the phone from Aaron's hand.

"Hi, Kim. I know you're upset about dinner, but, the thing is, I haven't seen Aaron in over four months, and if I didn't get him alone, I would've gone down on him right there on the rooftop. I'm pretty sure that's not legal here, so we had to leave."

I heard a little gasp and then silence. I considered telling Aaron to take notes so he'd know how to shut her up, but I needed to finish speaking to Kim.

"I'm sure we'll see you tomorrow, but we can't talk now because we need to eat and then get into bed, so we can, well, do you actually want to know this level of detail, Kim?"

A long pause and then a squeaky, "Oh, no, of course not. I'm sorry I interrupted."

"That's okay. Tell Dean thanks for picking me up. We'll call you tomorrow."

And with that, I ended the call and looked up at Aaron. He was still standing with one hand holding the spoon in the saucepan, but he was no longer stirring. His mouth was hanging open. Then he started to laugh and wrapped his free hand around me and pulled me close to him.

"You're my hero."

"Yes, that's me. I save big strong guys in distress from little damsels, using nothing but the power of speech."

Aaron smiled and leaned down to give me a light kiss. I stroked his cheek.

"You know, Aaron, it's okay to say no."

He furrowed his brow.

"I know it's okay. But I don't want to say no to you. I want everything with you."

I laughed.

"I meant, it's okay for you to say no to Kim and to Dean. You don't have to do everything they ask." Then I decided to lighten the mood a little. "With me, though, no isn't an option. I've captured you, and now you have to bend to my will."

His lips covered mine before I finished my sentence. When he finally pulled away, his eyes were moist.

"You have captured me, Zach. You do know that, right? I hope you won't let me go."

He was putting his heart out there, and I should've answered him or engaged in the conversation, but I still wasn't good with all the emotional stuff, and I needed some time to sort my head out. I hadn't had a chance to process the conversation I'd heard Aaron having with his friends or the strength of my reaction to seeing Aaron in person. So I decided to put a pin in the conversation and keep things light during dinner.

"Aside from the great tragedy of not having dinner with Dean and Kim, the other issue with leaving in a hurry is that my bag is in Dean's car. That leaves me without any clean clothes. Do you have anything that'll fit me?"

Aaron smiled.

"I like the idea of you wearing my clothes. Let's see what I have."

He turned off the burner on the stove and walked into the bedroom with me behind him. He dug through the drawers in his dresser and came up with a pair of boxers and a worn T-shirt.

"These might work. I'll get you a toothbrush too. Do you need anything else?"

I slipped the boxers on as he walked into the bathroom, but they weren't going to stay on my waist. The shirt was so long it reached to the middle of my thighs. Aaron came out of the bathroom and looked at me swimming in his shirt. His eyes got hot again. I glanced at his bulge and noticed he was hard.

"This turn you on, Aaron?" He nodded shyly and blushed. I walked over to him so our bodies were pressed together. "Why? Tell me what turns you on about me in your shirt."

"You look so cute in it. You look small, like I can wrap myself around you and protect you."

At that moment, I was torn. If I were being honest, which I always was, I'd admit that I liked the idea of him protecting me, of being wrapped in his arms. His size was part of what attracted me to him. The same was true for his strength and stability. I felt like Aaron could hold onto me and keep me grounded and secure.

But the problem was I didn't want to be another Michael, yet another person for Aaron to save and take care of without getting anything in return. And, I didn't want him to see me as weak and needy.

He must have noticed my internal conflict.

"I know that look. It's the same look you had before you left me the last time. I'm not going to let that happen again. Please talk to me, Zach. That's the only way this thing between us has a chance. We have to talk to each other."

He was right, of course. And, if I wanted us to have a chance, then what was the harm in telling him how I felt?

"Okay. We'll talk. But let's sit down to eat first. I'm hungry and dinner smells wonderful."

CHAPTER TWELVE

I WALKED into Aaron's kitchen and opened a cabinet to look for plates. It was empty. I don't mean sparse. I mean, there was literally nothing in it.

"The plates are in the cabinet above the sink."

I walked over to that cabinet and opened it. There were four white dinner plates, four white bowls, and four white salad plates. They had all clearly come from one of those mega-store box of dishes. I picked up two plates and handed them to Aaron.

"Glasses?"

"They're in the cabinet next to the fridge."

I walked over to that cabinet and wondered what I'd find. Four simple glass tumblers, four white mugs—I was guessing they came with the other dishes. That was it.

I picked up two glasses and filled them with water from the fridge. Then I looked around the kitchen and realized it was as empty and impersonal as the rest of the apartment. A wave of sadness washed over me that Aaron lived this way. He was such a warm, caring person, but his place was cold and empty. It didn't make sense.

I turned with the filled glasses and realized there was no table. Aaron was setting the full plates down on the counter-bar. I put the glasses next to them as he opened a drawer and took out two forks and two knives. You've probably already guessed that left two forks, two knives, and four spoons in the drawer.

"Do you have napkins, or should I grab some paper towels?"

"Oh, paper towels. I'm sorry, Zach. I guess you can tell I don't entertain much. Well, I actually don't entertain at all. You're the first person who's ever been here."

That pang of sadness came over me again and it hit deep in my stomach. I'd lived in lots of different places since I'd moved to LA. The first one was a room I'd rented in a house with a bunch of other guys. I saw it advertised in the WeHo News. I didn't know anyone when I first moved in because I was new to town, but by the time I moved out of that place a year later, I had lots of friends.

During that move and every move since, there were always guys helping me pack boxes, carry furniture, unpack—all the normal move things. And there were also lots of friends who came over to eat or hang out or fuck. Whatever. The point being, I'd always had many people in my life and at my place. I didn't make much money, so my place wasn't big, and my stuff wasn't expensive. But damn, I had more than one couch and a pre-packaged-college-dorm-supply-pack of dishes.

Aaron was twenty-seven years old, and he'd been living in Emile City for a year. That was well past old enough and well past long enough to have a life. So why didn't he?

I sat on one of the two stools next to the counter-bar and dug into the risotto on my plate. Now, you already know that I cooked for a living, so I'd had some damn good risotto in my time. My special mushroom parmesan risotto was pretty fucking awesome. Aaron was Mister Bachelor, and he'd already admitted that he didn't have people over for dinner or anything else. So, I assumed he couldn't cook very well. I was wrong.

"Mmmmm. Aaron, this is good."

I got the words out between large mouthfuls of risotto. He laughed.

"I'll try not to be offended that you sound so surprised."

I was still feeling sorry for him, for the isolated life he seemed to lead. The last thing I wanted to do was insult him. I clasped his upper arm.

"No. I didn't mean it that way. I'm a food snob. Occupational hazard, you know. You live alone, and you said you don't entertain so I—"

I have to say I was extremely grateful when he put me out of my misery by jumping in, because I had no idea where I was going with that sentence.

"It's okay. I understand. I was teasing you. Michael's parents had their hands full with the two girls and all of his medical stuff, so I tried to help out as much as I could in high school. My mom is a great cook, and she used to help me make meals I could bring over to their place. That was an easy way for me to ease their burden. As a bonus, I got to spend time with my mom and learn a bunch of her tricks and recipes.

"Then, when Michael died and his parents shut

down, I got in the habit of going over there to make dinner for the girls. And you know that when I moved away for vet school, I lived with your brother. Trust me when I tell you that you got *all* of the cooking genes in your family. Dean can't manage to make toast without burning it. And Kimmy isn't any better, so when we all three lived together after Simon was born, I was in charge of the kitchen. The same was true when I moved here and lived with them, so I've spent many years cooking for people."

Now, here's the thing. If you read that and said a big "awwww" that Aaron is such a sweet guy, then you'll probably think I'm a big asshole, because I felt even sadder. That story confirmed that Aaron had been living his life for other people. Not that there was anything wrong with caring for others. Fuck, I hadn't done enough of that in my life, which I'd realized after I met Aaron. But, there was a big, wide space between living your life like a self-absorbed bastard (i.e. me), and not living *your* life at all (i.e. Aaron).

"Well, while I'm here I've got kitchen duty, okay? I'm making all of our meals."

"Oh, you don't have to do that. I know you have to cook at work, and I'm happy to give you a break while you're here, Zach."

I rubbed his arm and looked into his eyes.

"I like cooking. That's why I chose it for a profession. Come on, let me show off a little. Besides, I want to take care of you."

"Really?" he said in a broken voice.

The surprise and underlying happiness in his

voice almost made me cry. Had no one ever offered to take care of him? I mean, no one had ever taken care of me. I'd essentially been on my own for as long as I could remember, or at least since my father died when I was eight. But Aaron had done so much for so many people. How was it possible they had never cared for him in return?

We finished eating, and I took our dishes to the sink and started washing. Aaron came up behind me and wrapped his arms around me. I leaned back against him and into his touch.

"I'll get these, Zach. You sit and relax. You must be tired after working this morning and then flying here." He kissed my neck. "Thanks for that, by the way. I'm so glad you were able to get here early."

I turned my head back and met his eyes.

"I'm glad too. Now, I'm washing these dishes, and that's all there is to it. You go get ready for bed. I'm standing around half-naked, wearing nothing but a T-shirt, and you're still fully dressed."

He ran his hand up my thigh and pushed the shirt up with his forearm as he brushed over my ass. I moaned and shuddered. At least I think it was me; it might have been him. It was probably both of us. Then he whispered into my ear.

"You have the most beautiful ass I have ever seen." I looked back at him, and he blushed. "Is that a weird thing to say?"

No, it wasn't weird. I'd heard it before. And, by the way, I did have a great fucking ass. (Read that last sentence however you want, it works on both levels.) I didn't say that, though.

I kissed him and said, "No, it's not weird. I'm glad you like my ass. I have high hopes that you're going to get intimately familiar with it soon."

He blushed even more and laughed before he walked away, shaking his head. I heard the shower start as I finished drying the dishes and putting them away. I put the towel next to the sink and leaned against the counter, taking yet another look around Aaron's apartment and thinking over what I knew about his life.

For the first time, I thought maybe he did need me; maybe I did bring something to our relationship. Yes, relationship. I said it. Now, fuck off.

I heard the shower turn off, and I hit the lights in the kitchen, made sure the front door was locked, and walked into the bedroom. Aaron was stepping out of the bathroom, toweling off his hair, thereby leaving the rest of his body exposed. I didn't know how it was possible, but he looked even better than I remembered. His skin positively glowed, he was all long, lean muscle, and even flaccid, his cock was spectacular.

Now, I know with all my talk about wanting to get fucked, you're expecting this part of the story to turn to one of us attacking the other and then fucking like rabbits. Well, that's not what happened. Believe me, you're not half as surprised as me at what I said next.

"You still up for talking?"

Aaron nodded and dropped his towel on the floor before sitting next to me on the bed. Yes, I asked him

,22,

to talk. That wasn't all, though. I followed it up with, "I think you need to put some clothes on. You can't possibly expect me to think straight with your naked body next to me in a bed."

Aaron laughed, but he didn't get up to get dressed. Instead, he scooted to the top of the bed, pulled the comforter down and slipped underneath. Then he held his hand out to me.

"Thinking straight is the last thing I want from you. Come over here. I promise I won't jump you...yet. I'll exhibit tremendous self-restraint while we're talking. But, I've been wanting to feel your skin against mine for months, and I'm not giving that up. Besides, other than that first time in Kimmy's kitchen, I haven't known you to have a problem talking, so I think you'll be able to deal."

I crawled over to Aaron, stripped his shirt off myself, and joined him under the covers. We were both lying on our sides, facing each other. I was propped up by one hand while my other hand traced circles on Aaron's chest. His head was resting on a couple of pillows, and his hand was petting my hair.

In all the beds (and bathrooms and living rooms and back rooms and alleys, etc., etc., etc.) I'd been in with those innumerable guys, I'd never once shared an intimacy like that. Just looking, touching, thinking, and...

"I really do love you, Zach. As much as I always wanted to find someone, I never knew it would feel this good."

"So, I'm not another Michael?" Huh, I could've worked up to that comment instead of spitting it right out. Oh well.

Aaron sat straight up.

"What do you mean?"

I lay down so I was flat on my back, looking up at the ceiling.

"I don't want to be someone you're with because you feel an obligation, or because you have some unquenchable need to save the world. I've been on my own for a long time, Aaron. I've been happy in this life I've built. You might not understand that, but it's true. I never thought I'd want anything else until you came along and showed me there is something else."

I sat up on the bed so we were facing each other.

"I'm not stupid, Aaron. I will know if you're in this because you think I need saving, if you don't mean the things you say. Don't say you love me if it isn't true. It might have been okay with Michael, but it isn't okay with me. I didn't even realize I was lonely until I met you. And if we end this now, I can still go back—no harm, no foul. But if I invest any more of myself in this thing, and then I realize you're skimming the surface..."

"No!"

His shout startled me into silence.

"I'm sorry for yelling, Zach, but darn it! Where do I start with how wrong you are? I told you about my real feelings for Michael because I thought they'd make you feel better, more secure about my feelings for you. How that story made you doubt my feelings instead is...well, let's just say, you're a deep thinker, and no one would ever think you're stupid, Zach. And while I may have been 'skimming the surface' in my understanding of how someone could misunderstand that story, my feelings for you are not shallow.

"I've meant every word I've ever said to you. I don't say things I don't mean. I don't lie, Zach. Not ever. I never told Michael I was in love with him. He knew, and I knew that what we had was friendship. I loved him like I love your brother and Kimmy."

He lowered his voice and tried to even out his breathing.

"I've never been in love with anyone before you. Oh, I wanted it. I longed for it. I've hated the loneliness. But like I'm not willing to lie to other people, I wasn't willing to lie to myself. I wasn't going to pretend I was into someone just so I wouldn't be alone. So I waited and waited. There were times I wasn't even sure what I was waiting for, but I knew, or maybe I hoped, I'd know him when I saw him. And I did, Zach. I knew the minute you walked into Kimmy's kitchen.

"Okay, what else? Oh, the saving. Is there something so wrong with me wanting to take care of you, protect you, make you happy, make you feel good? It doesn't mean I think you need saving. Or at least not that you need it any more than I do. Can we save each other, Zach?"

Aaron's voice was shaking. I wasn't sure if it was because he was angry, frustrated, or tired. Maybe he was all of those things. I remained calm. Talk about a role reversal.

I reached over and took his foot into my hand, pulled it onto my lap, and then rubbed the sole. I stretched my legs so they were also in his lap and then took his other foot into mine. He had to bend his knees and lay his legs over mine. So, there we sat, legs all tangled, hands giving foot massages, bodies naked, and no words being spoken.

I thought about what he'd said. Why did I have such an issue with Aaron wanting to take care of me? I recognized that, on an emotional level, I craved that aspect of what he offered. One of the first things that attracted me to Aaron was the warmth and strength he exuded. And that continued to draw me toward him. So, yes, I wanted him to take care of me. But yet, intellectually, I was fighting it. I knew my childhood was the reason behind this. The question was, was I going to tell Aaron about it?

CHAPTER THIRTEEN

DURING ALL our talks, we'd stayed away from any discussion of our families. It was the proverbial elephant in the room. I realized, as I sat there rubbing his feet, that I had to talk about it if I ever wanted to truly share my life with Aaron.

I looked up to meet his eyes. There was caring, compassion, and love in those eyes. But that wasn't what made me open up. The reason I started talking was because there was also loneliness and fear. And, as I thought about his bland apartment and his empty kitchen, I knew that he did need me. It wouldn't be one-sided. I could help him and support him. And he was scared that I wouldn't, that I would walk away and leave him in his lonely, solitary life. No, I wasn't going to do that. I wasn't going to run away from him this time.

"What has Dean told you about our family?"

The sound of my voice finally broke the silence. Aaron looked almost startled, but he recovered quickly and answered my question.

"He talks about your dad a lot. I know he died when Dean was starting high school. Sounds like he was a great guy."

He hesitated and looked at me, clearly unsure whether he should continue.

"I need to understand what you know, so I can fill in the pieces."

He nodded, but I could tell he wasn't sure how much to say. Still, he continued talking.

"Dean should've talked with you himself about some of these things. I've told him to do it for years. But he couldn't. I don't want to betray his trust, but I think he'll understand. Your mom had a drinking problem. When your dad was alive, he covered for her a lot. Then when he died, there was no buffer, and her drinking got worse."

"I was there, Aaron, it isn't a secret from me. What else?"

He seemed relieved.

"Ummm. Your mom remarried much more quickly than Dean would've liked. And he wasn't a big fan of your stepfather. But, from what I understand, Dean sort of checked out of the family after your dad died, so he didn't know your stepfather well. He said he spent most of his time in school or doing sports, and that he spent more nights at friends' houses than in his own bed. And when college came, he chose the farthest school he could, and he didn't come back to visit."

Aaron let go of my feet, put his legs on either side of my body, and did the same with mine. He scooted closer, bringing us chest to chest.

"You can talk to him about it, Zach. He feels terrible for abandoning you. He knows he should've been there for you, that he was supposed to take care of you. But he said he missed your dad so much he couldn't do it."

Quite a bit of our height difference was in our legs, so even though we still weren't exactly eye-to-eye, when we were sitting like that, I could kiss Aaron without him hunching down as much. I decided to take advantage of the proximity and pressed my lips to his. It was a soft, light kiss. Anything more than that and the conversation would've ended before it began. And I wasn't sure when I'd be able to re-gather the courage to talk about my childhood, so I pressed on.

"It's not about Dean. You're right about him, he was pretty much non-existent. And my mother did drink. A lot. That piece of shit she married after my dad died was no better. He never liked me because I was in the way, so I learned to stay away. I'd walk home from school and go to my room. When I got hungry, I waited to go to the kitchen until they were outside or in their bedroom or out of the house."

I shook with the memory of how scared I'd been in those days. I never knew whether to be relieved when they left me alone at home for hours because I knew they wouldn't yell at me, or to be scared because I was eight years old and by myself at night. Aaron wrapped his arms around me and stroked my back. It relaxed me.

"Hey, on the plus side, that's how I learned to cook. Anyway, that's how things went for years. We coexisted. They didn't talk to me or look at me unless they absolutely had to. And I did everything I could to stay out of their way. But when I was thirteen, it all changed."

I was resting my head on Aaron's chest, but we

were still sitting up in bed. It was late and I'd had a long day. Telling that story made me even more tired.

"I need to lie down," I mumbled into his chest.

He held on to me, turned his body, and then lay back so his head was propped on the pillows and my body was on top of his. Then he reached over for the blanket, raised his feet off of it, and pulled it up to cover my back.

"How's this? Comfy?"

His body felt warm and hard beneath me. My head was resting on his chest and his strong arms were circled around my back and holding me tight.

"Thanks. You're okay with me on top of you like this? My weight isn't too much for you?"

He laughed and the vibrations made my body bounce up and down.

"You're what? A buck twenty, maybe a buck twenty-five, soaking wet? You feel great on top of me, Zach."

"Yeah, well don't get too used to it, because I'm more of a bottom."

He squeezed my ass.

"Top, bottom, whatever. I don't care, Zach, as long as I'm with you."

Okay, time to stop deflecting.

"I'd always known I was attracted to guys. And by the time I was thirteen, I had a skateboard, so I was able to go all sorts of places after school. It's not like my mom ever noticed when I came home. One day, I met some guys at a skate park. A couple of them were clearly checking me out. They were a few years older, and they weren't bad-looking, so I started hooking up with them a little.

"Well, one time I made a dumb fucking mistake, and I let one of them walk me home. The house was dark when we got there, so we didn't think anyone was home. We played a little grab-ass out front, and then I went inside. My stepdad was standing by the front window. He was already three sheets to the wind by then, and seeing me make out with a guy set him off. I'd always known he hated me, but he hadn't ever touched me, until that night.

"It turned out, the five years he'd been ignoring me were the good old days, because the next five years were a fucking nightmare. He managed to stay away from me when he was sober, but that wasn't often. More often than not, the two of them would get drunk. I did everything I could to stay out of their way. I didn't eat dinner most nights because I didn't want to take the chance that he'd catch me outside of my room. But when he was drunk, he'd find some excuse to catch me—going to the bathroom or coming home early or some reason to come to my room."

I was shaking, even though Aaron was squeezing me tightly.

"Zach, we don't have to keep talking about this tonight. You're tired. We can rest and keep going in the morning."

I shook my head.

"No, I need to get through this. I don't want to drag it out, and you need to understand."

I buried my face in his neck and inhaled his scent. That calmed me. I reached my tongue out and licked him. I sucked on his skin. He whimpered.

"Most of the time it was body blows, or he'd whip me with his belt in places that would get covered by clothes. But every once in a while he'd lose control. After those times, I'd have to stay out of school until the bruises on my face healed. A couple of times, I had to go to the hospital—a broken arm one time, cracked ribs another. I told the doctors I fell riding my board."

"What about your mom?" Aaron asked softly as he stroked my hair.

"My mom never said much. She'd sit in the living room and drink. She rarely looked at me and spoke to me even less. Sometimes, I'd hear them talking in the other room after he'd hit me. She'd be apologizing to him for having a faggot for a son and saying I'd be gone soon.

"So that's what I did. I turned eighteen during the last week of high school. I waited for classes to end, and then I packed a bag and bought a bus ticket to LA. They mailed me my diploma because I was gone before graduation."

"Oh, Zach. I'm so sorry. I'm so, so sorry."

I could hear Aaron sniffling. I looked at his face and saw it was wet with tears.

"Why are you crying?"

"I'm sorry. I...I love you so much, Zach. I hate that you went through that. You're incredible. I always knew that, but I didn't realize how much you've overcome. I've never known anyone as strong as you."

I snorted out a laugh.

"Strong? I let him beat the shit out of me for five years and never did a thing to defend myself. I didn't even talk back to him. I've always hated myself for how weak I was."

Aaron met my eyes and held my head between his big hands.

"Zach, you were a kid. I've seen pictures of your stepfather. He's a big guy. He was probably twice the size you are now, back then. You didn't stand a chance against him physically. But you survived. No, you did more than that." He stroked my temples with his thumbs. "You light up a room, Zach. You have an amazing smile. You're funny, and you're fun to be with, and the joy you exude is contagious. You're so confident and so sure of who you are. Do you have any idea how rare that is? Do you know how many people go through life not sure of what they want or of who they are? I can't tell you how much I admire you."

Well, that was enough to make me cry too. I knew he meant those things. It wasn't lip service. Aaron wasn't capable of lying; his face was way too expressive. He hugged me tightly.

"You don't have to do this alone anymore, Zach. I'm here now, and I'll help you. You can let go, Zach. I'll take care of you, babe."

That was exactly what I was afraid of. My body went rigid.

"What? What did I say, Zach? Did I say something wrong?"

I pulled away from his embrace and glared at him.

"I'm not weak. I can take care of myself. I've been able to make it just fine on my own."

I saw frustration and maybe even anger in Aaron's eyes.

"Well, good for you! But I'm not fine, Zach. I'm tired of taking care of myself. I'm tired of being on my own. I'm so lonely it hurts. I felt like I was barely existing until I met you. I need you, Zach. I need your energy and your light. I need someone in my life who is there for me first. I thought you wanted that too. You never said it, but I guess...I guess I thought you...you... Never mind. I was stupid."

He rolled himself out from under me and got out of bed. I sat there as he stormed out of the room.

It took me a moment to calm down and think about what'd happened. He reached out to me by saying I was no longer alone, and I responded by taking his head off.

The weekend we met, Aaron had asked me to meet him at least part of the way. I'd been barely doing it. Over the months that we'd talked on the phone every night, he'd initiated every call. I looked forward to them, made sure I was home and ready to talk. But I never told him that, and I never picked up the fucking phone and dialed. And on every one of those calls, he told me he loved me. Damn, I looked forward to that. It warmed me deep inside. But I never said it to him.

I got up after a couple of minutes and found Aaron in the kitchen. He was facing the counter, grasping it with both hands with his head slumped down. It was dark, so I couldn't see him well, but his body language said everything. He was hurt and sad. That was my fault. I did that. I hated myself at that moment.

"I do love you, Aaron."

There. I said it. And you know what? It wasn't hard. It actually felt pretty damn good. What took me so long? I walked over to him until we were almost touching.

"That's what you were going to say, right? That I never said it, but you thought I loved you? Well, you're right. I do love you. So much. I'm sorry I never told you. I'm a fucking asshole. Can you forgive me?"

He turned around and hunched down to hug me. We pressed our naked bodies together and held on to each other. He mumbled an "of course" at the top of my head. It was that easy. I acted like a prick and hurt him, yet he accepted my apology without hesitation. Damn it. I wanted to be with him. I didn't want to lose that chance. No guts, no glory. Time to lay it out.

"I do want to let go and have you take care of me, Aaron. You have no idea how good that sounds. It's just... Aaron, you have to understand—no one has *ever* taken care of me. At least not since my dad died twenty years ago. It's so much safer this way. I can't get hurt if I don't care, and I won't be let down if I'm not counting on anyone else. I'm sorry I snapped in there. I didn't mean it. It's a reflex. Be patient with me, okay? I'll get better at this."

Didn't think I had it in me, did you? Well, ha! I'm a pretty self-aware guy. It'd be fun to say I learned all of this about myself because I'd fucked a few shrinks, but I actually do read, you know. I'd even been known to pick up some self-help books. Now, I may have also fucked some guys in the mental health field but, as I've previously told you, I tend to have very limited conversations with guys in bed. Mostly it was shit like "fuck me harder." Yeah, I know, deep stuff. Well, if it was good, it was deep, but that wasn't what I meant. Ha, ha.

"I won't let you down, Zach. I promise I won't let you down. And I *will not* hurt you. Not ever."

I believed him. And that made me feel good. But by that time, I'd been with Aaron for hours and, frankly, I was ready to feel good in another way.

"Hey, Aaron?"

He was gently stroking my hair.

"Yeah?"

"All this emotional stuff is great and all, but can we please move on to the fucking part of this evening's program?"

He laughed.

"You really are a sweet talker, Zach."

He reached down and picked me up, one arm under my legs and the other behind my back. Then he walked out of the kitchen and into the bedroom. Yup, he was that strong. And, yup, that was a big fucking turn-on.

CHAPTER FOURTEEN

WHEN WE got to the bedroom, Aaron lowered me onto the bed, then joined me. His hands stroked my neck and chest, and his lips followed. I enjoyed the attention, and his tongue and hands all over me were great. But we'd had months of foreplay by that point, and I hadn't had sex in all that time, so I wanted to skip the preliminaries and get to the main event.

I rolled on top of him so he was on his back and we were face-to-face. My cock was against his stomach, and his cock pressed against my balls. He thrust up against me, and that made us both groan.

"Where do you keep the supplies?"

As I was asking, I realized he might not have supplies. This was, after all, his first time having any guy at his place, and his first time fucking anyone. I had one condom in my wallet, but that was it. The lube and other condoms were in my bag, which was in Dean's car. Now, don't get me wrong, I like the burn, but not using any lube when I hadn't been with anyone in that long was going to be uncomfortable. Thankfully, Aaron was a boy scout. He reached over to his nightstand, opened the drawer, and pulled out a few condoms and new bottle of lube.

I raised myself off Aaron, took one of the condoms, and opened it. I squirted some lube into the condom and rolled it onto his dick, then took more lube and rubbed it all over his condom-covered cock. I wiped the rest of the lube from my hands onto my own dick and Aaron's stomach. I straddled him and lined his cock up with my hungry, begging hole, pressing it against me, and lowered myself down in one hard motion.

"Oh fuck! That feels so fucking good." I grunted out the words as I braced myself by leaning back and resting my hands on his thighs. I remained in that position with my eyes closed for a little while, letting myself adjust as my body shook with the depth of feeling I was experiencing. Eventually I opened my eyes and looked at Aaron.

He was lying on his back, trembling and gazing at me with wet eyes. He reached his hand up and stroked my cheek. Then he put both of his hands on my thighs and massaged them as he sighed deeply. He didn't break eye contact, and I could see his love for me.

Once I was adjusted, I began to raise myself up and down on him. I'd go up until only his crown was in me, and then drop back down until I was completely impaled on his dick. By leaning back the way I was, his dick hit my prostate on every drop. The physical sensation felt incredible, and I'd been waiting for so long to have Aaron's dick inside me that I knew I wouldn't last long.

Aaron reached over to my cock and started stroking me with one hand and playing with my balls with the other. I think he was moaning, but it was hard for me to hear anything above my own grunts, as I increased the pace and used every muscle in my legs to raise and lower myself onto his long, thick pole.

When Aaron took my balls into his hand and pulled them, I started shooting, my whole body tensed, and I could no longer move. He held my hips in his hands, pulled me up, and then he lowered me while thrusting his hips up and down. That allowed the feelings inside me to continue, and it made my orgasm last longer.

When I was finally spent, I collapsed onto Aaron's chest. He was still inside me, thrusting gently up into me as he caressed my back and whispered soothing words into my ear. Once I'd caught my breath, I raised my head and looked into his eyes. He put his hand on the back of my head and pulled me toward him for a kiss.

Lips and tongues blended together, first in a gentle kiss and then more passionate. Eventually, Aaron rolled us over so I was on my back, and he was pressed against me, still hard inside me. I wrapped my legs around his back and locked my ankles together. He nibbled on my neck and continued his gentle thrusts, alternating them with a slow circular movement.

It didn't take a lot to get me off, so I didn't usually last long, but I recharged very quickly. And Aaron's movements caused his stomach to rub against my dick, which was helping to work me up. We were both a bit sweaty, his stomach wet with lube and my cum, so the whole thing was incredibly arousing. Not to mention the fact that his cock was still deep inside me. I hardened in an instant and started meeting his thrusts.

Aaron moved his licks and kisses up my neck

until he reached my mouth. Then he started gnawing on my bottom lip. I could feel his heart racing, and his breathing was heavy. He slowly began increasing the pace and length of his thrusts. What started out as slow, short strokes, eventually turned into fast, deep strokes that took him almost completely out of my ass before he plowed back in.

"Oh, yes, Aaron. Fuck me! Fuck me!"

I moaned into his ear as he pummeled into me. Our bodies moved together, me pushing myself up and him pounding us both down. My dick was still pressed between us, rubbing against his wet skin. With all of those feelings combined, I felt another orgasm approaching. I clasped his back, dug my fingers into him, and begged him to fuck me harder.

That did it. He gave a few last, hard, deep thrusts, and I moaned his name as I shot off between us. His grunts joined mine as he grasped my shoulders and pressed as hard and deep as possible into me while he released.

After a couple of minutes, he pulled out and removed the condom, tied it off, and dropped it onto the floor next to the bed. He gently rubbed his hand over my ass.

"You okay?"

"I'm way better than okay. That was fucking fantastic, Aaron. Are you sure you've never done this before?"

I was only half-kidding. It wasn't that I didn't believe him. I mean, who would lie about being a virgin at twenty-seven? It wasn't exactly something to be proud of, you know? But he was good. He moved his body in a way that rubbed me in all the right spots. He lasted a hell of a long time. And he was sure of himself and took control, which I liked. That was why it was one of the best fucks I'd ever had. It wasn't only because of my feelings for Aaron. Yes, our feelings for each other made it better, but he also knew how to use his dick, and he fucked me through two orgasms. Even without being in love that would've felt good.

"Well, not in real life. But I have a remarkably active imagination." He laughed softly and then kissed my cheek. "I know you're beat, but what do you say to a quick shower before we go to sleep?"

I grumbled a little but eventually agreed. We were both sticky and a shower sounded good. We got out of bed, then Aaron picked up the condom wrapper and the used condom and walked into the bathroom. Ten minutes later, we were clean and back in bed. I immediately pressed my back against Aaron, so he was spooned against me. He wrapped his arm around my chest and held me close to him.

"I've wanted to fall asleep like this every night for the past four months."

I whispered the words, a little embarrassed about my feelings for him. I don't know why. I know it sounds stupid. But, hey, I still wasn't completely used to the whole thing. He stroked my chest and kissed my neck.

"I have, too, Zach. I want to fall asleep like this forever. I love you."

"Me too, Aaron. Good night."

I was asleep as soon as the words left my mouth. My nose was filled with Aaron's scent, my body was covered in his warmth, and my ass felt the very pleasant aftereffects of a thoroughly fulfilled longing.

A REPETITIVE, annoying knocking forced me to open my eyes. Aaron and I were still pressed together. He was on his back, and I was on my side with one leg and one arm thrown over him and my face buried in his neck.

I tried to ask about the irritating noise, but my mouth couldn't formulate words, so it came out in an incomprehensible growl.

"I think that's the door." He turned his head to look at the clock on the nightstand. "It's eight in the morning on a Saturday. No one ever comes here. I can't imagine who that would be."

"Ignore it. They probably have the wrong door."

I tried to close my eyes to go back to sleep, but I was already awake enough to feel and smell Aaron's skin. I decided sleep could wait. I reached over to his cock, when the knocking on the door turned into banging. Aaron groaned.

"They're not going to stop. Hold that thought, I'll be right back."

He got out of bed and pulled a pair of sweatpants out of his dresser drawer. I could hear him talking to the annoying fucker who'd woken us up as he walked to the door.

"I'm coming." Then I heard the door open. "Kimmy! What...what are you doing here?"

"Well, that's no way to greet someone. Where are your manners? Aren't you going to invite me in?"

"Oh, I'm sorry. Of course, come in."

I heard Kim talking to Aaron, but I couldn't make out all the words. She had her peppy voice on, and I heard my name a couple of times. I thought I should get out there, before she either talked Aaron into white-washing her fence or walked into the bedroom and started bouncing on the bed.

"I'm right here, Kim."

I managed to grumble the words out as I stumbled through the hallway.

"Oh good! He's awake. How are you this fine morning, sleepyhead?"

I made my way into the living room and saw Aaron and Kim standing in front of the couch. Her hair and makeup were all done, and she was wearing some sort of flowery thing. Fucking morning people. Why was she here? Had she never heard of a telephone? Pick. Up. The. Fucking. Phone. And. Call. How am I this fine morning you ask?

"I'm very well-fucked this morning, Kim. Thanks for asking. And, if Aaron's up for it, if you know what I mean, I'm hoping for another round. How are you?"

Kim made a hiccup sound, covered her mouth with her hand, and stared at me. I didn't know if it was what I'd said, or the fact that I was standing completely naked in front of her, but she mumbled something and then disappeared into the kitchen.

Aaron blushed, walked over to me, and wrapped me in his arms. Then he leaned down, kissed my neck, and pressed his body tightly to mine, so I could feel his hardening dick against me.

"I'm up for it," he whispered in my ear. "But your brother and the boys want to see you. Kimmy came here to invite us to their place for breakfast. Can we go over there for a little while? We can eat, play with the boys, and be back in bed within three hours."

I grumbled. Aaron covered my neck in little kisses.

"Well-fucked, huh?"

That made me laugh. I pulled my head back and looked up at his face. He had a shy, little-boy smile. As if he'd done something good, and he was proud of himself. Well, he sure as fuck had reason to be proud. He was damn good.

"*Very* well-fucked," I answered.

His smile broadened.

"I'm making it my personal mission to keep you in that condition as long as you're with me. Come on, let's get dressed quickly so we can go over there and then come back here and get back in bed."

With that, he took my arm and pulled me into the bedroom.

"Kimmy said your bag is in her car."

Aaron slipped a long-sleeved T-shirt on over his head.

"I'll run out and get it."

He walked over to me, bent down, and kissed my cheek. Then he looked at me and chewed on his bottom lip.

"Zach, I, ummm, I had a nice time last night. Thank you."

He blushed and then walked out of the room. I stood there thinking how fucking adorable he looked with that shy little smile. He also looked hot, and that made me hard again.

Three hours. I could wait three hours. And I did want to see Dean and the kids. Okay, three hours.

CHAPTER FIFTEEN

KIM LEFT Aaron's apartment after we promised to get dressed quickly and meet her back at her house. I washed my face, brushed my teeth, and threw on an old pair of jeans, a T-shirt, and a sweatshirt over it. I was tying the laces on my All Stars when Aaron walked out of the kitchen, holding a canvas bag. His eyes were gleaming as he looked me up and down, as though I was a prize. I raised my eyebrows at him, and he shrugged.

"You look hot."

I looked down at my outfit and laughed. I had lots of clothes designed to pick up guys, but worn jeans and an old sweatshirt were most certainly not on the list.

"Hot? This isn't exactly club-wear. If I were going for hot, the pants would be a lot tighter, I'd lose the sweatshirt, and the T-shirt would be a few sizes smaller."

"Well, I'm sure that would work too. I think you'd look great in anything, Zach." He stroked my cheek and ran his fingers through my hair. "You're beautiful. But, to me, you look especially good like this. You look relaxed and comfortable."

Relaxed and comfortable. That was how I felt. Well, one part of my body wasn't relaxed, but we'd have to handle that later. I adjusted my dick in my pants and noticed Aaron doing the same.

"You know, Aaron, being with you is like being thirteen all over again. Constant erections with no ability to control them."

I expected him to laugh, but instead he looked down at the ground. Then he raised his eyes to mine, put his arms around me, and pulled me up against him.

"Is...is that from being with me? We haven't spent that much time together in person, and it's not like I could see you while we were on the phone. Plus, I haven't been with you around other people, so I, ummm..." He sighed. "Never mind. I'm blabbering. Let's go."

He picked up the canvas bag, took my hand, and led me to the door. What was that? I went over Aaron's words in my head, trying to make sense of them. But I didn't understand. In case you hadn't noticed, I wasn't exactly the quiet, shy type. So as soon as we got into the car, I asked him.

"What did you mean back there? Do you not realize that I'm attracted to you?"

He reached over and held my hand. I enjoyed his constant need to touch me. Truth be told, I needed it too.

"I know you're attracted to me. I knew it from the first time we met."

Well, it wasn't an ego problem. I laughed.

"Okay, so what did you mean?"

He was quiet for a long time. When we got to a stop light, he turned and looked at me.

"I didn't mean anything."

"No way, Aaron. That's not going to fly with me."

He looked surprised. Frankly, so was I. I wasn't usually the one wanting to talk about feelings and emotions and all that crap. Of course, I'd changed so much since I'd met Aaron anything was possible with me.

I mean, if someone had told me six months prior that I would spend more than four months with nothing but the company of my own hand, and that I'd then choose to spend a Saturday with kids instead of in bed getting my ass fucked raw, I'd have told him to go fuck himself, and then me. So, at that point, what difference did a little conversation make?

"You were the one who said we need to talk about things, remember? You were the one who said we don't stand a chance if we don't talk to each other. So spill, Aaron."

He hesitated. I squeezed his hand. The light changed, so he turned back toward the road. Then he started talking.

"I didn't know if you have that reaction to every guy you're attracted to. That's all."

Did I have that reaction to every hot guy? No, absolutely not. I mean, I didn't have trouble getting it up. And if I knew sex was coming, my dick sprung to attention. But sitting around looking at someone didn't get me hard. When I was a kid, yeah. Staring at a good-looking guy turned me on. It probably wasn't just the staring, though. I used to look at guys and imagine what I could be doing with them.

But I'd been having very frequent sex for over

a decade (the last several months being a notable exception), so I no longer needed to imagine. Plus, I was long past being a teenager with raging hormones. That was, except when I was around Aaron. Then I seemed to have no control over my body. That was why I'd made that comment.

"No, I don't have that reaction to every guy. You get me worked up, Aaron. Not like anyone else. And it's not because I'm extra horny after all these months of celibacy."

He didn't say anything. I'd been looking out the window while we were talking, but I turned to look at him when he was so quiet. He was still driving, but his mouth was hanging open, and he was staring at me.

"Aaron! Eyes on the road."

He quickly turned back to the road, mumbled an apology, and managed to get us to Dean's house in one piece.

"I'm driving on the way back. I know I said I wanted to spend the day in bed, but I meant *your* bed. Not a hospital bed."

I was grumbling at him as I stepped out of the car. He reached onto the backseat, picked up the canvas bag, and followed me.

"I'm sorry. I got distracted." He looked down at the ground and rubbed the toe of his shoe into the driveway. "Late night, I guess."

We walked up the driveway and our hands met. I wasn't sure whether he reached for me, I reached for him, or we were drawn together. Whatever it was, I enjoyed it. We intertwined our fingers and made our way over to the kitchen door. I opened it and walked in, pulling Aaron behind me. I expected to see some food ready after Kim's early morning wakeup, but the kitchen was clean.

Aaron let go of my hand and walked over to the counter. He started unpacking the canvas bag. Flour, butter, eggs, spinach, an onion, feta cheese.

"They should have some milk and strawberries in the fridge and bananas in the bowl on the counter next to it. I was here yesterday, and there were plenty."

Aaron was pulling a mixing bowl out of the upper cabinet while he was talking.

"What are you doing?"

"Crepes. I'll sauté the spinach and onions and then sprinkle some feta on it to make a savory filling, and I'll cut up the fruit and mix it with some jam to make a sweet filling."

He started cracking the eggs.

"I don't mean what are you making. I mean, why are you cooking? I thought Kim invited us over here for breakfast. Didn't they already make something?"

Aaron laughed.

"I told you. Between the two of them, they can barely make toast. Don't worry, though; you'll like these crepes. I promise you won't go hungry. I have every incentive to make sure you have all your strength." He smiled, waggled his eyebrows, and turned back to his task. "I don't think they heard us come in. Go on in there." He motioned his head toward the door. "I'm sure Dean wants to see you and so do the boys. This won't take me long."

If it had been anyone other than my brother's family, I probably would've taken Aaron and dragged him the fuck out of there. This shit was nuts. Who invites you to their house for a meal and then expects you to bring the ingredients and make everything?

But it *was* my brother's family. And that meant it was my family. The only family I had. I hadn't had a family for so long and never thought I ever would, so that did mean something to me. I sighed and gave in to the insanity.

"I'll get the milk and strawberries out of the fridge. Do you want me to make the crepe batter, or should I sauté the spinach and onions?"

I walked over to the fridge and got the stuff out.

"And don't fucking say you're doing both. We're making breakfast together. It'll take half the time and then we'll both get to relax and hang out."

Aaron opened his mouth to object, but before he could say a word, I walked over to him, pulled his head down, and covered his lips with mine. He had an egg in one hand, but he took the other and rested it on the small of my back. I parted my mouth to let his tongue in and sucked on it.

When we finally separated, I whispered to him, "Don't argue with me about this, Aaron, or you'll have to give me a spanking when we get home."

His eyes were glazed, and he panted out a response.

"I think you have that threat backward."

I waggled my eyebrows at him.

"No, I don't. Why shouldn't I get a little bonus if you choose not to behave? Come to think of it, maybe you should spank me either way."

He laughed.

"I'll make the batter, you make the filling."

"That's more like it."

I kissed his cheek. Then I rinsed the spinach and looked through the cabinets for a cutting board.

"There's a narrow cabinet below and to the right of the sink. That's where they keep the cutting board. The knives are in the block next to the stove. And the frying pan is in the deep drawer next to it."

I got everything out and diced the onion. Aaron was stirring the batter and then got a crepe pan out of a drawer. We worked together in companionable silence. While we were standing next to each other in front of the stove, Aaron making crepes and me sautéing onions, I nudged him with my hip. He looked down at me, and I smiled.

"This is nice, Aaron."

He sighed, smiled at me, and in a wistful voice, said, "Yeah, it is. It's the best. I love you, Zach."

Just then, the door opened, and Dean walked in holding one of the babies. The kid looked much bigger than he had last time I'd been there.

"I thought I smelled something wonderful coming from in here." He set the baby down, came up behind us, and put a hand on each of our shoulders while he looked into the pans. "Crepes? Yum! I'll go get Kim. Ryan, sit down at your table and stay away from the stove. Uncle

Zach and Uncle Aaron are cooking."

The little guy ran over to a small, colorful table they had set up in the corner.

"Okay, Daddy."

"Wow! He wasn't doing that last time I was here."

"I know. It's amazing how quickly they develop at this age. They're both running around, and they're learning new words every day."

Dean walked out of the kitchen, calling Kim's name. I was still looking at Ryan in the corner. He looked like my brother: blond hair, blue eyes, stocky build. I turned back to the stove and noticed Aaron staring at me.

"What?"

He shrugged.

"Nothing. I like looking at you. I'm so glad you're here." He flipped the crepe from the pan onto the waiting plate and poured more batter. "I missed you, Zach. Four months is too long to be apart."

He was right. Four months was too long. Hell, four weeks or even four days would've been too long. I thought about when I'd next be able to return.

"Uncle Zach!"

I looked at the doorway and saw Simon running toward me. Kim was right behind him with Chad holding her hand. I hunched down on the ground, and Simon fell into my arms. I ruffled his hair.

"Hi, little man. You've grown."

"Yes. I'm big. I made you pictures, Uncle Zach. Want to see?"

"I sure do. But let's eat breakfast first."

The spinach was done, so I scooped it into a bowl. Aaron was almost through all of the batter. That left the fruit, so I sliced the strawberries and bananas. Kim set the table, and then we were ready to eat. The boys sat at their little table and the adults sat at the kitchen table. Aaron and I put everything out, so people could make their own crepes.

Aaron picked up one of the kids' plates.

"I'll make Chad's plate."

Kim picked up a plate and started putting together a fruit crepe. By the time she'd given the plate to Simon and turned back to the table, Aaron had plates ready for Chad and Ryan. She picked both up and set them in front of the boys at the little table.

"Thanks, sweetie," she said to Aaron.

Dean looked up from his almost finished empty plate, suddenly remembering some common courtesy.

"Oh yeah. This is delicious, guys, thank you."

Aaron sat next to me. He put his hand on my thigh and stroked it, then leaned down and whispered in my ear, "You're not eating. Everything okay?"

I'd been watching their interaction and wasn't thinking about food. I kissed his cheek.

"I'm fine. Sorry, mind wandered there for a minute."

I turned back to the table to put a crepe on my plate and noticed Kim and Dean were both looking at us and smiling.

"So, Aaron, have you made a decision about the clinic?"

Aaron looked over at me.

"Not yet. I want to talk to Zach first, and we haven't had a chance."

"Oh, I figured you'd have done that last night."

"I'm sorry, Dean. We'll talk today."

I had no idea what they were talking about, but I was tired of Dean and Kim acting like they needed to be the top priority in Aaron's every thought and action. And I hated constantly hearing him apologize to them. Especially considering how much he did for them. Did it never occur to them that we might have had other things to talk about and do last night? Like each other, for instance. I opened my mouth to tell my brother off when Aaron turned to me.

"Sorry about this. I know we're being rude leaving you out. I thought we'd get a chance to talk when we got back home, but I may as well fill you in now. Kimmy wants to sell the clinic. So I need to decide whether I want to buy it."

I looked over at Kim.

"Last time I was here, you said the clinic was doing well, Kim. Why do you want to sell it?"

"Oh, it's doing great, even better now than it was over the summer. But with your brother's promotion, we can afford to have me stay home with the boys, full-time. So, this is a good chance for me to get out. It's not like Aaron needs me there. He's doing practically everything himself anyway."

Aaron wasn't saying anything. He seemed to be making a career out of cutting up his crepe. I had no idea why this discussion made him uncomfortable, or why he wanted to talk to me before making a decision. It wasn't like I knew dick about vet clinics or running a business. Still, he looked uncomfortable, so I decided to change the topic. Dean had mentioned his promotion in one of his e-mails, but he hadn't given me many details.

"Congrats on getting tenure, Dean. Does it mean more work?"

"No. I've already been spending a lot of time writing and getting things published. I'll keep doing that. More than anything, it means security and a little more money."

The rest of the morning was nice. We finished eating and Kim and Dean managed to clean up their own kitchen while Aaron and I played with the boys in the family room. Simon wanted to color with me, and then we built a castle out of blocks. Ryan and Chad tried to mimic everything he did. I thought back to whether I'd ever been that way with Dean, but I couldn't remember much from before my dad died, and Dean hadn't been around after that.

After a couple of hours, Dean asked Aaron for some help with something out back. (You're shocked, I know. Try to hold it together.) Simon went to his room and brought out a few books. I sat on the couch, and all three boys sat on my lap and leaned up against me while I read to them.

"You're a big animal guy, aren't you, Simon?"

Each of the books he brought to me was about animals—one about cats and dogs, one about wolves, and the last one about birds.

"Yes. I like animals. Like Uncle Aaron."

I thought it was interesting that he didn't mention his mom. After all, she was a vet too. At around noon, Kim came in and called us into the kitchen for lunch. We'd eaten breakfast a couple of hours earlier, so I wasn't that hungry, which was good because she'd made macaroni and cheese from the box. Aaron saw the look of horror on my face and choked back a laugh.

"Kimmy, we'll help feed the boys, and then we're going to get going. I know it's about nap time for them anyway."

"Sounds good, Aaron. Do you two want some noodles?"

Aaron grinned at me.

"No thanks, Kimmy. I think Zach and I are both still full from breakfast."

Aaron and Kim helped Chad and Ryan into the chairs on their small table and made sure they got more food in their mouths than on their clothes. Simon sat in his booster at the big table so I could spend time with him. We talked about bugs. He seemed to know a lot about all sorts of insects and worms. Not that I had any idea whether his information was accurate, but I liked listening to his earnest little voice sharing his knowledge with me.

When the kids were done with lunch, Aaron picked up their plates, rinsed them, and put them in the dishwasher. We all said our goodbyes, and then Aaron and I were on our way back to his place.

CHAPTER SIXTEEN

"WELL, THAT was longer than three hours, but it was nice seeing everyone." I reached over and held Aaron's hand. "How often do you go over there?"

"Oh, I don't know. I try to make it over at least a couple of nights during the week to make dinner, and give Kimmy and Dean a chance to go out on their own for a little bit. The rest of the nights, I've been working late, getting everything fixed up at the clinic. That isn't taking as much time anymore, though. Things are in pretty good shape.

"When I got here, I started keeping the clinic open on weekends so we could build our client base back up. A lot of people left when Kim took over. But some of them have come back, and we have lots of new clients too. As we got busier, I reduced it to two weekends a month. I made an arrangement with an emergency clinic not too far from us for the weekends we're closed. We refer all of our after-hours calls to him, and he gives us a kickback. It's a nice way to earn a little extra without doing any work. Plus, it leaves half my weekends free, so I can help Kimmy out with the boys.

"I could actually cut weekends out altogether. We're so busy now that we almost need to turn new clients away. But, Kimmy's doing well, so she doesn't need as much help with the kids. And it's not like I have much going on in my personal life, so work gives me something to do."

Well, that was sad.

"What about your friends?"

Aaron sighed and shrugged.

"I guess I don't have many friends here."

I hated bringing up that party over the summer because I'd acted like such a prick. But I knew the guys there liked Aaron. And some of them were the same guys he was talking with at the roof party.

"What about your friends from that party you took me to?"

I looked at his face, nervous about how he'd react to that memory. But he didn't look mad.

"They're not friends. I mean, I see them quite a bit because we all do volunteer work with the gay rights group. But, outside of that, I don't see them much."

I didn't want to push him about this, but it was all part of what I didn't understand about Aaron's life, the emptiness in his apartment, his lack of social activities, unless you count taking care of my brother's family. I needed to understand, so I could help him. He deserved more out of life.

"You know, I'm pretty good at reading people, and those guys at the party like you. I could tell that they think of you as a friend. Why don't you spend more time with them?"

"Oh, I don't know. I'm not as good with people as

you, Zach. You're so outgoing and charismatic. Growing up, I spent most of my time with my family. There were so many of us cousins that we were each other's closest friends. Plus, the friends I had at school, I'd known my whole life. I didn't get to know many people in college because I was busy with Michael and his family. And then during grad school, I worked a lot and had classes. Most of my free time I spent with Dean and then with Kimmy, too, once they got together. And you know I lived with them for a year after Simon was born. That was a busy time. I guess I've never had a big group of friends. I'm okay focusing on a few close people."

I thought about what Aaron had said. Even though I had many more friends and people in my life, none of my friendships were as deep as Aaron's. He was extremely close to his parents, siblings, and several cousins—those were the important people during his childhood.

I knew he spoke with Michael's parents and sisters every week and visited them when he went home. And then there were Dean and Kim. He had rearranged his entire life to be with them, and they were all very close. Comparing my relationships, I realized that while I had a larger number of friends, his friendships were deeper and had lasted much longer. It took a lot more for Aaron to make friends, but once he connected with someone, he didn't let go.

That made me think of one of the books that I'd read to Simon.

"You're like a wolf."

"What does that mean?"

I laughed.

"You mate for life."

He turned his head toward me and gazed into my eyes.

"I sure hope so."

Jesus. I didn't mean it like that. Thankfully, Aaron turned back to the road, so he probably didn't notice the look of terror that I was sure crossed my face. We'd never talked about our relationship—what we expected from each other, or where we were going with things. It wasn't like I didn't know he wanted something serious. Of course I knew. But it was easier not to think about it. Why? Because I still wasn't sure whether I was capable of giving him what I knew he wanted—monogamy, fidelity, exclusivity. I'd never even considered that type of life before I met Aaron, and I still wasn't sure I wanted to live that way.

We were quiet during the rest of the drive back to Aaron's place. It didn't take long, so it wasn't awkward. Aaron put his arm around me as we walked up to his door.

"I'm going to put these things away in the kitchen. Do you want a drink?"

I considered asking for vodka to calm my nerves after that conversation. No, getting wasted was not the solution.

"How about some tea? I think I saw some in your fridge. I'll get it. Do you want a glass?"

"Sure."

I followed him into the kitchen. He put away the things he'd brought to Dean's house while I got two glasses down from the cabinet and poured us some tea. I leaned against the counter, took a sip of the tea, and started coughing.

"What the fuck is this?"

Aaron laughed.

"Sweet tea. You can take the boy out of the South, but you can't take the South out of the boy."

I set the glass down on the counter.

"From the taste of that, I think I consumed my daily allotment of calories."

Aaron came over to me and ran his hand down my chest.

"I don't think you have anything to worry about, Zach. You look great. Perfect."

Well, I wasn't going to argue about that. I was in good shape. I didn't have any extra fat on my body, and I wasn't fishing for compliments. Besides, Aaron's hand was stroking my chest and stomach, and that made me lose my breath. I wasn't sure I could formulate words, even if I'd wanted to.

He leaned down and licked the spot behind my ear, he sucked on my lobe, and then darted his tongue into my ear. While he was doing that, his hands worked on my pants—he unbuttoned my jeans and reached his hand into my boxer briefs. I moaned and pushed into him when he covered my cock with his big, warm hand.

"Bedroom," I whispered into his ear.

He ran his tongue down my neck and then up my chin. When he reached my lips, I curled my fingers through his hair, grasped the back of his head, and pulled him tightly against me, forcing our lips to mash together in a hard kiss. He moaned.

We eventually managed to stumble into Aaron's bedroom, though we never stopped groping each other. Once we were in the room, we quickly got undressed and into bed. The previous night, I'd been so desperate to feel Aaron's cock inside me that we'd skipped all the preliminaries. I would've been happy to follow the same course of action, but Aaron wasn't having it.

"Lie down, babe. Relax. Let me love you."

I didn't think relaxing was going to be possible, but I lay back on the bed and enjoyed the feeling of Aaron's hands and tongue working me over. He started with my neck and sucked so hard I was pretty sure he'd leave a mark. I turned my head to the side to give him more room to work. Then he focused on my chest, massaging my pecs, and sucking and gnawing on my nipples. Just when I thought I couldn't take any more of that, he lowered down to my stomach, running his tongue over every muscle and then dipping it into my bellybutton.

My cock was next. Aaron lapped at it like a cat, swirled his tongue around the head, then sucked on it. After a short time sucking, he took my whole cock into his mouth and throat, then hummed and swallowed. I bucked up against him and moaned. He released my dick and moved his mouth to my balls. He took one into his mouth while his hand caressed the other, and then switched sides.

I'd never had anyone worship my body that way. Obviously, when I fucked around in clubs, we didn't take off our clothes; we just made sure the important parts were exposed. But even when I went home with guys, we got to the main act pretty quickly. I mean, we were there to get off. Why postpone it?

The way Aaron was touching me and licking me, though...it was like that was the experience. His warmth felt so good on my body. And just when I thought it couldn't get any better, he started working on my ass. Holy fuck!

I'd been rimmed a few times over the years. If you're wondering why only a few times, considering how many guys I'd fucked around with, well, I think you've been watching too much porn. In real life, most guys don't like to put their mouth on a stranger's ass, even if they're about to fuck it. Maybe it would've been different if they'd felt they needed to encourage me or something, but I'd always been ready to go. Anyway, what Aaron was doing to my ass was nothing like I'd ever experienced.

At first, he ran his tongue up and down the cleft of my ass. But it didn't take long before he was tonguing and sucking on my pucker, and then he pushed his tongue into me and swiped it in a swirling pattern inside me. For a guy like me, who gets off on ass play, that was pure fucking heaven.

I put my hands underneath my knees and pulled my legs up toward my chest. That raised my ass up and gave Aaron more access. He took advantage of the situation by massaging my ass cheeks with his big hands and then spreading my cheeks and continuing his feast on my asshole.

I didn't know how long Aaron worked on me, but

eventually I felt like my heart was going to beat itself out of my chest, and I had to get off. I couldn't speak, and I couldn't move. Every part of my body was focused on my ass and the feelings Aaron was giving me. He must have sensed my need, because he moved one hand over to stroke my dick, while at the same time he pushed two fingers from his other hand into my hole alongside his tongue. That did it, and I started screaming as I unloaded.

I think I must have blacked out for several seconds. When I opened my eyes, Aaron was leaning over me, licking my cum off my chest. I looked into his eyes, and we gazed at each other as he ran his tongue over my body, lapped up my cum, and then brought it into his mouth and swallowed. Fuck, that was hot. He didn't stop until I was completely clean. Then he scooted his body up and started nibbling on my neck.

"I hope those are happy tears," he whispered huskily into my ear.

I hadn't even realized that I was crying. I clung to him and nodded my head against his shoulder.

"Good. All I want is to make you happy, Zach. I love smelling you, licking you, tasting you. I never want to stop." I think I whimpered at that point. Not very butch, I know, but Jesus, he was making me so fucking hot. "Are you ready for more?"

I was trembling and still couldn't speak, but I nodded again. He reached into the nightstand and got out a condom and lube. He pulled himself up off me, opened the condom wrapper, and rolled the condom onto his cock. When he reached for the lube, I managed to pull myself together enough to stop him.

"I think I'm wet enough from your mouth. I want to feel you pushing in. I...I want to feel the burn."

He hesitated and looked into my eyes. Then he set the lube down, pushed my legs back up, and returned his face to my ass. He didn't spend long down there, but I could feel the wetness from his mouth dripping down into the cleft of my ass and then his fingers pushing it in. Before long, he raised his body, lifted my legs up against his chest, lined up his cock with my asshole, and pushed his way into me in one smooth stroke.

I'd been propped up on my elbows, watching him, but when he bottomed out, I fell back onto the bed and moaned.

"Oh, Christ, Aaron. That feels incredible."

He fucked me slowly at first, holding my legs up and pumping his cock in and out of me with a gentle thrust of his hips. Eventually my left leg slipped down his side and lay on the bed. He clutched my right leg with both of his hands, pushed it all the way up against my chest so my ankle was by my ear, and then he straddled my left leg and continued pushing into me, increasing his speed.

That position changed the angle of his cock inside me and hit me in new places. Then he increased his speed and started to piston into me and moan.

"So good. So good. You feel so, so good."

When it seemed like he was about to come, I reached down to my cock, but Aaron beat me to it. Two strokes with his big hand, and I was shooting off between us, clenching my ass on his cock and forcing him to unload into the condom.

We were both spent, panting and coming down from our orgasmic highs. Aaron collapsed with part of his body on top of mine. He rested his head on my shoulder as I ran my finger through the cum on my stomach. Aaron took my hand in his, brought my finger to his mouth, and sucked on it. My tired cock tried to stir.

"Oh fuck, Aaron. You are *sooo* good."

He pulled his mouth off my finger, kissed the palm of my hand, and then pressed it against his chest. I could feel his heart beating.

"We're good together, Zach."

I rolled on top of him, buried my face in his neck, and clung to him so tightly I thought I might leave bruises. He wrapped his arms around me and held me as he stroked my back. I felt the wetness on my face and realized I was crying again. I didn't know why, but I couldn't stop. My whole body shook, and the tears kept flowing. Aaron continued holding me and stroking me. He rocked our bodies from side to side and whispered into my ear.

"Shhhhh. It'll be okay, Zach. You'll see. We're going to make this work. Shhhhh. I have you."

As soon as he said it, I realized he was right. I was crying because I didn't want to lose him. It felt so good to be connected to him like that, to love him, and to have him love me back. I knew he could make something like that work. He was Mister Dependable. His entire life was one long chain of permanent relationships. But me? Well, I had absolutely no fucking experience with anything in the neighborhood of permanent. Not with another guy, not with family, not with friends. Not with anybody.

I'd fuck it up. I knew I'd fuck it up. Even if I wanted to make it work. Fuck it, let's call a spade a spade—I *did* want it to work. But that sure as hell didn't mean I was capable of making it work. Was I?

CHAPTER SEVENTEEN

I STAYED in bed, lying on top of Aaron, feeling his strong arms around me, holding me, soothing me, until I finally calmed down. By then, my cum had dried and our bodies were stuck together. I turned my head toward the clock on the nightstand.

"It's two o'clock. We skipped lunch, and I'm hungry. What do you say to a quick shower and then some food?"

Aaron kissed my neck.

"That sounds good. Let's go."

He sat up and swung his feet down onto the floor. That moved my body so I was standing in between his legs while he was sitting on the bed. I looked into his eyes, stroked his cheeks, and leaned my forehead against his. We stayed like that for a minute, neither of us saying anything. Eventually, I sighed and took his hand.

"Shower. Food. Here we go."

We didn't fool around in the shower. Aaron did wash me, though, and he shampooed my hair. It wasn't sexual, but I enjoyed it. After we dried off, I hung my towel on the hook and walked into the kitchen with Aaron following me. No point in getting dressed, I knew we wouldn't be leaving the house.

"How about sandwiches? I have some good bread, cold cuts, cheese, and tomatoes."

"Perfect."

I got the fixings out of the fridge while Aaron cut the bread. Once we assembled the sandwiches, I poured us each a glass of water. Aaron took our plates and walked over the couch.

"The stools are cold. Plus, if we sit here, we can snuggle while we eat."

Yes, he said snuggle. What can I tell you? I found it fucking adorable. The old me would've ridiculed the new me to no end. Whatever. I liked the new me better.

We sat on the couch together and ate our sandwiches. I looked at Aaron's naked body, his glowing skin, his firm muscles, and felt a tightening in my chest.

"You're gorgeous. You're truly gorgeous."

He smiled at me.

"I'm glad you think so. But I'm nothing special. Not like you, Zach."

I studied his face. He was being sincere. How could he not know how good he looked? I thought about telling him I'd seen a lot of guys in my life, so I had a good frame of reference, but I didn't want to bring up other guys.

I tucked my left leg underneath my ass and raised my right leg, so my foot was on the couch and I could lean my arm on my knee.

"So, tell me about the deal with the clinic. Kim wants to sell it to you?"

Aaron took the final bite of his sandwich.

"Mmmm, hmmm."

He swallowed, drank some of his water, and then set his glass down on the floor.

"She's never liked working. She loves animals, but she gets stressed out pretty easily. She's always worried that she hasn't caught something, and whenever one of the animals dies, she gets super-depressed. The thing is, it's not all puppies and shots, you know?

"A lot of what we do involves animals that have been hurt or are old or sick. They're not all going to make it. And that's hard on Kimmy. So, I take those cases and leave Kimmy with the healthy ones. It works out okay, because that's not very many hours, and she only wants to work part-time. The truth is, though, we don't need a vet doing that work. We could have a tech do it and have one of us pop in to introduce ourselves. Kimmy knows that. And with Dean making more money now, she doesn't need to work anymore, which is great. Plus, they're no longer upside down on the clinic, so they can sell."

I looked around Aaron's apartment. He sure didn't live like a guy who could afford to buy his own business. Not that I knew how much a vet clinic costs, but he didn't even have a coffee table. I figured the lack of money was his hold up.

"Maybe you can get a loan to buy it. That's what Kim did, right?"

We were both done eating, so Aaron took our plates and set them on the floor, next to our water glasses. He leaned back into the corner of the couch and held his arms out.

"Come cuddle with me."

I almost laughed. Not to make fun of him, but because he was so damn cute. I lay down with my side against his chest and my head on his shoulder while he wrapped his arms around me.

"I don't need a loan. It's not like they own the building, so the value of the business is equipment and goodwill. I have enough put away to buy it."

"Really?"

I knew I sounded very surprised. Aaron made gentle circles on my back with his fingers as he spoke.

"Yeah, well, I had scholarships and a college fund that I used to pay for tuition and living expenses during college and vet school, but I still worked the whole time, except for that one year when I helped with Simon. It's not like I'm very spendy, so I put away a lot of money. Plus, I'd be getting the clinic at a good price.

"When I came down here to help out, things were bad. Kimmy was barely able to break even on a month-to-month basis. Actually, the first week I was here, she didn't break even. They had to dip into their savings to cover payroll. So when I stepped in to help, neither of us could pull a salary. I had all that money saved up and was living at their house, so that was fine with me. Dean didn't feel right about it. He wanted to pay me, but I refused because I was doing a friend a favor.

"Kimmy had stopped working because the babies were almost due, and then she didn't come back to work for a few months after that. So I was the only one covering the clinic. I didn't know anyone here except Dean and Kim, so I didn't mind spending all my days and evenings working. Eventually, Dean said the favor could last until we got the clinic back to where it was when they bought it. Any increase in the value after that would be mine. Sort of like a profit sharing thing. I didn't feel right about it, but he insisted. He said if I didn't agree, Kimmy would have to come back to work. I knew she didn't want that. She wanted to spend time with the boys, and her hormones weren't quite back on track.

"So that was our deal. I built the client base back up, and by the time the twins were a few months old and Kimmy was able to come back to work, we were in great shape. The clinic was worth more than they paid for it. Dean tried to talk Kimmy into selling it back then, so they could get out, but she wasn't ready to give up. She still thought she wanted to work, but only part-time. That meant I needed to stay around.

"By that time, we were netting enough to take some money home. At first, we split the net down the middle. Dean didn't mind, because we weren't making that much. But eventually, we started doing well, and Dean didn't feel right splitting the money evenly since Kimmy was only working part-time. In the end, we agreed to split the income based on the hours we worked. I felt bad; they did own the clinic after all. But the types of cases Kim saw were low-dollar deals—well-visits and immunizations. I had the sick animals, which have higher profit margins. So she was still getting a little extra, considering the type of work she was doing.

"But she's been reducing her hours little by little, and at this point she's working so infrequently that she isn't bringing much home. Plus, Dean put all the money she's been making over the past year toward their loan, and they've been able to pay half of it down. That means if they sell, they'll get cash out."

I was listening to Aaron's story and trying to absorb the details. One thing I definitely managed to take away was that he was damn good at what he did. How else would he have been able to take a sinking ship and turn it around so quickly? I also gathered that he'd been saving just about every dollar he'd made since he was eighteen years old. I guessed the saving was the reason for the small, empty apartment.

"Okay, so you've been able to save enough to pay them what they originally paid for the clinic. And that's all you'll have to pay, even though it's worth a lot more now?" Aaron nodded. "And if you don't buy it?"

"If I don't buy it, we sell. Kim and Dean get the purchase price up to what they paid when they bought the clinic, and I get the difference."

"Well, would you want to go work for someone else in town or open a different clinic?" He shook his head. "So, what's the question here? It sounds like a great deal. Why haven't you agreed to buy it?"

Aaron was quiet, looking intently at me.

"If I buy the clinic, I'll be committing to staying here. Making a life here."

I didn't understand the issue. Aaron seemed to like Emile City. Hell, even I liked Emile City, now that I saw the areas where Aaron spent time. It was nothing like the neighborhood where my family lived when I was a kid. Oh, of course! If he stayed here, he'd be away from his family. I knew how close he was to them.

"You're not sure if you want to settle down here, away from your family?"

He leaned his head back against the couch and closed his eyes.

"I do miss my family. And I used to think that eventually I'd move back to Bryerville. But that's not my holdup, Zach."

"What then?"

He was quiet for a long time, lying there with his eyes closed.

"It's not a what. It's a who."

He opened his eyes and sat up. I turned so we were facing each other, and Aaron leaned forward to press his lips softly against mine. We shared a few gentle kisses, then he sighed and pulled back. When he spoke again, it was in a very quiet whisper.

"I'll move to LA, if you want. Or we can live here, near your brother. I don't expect you to move to Bryerville. I realize you don't have any connections there, and it's a tiny town. But, Zach, I want to build a life with you. We can't do that if we only see each other for a few weekends a year."

My heart raced, and my breathing quickened. *Jesus! Is this what a panic attack feels like?* I tried to calm down and think about what he'd said. He wasn't asking me to do anything. He said he wanted to live in the same city. I wanted that too. No reason to panic. I concentrated on my breathing and my heart slowed down. Aaron stroked my back.

"Did I freak you out?"

Well, yeah, he did. But that was because I was emotionally warped. No reason to admit that.

"No, I'm good." Deep breath. "I want to make a life with you, too, Aaron but I'm not sure what that means."

I looked at him and waited for an answer.

"It means whatever we want it to mean. Whatever you're comfortable with. I won't push you. I'll take whatever you want to give."

I should've been happy about that answer, right? He wasn't pushing. But I wasn't happy, and I didn't know why.

"We don't have to decide anything right now, Zach. You're only here until tomorrow. Let's enjoy our time together. You think about this and let me know whatever and whenever you decide."

"But, what about Dean and the clinic?"

Aaron smiled at me and stroked my hand.

"At the end of the day, that's just business. What we're talking about is a lot more important. I don't want you to feel pressured to make a decision about our relationship just because Kimmy's ready to sell the clinic. I'll handle that. You take all the time you need."

Relief, right? I should've been feeling relief. Why wasn't I?

"Zach?"

I realized I'd been sitting there, staring at him and not saying anything.

"Yeah?"

"I love you."

And there it was—happiness and relief washed over my body. I scooted closer to Aaron, until we were chest-to-chest, wrapped my legs around him, and kissed his neck. If he loved me even half as much as I loved him, then I was one hell of a lucky guy.

"Me, too, Aaron."

AARON AND I spent the rest of that Saturday in bed. No, we weren't fucking the entire time. We played board games. Stop laughing. We had sex when we got back from Dean's house and we didn't go to sleep until at least ten hours later. Nobody can fuck for that long. Besides, it was fun. It turned out I was good at Risk. But he kicked my ass in Battleship.

"Aaron, you only own like, five pieces of furniture, yet you have every board game known to man. Even if you wanted to have people over to play these games, there'd be nowhere for them to sit. And I know you can't play these on your own. So what gives?"

He playfully smacked my shoulder.

"I've had these forever. I used to play with my cousins when I was a kid. And Michael and I played a lot when he was in the hospital. There was nothing else to do."

He hesitated and looked at me. I smiled back at him.

"It's okay. I don't mind hearing you talk about Michael. He was your friend. I get it."

I didn't mind. I wasn't jealous of the guy. I mean, first of all, he was dead. I wasn't going to be jealous of a dead guy. That was fucking stupid. Plus, I knew Aaron hadn't been in love with him. I believed what Aaron told me—that he loved him like a friend. And finally, I knew Aaron was in love with me. I could tell from the way he looked at me, the way he held me, the way he touched me when we made love.

Ugh! Did I say, made love? Mother-fucking hell! I'd been with Aaron for just over twenty-four hours, and I was already thinking like...like...

"Thanks for understanding. I love you so much, Zach."

He leaned down and kissed my cheek. I buried my face in his neck and inhaled his scent. Fine, I was thinking like a guy in love. Now, fuck off.

OKAY, SO you know how I've said Aaron has an expressive smile? Over the course of that weekend, I learned that it wasn't only his smile; it was everything he did with his mouth. And Saturday evening, he was using his mouth to express a hunger for my skin.

Now, in my experience, mouths played into sex by sucking cock. Sometimes they'd gnaw on a nipple or whatever. But that was about it. Aaron seemed to enjoy licking me. Not just my dick and not just my ass, although I will say he spent a good deal of time there, which I

absolutely fucking loved. But he licked other parts too—
my neck, the area behind my ears, my bellybutton, my feet,
and everywhere in between. He'd run his tongue over me
and massage me with his strong hands. And I'd alternate
between being so worked up I thought I'd explode and so
relaxed I thought I'd fall asleep.

I'd never had a lover like Aaron. Okay, I'd never
had a *lover* at all, just a series of fucks. But you know what
I mean. I'd never been with a guy who spent that kind of
time. It sometimes seemed like it wasn't even about getting
off. He was enjoying the moment, touching me, kissing me,
rubbing me, licking me, and I lost myself in those feelings.
I lost myself in him.

By the time the sun set that Saturday, Aaron had
tasted every part of my body, explored every square inch
of me with his fingers, and memorized the spots that made
me gasp and the ones that made me giggle. Now, before
you go thinking I was a completely changed man, I should
tell you—in the midst of all the soft touches, we sucked
each other off, and Aaron made love to me.

I was face down on the bed, with my head resting
on my arms and my knees tucked underneath my stomach.
Aaron's body covered mine like a blanket, and he thrust his
hard cock into me slowly and gently as he rocked his body
forward and back on mine. It took a long time that way.
The movements were slow enough to keep my orgasm at
bay longer than usual. By the time I came, I wanted it so
badly my entire body shuddered and convulsed, and then
I fell into a deep sleep.

I woke up with Aaron pressed against my back, my

legs tucked back against his knees, one of his arms under my neck, his other arm around my chest. I could hear his rhythmic breathing, and I could feel his heart beating against my back. I didn't ever want it to end—the feeling of being wrapped up in Aaron. But then my stomach growled and reminded me it was time to eat.

I insisted on making dinner that night—lime chicken kabobs. I couldn't get Aaron to sit down and relax, though. He stood directly outside the kitchen, shifting from foot to foot, biting his lip and watching me work. It was causing him so much anxiety to watch without helping, that I relented.

"Fine. You can help. Make the salad, okay?"

When I told him he could help, his entire body perked up and a big smile spread across his face.

"Great! I'd love to make a salad."

He rushed into the kitchen, dug through the fridge for ingredients, and started washing lettuce in the sink.

"I make a great Caesar dressing. I have some romaine here, and I can make croutons from the bread we have left from lunch."

After a few minutes, we were chatting and laughing, working together to make dinner. We were a good team, and we had fun. Every time I did anything with Aaron, it was fun.

Smart, kind, fun, and unfuckingbelievably hot in bed. My mind finally started catching up to what my body had known from the beginning—I didn't want anybody other than Aaron.

CHAPTER EIGHTEEN

AARON DIDN'T bring up the sale of the clinic or the idea of our living in the same town again during the rest of the trip. And I was having such a good time with him—laughing, talking, fucking—that I didn't think about it. Well, the truth was, I didn't let myself think about it. But that was practically the same thing, right?

Anyway, everything was great. He was happy. I was happy. I floated on a fucking cloud during the flight, remembering something he'd said, or something he'd done, and feeling all warm and shit inside. I didn't even stop to feel horrified at my sappiness.

The next day at work, though, everything changed. My friend, Brandon, came into the restaurant for a late dinner. I was pretty much done in the kitchen, so I sat with him at the bar while he ate.

"Hey, Zach. We missed you at Paul's house this weekend. Great party, but it wasn't the same without you. Where were you?"

"Oh, I was out of town visiting my—"

My what? Lover? Boyfriend? Partner? I had no idea what to call Aaron. That bothered me. Aaron had become the center of my world. Our nightly telephone calls had been the highlight of my days since I'd met him. And that weekend I'd spent with him had literally been the best forty-eight hours of my life.

Yet, he let me leave without planning another time for us to be together. He'd said he wanted to build a life with me. But then he dropped it, as if it wasn't a big deal. At some level, I realized it was me that had been avoiding the subject. But I was still fucking pissed that he let me avoid it.

My thoughts were interrupted by the sound of Brandon's voice. He'd taken the pause in my sentence as permission to move on, making me realize he didn't actually give a shit where I'd been that weekend. Whatever. It wasn't like I bothered to ask what he'd been doing.

"So, are you?"

"Am I what?"

"Are you going to come out tonight? He's going to be there."

"Who's going to be where?"

"Fuck, Zach. You weren't listening to a word I said. That hot redhead Paul was dating. I was saying he asked about you at the party on Saturday. Said you have a great ass. He's going to Fubar tonight with a bunch of other guys. Sounds like fun, so, I was asking if you wanted to go."

I didn't want to go out. What I wanted was to go to my place, get in bed, and talk to Aaron on the phone. The realization that I preferred a night alone in my apartment to a night of clubbing with my friends got to me. Plus, I was mad at Aaron for seemingly not caring about when he'd see me next.

"Yeah, that sounds good. I'm done here, but I need to change. I'll meet you there."

As I drove to my apartment, showered, and got dressed, I was getting progressively angrier. In retrospect, I think I was sad about being away from Aaron. I missed him desperately. But, in my fucked up mind, I interpreted that as being angry at Aaron. And I somehow managed to convince myself I was justified in my anger because he didn't push for us to be together. Yeah, I know, I have more issues than fucking *People* magazine. What of it?

When I got to the club, I headed straight for the bar and proceeded to get drunk. Very drunk. Aaron called a couple of times, but I didn't answer my phone. I stewed in vodka and righteous indignation. I was pretty lit, standing around talking with my friends, when the redhead came up to me.

My friend Paul had brought him to a party about a year prior. I thought he was hot, and I knew Paul was good in bed, so the three of us hooked up that night. I hadn't seen him since. I think Paul said he moved to Portland or something.

"How're you doing, Zach? It's good to see you here. I was disappointed when you weren't at Paul's this weekend. I thought I wouldn't get to see you before I leave tomorrow."

Honestly, I can't tell you what happened after that. I think I fell into my old habits. There I was, in a bar I'd been going to for years to pick up guys, standing next to a guy I'd had a fun night with back in the day. And I was drunk. And I was pissed at Aaron. So, when the redhead started walking to the back room and asked me to go with him, I did.

We hadn't gotten very far into the darkness, when he started groping my ass. His movements were rough and unfamiliar. His breathing sounded all wrong. Even his scent put me off. The bottom line was, he wasn't Aaron. I pushed him away.

"What the fuck, man?"

"Sorry. Look, this isn't a good idea. I'm seeing someone."

He laughed.

"Yeah, so what? I'm seeing someone too. But he's not here right now, and I'm horny. It's sex. I'm sure both our guys will understand. Hell, we can tell them the story later and get them hot."

I didn't move toward him, but I didn't walk away either. I thought about what he'd said. No way would a story about me with another guy get Aaron hot. When I told him about my past, I made very broad statements, and he never once asked for details.

"Oh, come on. I've heard a lot of stories about you, Zach. You're one of the biggest cockhounds I've ever met. Don't tell me some guy actually asked you not to fuck around?"

No, Aaron hadn't asked me for monogamy. I'd assumed he expected it. After all, he sure as hell wasn't fooling around with anyone else. Shit, he hadn't fooled around with anyone before we'd met in anticipation of the relationship he'd hoped to someday have. Now that we were together, I had absolutely no doubt that Aaron wouldn't fuck another guy.

But why hadn't he asked me to do the same? Was it because he thought I was incapable of keeping my dick in my pants? I could feel myself getting even angrier. Fuck him! If he didn't think I had enough self-control to remain faithful to him, then he didn't deserve my fidelity.

I stepped forward, toward the redhead. He gave me a smirk and rubbed his hand over his cock. And in that moment, a lucid thought made its way through my alcohol-rattled head: *I* deserved my fidelity. It wasn't about Aaron. No, that wasn't what I meant. Of course it was about Aaron. What I meant was, I needed to stay faithful to Aaron for myself, not for him.

Sex is fun. It feels good. So why limit myself to one guy? Sex is just sex, right? It doesn't have to mean anything.

I'd spent my entire life thinking that way, believing those words. And they were true. Sex had always been fun, and it had never meant anything. Because I had never let it mean anything. I didn't want that anymore. I didn't want quickies in back rooms with nameless guys. I wanted long nights in bed, passionate kisses, and Aaron's arms around me when I fell asleep. That was what I wanted sex to be. I wanted it to mean something. And it was up to me to make it that way.

I stepped back from the redhead and turned around.

"Where are you going?" he asked as I walked away.

"Home. I'm going home."

AS SOON as I got to my apartment, I called Aaron. It was late, but I was pissed and didn't want to wait to talk to him.

"Hello."

His voice was groggy. I'd clearly woken him up.

"Why didn't you ask me to stop fucking around?"

I was yelling.

"What...what do you mean?"

He sounded confused.

"You know what I mean! Why haven't you ever asked me to stop having sex with other guys?"

There was a pause. Then I heard sheets moving, and I knew he was waking up.

"Zach." He sighed. "I didn't ask because I didn't want to push you away."

That pissed me off.

"That's such bullshit, Aaron."

"What? Why? It's true."

"I know it's true. And that's why it's bullshit. I might have agreed. I might have been fine with it. But you didn't think that was possible. You didn't even give me a chance."

"Oh, come on, Zach! When I brought up the idea of us living in the same city, you looked like a deer in the headlights. And you expect me to believe you'd have been perfectly fine if I'd asked you to stop sleeping with other guys?"

Okay, he had a point. I did panic the one time he brought up anything about our relationship. And, he was right, he hadn't asked for anything more than sharing a fucking zip code.

"Fine. You're right. Maybe I would've been a little scared if you'd asked. But, so what? You could've stuck it out and fought for me. Aren't I worth it to you?"

I hated how whiny I sounded, but the words were already out there. And I meant them.

"Jesus, Zach! Of course you're worth it. You're worth everything. That's why I didn't ask. I can't risk losing you. I can deal with anything as long as I still get to be with you. Do you think I like knowing you're with other guys? It kills me. I swear to you, I literally feel sick if I let myself think about it. When you didn't answer your phone tonight, I thought I was going to get an ulcer. But I suck it up and deal, because you're worth it."

My anger dissipated when I heard those words. I thought back to the conversation when he'd brought up our relationship. He'd told me he wanted to make a life with me, but he didn't want to push me. He'd said he'd take whatever I wanted to give. Why hadn't I told him then that I'd stopped fucking around with other guys after I met him? Why didn't I give him that? It would've meant so much to him. I'd always known that on some level, but I'd held it back. Why? Because saying it would've been tantamount to agreeing to keep it up, that's why. Because saying it would've been committing to him completely.

He was right. I had been scared. And not just a little.

"Aaron?"

My voice was lower, no longer yelling.

"Yeah?"

"You deserve better."

He made a strangled noise, and then I heard a broken, "No, don't say it, Zach."

What did he think I was going to say?

"Aaron, listen to me. You can't keep putting your own needs and desires on the back burner. You can't keep living your life to make other people happy, not if you're doing it at your expense."

"Please, Zach. I love you so much. Please."

He was almost whispering and his words were interspersed with whimpers. It sounded like he was crying.

"What's wrong, Aaron? Why are you crying?"

He sniffled.

"I don't want to lose you. Please don't end things, Zach. Please."

Is that what he thought I was doing?

"I'm not breaking up with you, Aaron."

"You're not?"

He sounded so relieved.

"No, I'm not. I'm asking you to tell me what *you* need. I'm asking you to stop holding back. I'm asking you to honestly tell me what you want from me."

He didn't say anything for several long minutes. I could hear him breathing through the phone. Eventually, he spoke.

"I don't want you to let anybody else touch you. I don't want you to so much as hold another guy's hand, let alone his ass or his dick. I want you to be mine. Just mine. I want you to move in with me, so we can be together every day. The two of us, together, living our lives with each other and nobody else. I want us to be a family, Zach."

"Okay."

"Okay?"

He sounded surprised.

"Yeah, okay. I want those things too. Other than that drunken fuckup at your friend's party the first weekend we met, I haven't been with another guy since I first laid eyes on you. And I don't miss it. I want to live my life with you, too, Aaron. Just you."

I could hear his breathing getting louder. It sounded like he was gasping for air.

"You...you haven't been with anybody else? At all? It's been, what? Almost five months. And we've only seen each other for a few days during that whole time. And... and...I didn't even ask you to be monogamous. Nobody else? The whole time?"

I felt like such a shit, hearing the relief and the barely contained euphoria in his voice. Knowing I'd brought him to tears by doing nothing more than finally giving him what he'd freely given me from the beginning—commitment.

"That's right. You didn't ask. But I haven't wanted anybody else. I should've told you. I can be a fucking asshole sometimes, Aaron. I'm sorry."

He gave a little chuckle.

"Oh, it's okay. You've told me now. That's what matters. Besides, I like fucking assholes."

I laughed.

"I love you, Aaron."

I was expecting an "I love you too," but what he said instead, touched me more in that moment.

"I know you do, Zach. I know."

CHAPTER NINETEEN

I FUCKING hate packing. Fucking hate it. I never thought I had a lot of stuff, but when I started looking around my place, deciding how many boxes I needed to buy, I realized I was wrong.

For the first seven or so years I'd lived in LA, I'd probably moved almost every year. Sometimes it was because a landlord sold the place. Sometimes it was because a roommate moved out, so the rest of us needed to get a smaller place, or a new roommate wanted to join, so we needed a bigger place. But the last few years I'd been making enough money to live on my own, and I liked my apartment. I was in a good part of West Hollywood, had nice neighbors, and even a decent amount of storage space. Of course, storage space meant I'd filled it with things I now needed to pack. Damn it!

I was sitting in my living room, setting up boxes, when Aaron called.

"Hello," I practically growled.

"Hi, babe. Everything okay?"

"Fine. Just starting to pack. Fucking hate it."

"Oh, Zach. I'm sorry I can't be there to help."

I took a deep breath and ran my fingers through

my hair. It was just fucking putting things into boxes. No big deal.

"It's fine. Sorry. I was being unreasonably grouchy. Actually, I have good news."

"Yeah? What's going on?"

"Well, there are lots of chefs looking for work here, so my boss had no trouble finding someone in the stack of resumes she keeps in her desk. The guy she hired needs to start right away. So he'll be shadowing me starting tomorrow, and once he has everything down, I'm out of there. My boss said if I want to leave early, that's fine because that way they don't have to pay two of us."

"Hey! That's great. I get you even sooner than we thought. So when do you think you'll be ready to come home?"

Home. I'd never thought of Emile City as home, more like the place from which I had escaped. And, even though I'd been living in LA for ten years, it wasn't home either. LA was too big, too transitory to be home. So, I guess I'd never felt like I had a home, per se. Aaron was right, though. I did feel as if I was coming home. Not because of the city. No, home was Aaron.

Yeah, yeah. Fucking sappy as all get out. I know. I'm a lost cause. Get over it. I have.

"Well, if I pack before work and a little after work, I should be done by Thursday night. And I think the new chef will probably be all set by then too. So I can probably start the drive over on Friday morning."

Aaron didn't say anything. I actually didn't notice, at first, because I'd started putting boxes together again while I was talking. When he finally did speak, it almost startled me.

"Zach?"

"Oh. Yeah?"

"I, umm, I hate thinking of you driving here by yourself, and I can't take time off, because I want to close the clinic for the week between Christmas and New Year's so we can go to Bryerville for you to meet my family. Plus, you're going to be so tired if you pack all day and then work full shifts on your feet. Do you think maybe we can hire a moving company? They'll take care of the packing, and they'll drive your stuff here. You can fly."

Do I think *we* could hire a moving company? We both knew that was code for *Aaron* hiring a moving company. That was expensive, and I needed every bit of my savings to carry me through in Emile City until I found a job. Besides, I was perfectly capable of packing my own shit and driving it down.

"I'm not a kid who needs a babysitter. I can drive a fucking truck by myself. And I'm perfectly capable of putting things in boxes. I don't need your money, Aaron."

My growly voice was back in full force. Aaron sighed.

"Oh, Zach. I know you're not a kid. You're older than I am, and a better driver. You said we could be a family, Zach. When you get here, we're going to need to talk about what that means. I'll be so happy when we're finally together and we can look at each other when we talk about these things. Or, even better, touch each other while we're talking."

Now, you tell me, how could I stay mad at him when he was being so fucking sweet? I couldn't.

THE WEEK flew by. The new guy caught on quickly at work, so Thursday would be my last day. I spent every free minute packing.

My kitchen took the most time. I didn't make that much money, but anything extra I had went to cooking tools. I had great knives and a good collection of pots, pans, and baking trays. Plus, a few fun gadgets. My dishes weren't anything fancy, but they were mine. I'd picked them out at yard sales and resale shops. They were mismatched, but they coordinated nicely. I loved how colorful they looked when I set the table. I went through a roll of bubble wrap in that room alone.

After the kitchen, I focused on books. I liked to read. I always had a few books from the local library, and I read online, but I also had a good collection of my own books: novels, biographies, historical references. I had small boxes for those so they wouldn't get too heavy.

With the kitchen and books packed, I turned to art. First, my art supplies: paints, canvases, brushes, some scraps of fabric, metal, and other things I used to make mixed-media pieces. Well, that was what I used to do back when I was taking time to paint. I promised myself I'd get back to that when I got settled in Emile City. In addition to my supplies, I had a good collection of paintings and ceramics. Some of the paintings were mine, but most of them and the ceramics were things I'd gotten in trade from other artists. I thought a few of the pieces were likely worth something because the artists had since made it pretty big.

Looking at my furniture with a critical eye, I decided to bring my coffee table, a small round wooden table that a friend who was into woodwork made for me, two comfortable armchairs, and an armoire. Everything else wasn't worth dragging hundreds of miles. Even most of the things I was bringing were resale finds, but they had a cool, retro vibe, and it'd be hard to find pieces like them again.

Wednesday night I forced myself to stay up until my clothes were all packed, (fucking hell, I had a lot of clothes), and I was done. I worked until five Thursday night, and then left the new guy to handle the dinner shift and went home. A few of my friends came over to help me load the moving truck. An hour and a half later, I was headed to my friend Clark's place with all of my belongings. He was putting me up in his guest room for the night, and the next morning I'd be on my way to Emile City.

When I pulled up to Clark's house, I noticed lots of familiar cars on the street. I picked up the bag I'd packed with the things I'd need until I got to Aaron's, and walked up to the door. As soon as I knocked, it swung open, and I saw dozens of guys crowded inside the place.

"Zach!"

"Hey, guys. What's going on?"

"You didn't think we'd let you leave town without one last fiesta, did you? Clark's throwing you a goodbye bash."

That sounded nice. Spending time with my friends, having a few drinks and some fun after the last few days was exactly what I needed. I'd still get to bed early enough because Clark's house was a pre-party place, not one for an all-night shindig.

He had a couple of neighbors who were fucking ridiculous about noise. I swear, if he sneezed too loud, they complained. So, whenever he had parties, they called the police. Clark finally reached an unspoken agreement with the cops—they wouldn't come out on the noise complaints until after ten thirty, and he would make sure that parties were shut down by then.

I hadn't seen most of my friends since I'd decided to move, so I spent a lot of time answering the "why are you going?" question and then looking at shocked faces when I told them I was moving to be with my boyfriend. Their shock didn't surprise me. The fact that I wasn't anxious about it, though, did surprise me.

By ten fifteen, almost everyone had given me goodbye hugs and kisses and headed out to the bars. I was walking out of the bathroom when I almost stepped into a tree of a man. I looked up to see tall, dark, and handsome.

"Hey, James. You heading out? I'm glad you came."

"Well, I haven't yet, but I was hoping we could do something about that."

I chuckled.

"No can do. I'm seeing someone. He's the reason

I'm moving, so..."

"I can't believe you're actually leaving for a guy, Zach. I never saw it coming."

"Yeah? Neither did I."

James was standing way too close to me. At least, he felt too close at that point. There was a time when I would've dragged him back into the bathroom and made sure we got a whole lot closer. I tried to walk around him, but he somehow managed to get even closer.

"If you're looking to party, James, you should hit the clubs. I think that's where everyone went. I need to leave early tomorrow, so I'm going to bed soon."

"Bed sounds perfect, Zach."

He reached his arm around me and rested his hand on my ass. What part of boyfriend was he not getting? I sighed and removed his hand.

"I'm off the market, James. Let's go, I'll walk you out."

"Oh, come on, Zach! What are you afraid of? Don't worry, you won't get dumped. Your guy will never know about this. And we have fun together, remember?"

No, I didn't remember. Oh, I knew I'd fucked around with James a few times. And he was a good-looking guy. But I didn't remember any details. All those times with all those guys had blended in my mind, so I couldn't remember exactly what happened with which one. Why did it matter? Those times had been for the moment. Fun while they lasted, but that was it.

"He wouldn't dump me, even if he did know. That's one of the reasons why this isn't happening, James. And the other reason is, *I'd* know."

I'd promised Aaron there wouldn't be other guys. That was what he'd asked for, which was fine with me. But I knew that if I broke the promise, he wouldn't leave me. He'd probably be hurt, but he'd accept it and keep going. That was who he was. The man walked through life doing everything for everyone else and never demanding a damn thing for himself. Well, I wasn't going to be like those other people. He deserved better than that, and he was going to get it, at least from me.

I briefly wondered whether the fact that I could get away with everything when it came to Aaron was the very reason why I didn't want to do anything to hurt him. Maybe I wouldn't be so willing to be faithful if I felt as though I was doing it under some sort of threat or demand. Whatever. The whys didn't matter.

James was surprised by my response, so he'd softened his stance a bit, and I was able to squeeze past him. I walked into the kitchen and helped Clark clean up.

"You look happy, Zach."

I leaned back against the counter and looked at Clark.

"I am. I really am. I'll be even happier when I'm done with all this moving shit, but, yeah, I'm happy."

Clark shook his head.

"This Aaron must be some guy. I never thought you'd want to do the whole settle-down thing, man."

Now, I may have turned into a sappy motherfucker, but I wasn't about to start waxing poetic about Aaron to my friends. Those feelings were personal. So I shrugged, waggled my eyebrows, and said, "Well, he has a big, thick dick. I couldn't walk away from that."

Clark chuckled and turned back to the sink to finish the dishes.

"If you couldn't walk away, Zach, your guy isn't doing it right. Tell the man to learn how to handle his equipment."

I snapped Clark's ass with a towel.

"Fuck you. I'll do a walk around and see if anyone left bottles or other trash."

As I walked into the living room, my phone rang, and I saw Aaron's name on the screen.

"Hey, big guy. How was your day?"

"Hi, babe. My day was good, but long. Where are you?"

"My friend's house. We got everything loaded in the truck, and I'm staying here tonight, then heading your way tomorrow, remember?"

"Yes, I remember. But the cab driver needs an exact address. Turns out 'Zach's friend's house' isn't enough of a description."

He sounded tired.

"Cab driver?"

"I'm in LA, babe. Pulling out of the airport now. Kimmy is going to cover the clinic tomorrow. With both of us driving, we'll be able to make it back to Emile City before Monday, when I have to be back at work."

I should've known Aaron backed away too easily from the moving company discussion. I probably should've been angry, or something, that he didn't think

I could drive myself, or whatever. But I was so fucking excited that he was in town, I couldn't work up any anger. I gave him Clark's address and then went into the kitchen to make sure Clark was okay with having another houseguest for the night.

CHAPTER TWENTY

I WAS so fucking happy that Aaron was in town I practically skipped to the kitchen.

"Clark, Aaron decided to fly down here so we can drive to Emile City together. Can he stay here tonight too?"

Clark winked at me.

"Are you kidding? Of course! I can't wait to meet the guy who managed to tame you. Besides, it'll give me a great chance to teach him a thing or two about how to use that big, thick dick you were bragging about."

Yeah, right. Clark was oral only, as far as I knew. Not into penetration in either the giving or receiving role. I'd always found that odd, but I knew there were guys who didn't ever get into it...or let it get into them, as the case may be. Different strokes, right?

"Not gonna happen, Clark. Keep your teaching techniques to yourself."

We laughed and finished cleaning up. I liked Clark. He'd grown up in a suburb of Emile City, and even though we hadn't known each other then, the shared background was enough to start our friendship when we met in LA. He was different from my other friends. He went out with us, partied, and all that. But there was an underlying seriousness to him. Or maybe it was sadness.

A couple years back, I'd noticed framed pictures of a guy in Clark's bedroom. In one of them, Clark and the guy are wrapped up together like puppies, sleeping on a sofa. He looked a few years younger in that picture than he was when I first met him.

There was something incredibly moving about the picture. I asked him who the guy was once, and he told me he was the love of his life. He wiped away tears as he said it, and I was uncomfortable talking about that sort of thing at the time, so I dropped it. Now, I wondered what the story was with the photo guy.

"Hey, Clark?"

"Yes, sir?"

"You ever think about settling down with one guy?"

It was a weird conversation to be having. I hadn't ever talked to any of my friends about relationships and shit. Well, I guess it wasn't something I'd ever thought about. Clark put both of his hands on the counter and looked down.

"I think about it all the time. But it won't happen, not for me. I had my chance, and it didn't work out."

Damn it. Why did I bring this up? He sounded sad, and I wasn't exactly good at dealing with emotional situations. I put my hand on his shoulder.

"There are other guys, Clark."

He shook his head.

"Not for me. There'll never be another guy for me. Come on, let's make sure I have enough clean towels in the bathroom for your man."

I was grateful for the change in topic because I was all out of advice and completely out of my element, so I shut the fuck up and followed him into the bathroom. After that, I stood in the living room, looked out the window, and wondered how long it took a fucking cab to get there from the airport. When I finally saw the cab pull up, I ran out the front door.

Aaron stepped out of the cab. His golden hair was messy, and it stuck up in the back, probably from resting on the airplane seat. His clothes were crumpled, and his eyes looked tired. When he saw me, he gave me a smile that took over his entire face. Damn, he was so beautiful my heart ached.

I walked over to Aaron to give him a hug, but he had other ideas. He dropped his bag, wrapped his arms around me, cupped my ass, and lifted me up. I wrapped my legs around his waist and my arms around his neck, and leaned in for a kiss. After that, it was tongues and tasting, warmth and rubbing. One of us was moaning, or maybe it was both of us, and then I heard Clark's voice.

"You boys might want to take this inside. I think you're making the neighbors jealous."

Aaron loosened his grip, and I reluctantly slid down his body. He picked up his bag and looked at me sheepishly.

"Umm, hello. I'm glad you're here. It's nice to see you."

I laughed at Aaron's repetition of the greetings I'd suggested after our explosive elevator ride leaving that roof party.

"We do tend to skip the normal greetings, don't we? Come on, you can meet a few of my friends." I held Aaron's hand as we walked toward the front porch. Then I lowered my voice and turned to him. "You could always try 'come for me' again. That was great, last time."

"Zach, don't. I'm doing algebra in my head here to, umm, get things to go down. Reminding me of that is counterproductive to the cause."

Aaron was such an odd juxtaposition of characteristics. He was an amazing lover. Completely free, passionate, expressive. When we were in bed together he made all of my senses come alive, and the times with him had been unparalleled. Yet, he was embarrassed at the prospect of a few guys noticing he had a hard-on. Guys who, by the way, would happily drop trou if they thought he was even slightly interested.

We got to the porch, and I introduced Aaron to Clark. Clark held his hand out, and I could tell Aaron was conflicted. He was holding his bag with one hand, carrying it in front of his package, no doubt on purpose. And I was holding his other hand. I dropped his hand, reached over and took the bag, and made sure to rub against his dick as I did it.

"I'll put this in the guest room."

I gave Aaron my best butter-wouldn't-melt-in-my-mouth smile and almost laughed out loud at his red face. I was a bastard, I knew. But it was too damn fun to make him blush. After I put the bag down, I got a glass of water from the kitchen and went into the living room.

Aaron was sitting on the couch talking with Clark

and the other two guys who hadn't left. He was smiling and combing his fingers through his golden hair. His shirt was draped across his chest in a way that highlighted his broad shoulders. I stopped to catch my breath. Fuck, I wanted him. Well, that wasn't happening with a bunch of other guys in the room, but at least I could get close to him.

I walked over, handed Aaron the water, and curled up in his lap.

"Thanks, babe."

He kissed my cheek, took a drink of water, and wrapped his arm around me, pulling me tight against his chest. Then he dropped his hand and stroked my thigh as he told my friends about some work he was doing at the Emile City Zoo. I let the sound of Aaron's voice wash over me, his scent fill me, and I reveled in the feeling of his body touching mine. My shoulders loosened, and my entire body relaxed. Home.

I GUESS the day of working, then loading the truck, took more out of me than I'd realized, because before long, I was asleep on Aaron's lap. Soft voices were the first thing I noticed when I started waking up. I opened my eyes and realized that it was probably very late. Aaron and I were on the couch, Clark was sitting in an armchair next to us, and everyone else was gone.

"How long was I out?"

Aaron stroked my hair and kissed my forehead.

"A couple of hours. You must have been tired. Let's go to bed."

"I was tired. Glad I got that nap, now I have enough energy to ravish you."

Aaron blushed, and I shook my head. How was that embarrassing? It wasn't like Clark didn't know we were having sex. Hell, it would've been embarrassing if we weren't. I got off the couch and pulled Aaron up behind me.

"Night, Clark."

Clark got up and hugged Aaron, which seemed a little strange. Well, they'd been talking for hours while I was sleeping so...whatever. Time to get naked.

"Goodnight, guys. And don't worry about keeping it down. I haven't been with anyone in way longer than I care to mention so I could *really* use some excitement."

I laughed, Aaron continued with the blush.

"Come on, big guy. I need to get your clothes off, so I can see if that blush goes all over. It's fucking adorable."

I think the poor man gave up on talking. He just followed me to the bedroom and closed the door. After that, I couldn't keep teasing him because I found myself spread on the bed, with my shirt off and my pants at my ankles. How did he do that?

Aaron was leaning over me, licking my balls, as he untied my shoes and then pushed them off, followed by my pants. Then he spread my legs and nestled in between them. He licked my thighs, sucked on my balls, and then treated my dick like one of those bullet popsicles—long licks with his tongue flattened, all the way around. When he got to the crown, he sucked softly, then pressed his tongue into my slit.

"Ungh!"

Shit, that felt good. Aaron dropped his head down and swallowed around my cock. Just as I got close to the edge, he pulled off. I whimpered.

"Aaron? Please, please, I...I need."

He moaned in response.

"Don't worry, babe. I'll give you what you need, I promise. I want to taste all of you first." His deep voice was husky. "Love how you taste, how you smell. Dream about it. Mmmm."

He put his hands under the back of my knees, and pushed my legs up, burying his face in my ass. Damn—just, damn. He was moaning and pushing his face into me, tongue darting out. I reached my hands down, grasped my ass, and pulled the cheeks apart.

"Yes, Zach. So good."

Those were the last words I could understand. After that, there were just moans as Aaron licked and sucked every inch of my cleft, finally making his way to my hungry hole, where he curled his tongue and darted it in past the ring.

I knew I was making noises, but I wasn't sure if they were words or groans. I was well past incoherent by then, wondering how, if the sounds coming from Aaron were any indication, I'd managed to find a lover who seemed to enjoy eating my ass as much as I enjoyed having him do it.

Aaron moved one of his forearms sideways, so

it rested underneath both of my knees and held up my legs. He took his free hand and reached up to my mouth, putting a finger at my lips.

"Suck, babe."

I opened my mouth and sucked on his finger as if it were his dick. He moved it in and out of my mouth, in time with what he was doing to my ass with his tongue. When he pulled his finger out, I knew where it was going and moaned in anticipation. And then his finger was buried in my ass, right next to his tongue.

"Aaron! *Yes!*"

I moved my hands to the back of his head and pulled his face into my ass. I swear, I'd lost all control by then. Otherwise, I surely wouldn't have done that. Not that Aaron seemed to mind. His moans got louder, his tongue did that swiping thing in my hole, and his finger pressed insistently inside, finding my prostate.

"Oh, yes. Oh, Christ. Aaron...Aaron...I'm gonna—"

He pulled his head free of my grasp and lowered my legs, bringing my cock in line with his face.

"In my mouth, Zach."

The first shot hit his face. After that, he managed to get my cock buried in his mouth, and he sucked for all his worth, while I shot down his throat.

I lay on the bed, panting, when Aaron finally pulled his mouth off my cock. I looked down to where he kneeled at the end of the bed, and realized that even though I was completely naked, he was still fully clothed. Fuck, why was that so hot?

Our eyes met, and he held my gaze as he wiped

my cum off his face and then licked it from the back of his hand. I groaned and my dick twitched, trying to harden again. Then Aaron unzipped his pants and took his dick out through the fly on his briefs. He stroked himself firmly as he put first one knee and then the other on the outside of my legs, so that he was bent over me. Then his head flung back, and he moaned as ropes of cum flew out of his dick and onto my neck, chest, and stomach.

I put my arm over my eyes to block out any visual stimulation, and tried to get my heart to beat at a normal rhythm and my breath to come out in something other than gasps. I felt Aaron get off the bed, heard a rustling of clothes, and then there was fabric wiping my chin, neck, chest, stomach, cock, and ass. When the bed dropped next to me, I moved my arm and opened my eyes to see Aaron, lying beside me, and looking concerned.

"Are you okay? Was that too...too—"

Dirty? Out of control? Wild? *Fucking perfect?*

"Was it too much?"

I pushed up against him until he was on his back and I was on top of him, with my head buried in his neck.

"Too much isn't possible. Not with you. I can't get enough of you. You make me feel so good, Aaron. I never knew it could be like this. You're an incredible lover. I'm so lucky."

He let out a sigh of relief and wrapped those strong arms around me.

"We're both lucky. I love you, babe. Goodnight."

I DIDN'T wake up as early as I'd planned the next morning, but that wasn't my biggest concern. What bothered me was that I woke up alone, and when I ran my hand over Aaron's side of the bed, it was cold. How long had he been up?

I stumbled out of bed, put on my briefs, and walked out of the room. I started walking to the kitchen, but turned the other way when I heard voices coming from Clark's bedroom. I walked past the bathroom and up to the open door at the end of the hallway. Then I froze.

Aaron was sitting on Clark's bed, wearing nothing but a towel, with his arms around my completely naked friend.

CHAPTER TWENTY-ONE

I'D NEVER been one for jealousy. Really, when would that feeling have come up? I hadn't ever had a boyfriend, so seeing other guys together was like a bonus—live porn. It got me hard, and I usually jumped in. So, at first, I couldn't identify the hot feeling in my head and the clenching in my stomach when I saw Aaron and Clark, wearing one towel between them and holding each other on Clark's bed. That was when I knew how much seeing two guys together could hurt. At least, when one of those guys was supposed to be mine.

"What in the fuck is going on in here?"

It wasn't a yell, more like a sob. And as soon as Aaron heard it, he pushed Clark off his lap and ran to the door. I held my hand out to keep him away.

"No. No, don't. What...what—"

"Shhh, babe. We were just talking."

He pushed his way past my hand and hugged me tight, refusing to let go as I tried to wriggle free. His voice was soft as he explained.

"I heard him crying when I got out of the shower, so I came to check on him. He's had a rough night, babe. A rough few years. He needed someone to listen. Nothing happened, Zach. You're the only one for me. You know that."

He'd started rocking me from side to side as he spoke, and I could feel my body calming. Yeah, I did know. Funny, I wouldn't have thought it would've mattered, though, if he had wanted to fuck around with other guys. I thought I was doing the whole monogamy thing because it was what Aaron wanted. Guess I wanted it too.

"I'm sorry."

Clark's sad, weak voice broke me from my thoughts. I pulled my head away from Aaron and looked over at Clark. He was standing next to his bed, clutching a picture frame. His eyes were red, with dark circles underneath them. As I took in the whole scene, I noticed a few photo albums and letters strewn about the bed.

I walked over to my friend and put my hand on his arm.

"Nothing to be sorry about. I was...startled. You okay?"

He wiped his eyes with the back of his hand and seemed to notice the picture he was clutching. It was the one of him and the guy sleeping together. The one I'd noticed the first time I was in Clark's bedroom.

"No, I'm an idiot. A self-righteous idiot. But, at least I finally realize it. Now, according to your guy, I can finally get off my ass and do something about it. If it isn't too late."

Then he shook his head and put the picture down, next to everything else on his bed.

"I'm going to take a shower, and then I'll see you guys out. I have a busy few days ahead of me."

He walked into the bathroom that adjoined his bedroom and closed the door. I looked over at Aaron who was still standing by the bedroom door.

"We'll call him when we get back to Emile City, after he's had some time to think. Don't worry; your friend will be okay."

I walked up to Aaron, hugged him tightly, and rested my head on his chest.

"I've known Clark for three years, ever since he first moved to LA. He's one of my best friends. We probably see each other at least once a week. I think we even fooled around a long time ago. You've been here for two seconds, and you've got him spilling his guts and baring his soul, on the road to healing, or whatever, that I didn't even know he needed."

I stroked Aaron's chest, looked up, and met his eyes, feeling as though I'd won the fucking lottery when I walked into Dean's kitchen that summer day.

"Thank you for helping my friend."

WE DROVE in shifts and made it to Emile City Sunday evening. Aaron had to work the next day, but Dean didn't have class until the afternoon, so he was going to come over to help unpack the moving truck. With that plan set, we didn't have to do any unloading or unpacking when we got in on Sunday. Thank fuck for that, because we were both tired. Aaron dialed a local pizza place, and we flopped onto the couch.

After we ate our pizza, I lay back on the arm of the couch with my feet in Aaron's lap, and he massaged them.

"There's a great new Italian place in EC West that everyone keeps talking about. Maybe we can try it this weekend."

EC West was the gay-friendly neighborhood, where Aaron had that roof party for the gay rights organization and where we'd eaten dinner.

"Mmmhmm. That sounds good. Hey, Aaron?"

"Yeah."

"Why don't you live in EC West? I know you like spending time there, and it's a really friendly part of town."

"I know, right? It's great. And I don't think you've seen it in daylight. There are nice neighborhoods with historic houses. We'll drive around sometime. I don't live there because when I moved out of Kimmy and Dean's, I didn't know how long I'd be staying in town. I needed a place that rents month-to-month and one that wasn't too far from their house and the clinic. This place fit the bill. But we can live anywhere you want, Zach. And EC West would be great."

"You don't mind leaving your apartment?"

Aaron laughed.

"You have looked around here, right? I never intended it to be long term. We can go house hunting this weekend."

House hunting with Aaron. That sounded...nice. Domestic as shit, but nice.

"Let's wait until I find a job so I know how much I

can afford. Then we can go."

Aaron's hands stopped moving on my feet, and he dropped his eyes.

"Aaron?"

No response. Shit. What did I do? I thought back to what I'd been saying, totally innocuous. Maybe Aaron was having second thoughts about us. No, that didn't make sense. He was just talking about getting a place together. Maybe something was going on with Dean. No, he would've told me that himself. Shit, I wasn't a mind reader.

"Aaron? What's wrong? Did I say or do something wrong?"

"No, no, it's not that. I...I'm trying to figure out how to talk to you about something without making you mad."

Fuck this whole relationship, talking shit. It was hard. I rolled my shoulders, relaxed my body, and reminded myself that I was a grown man in control of my emotions.

"Go ahead and talk, big guy. I promise to stay David Banner over here and not get all Incredible Hulk on you, okay?"

Aaron laughed and squeezed my foot.

"Okay. I think we need to talk about our relationship and how we're going to handle things."

I'd moved to be with him and promised to stop fucking other guys. What other *things* did we need to handle?

"You've lost me, Aaron. What things?"

"Money. I'm talking about money, Zach."

I opened my mouth to say something, not sure

what, but it most likely would've been pissy or sarcastic.

"Wait, please. Zach, I want to get this out, and I don't want to fight. Do you think maybe you can hear me out completely and think about what I have to say before you answer? After that, I'll do the same."

I held back my growl. Fine. He could talk. I'd listen before saying anything. It wouldn't do shit to change my thoughts about Aaron's whole "Zach is a charity where I can contribute my money" speech, which I knew was coming. But, fine, I'd listen.

"It's a deal. I'm listening."

"Thanks, babe."

He gave me a genuine, but anxious smile, and then he started back on the foot rub while he spoke.

"Zach, you gave up your job, your apartment, your friends, your whole life, to come here for me. If we could get legally married, I would've proposed before asking you to do that."

"What? Aaron, you're not even twenty-eight years old!"

I knew I wasn't supposed to interrupt, but marriage? Shit. Aaron shrugged and laughed.

"Hey, my parents got married when they were twenty, had my brother when they were twenty-two, and by the time they were twenty-eight, they had three kids and a mortgage. What can I say? Small Southern town, not a lot to do, family values and all that. But that's not my point.

"What I'm saying, Zach, is that we agreed to be a family. Husbands isn't legal, *yet*, so I guess partners is the right word, but the meaning is the same. We can't have a marriage license, we can't make babies that are half-me and half-you, but we can have the rest of it, Zach, if we want it.

"We can bind ourselves together, live our lives as one unit. Not a yours or a mine, but an ours. That means that what we earn belongs to both of us equally. The law doesn't recognize that, but I surely do. So, yes, we should figure out what *we* can afford before we look for a place. But the money is ours. I'm not giving it to you. It's already both of ours. Do you get that? *Our* family, *our* income, *our* house, *our* expenses.

His voice got softer, and he looked down.

"These past months, being apart from you, were killing me. I felt like I couldn't breathe sometimes. And nights when you were out, sometimes I couldn't get my mind to stop imagining you with other guys, and I thought I'd throw up, I swear. But I love you, Zach. That wasn't going to stop. And I didn't want it to stop."

He looked up and met my eyes.

"I think that's why Kimmy kept trying to hang around us last time you were here; she was worried you were going to hurt me or something. But I know you won't hurt me. And when you told me there hadn't been anyone else the whole time, and agreed to move here, Zach, my heart felt like it was flying.

"I guess what I'm doing here is, I'm asking you to own this. Really own it. I know you're not used to counting on anyone but yourself. I'm not used to this either. I'm the guy who always takes care of other people, not the one who needs someone else. But I do need *you*, Zach. It's scary to trust another person, I get it. But this thing we have between us, it's right. I know it's right. And I trust you, babe. I trust you with everything.

"So, think about it, okay? Let your walls down for me. All of them. I don't want part-of-the-way anymore. We're past that. Meet me halfway, Zach. Please, trust me to be your family."

As it turned out, it wasn't all that difficult not to respond right away to Aaron. By the time he finished talking, I had a lump in my throat, and I didn't have any words. So, I nodded and crawled across the couch until I was straddling him. He wrapped his arms around me as I nuzzled into his neck.

I had a lot of thinking to do, and we were both exhausted from the long drive. But my dick didn't seem to care about any of that. It got hard and pressed insistently against Aaron through our clothes. I reached up for a kiss—first soft lips, pressing together, then my tongue, swiping at his lips.

"Mmmm. Want you, Aaron."

He pushed his cock up against mine, showing me the feeling was mutual. Damn, that was good. He snaked his tongue out of his mouth and licked my tongue, then swirled his around it. That reminded me of what he did inside my ass with that tongue, and I almost came on the spot. I never thought I'd find anything I enjoyed more than being fucked, but Aaron's face buried in my ass was a serious contender for first place.

I whimpered and sucked Aaron's tongue into my

mouth. Then we got into a rhythm. Back and forth we went, sitting on the couch, with me grinding down on him and him pressing up to meet me. Aaron's arms wrapped around my back, mine around his. It was slow and easy, and I felt as though we were a couple of randy teenagers, making out on the couch.

"This okay, Aaron? Ungh. Because, if we don't stop… ahhhh…if we don't stop, I'm gonna come in my pants."

He reached between us and opened my pants, then his. After that, he took both our cocks into his big hand and started stroking.

"Ungh. Feels good."

I leaned back in for more kisses, as we reestablished our rhythm. Aaron stroked, and we continued to push together, forcing our cocks through his fist. I came first, liquid heat rolling down Aaron's hand and both of our cocks. He used it as lube to help finish himself in a few more strokes. Then he was moaning into my mouth and kissing my neck.

"Mmmm, 's nice. Love you, babe. So glad you're finally home."

"Me, too, Aaron. Shower, then bed?"

He nodded against my shoulder. Ten minutes of warm water and slippery soap later, we were snuggled together in bed, legs all tangled, my back against Aaron's chest, him holding me tightly, with his arm wrapped around my chest. And I felt happy and content.

CHAPTER TWENTY-TWO

THE NEXT morning, I woke up to a tongue bath. Of my dick. Warm bed, soft sheets, and Aaron's wet tongue treating my dick like a fucking ice cream cone. I stroked his head to let him know I was awake.

"Love how you taste. Want you all the time."

He practically purred the words out. Then he brought his mouth down over my crown, pressed his tongue into my slit, and took me down to the root. I moaned and reflexively bucked my hips, pushing my dick as far as possible into his mouth.

Some guys hate that. They'll even hold your hips down while they're blowing you, so they keep complete control over the act. Which, as long as they're sucking your dick, is totally their prerogative, right? Aaron, on the other hand, moaned, put one hand on my ass, and pulled me toward him.

I could feel his other hand moving across my leg as he pumped his cock, his moans vibrating on my dick. Knowing he was getting so worked up from sucking me made me hotter. Before long Aaron's happy sounds, swirling tongue, and hard sucks did me in. I shouted his name and poured myself down his throat as I heard him groan and felt heat splash on my leg.

Damn, my man loves to suck cock. And ass. Total oral fixation. Plus a big dick. Yeah, you're jealous, I know. Too fucking bad. I'm not letting him go.

"Morning, big guy," I panted, still trying to catch my breath.

He kissed and licked his way up my body and then nuzzled my neck.

"I think you're turning me into a morning person. My mom has always sworn that could never be done. Of course, she's never had the pleasure of sleeping next to you, knowing how you smell, tasting your skin, sucking your balls—"

"Are we still talking about your mother? Because, I'm totally fine with kink, but this is kinda grossing me out."

Aaron chuckled.

"Point taken. No more mom talk in bed."

Aaron took a fast shower, ate two bowls of cereal, and left for work. I went through the kitchen to see what we needed to buy, which was just about everything. Then Dean came over with bagels and coffee.

"I know I said this on the phone, but I want you to know how happy I am that you decided to move here. I've missed having you in my life all these years. And having you here, so the boys will grow up knowing their uncle, means the world to me, Zach."

He squeezed my shoulder and took a sip of coffee. Damn. My stomach felt all tingly. Last Christmas I didn't have any family, and it didn't bother me, at least not much. Now I had a partner, a brother, three nephews, and a sister-in-law who was a mix of amusing and a little scary. What a fucking difference a year makes.

"All right, old man. Let's get my stuff in here, so we can drop the truck off."

We went outside, took my car off the trailer hitch where it was attached to the moving truck, and started unloading. The furniture was easy to place, given the fact that Aaron had practically no furniture in the apartment. We stacked the boxes against a wall in the bedroom. I figured there was no point in my unpacking if Aaron and I were going to look for a new place. I opened up a few of the clothing boxes, but the rest of my shit could stay packed.

When we were done unloading, I drove the moving truck to a local drop off location, with Dean following in his car. Then Dean took me home.

"Thanks for your help."

"No problem, Zach. Hey, listen, I need to talk to you about a few things with mom's estate. Maybe we can grab a bite when you're settled?"

Mom's estate? The woman had been dead for six months, what was there to say?

"Yeah, sure. Catch you later."

I'd noticed that the fridge was almost empty and the pantry was missing some staples, so instead of going back into the apartment, I got into my car and headed for the grocery store. While I was there, I picked up a couple of local papers for the job classifieds. I figured between those and some websites, I'd be able to find a job pretty quickly.

When I got home from the store, I put the groceries away and started dinner. Once the meal was in the oven and I'd cleaned up the kitchen, I started looking through the job postings. Five minutes into that, I realized I had a problem.

In my industry, the good jobs are dinner and weekend shifts in high-end restaurants. Some of those places aren't even open for lunch. Even the places that serve daytime meals don't have their head chefs working then. But Aaron worked weekdays, so if I worked nights and weekends, I'd get home when he'd be sleeping, and we'd basically never see each other.

I saw a few listings for lunch cooks and thought about whether I should apply. Those jobs were usually stepping stones for people who couldn't get hired on for dinners. I'd worked at some pretty damn good places in LA, and my last job was second-in-command at a well-known restaurant there. That meant I'd have no trouble getting a gig as head chef at almost any place in Emile City. So, for me, getting a day shift wouldn't be a stepping stone, it'd be a dead end.

How I hadn't realized this would be an issue, I couldn't say. Maybe it was because I was so busy with all the shit related to the move. Whatever the reason, I was suddenly faced with the realization that my personal life was in direct conflict with my professional one. Getting a good job would most certainly mean almost no time with Aaron.

I set the papers down and walked away from the

computer. Not going to happen. I didn't fucking move all the way to Emile City so I could see Aaron every once in a while. Nothing was worth that, not even my career. Funny thing, I didn't feel like I was sacrificing anything, even though I was effectively ending any chance I had to be a successful chef. Our relationship came first. That was a joy, not a sacrifice.

THE CLINIC closed at five, so when my phone rang at a quarter 'til and I saw Aaron's name on the screen, I figured something was up.

"Hi, big guy."

"Hi, babe. I'm sorry, but I'm going to be late. It's been a nightmare of a day. Anything special you want me to pick up for dinner on my way home? I'm too tired to cook, and I think the kitchen's pretty bare anyway."

"I already made dinner. It'll keep until you get home. And I went shopping today, too, so that's done. Sorry you've had a rough day, want to tell me about it when you get home?"

I heard a deep sigh, and then Aaron's voice came back, sounding a little gravely.

"Oh, Zach. I love you so much. Thanks for doing all that, for taking care of me. I should be done here by six thirty and home by seven. And, yeah, I'd love to tell you about it when I get home."

My heart warmed with the knowledge that I could

make him so happy. Yeah, I could've focused on the fact that maybe it was sad it took so little, as though no one else had ever bothered. But the past didn't matter. I was here now, and I'd make sure he always felt taken care of. He did the same for me, after all. Halfway, wasn't that where Aaron asked me to meet him? I could do that.

"THIS IS so good, Zach. I've never had better pot roast and mashed potatoes." We were sitting on the stools at the kitchen counter, finishing our dinner. And I was basking in Aaron's praise of my cooking. "Just don't ever tell my mom I said so. Not that she'd disagree, if she ever had the pleasure of tasting this. It's that good."

He scraped his plate with his fork, trying to get every last bite. Then he put the fork in his mouth and sucked off the last of the food, with an almost blissful look on his face. That reminded me of how he looked with his mouth wrapped around my dick, and I moaned. Damn, my guy was fucking hot. But he wanted to talk about whatever happened at the clinic, so sex would've to wait. I thumped my dick to stop what felt like rapidly approaching spontaneous combustion. Look at me being all adult.

I grabbed our plates and walked around the counter.

"I'll clean up, Zach. You made dinner."

"Everything's clean. I'm putting these in the

dishwasher, and we're done."

I walked into the kitchen, put the dishes away, and turned to find Aaron right behind me, with a soft, loving look on his face. The way that man looked at me, as if I was, I don't know, precious or something, made me weak in the knees. He scooped me into a hug and talked into my neck.

"I love this. Love coming home to you. Love being with you. Love your cooking. I love you, Zach."

Yeah, I know. He says love frequently. You'd think that not having heard it in my life, at least not after the age of eight, that it would bother me or make me uncomfortable. But it didn't. Every time he told me he loved me, my heart beat a little faster and a space inside me I didn't even know was empty, felt like it was filling up.

"This is good, yeah?"

More nuzzling, and Aaron nodding into my neck.

"Yeah. It's good, Zach. It's very, very good."

After a few more seconds of Aaron holding me and kissing my neck, I thought I should start the conversation before I lost all control and started shedding clothes.

"So, what happened at work today?"

He set me down, and we walked over to the couch. Aaron sat on the end and pulled me onto his lap, which was well on its way to becoming our standard hanging out position.

"Oh, well. On my way in, I got a call from Tina, my receptionist, saying her mom's sick so she has to go to Wisconsin. And she doesn't know when she'll be back. So,

I didn't have anyone to work the counter today. The two techs had to keep running up there. And the three of us took turns answering the phone. Doing all of that meant we couldn't get through our appointments on time, so everyone was kept waiting.

"And, I love Kimmy. I do. But, honest to goodness, I don't understand what that woman does sometimes. The paperwork and filing from Friday were a complete disaster. It took me over an hour to sort through it, and I'll probably have to spend another hour tomorrow undoing and then redoing most of it."

He leaned his head on the back of the couch, closed his eyes, and sighed.

"Maybe I can get a receptionist through a temp service or something. We have three more weeks before we close for the holidays, and I don't think we can manage that long without someone out front. I can't imagine Tina will be back before then, she was going to go home for Christmas anyway."

Aaron looked stressed out and bone tired.

"I can help." He lifted his head and looked at me. "Answering phones and greeting people when they come in for appointments, right? I think I can handle that."

"Of course you can handle it, babe. But I'd never ask you to do that. I know how anxious you are to find a good restaurant here."

Good a time as any to tell him about my issues on the job front.

"Yeah, well, it turns out there are some problems there I need to think through."

Aaron's expression became concerned, and he started rubbing my back.

"What problems?"

I told him about the dinner shifts and how we'd never see each other if I took that type of job. And, about how the lunch shifts were low-paying, and in my case, a dead end. He looked so miserable that I almost laughed.

"Come on, big guy. It's not that bad."

"I don't want to keep you from your career, Zach. I know how much you enjoy it and how hard you've worked all these years to get where you are. If you give that up, I'm afraid you'll end up resenting me or regretting moving here."

I sat up a little so that we were eye-to-eye and then lightly kissed him.

"It's." *Kiss*. "Just." *Kiss*. "A." *Kiss*. "Job."

"Yeah? You're not upset?"

I shook my head.

"I'm not upset. I have some thinking to do, but I'm not upset. I get to see you every day now, Aaron. That matters to me more than any job."

He hugged me tight, and then gazed into my eyes.

"Family first, yeah?"

I thought back to our conversation the previous evening in the context of my job situation. I was giving up a career so Aaron and I could have time together. I could see the question in his eyes and the hesitation about bringing the conversation back up.

It was hard to rely on someone else to support me. Some of it was probably some macho pride bullshit, but the rest was fear of being at the complete mercy of another person. That hadn't gone so well for me when I was a kid.

I stroked Aaron's cheek and looked deeply into those warm blue eyes. He wouldn't let me down. I felt it all the way in my core. I'd always be safe with Aaron.

"I'll cover for your receptionist until she gets back from Wisconsin. And I'll figure things out on the job front as soon as possible." I swallowed, took a deep breath, and crashed through the last fucking wall, leaving rubble in its wake. "How long can we afford for me to be out of work?"

I'm not sure how I expected Aaron to react, but it wasn't with tears. Yet, that was what happened. His eyes got misty, and he clutched me so tight I was struggling to breathe.

"The clinic's doing well, babe. Very well. And, even after paying Kimmy and Dean the sales price, which we need to do before the end of the calendar year, we'll have plenty left in savings. There's no rush to figure things out on the job front. Take your time. We can go over the accounts this week so you know exactly how much we have and where. And we'll get your name added to all of them."

I stiffened a little, but then shook it off. Ours, not mine or yours. That was what he'd said, and it made sense. That was how families operated, right? Not that I'd know from personal experience, but that seemed to be how things worked. I could see that from looking at Dean's family.

"Okay. Thanks, Aaron."

"Thank *you*, Zach, for trusting me."

He stroked my temples with his thumbs and kissed me softly.

"You don't mind working at the clinic? 'Cause it'd be a huge help. Plus, I'd get to see you throughout the day. That's like a dream come true."

Aaron blushed a little at the last part. Nice to know his sap-meter wasn't totally faulty. Not that I hadn't had the same thought, I'm just way too cool to say it out loud. Or something like that, right?

CHAPTER TWENTY-THREE

AFTER TWENTY minutes of snuggling on the couch, I was ready for bed. Not sleep, mind you, bed. Naked. With Aaron's dick lodged in my ass.

"So, how tired are you?"

Aaron had been rubbing my back with his eyes closed. He opened them and looked at me. I wasn't sure what he saw in my eyes, but his cheeks flushed, and he got up off the couch, holding me in his arms.

"Not that tired. I'd have to be dead to be too tired to, ehm, be with you."

He walked us into the bedroom, stripped off my shirt, and unbuttoned my pants. I kicked off my shoes, shimmied out of my pants, and started working on his, while he gave up with the buttons on his shirt and pulled it off over his head. Why was it, getting undressed never seemed to take long when I was alone, but the fucking clothes were like handcuffs when I was with Aaron?

When we were *finally* naked, I got on the bed and scooted until my head was on the pillows. Aaron climbed on top of me, resting his body over mine, but holding himself up with his forearms. He kissed my ear, neck, and mouth. I let my hands wander over his body, counting ribs, dipping in his belly button, tugging gently at the hair around his dick. Of course that led to touching his dick, which made my asshole twitch.

"Want you inside me. Now." Aaron gave one last kiss to the spot behind my ear, which he'd been working on, then he leaned over and got the condoms and lube out of the drawer. "When was the last time you were tested?"

There was that blush again. Honestly, I needed a reference manual to figure out what embarrassed that man. Asking about a fucking test people talk about over lunch was cause for a red face, but having me pull his face into my ass so hard I wasn't sure how he was still able to breathe was perfectly fine.

"I, umm, I got tested before you came out here for Thanksgiving."

"All clear?" He nodded in response to my question. I kept talking. "I get tested every three months. Done it twice since that first weekend I was here. No guys, except you in that time." I lifted up and kissed him. "Think we can lose the covers? I've never done it bare, and I'd like to know what that feels like. Just your skin on mine."

I could feel Aaron's heartbeat increase, and his breathing turned into gasps. Well, I do believe something was turning my guy on. I wasn't sure whether it was the idea of going bareback or the dirty talk in general, so I kept going.

"Plus, that way, when you come, it'll be inside me."

Aaron groaned and started sucking up a mark on my neck, humping down on top of me. Oh, yeah, he liked the talking.

Now, here's the thing with dirty talk. Some guys

get into it, others think it's gross. You'd think that Mister Blush-when-I-asked-when-he'd-been-tested would fall under the think-it's-gross category. But, based on the way Aaron reacted to my words and how fucking expressive and open he was when we were actually having sex, I thought he'd probably get off on dirty.

"You like that, Aaron? The idea of your cum in me? Wonder how long it'll stay inside. Do you think I'll feel it running out, down my balls, while I'm sleeping?"

"Oh, Zach. You're driving me crazy, making me want—"

I hadn't noticed him putting lube on his fingers, but he must have, because one, and then two, wet fingers found their way into my ass in rapid succession.

"Ungh."

I arched my back and ground down on Aaron's hand, taking his fingers all the way in. One deep, long kiss later, I was gasping for air and riding three fingers.

"Ready for me, babe?" He was practically vibrating with need. "I don't know how much longer I can wait."

His heavy cock rubbed against my thigh, leaving a wet trail. Now, I already knew Aaron had tremendous staying power, so if he was that close, I'd been doing something right. I made a mental note to talk dirty to him in the future, then I shut off my brain and focused on his dick.

"Don't wait."

I reached down and stroked his slick cock, leading him to my opening. Then I lifted my legs and pulled my knees up and out.

"Oh, Jesus, Zach. That's so hot."

And then he slid into me, nice and slow, until he was seated all the way, and I could feel his pubes against my balls. The feeling was warmer and silkier, though not all that different than with a condom, but knowing there was no barrier between us was a major turn-on. We moved together, long strokes bringing Aaron in and then out of me. I tilted my hips and the angle caused him to hit my prostate on the next downstroke.

"There!"

Aaron moaned, nipped at my ear, and then used short, powerful strokes to hit that spot, over and over again. I grasped my dick and started tugging furiously, meeting the speed of Aaron's pounding.

"Come in me, Aaron. Make me feel it."

"Oh! Zach, Zach, Zach!"

And then my chest was covered in wet heat, and Aaron clutched my hips hard enough to leave marks as he buried himself deep inside me. I could feel his dick pulsing as he moaned and gasped.

"Oh, oh, oh. That was...that was... Oh, Zach."

Aaron collapsed on top of me, then scooted to the side so that most of his weight was on the bed. I wanted to rub his back or say something, but I was too focused on getting air into my lungs. He ran his hand gently over my chest and ass.

"You okay?"

"Ummhmm. But I'm too tired to shower tonight. Mind waiting until morning?"

The power of speech wasn't there yet, and there

was no way my legs were going to work. Aaron nodded, reached over the edge of the bed until he came up with something, my briefs I think, then he wiped the cum off me. I turned my back to him, getting into our regular position. He pulled the blanket over us, wrapped his arm around my chest, and kissed my neck.

"Wake me if you feel it running down your balls. That's something I've got to see. Just thinking about it makes me want to start all over again."

I groaned. Yup, dirty talk was a definite go.

THE NEXT morning, Aaron and I headed to his clinic. I was surprised when we pulled up to a nondescript strip mall in a nondescript part of town. My face must have shown some of what I was feeling.

"Yeah, I know. The location is questionable and the building is nothing to write home about. But, on the plus side, we're paying way too much in rent."

I raised my eyebrows at him, and he laughed.

"I'm kidding. Well, kidding about it being a plus. The rent is outrageous. When Kimmy bought the clinic, the landlord refused to assign the lease unless she agreed to pay thirty percent more than the previous owner. Why she didn't get a new place, I can't explain. There are lots of buildings in the area, and the real value of the business was in the equipment and goodwill."

We got out of the car and walked up to the door.

Aaron unlocked it and turned on the lights.

"Sounds like business isn't her thing."

Aaron shook his head.

"No, it's not. She can charm the socks off anyone, make friends at a funeral, and cause men twice her size to grovel. But she hates dealing with the business end of things. That's why she had all those problems running this place. The good news is, most of the equipment was new when Kimmy bought it, and we have a loyal client base now."

We walked through the clinic, and Aaron showed me around. It was fine. Nothing special. That loyal client base had to be due to Aaron. There was no other reason why people would flock to the place.

"So how long are you stuck in the lease? Maybe you can move."

Aaron nodded.

"The lease is up the middle of January. The landlord offered me a good rate on a renewal, after I told him there's no way I'd agree to the current terms. But I haven't signed it yet. I was thinking it might make better sense to buy a building. That way, instead of throwing money away on rent, we could build equity. What do you think?"

Aaron was looking at me as if he expected me to answer the question. I cleared my head and thought about it.

"Yeah. That makes sense. I guess it depends on how much it would cost to buy, including the interest on the mortgage, versus how much you'd pay in rent. Would there be a substantial amount going to equity?"

"You know, I haven't run the numbers yet, because I haven't had time to look at any buildings. You're right, though. We should probably talk to the bank to figure out the rates on commercial loans and call a Realtor, so we have a better idea of what things cost."

The "we" didn't go unnoticed. It slipped out of Aaron's mouth like it was the most natural thing in the world to think of the business he'd been building as being ours. Could it be that easy?

"I can call the bank today. And I'll see if I can find a Realtor to show us listings one night this week. Sound good?"

Aaron was giving me that same loving look, this time mixed with a hint of wonder.

"That sounds perfect, Zach. I've been meaning to do that for weeks, but haven't found the time. Check the Gay Chamber's website for Realtors. I'm sure there are a few listed, and I like to support the community whenever we can."

THE DAY went by pretty quickly. I met Aaron's techs, John and Marvin. Early twenties, somewhat cute, terminally straight. I answered phones, made appointments, and greeted people as they came in. And, in-between all of that, I spoke with the bank and got information on commercial mortgage rates, which were much higher than I expected.

I also talked to a few Realtors I found through the Gay Chamber and promised to set up a meeting with the one I liked best after I got Aaron's schedule.

I asked him to find us a few places close to Aaron's existing clinic and a few places in EC West. I hadn't talked with Aaron about moving locations, but if his client base truly was loyal, they'd probably follow him there. And if we were going to live in EC West, it'd be nice for him not to have the commute.

I got all of that done by noon. Aaron had told me he didn't take lunch breaks because some people could only bring their pets in during their own lunch hour. So, I decided not to take a break either. I ate a PowerBar and then found some cleaner and wiped down the front counter and desk. Granted, I was used to kitchens, not vet clinics, but there was no reason things couldn't be clean there. The dogs weren't behind the counter, standing on the damn desk.

The other thing that occupied my time was figuring out the situation with pet food. There was a corner in front where bags of pet food were stacked. I noticed that most of the customers bought food on their way out. The food was surprisingly expensive, so I asked Aaron about it during one of the many times he came up front, in between customers.

"Things look great out here, Zach. Really great. Did you clean and organize?"

He looked so happy and so fucking adorable I wanted to hug him. But I wasn't sure what the rules were at work, so I held back.

"Yup. I had time."

Aaron stroked my ass and pressed against me as he leaned over my body, allegedly to look around.

"Tina is super-sensitive about any of us getting near her space, so I've never bothered to organize up here. This is so much better." He kissed my cheek, gazed into my eyes, and brushed my hair back. "Thanks, babe. You've only been here a few hours, and you're already improving the place."

Okay, so affection at work was acceptable. Good. I put my arm around him and stroked his back.

"What's the deal with the food?"

"What do you mean?"

"It's expensive. I didn't realize dog food cost so much."

"Oh, it usually doesn't, at least not all the brands. The brands we carry, though, are specialty foods, some vegetarian, some prescription, all organic. They're not available through the big pet store chains."

"Do you order from a catalog or online? I was thinking I could see if they have biscuits or other treats. A few customers asked for those when they bought the food."

Aaron started looking through the appointment schedule and then peeked out over the desk to see how many people were waiting. We were on track, not running late.

"Yeah, people ask for that all the time. I can't figure out why those companies don't make them. The markup on the food is really high; we bring in a lot with it. But they just make the food—dry and canned. No treats."

A squeeze to my shoulder and another kiss on the cheek, and then Aaron took the next pet in line—a white bunny that would have been cuter if its owner didn't have bandages wrapped around half his fingers. I had no idea what that Tina did during her downtime, but I wasn't used to it. Working at restaurants, there was no fucking downtime. We were always on our feet, running around, trying to get things out.

I shuffled some papers, checked my e-mail, and then decided to look at the ingredients in the food we carried. Hmmm. Not different from human food. That gave me an idea. I went online and looked up animal treats, read their ingredients, and researched recipes. By the time we shut down for the night and headed out, I had a plan.

CHAPTER TWENTY-FOUR

"READY TO go?"

We'd finished seeing the last animal on the schedule thirty minutes earlier. The techs left right after that, and I filed the paperwork for the day, turned off the lights, computers, and machines, and then went to find Aaron. He was sitting at his desk in the back office, looking over charts.

When he heard me come in, he looked up and our eyes locked. I gasped. He was devastating, absolutely devastating. Hair all askew from running his fingers through it, shirt sleeves rolled up to his elbows, shirt crumpled, with the top few buttons open. Looking at him made my chest tighten and my lungs constrict.

"Come here."

His voice was rough with something that sounded like need. He rolled his chair back from the desk, leaving room for me in front of him. He tracked me with a predatory gleam in his eyes as I walked over to him, and I shuddered in anticipation. When I stood right before him, he reached up to my head and ran his fingers through my hair.

"Take off your belt."

His words were firm, his voice low and husky. I

unbuckled my belt, slid it out of my pants, and set it on the desk.

"Now your shirt."

I unbuttoned my shirt and let it slide to the floor.

"Pants."

It was an order, not a request. I swallowed hard, shocked at how much the sure tone of his voice and his control over the situation was turning me on.

I squatted down, took off my shoes and socks, then stood and moved my trembling hands to my pants. Aaron reached his hands to mine, gently lifted them to his mouth and kissed the backs of my hands and my palms. He looked at me intently, trying to read my emotions. I guess he was satisfied with what he found in my eyes because he lowered my hands and repeated his order.

"Take them off."

I opened my pants and let them drop to the ground and pool at my feet. Then I stepped out of them and kicked both my shirt and pants to the side.

Aaron groaned and looked at my body appreciatively. He reached behind me and took the charts and papers off the desk and gathered them into a pile.

"I'm going to take you on this desk, Zach. Gonna bury my dick in your ass and claim you. And when I'm done, I'm going to come all over your handsome face."

I gasped at his words and my hard cock twitched, wetness forming at the head. Aaron put his hands on my waist and lifted me so I was sitting on his desk. I was so fucking turned on, I couldn't see straight. I reached down and stroked my cock, desperate for relief. Aaron shook his head.

"Uh, uh, uh. No touching."

He took my hand off my cock and moved my arm behind my head. Then he added my free arm to the one behind my head. He bent each of my arms at the elbow, so that my forearms were pressed together and each hand was on my opposite elbow. He took my belt and wrapped it around my forearms and wrists until my arms were bound behind my head, and lowered me onto the desk, so that I was lying on my back with my arms behind my head like a pillow.

I was completely immobile. Aaron stood between my naked, parted legs and ran his strong hand down my chest, then twisted each of my nipples in turn. My breath came out in gasps, and my dick ached.

"Aaron, please."

His eyes hadn't moved from their lock on mine and had grown progressively darker. There was passion and possession in those eyes. His gaze was primal, and it aroused me to no end.

"Please what, Zach? Do you want me to take you? Want me to fill you?"

I could only nod; my mouth was so fucking dry and my need so great.

Aaron rubbed his big hand over my cock, causing me to thrust up in the hope of getting more friction. Then he stepped back, walked to a cabinet by the wall, poked through a box, and came back with a bottle of some sort of lotion or cream.

After he reclaimed his position between my

thighs, Aaron started stripping off his clothes. First his shirt. He opened one button at a time until it hung open, his muscular chest exposed. Then his belt buckle, pants button, and pants zipper. With his clothes all open, and barely remaining on his body, Aaron kicked off his shoes and then let everything else drop until he stood before me wearing only his low-rise boxer briefs.

I longed to reach my hand to his chest, to feel his muscles rippling beneath his skin, to trace the triangle on his chest down the happy trail to that dick that made me so fucking happy. When I moved my arms to fulfill that wish, I remembered that I was tied up, unable to move, and at Aaron's mercy. Shouldn't be a turn-on, should it? But it was, oh my fucking Christ, was it ever a turn-on.

Aaron slid his briefs off and smeared a generous amount of cream on his dick. When he reached for my ass, I drew my knees up and spread them as much as I could without the use of my hands.

"God, I love how much you want this, how much you enjoy it. Makes me want you even more. I can't get enough of you, Zach."

That gravelly voice and feral gaze killed me. I groaned and wiggled my ass, hoping he'd get the idea and shove his thick cock in there. Thankfully, my man was smart. Or maybe horny. Well, he was both. Anyway, he spread the lotion in my cleft, pushed a little into my hole, then lined up his slick cock with my entrance and pushed his way into my chute with one long, fast stroke.

"Ugh!"

Damn, that almost hurt, in the best possible way.

My dick was leaking a puddle onto my stomach as Aaron stood between my legs and plowed into me. I reveled in the sound of his groans, the smell of his skin, and the sight of his tense, sweaty body working above me.

His hard pumps into my channel pushed me farther back on the desk until Aaron crawled up, too, bracing himself with his arms and knees. I wrapped my legs around his waist and pushed up to meet each of his hard thrusts down.

Aaron moved his hand between us and rubbed my cock until all the remaining lotion was on me. Then he put both hands on the desk and turned his already hard pumps into a punishing pounding. The sound of my ass hitting the desk with every downstroke and the accompanying grunt that left my body combined with Aaron's moans. I could feel my slick cock rubbing on his sweaty stomach as his big dick pounded my ass and poked at my sweet spot with almost every stroke.

"So tight, so good, so close."

He grunted out his pleasure. I hadn't said any words up to that point. My only sounds were primal moans. But I needed Aaron to see what he did to me.

"Look at my dick, Aaron. Watch what you do to me."

Aaron lowered his forehead to mine, and we both looked down in between our bodies as he continued to piston into me. Three more hard thrusts, and my dick exploded between us, spewing cum onto my stomach and chest.

"Ohhh!" I shouted and almost convulsed with the

pleasure riding over me.

When my cock finally finished twitching and releasing, Aaron pulled out of my ass, crawled a bit farther on the desk so that he kneeled over me with his cock over my chest and neck. Then he tugged on it.

"You're mine, Zach."

I nodded, no doubt in my mind about that. I could never go back, could never be anyone else's, wouldn't want to be.

"Yes, I'm yours."

Aaron moaned when he heard my words. Ropes of cum flew out of his cock and covered my face, all the while his eyes were locked onto mine, the depth of his feeling for me shining through.

As his breathing slowed, Aaron remained crouched above me. He rubbed his cum into my forehead, my cheeks, and finally my lips. I darted my tongue out so that I could get a taste. He moaned, then let me lick it off his finger. When I got it all, he gathered more of his cum onto his finger, returned it to my mouth, and continued the pattern until he'd fed me all of his cum. His gaze was so intense it made my breath hitch.

"It keeps getting better, Aaron. Didn't think there was room for better, but, damn, you're the hottest fucking thing I've ever seen."

He smiled and reached up to my arms, undid the belt, and rubbed my forearms and wrists. I slipped my arms around his neck and pulled him down to me for a kiss. Sweet, soft, and a little bit of tongue.

"You're everything to me, Zach. I love you so

much."

"LET'S TALK about our schedule for the week, big guy, so I can set a time with that Realtor. I know you have meetings for the gay rights group on Thursday evenings and that you usually help Dean and Kimmy out with the kids on Fridays. Anything else?"

Aaron was driving us home with a smile on his face. We'd cleaned up in the shower Aaron said they sometimes used for the animals. Yeah, that's a little disconcerting, I know. But the shower looked clean, and we'd both been sticky and sweaty.

"You remember my schedule. And you took care of looking for a new place. And you made everything up front look so great today. And I got to see you, like, every hour instead of every few months. And don't even get me started on how wonderful it was to have you there at the end of the day. You make me so happy."

I couldn't tell whether he was talking to me or thinking out loud. But his happiness was contagious, and he made me feel so wanted. I reached over and took his hand, raised it to my lips, and licked my way up his palm. Aaron shivered and moaned.

"I'm happy too. So, the schedule?"

Aaron shifted in his seat, probably trying to find a comfortable position for the big hard-on he was suddenly sporting. I thought about how dangerous it would be to lean across the seat and blow him. I shook my head—bad idea.

"Yeah, you're right. That's usually what I do. But none of it is set in stone. I figured you'd go with me to Kimmy's on Friday, so we can both spend time with the boys. You're welcome to come to the Thursday meetings too."

I squeezed his hand.

"Of course I'll go hang with the boys. It's going to be nice to be a part of their lives. The meetings on Thursdays aren't my thing, though. I was thinking I'd take that time to paint."

"Yeah? That's great. I'm glad you're going to get back into painting. I'm looking forward to seeing your work."

"I'll set up a meeting with the Realtor for tomorrow. We can look at a few places after work. And maybe we can go again this weekend, unless you want to go apartment hunting then."

I looked out the window and refamiliarized myself with my hometown.

"Why can't we do both? Can the Realtor show us houses and spaces for the clinic?"

So many things had changed since I'd left Emile City. It was much more built up. Prettier. Or at least it seemed that way to me. I answered Aaron absently.

"I think he helps people buy, not rent. I can look around online to find apartments in EC West."

Long minutes of silence stretched by as we drove. I was still looking out the window, taking things in.

"What if we buy a house, Zach?"

His voice was almost a whisper, and he sounded scared, like he expected me to go off on him. Hell, three days prior I would've done exactly that. I closed my eyes and rubbed them with my hands. He knew I didn't have much money put away, so he'd have to handle the down payment. And he'd also have to pay the mortgage, since I didn't have a job. I wasn't ready to deal with that yet. Everything was happening too fast. So I changed the subject, hoping he'd let it go for now and give me time to think.

"What do you want to do for dinner? I stocked up when I went to the store yesterday."

Aaron barely skipped a beat.

"Is there any more of that pot roast? That was so good. I'd love to eat it again."

I relaxed.

"We have enough left. If we're not cooking tonight, I have an idea of something I want to make for tomorrow."

"What?"

"Organic dog biscuits."

Aaron laughed.

"Seriously?"

"Yeah. I looked up some recipes, and I can get everything at a regular store. Even if we buy organic ingredients, they won't cost that much to make. We'll package the biscuits in simple bags, that'll save money and go with the whole homemade thing. Your customers are paying out the nose for that organic food, and they were asking for treats, so we might as well give it a shot."

"Great idea, Zach. I'll do a little research and come up with pricing. And put me to work in the kitchen too. Baking isn't my best skill, but I can follow instructions. This sounds like fun."

And it was fun. We stopped at the grocery store to get what we needed to make the dog biscuits, and I could honestly say that I'd never had a more enjoyable shopping experience. Aaron was super-affectionate—holding my hand, rubbing my back, squeezing my shoulder. His face was glowing and covered in an ever-present smile. And he couldn't keep his eyes off me. Whenever I looked at him, there he was, gazing at me, his blue eyes twinkling.

The rest of the evening was mellow and comfortable. We ate dinner, baked the biscuits, and snuggled together on the couch, reading. Yeah, I know, it sounds boring. But it wasn't. It was nice, a perfect ending to a really good day. And a good example of what my days would be like going forward. Lucky me.

CHAPTER TWENTY-FIVE

THE DOG biscuits were a huge hit. I'd only made a couple of batches, because I didn't know whether or not people would buy them. Turned out they did buy them. All of them. We sold out in the course of three hours and two of the customers called to say their dogs loved them and they already wanted more. I was so excited I ran to the back to tell Aaron. I thought he'd be in the office, so I walked in without knocking. Big fucking mistake.

John and Marvin had their backs to me. They were watching porn on the computer. Straight porn. Big hair, lots of makeup, and a close-up of a woman's body part I'd hoped never to see in my entire fucking life.

"Oh fuck!" I turned my head. "I'd comment about how totally unprofessional this is, but I have to take a moment to first scratch my eyes out and then throw up."

The techs turned, surprised to see me, but not concerned about what they were doing.

"Dude, you have to see this. Marvin pulled it up to show me. This chick can take two guys up her—"

"*Stop!* I don't need to see that. I'm out of here."

I turned to walk out the door and bumped into Kim. She was standing there, holding a bag from a local sandwich shop, and staring at the screen.

"Huh. She's completely shaved."

Really? That's the take-away here? She walked into a place-of-work to see something that, as far as I'm concerned, should only be seen that closely by a medical professional, and she's fascinated by grooming? Add that to the never-fucking-ending list of reasons I'm glad to be into dick. I'll never understand women.

"Let's go out front, Kim. I was heading that way."

She followed me, but kept her head turned back toward the computer until we rounded the corner.

"What can I do for you, Kim?"

"Oh, yeah. I brought you lunch."

Hmmm. That was unusual.

"Thanks. I'll eat it at my desk."

I walked up front and sat behind the desk.

"Tuna sandwich okay?" I nodded and started unwrapping the sandwich she handed me. "I'll join you, Zach."

Kim sat in the seat next to me and picked at a salad.

"Did you notice that the actress in that movie was completely shaved?"

Ummm, no, that wasn't my focus. I was too busy trying not to throw up in my mouth.

"No, Kim. Can't say I noticed. Gay, remember? Not my scene. I looked away as soon as possible."

The sandwich smelled pretty good. I took a bite.

"Do you think Dean would like it if I shaved myself down there?"

She was actually pointing south. Swear to God. And

then, when I didn't answer, she looked at my sandwich and added, "You know, my tuna. Should I shave it?"

I choked a little and pushed my sandwich away. My fucking appetite was gone. Not sure I'd ever be able to eat tuna again.

"Jesus fucking Christ, Kim. I have no fucking clue what Dean would like. And I know dick about pussy. Why don't you head to the back office and ask Hugh Hefner and Larry Flynt?"

I tossed the sandwich in the trash. Kim was still sitting at the desk, a thoughtful look on her face.

"Anything else you need, Kim? Or was this just an ironic and disgusting lunch coincidence?"

That question seemed to snap her out of the vaginal-induced trance.

"Oh. Yeah. I was wondering if you could please do me a huge favor and watch the boys on Thursday night. I have plans to go out with my girlfriends, and Dean's boss scheduled a faculty thing. I know Aaron has his meetings Thursday nights, so I was hoping…"

I nodded.

"Sure. No problem. I'll come by after work."

She gave me a hug and a squeaky thanks and walked away. I was pretty sure she was still muttering about "no hair" under her breath. So this was what it was like to have family? She was fucking nuts. I wasn't sure how my brother got through the day. But I liked her. A lot. Go figure.

"SO DID he give you any idea of what he'd be showing us?"

Aaron and I were driving to EC West. We closed the clinic right at five, and we were going to meet the Realtor at five thirty, look at some places, and then have dinner out there.

"No. I asked him to check them out first, so we wouldn't waste our time looking at dumps. But, other than that, he said today we'd look around EC West. If we don't like anything there, he can find places close to the current clinic location."

Aaron reached over and squeezed my hand.

"I like the idea of moving the clinic to EC West. It'd be great to live and work in the same community. Especially there. We might lose a few customers by leaving the area, but we'll gain new ones. Thanks for thinking of that, Zach. I'm so lucky to have you by my side."

He squeezed my hand, and I smiled to myself. Cheesy, yes. Still felt nice to hear it. Now fuck off.

We pulled up to the Realtor's office and went inside. A woman with short blond hair and bright green eyes was sitting at the desk.

"We're here to see David Miller."

Aaron was standing next to me, holding my hand. The woman looked down at an appointment book and back up at us.

"Are you Zach Johnson?"

"Yes. And Aaron Paulson."

"Okay, Mr. Johnson. I'll let him know you're here. You can have a seat."

The receptionist picked up the phone as Aaron and I walked over to the sofa. It was a long leather piece. Probably enough room for five. We sat pressed together in the corner. Aaron had his arm around me, and I rested my head on his shoulder. I didn't even realize I was tired, but I must have dozed off because I was startled by a voice that came from someone standing right in front of me.

"Sorry to keep you waiting, I...oh, is he sleeping?"

I opened my eyes and looked up. Black hair, blue eyes, very muscular build, mid-thirties. Nice.

"That's okay. Are you David?"

I stood up and reached out my hand. Aaron stood behind me, his hand on the small of my back. He didn't say anything and didn't offer his hand.

David shook my hand and smiled.

"I'm Zach Johnson and this is Aaron Paulson. Thanks for helping us out on such short notice."

"Don't mention it. Let's go back to my office so I can show you what I've got lined up for us tonight. Then we can look at the places that strike your fancy."

Aaron had a death grip on my hand as we followed David into his office. Nice ass, by the way. When we got to the office, David sat at his desk and I sat across from him. Aaron hesitated, scooted an empty chair closer to mine, and then sat down, never letting go of my hand.

"So, I wasn't sure about what square footage you'd want. You mentioned Mr. Paulson's clinic—"

"Aaron."

Aaron's voice was strained. And it sounded almost like he was growling, not his normal tone. I looked over at him in surprise.

"You mentioned Aaron's clinic, so I looked up the address and then checked the county records to find the size. I found buildings that are the same size, some that are smaller, and some that are bigger. Let's talk about your needs, and that'll help me narrow down the focus right away."

David looked at both of us as he spoke. He had a warm smile and intelligent eyes. I liked him. I turned to Aaron, expecting him to answer, but he was quiet and tense. Jesus, this was awkward, and I had no fucking clue what was going on. I turned to David.

"Umm. You know, David, we haven't talked about that. Can you give us a minute?"

David smiled.

"Sure. It'll give me a chance to call my partner and see how he's doing." He paused as he walked by Aaron. "He had to fill in at his family's business tonight, which is the only reason I could meet you. I don't normally work nights because we spend them together. *Exclusively.*"

Aaron laughed, let go of my hand, and dropped his head into his hands.

"That obvious, huh?"

David squeezed his shoulder.

"Afraid so. Still want me to leave?"

Aaron shook his head.

"No. But I could use a drink."

David nodded.

"I have water, diet, regular, and coffee."

"Water would be great, David."

David looked at me.

"Diet soda."

"One water and one diet soda coming up."

He walked out of the office and closed the door. I looked at Aaron.

"Want to fill me in?"

Aaron played with a loose string on his pants and wouldn't look at me.

"I'majealousfreak."

I couldn't decipher the mumble, so I got up from my chair and squatted in front of him, taking his hands in mine to stop him from pulling the damn pants apart.

"Hey, stop it. I like these pants. They look great on your ass. Now, tell me what the fuck happened here."

He sighed.

"I got jealous."

"What? Why?"

Aaron blushed and looked down again. He shrugged.

"I don't know. Because he's really handsome. And you're so darn wonderful and gorgeous that I know every gay guy we meet will want you. How can I compete with that?"

Huh. Jealous and insecure. Well, I knew how to handle that situation. I got up, straightened my pants, and gently ran my fingers through Aaron's hair. Then I smacked him hard upside the head.

"Ow! Why'd you do that?"

"Because you're an idiot. It's not a fucking competition, Aaron. I love you. I don't want anyone else, including the hotty Realtor. Now, pull your shit together because he asked some good fucking questions, and we need to figure out the answers."

Aaron rubbed the back of his head and nodded.

"So, do you want a bigger place? I can't imagine you'd want less space. You don't have much room as it is."

"Yeah. You're right. If we had a bigger space, I could get another tech and see more animals every day. And I've always wanted to carry more food and maybe some toys. That's easy money without any effort on our part, but I don't have room to store inventory or to display anything, so I'm limited now."

"Good thinking. Now, when David gets back, do you think you can talk in complete sentences and drop the caveman shit? Or do I need to blow you right in front of him to settle your ass down?"

Aaron laughed and pulled me onto his lap for a hug.

"I'll behave. Sorry, babe."

I kissed the top of his head.

"It's okay. Sort of cute even."

There was a knock on the door, and David walked in, holding a bottle of water and a diet soda. He saw me sitting on Aaron's lap and smiled.

"We're good?"

I nodded, got up, took the drinks from him, and handed Aaron his. David sat at the desk.

"So, square footage?"

TWO HOURS later, we'd seen the buildings David found in EC West that met our size requirements, and we'd made a new friend. David was fun, interesting, and smart. He and Aaron seemed to get along well.

"Once you've had time to talk, let me know what you think. If you want to go back and look at any of these again, we can do that. And let's set something up for this weekend. Maybe you can come to our place for dinner."

Aaron shook David's hand.

"Thanks, David. That sounds great. We're looking forward to meeting your partner. I liked a couple of the places we saw today, and it'll be great to relocate the clinic to EC West once we move here. We like the area. We'll talk about it and get back to you."

David arched his eyebrows.

"You're moving here? You mean you guys don't live in EC West now?" I shook my head. "Do you already have a house picked out?"

I tensed a bit in anticipation of where the conversation was going. He was probably going to try to sell us a house, and I wasn't sure yet whether I felt comfortable with that level of financial support from Aaron. I think Aaron could sense my discomfort, so he didn't answer the question. Well, if the silence continued much longer, we'd seem rude, so I answered.

"We haven't started looking yet."

A huge smile spread across David's handsome face.

"I have to show you one more place."

I was tired and hungry.

"I thought we already saw all the buildings that meet our requirements in EC West."

David nodded.

"Well, yeah. But that's because I didn't know about all your requirements. This place is perfect for you. I didn't show it to you at first, because it's much bigger than what you said you want. But, a lot of that is a residence, so if you want space to live and work, you can't beat it."

I felt Aaron shift behind me. I looked back and could see he was getting excited by the idea. He met my eyes with a questioning, hopeful look. Damn. I turned to David and spoke up.

"That sounds interesting, David. We'd love to take a look."

"Yeah? That's great. Seriously, you'll love this place. Let's go."

CHAPTER TWENTY-SIX

WE PILED into David's car, and ten minutes later we turned onto a beautiful street. There was a wide jogging path on one side and a brick sidewalk on the other. Huge, old trees lined the entire street and met high in the air, making an arch over the road. Instead of businesses facing the street, which was what I'd have expected on such a large road, there were houses. Each house was different from the one next to it, but they were all beautiful. Victorians, Colonials, mid-centuries. The lots were large, so the houses were surrounded by grassy areas and gardens.

"David, this neighborhood is fabulous."

He looked over at me and smiled.

"It's the best. My favorite part of EC West. The neighbors are all friendly. We have neighborhood parties on holidays and progressive dinners at each other's houses."

"You live here, David?"

"Yup. We live right behind this place."

He pulled into the driveway of a gorgeous two-story Craftsman. Redwood shingles alternated with gray stone to give the house a warm, woodsy feel.

"It's beautiful."

Aaron got out of the car and opened my door. He put his hand on the small of my back and rubbed circles as we followed David to the front door. Have I already mentioned how Aaron always seems to find a way to touch me? And how much I fucking love that?

"You can see that the driveway curves to both sides. They took out the side yards and turned them into parking. They used dark concrete pavers made to match the stone in the house, not asphalt. They kept the vegetation in the front yard, so that the look of the neighborhood from the street is consistent. And they kept the backyard intact, except for adding a pool in half of it."

"Pool?"

I had visions of skinny dipping with Aaron under the moonlight, which led to an uncomfortable tightness in my pants. I adjusted myself just as David looked back to answer me.

"Yes, it's a nice one, too, with a built-in hot tub." He followed the movement of my hand on my dick and then looked back at my face with a knowing smirk. "And the entire perimeter is lined with trees and bushes. Complete privacy."

I laughed.

"Fuck you, David."

"Oh, I don't think so. I value my balls, and I think your man there would rip them off."

Aaron raised both hands in the air and chuckled.

"Okay, okay. I said I was sorry."

I was glad we could all laugh together. David was a

nice guy, and Aaron could use more friends. Hell, so could I, considering the fact I didn't know anyone in Emile City other than Aaron, my brother, and my old friend Luke.

David opened the lockbox, took out the key, and let us into a big open room. He turned on the lights.

"The previous owner was a dentist, and he wanted to work from home. He converted this house to meet those needs. The first floor was his dental clinic and the second floor was his residence. We're standing in the waiting room."

Aaron and I looked around. The floors were covered in dark slate tiles, the walls were a muted green, and the wood trim looked original. There was a large curved desk toward the middle of the space. It was made of dark wood and the top was granite.

"This is a great room. We could put plenty of chairs or sofas around the perimeter and still have enough space for the animals while they're waiting. And that desk is perfect for a receptionist. It's bigger than what we have now."

Aaron walked over to the desk and ran his hand over the granite counter.

"We'd have room for more than one person up here, if we needed."

I could hear the excitement in Aaron's voice.

"Okay, so to the right is the space the previous owner used for an office."

David opened two large sliding doors, and we walked into a huge open room.

"This was a dentist's office?" Aaron asked.

"No, not his office. His partner's office. Jose is a dentist. His partner, Adam, is a stockbroker. He had televisions everywhere, following markets all around, and a few computers, each on a different desk. He worked crazy hours, so he had a couch and a mini fridge here so he could rest."

I looked over at David. "You sure know a lot about these guys."

"Of course. They were our neighbors and good friends. Great guys."

"Why are they selling?"

David shook his head and chuckled.

"Because they're lucky as hell. Adam, the stockbroker, got in on the ground floor with a new tech company. The company went public, and Adam and Jose became multimillionaires overnight. In this economy. Can you believe it? Anyway, they don't need to work anymore, so they're traveling the world for a couple of years, and then deciding what to do next."

We followed David out of that room, across the waiting room area, and to the other side of the space. It was a wide hallway with doors lining the sides. David opened one door and stepped inside. We followed.

"Each of the rooms is identical. There are five of them. You can see there's a sink in the corner and built in cabinets. These were the patient rooms. Jose had huge dental chairs in the middle, but you can put anything here. Should be enough room for what you do, right, Aaron?"

Aaron was walking around the small room. He looked out the window and ran his hand over the granite counter that covered the built-in cabinet. They were the same colors as the receptionist desk out front.

"It's perfect. We'd just need to put a treatment table in the middle and a chair against the wall, and we'd be ready to go. We already have three at the clinic, so we'd just need to buy two more."

We walked out of the room and peeked in each of the other four as we made our way to the end of the hallway. The last door led to a big space with more built-ins and sinks around the perimeter. There were electrical outlets built into the floor.

"This was his back-office space. Billing, lab, that kind of thing."

Aaron had lost that initial excited look and had gone to being almost mesmerized. I had to admit, the place was spectacular.

"This is perfect. We'd have space to add an x-ray machine and lab equipment. And there's plenty of room to house animals that need to stay overnight. Perfect."

David had a huge smile on his face. He rubbed his hands together.

"Want to see perfect? Let's take a look at the residence."

We followed David back to the entry. We'd looked at the large office on the right and the rooms off the hallway on the left. This time, he walked straight back to a glass door that led to the backyard. He flipped the switches next to the door and bathed the backyard in light.

"So, that's the yard. And this—"

David turned, and I noticed a short hallway that had been hidden from the angle in the waiting room. He opened a door, and we were looking at a wooden staircase.

"This is one way to get to the residence. There's also a separate entrance accessible from the side of the house."

We followed David up the stairs, through a large wooden door, and into another open space. One entire wall was made of windows overlooking the backyard. The rest of the walls were a golden-yellow.

There was a fireplace on one wall, flanked by built-in bookcases. And the floors were a dark stained wood.

"This is the entryway and living room. There's a powder room right over there." David gestured to a small door to our right. "And the bedrooms are this way. Two rooms, each with its own full bath."

We followed David and looked at the bedrooms. One decent-sized room and one large bedroom with a sitting room off of it and a fireplace.

"This is the master. Jacuzzi tub and steam shower in the bathroom."

Aaron and I went in, and I gasped. The fixtures, the cabinets, the tile work, it was the most gorgeous bathroom I'd ever seen. The wall next to the tub had a fireplace.

"This place is incredible."

David smiled.

"I knew you'd like it. Jose has exquisite taste. And Adam lets him have whatever he wants. Come on, you have to see the kitchen."

We walked back across the living room, through

a wide archway, and into a large, bright room. One wall was full of windows. There was a full-size freezer next to a full-size refrigerator, an extra-wide double oven, and an eight-burner stove, all in stainless steel. The countertops on the perimeter of the space were marble and the long island in the middle was covered in butcher block.

"Holy fuck. This kitchen is incredible. I take it they liked to cook."

David laughed so hard he had tears in his eyes.

"No. They don't. I don't think they used anything but the fridge and maybe the dishwasher. They ate out almost every night, and when they did eat here, it was almost always takeout on paper plates."

I furrowed my brows.

"Then why did they build this kitchen?"

More laughter from David. Then he shrugged.

"Because Jose thought it'd look pretty. He saw a picture in a magazine when they were designing this space."

I looked at him in disbelief. The stove alone cost more than my car.

David put one hand on his heart and raised his other hand as if he was taking an oath.

"Seriously, that's why."

"It's amazing, David. Perfect. But I can't imagine how we could afford it."

I clearly couldn't afford it. And I didn't know the details of Aaron's finances, but that house had to be out of the ballpark.

"I'll send you home with paperwork and e-mail

you tonight with pricing for other residential properties this size in the neighborhood. If you add the price of the commercial buildings you liked today to the price of houses the size of the residence portion of this building, you'll see that this place is actually quite a bit cheaper. And I don't know whether you've talked to a lender yet, but commercial loan rates are almost twice as high as residential. This place is in a residential neighborhood, and it is technically a house, so you could probably get a traditional mortgage for it and save a bit that way."

Aaron had been quiet during most of the house tour, but now he turned to David.

"Why is it less expensive? This house is gorgeous, the fixtures and details are incredible. And the clinic space is top of the line. It's perfect."

"Well, yeah. For you. But you have to understand. This entire neighborhood is residential. It's on the main egress street and not on the side streets, so Adam and Jose were able to get the zoning changed to mixed-use. But there's a stipulation, business hours are limited to keep down noise and traffic. Eight to Six. Because of that limitation, no restaurants or bars are interested. And it's too big a space for a boutique. Also, the zoning won't allow a conversion to make it fully commercial. They can't increase the ratio of commercial square footage to residential square footage. So, it's limited as far as businesses are concerned.

"Someone looking for a regular house could probably convert the zoning back to residential, but they'd have to put in a lot of money to remodel it. One couple looked into it, but they'd essentially have to take it down to the studs and start over. At that point it'd be way too expensive. So this place has sat empty for six months. And it's not like Jose and Adam need the money. They just want it off their books, and they want all of us to stop calling them and complaining that they're making a blight on the area by leaving this property vacant. They've reduced the price three times, and I bet they'd go down even more."

Aaron nodded and looked at me.

"Thanks, David. E-mail us the comps and the other information and give us a couple of days to talk this over."

"Will do. I'm going to go downstairs and make sure all the lights are off, and we're all locked up. You can have a few minutes to do another walk-through up here."

David went downstairs, and Aaron pulled me up against his chest.

"Your eyes started twinkling when you saw this kitchen."

I didn't say anything. It was true. The kitchen was fucking amazing. Didn't mean I could afford it.

"I'm going to use the bathroom. Be right back."

I took a walk through the living room, down the hallway, to the master bathroom. After I washed my hands, I leaned over the bathtub to examine the glass tiles covering the walls. The detail work in that house was truly outstanding. It looked like each tile was handmade.

I heard a groan and looked back over my shoulder. Aaron was standing just inside the bathroom, staring at my ass, and rubbing his hand over a rapidly inflating bulge in his pants.

"Promise me you won't ever do that when other people are around."

"Do what, big guy?"

He walked over to me, put his hands on my waist, and pulled my ass back against his crotch.

"Bend over. No one could possibly resist your ass."

Then he folded his body over mine and whispered into my ear as he gently pumped his hardening cock against my ass.

"I want you, Zach. Right here, right now."

I straightened my body, and Aaron raised himself with me.

"David's waiting for us. We don't have much time."

The words sounded like a protest, but the speed at which my hands were working the button and zipper of my pants made it abundantly clear that I was absolutely willing.

"We'll be fast, babe."

My mind was getting to the realization that we didn't have any lube when Aaron's head dropped from over my shoulder, his warmth left my back, and I felt his tongue working its way into my ass.

"Oh, Aaron. Fuck, that feels good. So damn good."

He drooled into my cleft and then pushed his saliva into my opening with his tongue. It seemed to me that he took more time licking my hole than was necessary if lubrication was his only goal.

"Jesus, Aaron. You're going to make me come from eating my ass. Get up here. I want you inside."

He raised his body back up so his chest was pressed against my back. He squatted, lined his cock up with my pucker, and pushed in.

I felt Aaron rub his hand under my shirt and down my back. Gentle strokes on my skin calmed and relaxed me as my body got used to his invasion. When I was ready for more, I reached one hand behind our bodies and squeezed his ass.

"Hard and fast, Aaron. Make me feel every fucking stroke."

And he did. He wrapped both arms around my chest and enveloped my body in his. Then he pounded his dick so hard into my passage that at times he lifted my body off the fucking ground.

"Ungh, ungh, ungh. I'm there, Aaron, gonna, gonna—"

His warm hand made its way down my chest to my dick. He stroked and made sure we were leaning over the tub so that when I came, I shot into the tub and not onto the wall.

As soon as I started my release, Aaron joined me with his dick buried deeply in my ass. We were both bent over the tub, panting, when we heard David's muffled voice.

"You guys still up here?"

"Fucking hell, Aaron. I'm not sure if my legs still work. You might have to carry me out of here."

We both stood and did up our pants. Aaron ran the water for a minute to clean things up and then he shut off the lights and put his arm around me as we walked back to the entryway.

"Enjoy the tour?"

David was smirking. No doubt he knew what we'd been up to...and into. Our shirts were untucked, our hair mussy, and I was probably walking with a slight limp.

"Yeah. That bathroom's fabulous."

Aaron blushed, and David had the good sense to keep his mouth shut.

CHAPTER TWENTY-SEVEN

DAVID DROVE us back to his office, where we'd left our car, and we said our goodbyes. Aaron and I got into his car. I turned to look at him and saw a thoughtful look on his face.

"Hungry?"

It was almost nine o'clock. He had to be hungry. I sure as shit was. Aaron nodded.

"Yeah. I could eat. What are you in the mood for?"

He seemed distracted. I could tell he was thinking about the house. It was time for us to figure out what we were going to do. But not on an empty stomach. I was already halfway to an anxiety attack. Talking before I had a chance to eat would not be a good idea.

"How about we try that Italian place you mentioned?"

Pasta, red sauce, comfort food. That was what I needed.

"Mmmm, that sounds good. It's down the street."

We pulled into a parking lot that had once been the backyard of a pretty Colonial. The house itself had been converted into a restaurant with sparkling white lights draped around the perimeter of the building and the trees in front. The entire street was like that—houses converted into restaurants, antique shops, salons, and boutiques.

Delicious smells met us as we walked in the door.

"Table for two, please."

Aaron had his arm around me, and I was leaning against his chest. He bent down and smelled my hair, moaned appreciatively, then kissed the top of my head.

"Right this way."

The hostess picked up a couple of menus and began leading us to a table.

"Aaron!"

We both turned to the side to see a group of guys sitting at a large round table.

"Come join us."

Well, at least this would get me a slight respite from the house purchase conversation. And I wanted to encourage Aaron to make friends.

"Come on, big guy. Let's go sit with your friends."

He looked at me in surprise.

"Why? We can get our own table. They're not my friends. I just know one of those guys from the spring baseball league I play in."

I rolled my eyes. Therein lay the problem. I dragged Aaron toward the table.

"It'll be fun. Besides, I want to get to know your friends."

By that time, we were too close to the group for Aaron to continue his protests. Good. We'd eat, relax, and Aaron could expand his social circle. Hey, I'd expand mine too. Well, that was the plan anyway. What was it they said about good intentions?

As soon as we got within arm's distance of the table, the guy who called us over stood up and hugged Aaron. He was almost Aaron's height, and he had a huge chest and bulging biceps. He was wearing pants that were loose on his thighs, so I gathered that he worked the top half of his body and ignored the rest.

Now, as you already know, Aaron is a warm, affectionate guy. That's why I was surprised when his body stiffened as soon as his friend hugged him. He reached over to me and pulled me up against his side.

"This is my partner, Zach Johnson. Zach this is Nick..."

"Gallaway. Nick Gallaway. You know that, Aaron!"

Nick hadn't removed his hand from Aaron's arm. And he hadn't turned his head in my direction.

"Right. Nick Gallaway. Of course."

"Here, sit down."

The guy sitting next to Nick had moved, leaving his seat empty, and Nick was pointing at it. Aaron frowned.

"It looks like there are two free seats at that end of the table; we'll sit there."

That was clearly not what Nick had in mind. His forehead creased like he was trying to make a decision. I don't know where he ended up with that, because Aaron had walked us over to the two empty seats. We sat down and Aaron rubbed my knee.

I could tell he was tense, so I smiled and introduced myself and Aaron to the guys sitting around us.

"Nice to meet you, Zach. I'm Seth. Aaron, we've

CARDENO C.

met. I think it was at the rally last spring. Or maybe at the dinner gala."

I knew the gay rights group Aaron volunteered with had an annual gala, and I figured they had their share of rallies too. Sounded like this guy was involved. I sensed Aaron relaxing, so I looked over at him for confirmation. He was smiling and nodding.

"That's right. Hi, Seth. Nice to see you again."

"You too. This is my partner, Eli."

Seth was probably in his mid-thirties, but Eli looked much younger. I'd be surprised if he was old enough to order the beer sitting in front of him.

"Hi, guys. Aaron, I don't know if you remember me, but we met at the Gay Youth Center last year."

"Of course I remember you, Eli!"

Youth center? Damn, he was younger than I thought. I assumed he must have reached legal age since the youth center days or else Seth wouldn't risk jail time by being so public about their relationship.

"Frank mentioned you're starting at the university next year. That's great."

I cringed when I heard he wasn't out of high school, yet. I supposed he might be eighteen, some people have early birthdays, but damn, that was a whole different stage in life.

"I'll be twenty-eight next month."

Eli was looking at me with a big grin on his face.

"Huh?"

Yeah, I know. Fucking eloquent. That's me.

"You were wondering how old I am. Probably

assumed I was still in college, but actually, I'm teaching music at the university next year."

I chuckled.

"Nah, I didn't assume you were in college."

He raised his eyebrows in disbelief.

"No?"

"No. I thought you were still in high school."

Seth choked on his beer.

"Damn it, Eli. When are you going to have the decency to get a wrinkle or something? The nine year age difference is hard enough. I don't want people to think I'm corrupting a minor."

Eli rolled his eyes.

"Darlin', if there's any corrupting going on, it's the other way around." He turned to me. "I was already in my twenties when we got together. Totally not a minor."

Eli and Aaron started talking about the California District Court's decision to overturn Prop 8 and what they thought would happen on appeal. Seth was talking to a guy on his other side. I leaned into Aaron.

"I'm going to find the bathroom. Will you order for me if the waiter comes? Whatever sounds good, I don't care."

Aaron nodded and kissed my cheek. Then he turned back to Eli and continued the discussion. I admired Aaron's commitment to our rights and his knowledge of all the pending laws. It wouldn't hurt me to learn more about those things. It was my life after all. Perhaps I should give a shit and get more involved in the work people were doing to make it better.

I was standing at the sink washing my hands when Nick, Aaron's Muscle Mary friend, walked in.

"You're not good enough for him. You know that, right? He's going to figure that out any minute and dump your ass."

Wow. Don't hold back, man. Tell me how you really feel. I ignored him and reached for a paper towel.

"I was at Micah's party last summer. You were fall-down drunk and then you let Micah's cousin and his friend fuck you at the same time. And I heard you up and moved here without a job, so you're unemployed. You're cute, I guess, but who wants to be with a guy who's so small?"

I turned to Nick, leaned back against the sink, and crossed my arms.

"That would be Aaron."

"What?"

"You asked who'd want to be with a guy who looks like me, and I answered. I've got to tell you, Nick, that if I'm as awful as you seem to think and Aaron still chose to be with me and not you, then you must be a real fucktard."

He clearly hadn't expected that to be my response, because he stood there dumbfounded.

"There you are, babe. Everything okay?" Aaron walked into the bathroom, scowled at Nick, then put his arms around me. "Seth and Eli left. Turns out everyone had already eaten. They were just finishing their drinks. Do you want to stay and eat here or should we get something to go? It's getting pretty late, and we still need to talk about whether we want to put in an offer on the house."

"House? You're buying a house together?"

Damn, was that fucking gnat still standing there?

"Nick was educating me about how awful I am and explaining that you're about to break up with me. I think the next part of the story was going to be about how he'd be there for you to pick up the pieces."

Aaron's face turned red, and he was shaking.

"He said what? I've made it very clear to him that I'm not interested in dating him."

I clasped his arm and made sure he didn't move toward Nick.

"It's a good thing I'm here, big guy, because you have shit taste in friends."

Okay, I said the last part intentionally, knowing how Aaron would react. And right on cue, Aaron said, "He's not my friend!"

"Well, I guess that settles it, Nick. You're not going to be rebound guy because, despite your predictions of woe, Aaron and I aren't breaking up. I'd say that we'll see you around, but I doubt that'll happen since you don't even rate friend status."

Nick was standing in front of us with his mouth gaping like a fish and his cheeks reddened in humiliation. I almost felt sorry for him.

"Let's get takeout, so we can go home and eat in our underwear." I pulled Aaron out of the bathroom before he could do or say something that he'd regret. That dickhead wasn't worth it. "Do you think it'll take them long to make the food?"

Aaron stopped walking and pulled me up against his chest.

"You okay? I hate that he talked to you that way."

I rubbed his back.

"I'm fine, big guy. I have a thick skin and a lot of self-confidence. Guys like that don't bother me."

Aaron smiled.

"That's one of the many things I love about you, Zach. Your strength."

I SET the takeout containers down by my feet and leaned my head back against the seat. I hoped Aaron would wait until we got home to start talking about the house. I wasn't kidding about the eating in our underwear thing. The sight of Aaron's body turned me on so much most of my damn blood went down below. I figured being lightheaded during the conversation would be a good idea. That way my brain could calm the fuck down.

"I have a business proposition for you, Zach."

"You know I'd love to have you proposition me, big guy."

I waggled my eyebrows at him. He laughed.

"I'm serious."

"So am I. Give me your hand, and I'll let you feel how serious."

"Zach! I mean it." But he reached out his hand. I placed it on my lap. He found my hard dick, squeezed it, and groaned. "It's a good thing we're in the car. Otherwise, I'd never be able to keep myself off you long enough to talk."

A final squeeze to my dick, and then he put his hand back on the steering wheel.

"So, I'd totally understand if you don't want to do this. No pressure. But instead of looking for another job, what do you think about expanding the organic biscuits idea?"

I mulled the idea over. It sounded good. But I wasn't sure how baking dog biscuits could keep me busy full-time.

"I'd love to make the biscuits. No problem there. But it's not a full-time job, Aaron."

"It could be."

I turned to him.

"What do you mean?"

"Well, they're a huge hit. People have always wanted them. And if we buy that house, we could turn the stockbroker's old office into a shop. There's enough room in there for us to sell more food than we currently carry, and other things too. I was thinking we could put in a dog bakery. You could use the kitchen upstairs to make different types of biscuits and treats. We might even be able to sell some online, depending on how much you can produce.

"And I think we'd also have space to sell other things. Maybe we can find high-end specialty products. Pet tags made by artists so they're more like jewelry. Handmade pet clothes and costumes for Halloween. Same thing with toys and beds. I once saw a cat bed made out of a gourd.

"The thing is, I can't manage that. Dealing with the clinic keeps me busy as it is. If I hire another tech, that's one more person to supervise and a third more animals to see each day. Plus I'd like to add more testing equipment, because there's space for it in that back room. That'd help us get more interesting cases, which would take more time. So if we wanted to expand the retail end of things, we'd need someone else to run it. If you're interested, I mean."

"You trying to keep me busy? Give me something to do so I don't feel like a freeloader?"

Aaron gripped the steering wheel so tight his knuckles turned white.

"You're not a freeloader. We're partners. I don't care if you decide not to find a job and you paint all day. I'm suggesting this because it's a good business idea, Zach. We have people coming in with pets all day. They already pay for premium food. The biscuits you made sold out in a few hours. And I know our customers would like unique products, things they can't get in the big chain stores. But those things aren't easy to find. We'd have to work with artists, figure out what they can make, deal with inventory and probably special orders. And creativity isn't my strong suit.

"We'd need someone artistic. Someone who could find the right products to carry. Maybe even design some things and find people to make them. The bakery part would take time, obviously, because we'd have to actually make the products. Does that sound busy enough for you? I'm not sure one person could manage all of it, but I thought I'd ask."

Huh. Baking and working with artists. Two things I was fucking good at. I could also deal with inventory and ordering. I did that in the restaurants.

"You think we can make money doing that?"

Aaron relaxed and nodded.

"I know we can. If I know one thing, it's my customer base. And in EC West it'll be even better. A bunch of gay men who treat their animals like children. Lots of disposable income. Trust me. They'll love this and there are no other animal boutiques here. It'd be a great profit center, Zach."

That made sense. And it'd be fun to work for Aaron. I'd enjoyed the last couple of days at the clinic.

"So if I do this, do I still get to fuck the boss?"

I chuckled at my joke. But Aaron wasn't laughing. His jaw went back to being clenched, and he spoke through gritted teeth.

"Partners. We're *partners*. If we do this, then we do it together, Zach. I'll head up the clinic, and you'll head up the dog bakery and pet boutique."

My instinct was to argue. To point out that his money would be setting this up, that it was his idea, that he was the one with the successful vet clinic. Well, that was one instinct, anyway. My other instinct was to do anything I could to take the frown off his face and relax his shoulders, to make him happy. Want to guess which instinct won?

CHAPTER TWENTY-EIGHT

OKAY, SO in case you haven't been paying attention enough to figure it out for yourself, I agreed to manage the dog bakery and pet boutique, and Aaron agreed to fuck me into the mattress. I think I got the good end of that deal.

We were naked in bed. I was on my hands and knees and Aaron was tracing the length of my spine with his tongue, leaving goose bumps in its wake.

"Gonna see you every day when we work together."

He was mumbling into my skin, making his way down my body.

"I was thinking about that when we were in the house today."

He was caressing my ass and rubbing his cheek against it.

"Did you feel those granite countertops?"

He burrowed his face into my cleft, licked his way down to my balls, nuzzled and sniffed.

"Mmmm. You smell so good."

Sometimes it seemed the man was part canine.

"I imagined you bent over those counters, the coolness against your skin and my heat behind you, inside you."

Fingers and tongue plunged inside me.

"Oh, Jesus. Aaron! Fuck."

"Yeah. Okay."

I barely made out his words before he was shoving that thick dick into me.

"Ahhh!" Damn, that was big and full, and it burned. Fucking wonderful.

Aaron's teeth were on the back of my neck, grazing on me as he pumped into me. Okay, this really was doggy style. I think the man was even growling. I know I was whimpering.

In and out. He kept up a steady, punishing rhythm. I could feel his breath against my neck, his teeth working me. And if I didn't come soon, I knew I'd lose my mind.

"Aaron, please, I...I need it."

His fingers dug into my hips, and he increased his speed.

"Take what you need, Zach."

Fucking hell. I ground back, meeting his pushes, feeling his balls slap against me.

"Take it. Take it. Take it."

He grunted out the words as he moved higher, changed the angle of entry, and made his cock hit my spot on every thrust. I reached down and gave myself one stroke. That was all it took, and I was shooting off.

"Ungh! Ahhh. Yes, yes, yes!"

I was still on my knees, leaning down on one hand. The other was wrapped around my cock, dripping with my release. Aaron held my hips. He wrapped one strong arm around my stomach, the other around my upper chest, right below my neck. Then he lifted me, so that we were both on our knees, with his still hard dick buried inside me and his hips continuing their thrusting motion.

I moved my hand over my cock. I wasn't soft yet. Actually, I was getting harder with each of Aaron's pushes inside me. I stroked my cock in time with his thrusts and bounced back against him, into his lap, feeling his arms grip me tightly and his cock fill me.

The mattress squeaked and the smell of cum permeated the air. Aaron was grunting and growling. I was moaning and whimpering. I turned my head back to him, found his lips, and we exchanged a wet, messy kiss. Then I peered into his eyes and gasped at what I saw. His look was feral, primal, and fucking erotic as hell.

"Jesus, fuck, Aaron."

I threw my head back against his chest and increased the force of my thrusts back and the speed of my strokes.

"Fuck me, Aaron. Fill me."

He groaned and pumped more forcefully. It still wasn't enough.

"Harder. Fuck me like you mean it. Make me feel it all day tomorrow, Aaron."

His hands gripped my skin like claws, and he shoved his dick into me so hard I could hear the sound of our skin meeting like slaps. He leaned back, pulled me off the bed, and then pushed forward and plunged back into me. Then his pants turned into almost shouts, he called my name, and filled my guts with his seed. Somewhere in that time I must have come again, because my hand and body were wet and sticky.

I collapsed onto the bed, rolled onto my back underneath him, and pulled him down on top of me and into a deep kiss.

"You okay?" His voice was soft, and he was gently stroking my ass. He did that frequently after we'd had sex. "I know that I don't have much or, well, any experience, but is it okay?"

Okay? Talk about an understatement. Funny, his lack of experience had concerned me a little at first. At least, I thought it had, hard to remember now. But there had never been anything virginal about Aaron in bed. The man was strong, self-assured, and in control. And that was hot, hot, and really fucking hot.

"You're an incredible lover. I never knew it could be like this. It's like my skin burns for you sometimes, Aaron."

Jesus! Who talks like that? I sure as hell never had, until that moment. I lowered my eyes. Aaron lifted my chin so that our eyes met again.

"You make me feel so much, Zach. I can't get enough of you, as you may have noticed."

Our eyes stayed locked together for a few long moments.

"That's good, because I wouldn't want to be alone in these feelings."

He smiled and touched his forehead to mine.

"Let's get cleaned up and go to bed. It's been a long day, babe. I know you must be tired."

We showered, changed the sheets, and went to sleep wrapped in each other's arms. Well, I went to sleep, anyway.

I woke up way too fucking early and noticed I was alone in bed. Aaron's heat and steady breathing was missing. Funny, I'd slept alone all my life, and it'd never been a problem. Yet, I couldn't imagine sleeping apart from him now. I missed his skin.

I blinked and tried to make out the numbers on the clock. Six thirty—we didn't need to be at work for at least two hours. Where the fuck was he?

"Aaron?"

I called his name as I made my way out of bed and padded into the living room. He looked up when he heard me come in.

"What are you doing?"

He was wearing sweats and a T-shirt, curled up on the sofa with the laptop on his lap (that's why it's called a laptop, assholes) and papers strewn around him.

"I'm running numbers, figuring things out with the house. I think we can do it. Do you want to see the spreadsheets?"

Spreadsheets? Really?

"Ummm. Sure. Let me get some coffee. I'm not completely awake."

I rubbed my eyes and stumbled into the kitchen.

"There should be a fresh batch in there, babe."

Sure enough. I took a mug from the cabinet, poured a cup, and drank half of it down. Then I refilled it and walked back to the living room. Aaron had cleared the papers off the couch and made room for me.

"Okay, so this spreadsheet will show you—"

I put my hand on his knee and squeezed.

"Hey, big guy, spreadsheets aren't my thing. Do you think you can explain what you figured out?"

He gave me a sheepish smile.

"Sorry. I'm a big geek sometimes, aren't I? Did I tell you that I majored in business with an emphasis on accounting in undergrad? I love spreadsheets."

I kissed his cheek. Fucking adorable. And smart. And have I already mentioned hot?

"Yeah, you told me. I think it's great. So what's the story? Can we afford the house?"

Yes, I said "we." And it earned me a huge smile and a kiss. With tongue. Totally worth it.

"Okay. So we can definitely afford to buy it. I ran the numbers, and if they lower the price ten percent, and we get a residential mortgage, we'll pay less per month for that house than we're paying now for the apartment and the overpriced rent on the current clinic."

"Really? How is that possible?"

"Well, we're paying crazy amounts now, for one thing. Month-to-month places charge a premium, and you know the story with the lease Kim agreed to for the clinic. And, for another thing, David was right. The cost of that house is quite a bit lower than the prices of a commercial building and a house combined. He was also right about the mortgage rates. They're a lot lower for residential property."

Okay, now I was getting excited. The house was

beautiful. I never even imagined living in a place like that. And the neighborhood sounded great. A place where we could make friends and build a life. Last, but not least, I liked the idea of opening the dog bakery and boutique. I wouldn't be cooking for people, but I'd still be in a kitchen, and I'd use my creativity in different ways.

"That sounds great, Aaron. Really great."

He smiled all the way up to his eyes.

"So there's one downside. We'll need to use a lot of our savings for the down payment. And we'll also need to use savings to buy inventory and fixtures for the bakery and boutique, because the mortgage will be for the house itself. After we spend all of that, we won't be able to buy the new lab and diagnostic equipment, and we won't be able to buy furniture for the house. Not unless we completely deplete our savings, which I'd rather not do."

"Okay. So what do you think, then? Is it still a good idea?"

I felt—I don't know, disappointed? I knew I'd been hesitant about buying a house together, but once I'd decided to let go of the damned anxiety and agreed to it, I'd realized that I wanted it. Really, really wanted it. The house, the job, the life. All of it.

Aaron set the laptop down on the floor, pulled me onto his lap, and wrapped his arms around me. I buried my face in his chest.

"It's absolutely a good idea. The location is perfect for us, the residence is everything we could want, and the business space is even better. And, like I said, we'll actually be paying less than if we bought the clinic and the house separately.

"Buying two exam tables and waiting room chairs is no big deal, so we can do that right away. We'll be able to save up for the new diagnostic and lab equipment in about six months, according to my projections. And that's assuming it'll take us that same length of time to replace the customers I think we'll probably lose because of the new location. If we don't lose as many customers as I projected, or if we get new customers faster, then we'll be in even better shape."

Well, that all sounded great to me.

"So where's the downside you mentioned?"

"Oh, it's not on the business end. That's a good deal all around. But on the personal front, we'll have to wait on things. The residential space is bigger than what we have now, and we don't have anywhere near enough things to fill this apartment. That means the new space will be almost empty. Buying everything we'll need to start the boutique and bakery means we can't buy things for the house. Well, not for a while, anyway. It could take a year or more, depending on how well we do and how much the things we want cost. I'd hoped that when we bought a house, you'd be able to furnish it in a way that you like, so it'd feel like home to you."

"Home is with you, big guy. I'll feel that way if we stay here or if we move. Doesn't matter where and doesn't matter what we have."

Have you ever felt like you were melting? Damn! The way he gazed at me when I said that, touched me to my core.

"Yeah?"

I nodded and put my forehead against his.

"Absolutely."

We stayed like that for several minutes. Aaron was rubbing my back. I was stroking his head, running my fingers through his hair.

"So what do you want me to do today? I can call David and let him know we want the house. And I can get forms from lenders. I can try to fill them out, but I don't know if I have the information they'll need."

"You're wonderful, you know that, Zach?"

I raised my eyebrows at him.

"I mean it. I can't tell you enough how much it means that you're here with me. That I'm not doing things alone anymore."

He sniffled a little and then kept talking.

"I already added you to all of the accounts. I faxed over all the forms for that yesterday. So when we get to the office, I'll give you the paperwork, and you'll have everything you need to get access. That should give you enough information for the lender to fill out the mortgage application over the phone and then they can e-mail it to us to review and sign. And, yes, please let David know. We'll need to sign an offer so he can submit it to the sellers."

"Sounds good, big guy. I have it covered." I got off the couch and pulled him up behind me. "Do you want to drive in together today or separately? Remember, I'm going to watch the boys while you're at the meeting for the gay rights group."

"I remember. I can drop you at Dean and Kimmy's house after work and then come pick you up. They don't live too far from the clinic. Besides, I don't want to lose any more time with you than is absolutely necessary."

I chuckled.

"You're a big sap, you know that?"

He nodded.

"Your big sap."

Mine. Yes, he was.

CHAPTER TWENTY-NINE

"THANK YOU so much for agreeing to watch the boys, Zach. I've been looking forward to this mom's night out for weeks."

Kim and I were standing in her kitchen, and she was pouring herself a glass of water. Aaron had his gay rights group meeting, and Dean was working late again.

"No problem. So, where are you going?"

I ran my eyes up and down her outfit. Fuck me heels, short, tight dress, lots of cleavage. Too much cleavage. It wasn't like I was into that kind of thing, but I thought I would've noticed earlier if Kim were stacked.

"We're going dancing." She must have caught my eyes resting on her chest. "What? Don't they look okay?"

They? She set her drink on the table, looked down at her breasts, cupped them in her hands, and shifted things.

"Damn water bra. I paid an arm and a leg for it. The sales girl promised that they'd look natural."

"Umm, they look fine, Kim. I was just surprised by the whole outfit, since Dean won't be with you."

She picked her drink back up, then looked at me and smirked.

"I'm not going to cheat on your brother, Zach. Not

unless Aaron changes teams, which seems continuously more improbable."

"I think the word you're looking for is impossible, and it's not you I'm worried about."

She patted my arm.

"That's nice, but I can handle myself. If a guy doesn't take no for an answer, I'll shove one of my shoes up his ass. No guy wants that."

She batted her eyelashes as she spoke and then she took a sip from her glass. I looked down at her shoes.

"What are those, about four inch heels? You're right, that's not enough for any guy."

Kim laughed and water came out of her nose and mouth.

"Damn it, Zach! Now I have to touch up my makeup."

She picked up her purse and walked out of the kitchen and into the bathroom. I followed.

"Any last minute instructions, Kim?"

She was applying any number of lotions and potions to her face.

"No. If they're tired and you're able to get them to go to bed, that'd be great. But Dean can't seem to manage that, so I don't expect anyone else to do it either. Well, except for Aaron, of course."

"Of course."

Have you ever spent two hours with three children under the age of five? I've run a marathon, and it took less fucking energy. All the crawling around and chasing them through the house finally had a welcome effect—Chad and Ryan fell asleep. I carried them into their room and put them in their cribs. That left Simon, and he could be occupied with more relaxing tasks.

"Want to color, bud?"

"Oh, yes! I'll go get my things, Uncle Zach. I have to hide them in my drawer so the twins don't get to them." He rolled his eyes. "It's hard having little brothers."

I choked back a laugh at his serious little face.

"I'm sure it is, bud. It's just us big guys now, so go get your art stash."

He bounced back to his bedroom and came back with a handful of markers and papers.

"Birds, Uncle Zach. Let's work on birds."

So we did. I spread the papers out on the coffee table, found the ones with the most white space, and taught my nephew how to draw birds. I knew the kid was only four, but I found myself thinking he had real potential. I was having fun, but when his hand started losing grip on the markers, and he was yawning almost continuously, it was time for bed.

"Let's go, little man. Bedtime."

"I'm not little, Uncle Zach. I'm a big guy, remember?"

He got up and walked toward the bedroom as he spoke.

"Oh, right. Sorry about that. Let's brush your teeth and put on your jammies. Then I'll read you a story."

I was halfway through the story when I heard the doorbell. Thankfully Simon was already asleep. I set the book down, turned off the light, and quietly closed the door.

I assumed that Aaron, Dean, or Kim had somehow managed to lose their keys, so I didn't look through the peephole before I opened the door. That meant I had no warning before the unwelcome trip back through time made the air whoosh out of my lungs.

"Lawrence!"

The black eyes that had haunted me through any number of nightmares, both real and imaginary, peered down at me. They were followed closely by the trademark scowl. And then my stepfather pushed his way past me and into the house.

"What are *you* doing here? Where's Dean?"

Get out. Leave now. You're not welcome here. Any of those would've been the right thing to say.

"Dean's not here. He had to work late."

Lawrence's eyes widened, and he spat the next question out at me.

"Where's that pretty little wife of his, then? I know he didn't leave your faggot ass here alone with his sons."

Okay, that was it.

"Lawrence, I'm going to have to ask you leave now. I'll let Dean know you stopped by."

I walked over to the door, opened it, and held it open for him.

"You can't tell me what to do, boy."

He marched into the kitchen calling Kim's name. I was worried he'd wake the boys, so I followed.

"Kim isn't home. She's out with friends, and she asked me to babysit. The boys are sleeping, and you're going to wake them, so stop yelling and get out. I'll tell

Dean you were here."

Those were my last words before I found myself pressed up against the wall in the kitchen with Lawrence's rough hand around my neck.

"You don't tell me what to do. I don't know what that little girl was thinking leaving you here with those boys, but I'm not going anywhere until Dean comes back."

I was struggling to breathe, but I managed to find enough strength to knee his balls. His grip on my neck loosened, and I squirmed away.

"Get out of this house, Lawrence."

I tried to get to the phone, but he caught my arm and spun me around.

"I guess you forgot the lessons I taught you. Well, I'm happy to remind you."

He pulled his arm back in a pose I remembered from my childhood.

"I'm not a kid anymore, and you don't scare me."

Okay, so I was scared. But I wasn't going to tell him that, and I wasn't going to back down. Not ever again.

"No, you're not a kid. But you're still a fucking fag, and I can still remind you what happens to fags. Those broken ribs and bruises will be a happy memory when I'm done with your homo ass."

I could see anger in his eyes. I was trying to pull my arm away from his grasp when I heard a chair scraping across the floor, followed by Dean's voice.

"What did you say?"

Lawrence was startled. Neither of us had heard Dean come in. Lawrence let go of my arm and turned toward my brother.

"Did you know your wife left *him* here alone with your sons? I was doing you a favor and making sure he stayed away from them."

I'd always thought of Dean as a gentle guy. He was a blurry memory from my childhood, but a quiet one. And now that I'd gotten to know him as an adult, I saw him as a loving husband and father, a caring brother, but not someone particularly strong-willed. Frankly, Kim ran that house and nobody would deny it. That was why I almost didn't recognize the man standing before me.

Dean's eyes were squinted together, and the little I could see of them looked black, not blue. His mouth was drawn in a tight line. And his entire expression and the way he held himself looked tense and furious. He was shaking and speaking through bared teeth as he walked toward me and Lawrence.

"He's gay, Lawrence. That means he's into men, not kids. Now, I asked you a question. Did you say you hit my brother?"

Lawrence hesitated for a moment before answering.

"I was doing your mother a favor. Trying to make a man out of him. He's nothing but a—"

I wasn't sure what he was going to say, because that was when Dean's fist connected with Lawrence's jaw and all hell broke loose. Lawrence wasn't a young man, but he was still big, bigger than Dean by a few inches and more than a few pounds. But Dean was in some kind of crazy rage, and he wasn't going down. In the blink of an eye, Lawrence was on the ground bleeding, and Dean was on top of him landing punch after punch on his face. I was in shock, but managed to snap out of it before Lawrence passed out, and we'd be dealing with a criminal situation.

"Dean."

He was muttering something I couldn't understand and striking Lawrence, who by that point was just trying to shield his face.

"Dean!"

I clutched his shoulder and shook him, wincing internally in fear that he'd hit me next. But he didn't. The sound of my voice and the feel of my hand seemed to break his trance.

"Stop, Dean. It's over. Stop."

He looked at me and blinked his eyes.

"He hit you? When we were kids, he hit you?"

I nodded and tried to pull him off our stepfather.

"It was a long time ago, Dean. I'm fine. Get up."

As if the anger and fighting weren't enough of a surprise, Dean's next move was even more shocking. He got off Lawrence and fell to his knees in front of me, hugged my legs, and started crying.

"I'm sorry. So sorry. Please forgive me. Dad asked me to take care of you. I was supposed to take care of you. This is all my fault. I'm sorry."

God damn. I was standing in my brother's kitchen with one large man sprawled on his back, bleeding, and another wrapped around my legs, crying. I didn't know what the fuck to do at that point. Thank goodness Aaron came in.

He walked through the kitchen door, looked over at me then down at Dean and Lawrence. His eyes ran over the scene for a few seconds, and then he laughed.

"Lawrence, right?" He walked up to Lawrence and stood over him. "I've heard a lot about you. None of it good." Lawrence sat up and reached his hand to Aaron, trying to get help standing. "Oh, I don't think so. I'm a total pillow biter, you don't want my cooties. Now get your hateful ass up and get the fuck out."

Hmm. Aaron was cussing. Hot. Well, everything Aaron did was hot, so that was no surprise.

Lawrence stumbled up and made his way to the door, with Aaron right behind him. As they reached the door, Lawrence turned back to Aaron.

"Your kind makes me sick. You'll get what's coming to you."

Aaron's side was to me, so I could see his expression. He smiled sweetly at Lawrence and then spoke with a thick Southern drawl.

"It's nice to know you're done picking on kids and ready to fight a man your own size. But remember one thing, this fag bashes back. I can take anything you can dish out, you piece of shit."

And with those words, Aaron grabbed Lawrence's shoulder, pushed him toward the door with one hand, and opened the door quickly with the other. That caused a door-to-head collision that made Lawrence's knees buckle. Before he could land on the kitchen floor, Aaron had the door open, Lawrence pushed out, and the door slammed. I wasn't sure whether he fell on his feet or his face. Not that I cared.

"Take your brother into the bathroom and get the blood off his knuckles. I'll clean up in here. If Kimmy sees this mess when she comes home, we're all going to be in huge trouble."

The sound of his wife's name brought Dean to his senses. He got up and started walking toward the door.

"You need to take my shirt with you. Kim takes the clothes into the dry cleaners, and she'll kill me if she sees blood."

And, with that, three grown men who took down a six foot five inch, two hundred fifty pound giant, scurried around like little mice to cover things up before they were discovered by a barely five foot, barely ninety-pound woman. Go ahead and laugh, you'd be doing the same thing if you knew Kim.

"I DON'T know how to make it better, Zach. I wish I could go back and do things differently. I'm so sorry I wasn't there for you when you needed me."

Aaron, Dean, and I were sitting on the living room couch. Dean had taken a shower and changed into sweats. We hid his bloody shirt in Aaron's car. The kitchen floor and door were clean, leaving no traces of Lawrence's visit.

"Seriously, Dean, it's fine. I'm fine. It wasn't your responsibility to take care of me. You were a kid."

He looked so damn miserable.

"It *was* my responsibility. I'm your brother. I'm supposed to take care of you. And I promised Dad. I can't imagine what you went through, Zach. I should have been by your side."

I rubbed his arm.

"Yeah, those were bad years. Very bad. But they led me to this place in time. They made me who I am now. And I wouldn't change that for anything. I happen to like who I am."

Aaron was sitting quietly next to me, letting my brother and me work through things. But when he heard those words, he pulled me onto his lap and kissed my ear.

"I like who you are, too, babe. I'm so lucky to have you."

"Good, everyone likes me. Now that we've got that settled, Dean, do you have any idea why father dearest decided to drop by tonight?"

Dean leaned his elbows on his knees and dropped his head into his hands.

"Money."

Ummm, what did that mean?

"Feel free to use as many words as you need to get your point across here, Dean. We're not charging by the syllable."

He got up and walked down the hallway. I heard a door opening, some other noises, a door closing, and Dean came back into the room holding a check. He handed it to me.

"I told you I needed to talk to you about Mom's estate. We finally got her house sold and everything settled. That's your half."

I looked down at the check. It wasn't enough money to live on, but it was definitely enough to furnish our new house or buy the equipment Aaron wanted for the clinic. I noticed the check was from Dean and Kim's personal account.

"I still don't understand why Lawrence was here. They'd been divorced for years before she died. And if this check is from Mom's estate, why is it coming from your account?" Dean wouldn't meet my eyes. He looked around the room like some sort of caged animal. "Dean! Start talking."

He sighed and his shoulders slumped. He looked down at the ground as he spoke.

"He was here because he's a dumbshit, and he's been trying to get me to give him some of the money, which I've refused to do. And the check is from my personal account because Mom left everything to me." His voice lowered to a whisper. "I'm sorry, Zach. I didn't want you to know that, but I don't want to lie to you either."

Huh. Surprisingly enough, that didn't hurt. Not even a little. The woman hadn't nurtured me at any time in my memory, she barely spoke to me and let her husband beat the shit out of me, and she hadn't tried to get in touch with me even once during the decade I'd been gone before she died. Not including me in her will was low on her shitty-things-to-do-to-Zach list.

I looked up at Aaron and handed him the check.

"Do we need this, Aaron, or are we going to be okay without it?"

He didn't even look at the check. Instead, he stroked my cheek and kissed my neck.

"We're fine, babe. Promise."

I turned back to Dean and returned his check.

"I don't want it."

He looked surprised.

"What? Why? You guys bought the clinic, and you're about to close on a house. And you don't have a paying job yet, Zach. She was your family as much as mine. The money is half yours."

Maybe before I understood what family meant, that would've made sense. Not any longer, though. I shook my head.

"She made me, but she wasn't my family."

I lifted Aaron's hand to my mouth and kissed the back. Our fingers were entwined.

"He's my family. And we don't need any of the past to start our future. We're fine. We have enough."

Dean stood up and raised his voice.

"Aaron, this isn't right. Talk to him. He needs to—"

Aaron squeezed me and kissed my neck.

"Put the money in the boys' college funds if you feel guilty. Zach's right, we don't need her money, and we don't want it."

He stood up and took me with him. Then he patted Dean's shoulder, put his arm around me, and walked us to the door.

"Get in bed before Kimmy gets home. If she gets one look at you like this, you're going to be faced with twenty questions."

CHAPTER THIRTY

IT WAS Sunday evening, and Aaron and I were cleaning up after dinner. Our offer on the house had been accepted and the sellers agreed we could move in at any time. The lender approved our loan request and promised to expedite the paperwork so we could close by the end of the year. Aaron had already planned to shut the clinic down for the week between Christmas and New Year's, which was great because we'd have time to get everything moved to the new space and be ready to open for business without missing any extra days. Unfortunately, that meant we wouldn't be able to spend as much time visiting his family as Aaron had planned.

"Okay, at the risk of exposing my inner geek, can we please make a list of what we need to do?" Aaron said. "I feel like the next couple of weeks are going to be crazy, and I don't want anything to slip through the cracks."

I got a pad of paper and a pen out of the drawer, sat down at the counter, and started writing.

"We need to tell the apartment manager that we'll be out by the end of the month, and let the landlord for the clinic know we won't be renewing the lease. We need to find a mover who can pack up the clinic files and things after hours and then move everything to the new space the day after Christmas, so we have the most possible time to unpack before leaving for Bryerville. We need to get the utilities set up at the new house. We need to make sure all of the people associated with the clinic—clients, vendors, etc.—know about the move.

"We need to order those two extra tables and chairs you mentioned for the new clinic space. And we need to figure things out for the boutique and dog bakery—how we want everything laid out, what types of display shelves we should get, and it'd be great to find at least some products for the boutique for opening day. I imagine a lot of that will be a work-in-progress, though. I'd like us to change our inventory out every few months, so there's always something new for people to buy."

"Wow. You're good." Aaron moved behind me and read over my shoulder. "This is a lot of work, Zach. I'm not sure we'll be able to get everything done in time."

I leaned back against him and enjoyed his warmth.

"We have two weeks. I can do a lot of it during the day, especially the calls and the change of address stuff. And we can do the rest after the clinic closes. There's not much to pack here. My stuff is already in boxes, and I think we can pack everything you own in less than two hours."

That wasn't a joke. The man had less stuff than anyone I'd ever met.

"Thanks, Zach. You do so much for us."

He was massaging my shoulders. It felt great.

"I don't mind. There's a lot of downtime working reception."

He kissed the top of my head.

"I don't know how I ever survived without you. It's hard to imagine being apart now."

I turned around and nuzzled his neck.

"Don't want to imagine it," I mumbled into his skin.

How weird is that, by the way? I'd gone over twenty-eight years without him in my life and at least twenty of those years being truly alone, and feeling fine with that. But a half year after meeting him and a week after moving in with him, I *needed* Aaron, an all-consuming, can't sleep without him next to me, want to touch him all the fucking time, crave his taste kind of need. There was no way to go back, which was fine with me. The last thing I wanted was to go back to a time before he was in my life.

Aaron was being oddly quiet, so I pulled back and looked up at him. He didn't meet my eyes. Instead, he moved to the sink, dried the last pot, and put it in the drawer. When that was done, he started fidgeting with his shirt hem and biting his bottom lip. Something was on his mind.

I got off the stool and pulled him to the couch. He sat down, then I curled onto his lap and looked into his eyes expectantly. I didn't need to say anything; he knew I wanted him to talk.

"I want to ask you something."

I ran my hand down Aaron's chest and reveled in the feeling of the hard muscles underneath his shirt. I leaned into him and inhaled his scent. He wrapped his arms around me and rubbed the back of my neck.

"Go ahead, big guy."

"I, umm, I know you said you prefer to be on the receiving end, but..."

Sex? That was what he was nervous to ask about? I should've known.

"Yeah, I do. But that doesn't mean I won't top. You want to try that, Aaron? Is that what has you all fidgety?"

I chuckled when he gave me a relieved smile and a little nod.

"I swear I will never figure out what makes you embarrassed and what doesn't."

I stood up and took his hand. He followed me into the bedroom without saying a word. I got the lube from the nightstand and set it on the bed next to us. When I looked up at Aaron, I noticed he was nervous.

"I won't hurt you, big guy, don't worry. I may not have a lot of experience on this end, but I've done it before." I rubbed circles on his stomach as I spoke. "Besides, you've got more than two inches on me, and I take you just fine. You won't have a problem. It might feel a little weird, but it won't hurt."

I didn't know whether Aaron would enjoy getting fucked, but I knew I wouldn't hurt him. The reality was that Aaron was much bigger than me, and I wasn't talking about his dick. He was much taller, much broader, just bigger. And a big guy like that could most certainly handle what I was packing. My dick was proportional to my body, which meant it wasn't anywhere near the size of Aaron's. It was nothing to be ashamed of, but as far as length and thickness, I was average, which was fine with me. I'd never been out there trying to attract size queens.

I really did prefer bottoming.

I stripped off my shirt and pants, then wrapped my arms around Aaron's neck and pulled him down for a kiss.

"This works better if you're naked."

I pulled down his sweatpants and briefs and kneeled before him to help him get them off past his feet.

"Take off your shirt, Aaron."

He pulled his shirt over his head, muscles working and flexing. Damn, he was so incredibly beautiful. I rose to my knees and found myself face-to-face with Aaron's dick. Yum.

I licked his balls, sucking each into my mouth. Then I ran my tongue up his cock, swirled around the crown, dipped into his slit, and sucked his thick dick into my mouth.

"Zach! Feels so good, babe."

Aaron twirled his fingers through my hair and moaned. I moved my hands to his hips, and nudged him until the back of his knees met the bed. He got the picture and sat down as I raised my body slightly so that I could continue sucking.

When I heard Aaron's breathing become faster and felt his balls draw up, I pulled off his cock.

"Lie down," I said as I picked up the lube.

He lowered himself onto his back and not surprisingly, his previously raging erection waned. My guy was scared.

I crawled on top of his body and kissed his neck, ear, and cheek.

"We don't have to do this. I don't miss it, don't crave it. I'm happy with our sex life, Aaron."

Okay, that last comment deserved an award for biggest fucking understatement of the year. I was way past happy with our sex life. Aaron was an animal in bed, completely raw, uninhibited, and powerful. Plus, he was totally hung and could go all night. And, as a final bonus, living with him meant that not only was the sex fucking awesome, it was frequent. Very frequent, as in multiple times per day. My balls sometimes ached from the sheer amount of use they were getting.

Now, if the man had told me he wouldn't fuck me anymore, we'd have had a problem. I probably wouldn't have liked giving up blow jobs either. And now that Aaron had introduced me to how good it felt to have my ass eaten, I think I'd put up a protest if that were being removed from the menu. But fucking him had honestly never crossed my mind. Like I said, not my favorite thing.

"I want to. I'm sorry I'm being such a baby about this."

His cheeks were red and his breathing fast. I wasn't upset with him, but I will say that I couldn't relate. I hadn't been nervous my first time. Well, not that nervous, anyway. Of course, I was pretty well sloshed back then, so that may have had something to do with my more relaxed state.

Aaron was lying on his back at the end of the bed, with his feet draped over the edge. I kissed him deeply and stroked his cock. When his body relaxed and his cock returned to full-mast, I moved my hand down and slowly lubed his ass then I scooted until I was standing in between his thighs, bent down, and took his cock into my mouth for another quick suck. He moaned happily and thrust his hips slightly. I moved off his cock, kissed the head, then stood and raised his legs so they were on my chest and his feet were over my shoulders.

Before I even touched his pucker, I put my hand on his cock and gently stroked him. His eyes were closed, and his arms were down at his sides with his hands clenched into fists.

"Relax, big guy. Try to enjoy this."

I wasn't sure at that point why we were even doing it. Well, I guessed maybe he wanted to at least try, which I understood. Deciding that the anticipation of starting with fingers would probably cause him more anxiety than accomplish any kind of preparation, I lined my cock up with his entry and tried to push in. That was a no-go. The man was so damn nervous that he was impenetrable.

I took the bottle of lube, added even more to his crack and my cock, then massaged the tight ring of muscles gently.

"Aaron?"

"Hmm?"

He didn't open his eyes. I moved my cock back into place and stroked his.

"Aaron, open your eyes and look at me."

His eyes fluttered open and met mine. I smiled at him and tried to show him with my expression how much he meant to me.

"Thank you for sharing yourself with me like this,

big guy. It means a lot. I love you."

I could literally see his body relax as he took in my words, and with them my cock, because I pressed forward as I spoke. Once I started, I decided to keep going until I was fully seated, then I kept my dick still and increased the speed of my hand on his cock.

"You okay, Aaron? Ready for me to move?"

He looked into my eyes and nodded.

"I'm good. Doesn't hurt, just feels...full, or something. Love you."

His words came out in pants, and his forehead was creased in concentration, but he didn't seem to be in pain, so I started the age-old back and forth motion. It'd been a long time since I'd been on the giving end of a fuck. Years, probably. I'd forgotten how good the friction and heat felt. Or maybe it had never felt quite that good because I'd never done it bare.

I lost myself in the motion and the feelings, so when I heard a moan, I was almost surprised that it came from me. Then I heard Aaron's responding moan, and I opened my eyes to meet his gaze.

"Love you, big guy. This feels so good."

I held on to his thighs and continued pumping into him, feeling my pleasure build with each thrust and each moan. Aaron moved his hand to his cock and stroked himself in time with my pushes. When I couldn't hold my orgasm back unless I stopped the friction, I froze over him.

He gave me a questioning look.

"It's too good, big guy," I grunted. "I don't know

how much longer I can hold back."

What could I say? I didn't have his stamina. Aaron moved his legs down from my shoulders and wrapped them around my waist, pulling me toward him and even farther into his channel.

"Don't hold back. Let go, babe. Give it to me."

So I did. I pulled out and pushed back in a few more times, and then I released and unloaded into him with a triumphant shout.

Once I caught my breath, I pulled out of his ass, bent over his cock, took him into my mouth, and sucked like a fucking Hoover until Aaron thrust his hips up and pulled my head down, filling my mouth with his seed.

I crawled up on him, and he held me as he scooted backward on the bed so that his entire body was lying on it.

"So what did you think?" I mumbled into his chest.

He kissed the top of my head.

"It felt good. Not as good as the other way, but it was nice. Is that okay?"

I chuckled and nibbled on his chin.

"Of course, that's okay. Just so you know, it does get better. Getting fucked is one of those things where practice makes perfect. Your body isn't used to the feeling."

"Thanks for being patient with me, Zach. I promise not to be so weird next time."

I reached down and pinched his ass.

"Ow! What was that for?"

"Trying to lighten the mood. Now stop apologizing.

This was nice. Besides, it's not like I want you to become some sort of dedicated bottom boy. That would put a real damper on things."

I didn't even have to look up to know he was blushing; the heat coming off his face was that intense. And the sex had been nice. Not the best, of course. That would be a tossup between the times that Aaron had his dick or his face in my ass. But still, it was sweet and loving and, well, nice.

CHAPTER THIRTY-ONE

I RELAXED in my seat and closed my eyes. Aaron and I were sitting on a plane on our way to Bryerville to visit his family. It was the first chance we'd had to be still in the past two weeks. My muscles were sore from packing, moving, and then unpacking. On the plus side, we'd managed to get the clinic completely organized and ready to go before we left. The residence was still in boxes, but we'd deal with that when we got home.

And we'd celebrated Christmas with Dean, Kim, and the boys. If you haven't watched kids open presents on Christmas morning, you need to do it. Their eyes light up, and they bounce around, all excited. Oh, additional bonus—watching Kim cuss up a storm trying to get toys out of their plastic jail cells. Seriously, that shit was encased in a hard plastic that couldn't be opened without heavy-duty scissors, and even then there was risk of lacerations. When the plastic finally came off, the fucking toys were tied down with some industrial twist wraps. I'd never seen anything like it.

"So Zach…"

I turned my head to face Aaron.

"Yes?"

“Now that I have you trapped on a plane, do you know what I’m going to do?”

“Join the mile high club?”

Aaron snorted out a laugh.

“You have a one-track mind.”

I raised my eyebrows at him.

“Is that a complaint?”

He shook his head furiously.

“No, sir. I like that track. I’ll happily run around that track all night. And all day. Wait, you’ve distracted me. What was I saying?”

Adorable. Absolutely fucking adorable.

“You were saying that you have me trapped on a plane, and you aren’t going to show me your snake, but...”

I paused and waited for him to finish the sentence.

“Oh, right. I thought you might want to get a little background on my family before you meet them.”

I furrowed my brows. Huh. I guess we hadn’t ever talked about his family. Pretty amazing considering how much time we’d spent talking on the phone before I moved to Emile City and then in person since I’d gotten there.

“I don’t need to be trapped for that. Give me the skinny.”

I turned my body toward him and tucked my leg under my ass. Aaron was in the aisle seat, stretching his long legs out. I was in the middle, and next to me was a man who kept sneaking glances at us, especially at our joined hands. I hadn’t determined whether he was curious, turned on, or horrified. Whatever.

"You don't mind?"

"Of course not! Why do you think I'd mind hearing about your family?"

"Well, I guess because you never asked about them."

Hmmm. Valid point. In retrospect, I hadn't asked him when we were first getting to know each other because I was recovering from my mother's funeral. After that, I didn't ask because I didn't want to tell him about my own fucked up childhood. And once that was out of the way, I didn't think about it. Truth was, family wasn't exactly something that occupied my mind, given the fact that I'd never had one.

I rubbed Aaron's knee.

"I'm sorry, big guy. I never thought about it. You know how things are for me. I have you and now Dean. But that's all new. Family has never been part of the picture for me, so I didn't think about yours. But I want to know about them."

Aaron turned his entire body toward me. He kissed my forehead and took both of my hands in his.

"My brother, Brad, is two and a half years older than me. His wife's name is Janie, and they have two boys. Donald is seven and Derrick is five. They want more kids, but haven't had any luck getting there. They're still trying."

I didn't say anything, but it struck me as odd that Aaron knew that level of intimate detail about another person. It seemed so personal, like the kind of thing only... huh, the kind of thing only family would know. Okay, it made sense.

"Diana is two and a half years younger than me. Good planning on our parents' part. Her husband's name is Cliff and they have four kids."

"Four kids!" Quick math in my head. "And she's only twenty-five years old!"

Aaron laughed.

"They got married right out of high school. Well, right when she graduated. Cliff is two years older. She worked while he finished up the last two years of college. They got pregnant nine months before he graduated. That wasn't an accident. And Diana has refused to use birth control since then. I'm not sure when she'll be done, but I know it's not now. Their youngest, Shawn, is six months old. If history holds, she'll be pregnant again within a year."

He paused in his story and waited for my expression to come back to normal. I had no idea why I was finding this so odd. I guess it was different from what my life had been. Truly, my circle of friends was around my age, so that made them older than Aaron's sister and around the same age as his brother. But none of them had kids. Well, none of them had relationships that lasted since high school either, or at all. Okay, so we came from different worlds. I already knew that.

"I'm good, Aaron. Keep going. Tell me what they do for a living."

"My dad is an accountant and my mom helps in his office. Cliff majored in accounting so he could go to work for my dad, which is what he does. He'll take over the practice one day. Diana takes care of the kids. Brad and Janie both work for my cousin's medical practice. Janie is a nurse, and Brad is the office manager."

That sounded so nice and so straight-out-of-fucking-television normal. It struck me that his siblings all worked with other family members, making me realize even more how close they all must be.

"Your family sounds close."

He nodded.

"Very. Not just my immediate family, but our uncles, aunts, and cousins too. I have sixteen aunts and uncles plus their spouses, sixty-eight cousins plus their spouses and kids. Almost everyone still lives in Bryerville."

I suddenly wondered if Aaron regretted settling in Emile City. I knew he'd considered going back until he met me. Was I keeping him from his family?

"Do you miss it, Aaron, living close to them?"

He leaned his head back on the chair and rubbed his thumb over the back of my hand.

"Of course I miss them; I love them. But I had to make my own family."

He opened his eyes and looked deeply into mine.

"When I was finishing college and trying to decide where to go to vet school, my cousin, Jake, called me. I'd gotten a scholarship to a great school out of state, but I wasn't sure I should go. Somehow, Jake found out. He was living in New York at the time, so he understood what it was like to be away. Anyway, he told me he understood how I felt about leaving home, but that I needed to build my own family, and we both knew I wouldn't be able to do that in Bryerville.

"That's why I left for school, which is where I met your brother and Kimmy, and they're how I met you. So he was right, I had to leave so I could build my own family. Best decision I ever made."

My heart started racing, and I felt tears forming in my eyes.

"Damn, Aaron. The things you say."

He raised our joined hands to his mouth and kissed the back of my hand.

"Damn, Zach. The things you make me feel."

"I'd like to cop a feel right now, but our friend here"—I motioned with my head toward the guy next to me—"might freak out. Or ask to join us. I'm not sure which would be worse."

Aaron laughed, then leaned down and kissed me.

"Based on the way he's looking at you, I think it's the latter. But he's destined for disappointment. You're mine, and I won't share."

"LOOK FOR a blue pickup truck."

Aaron and I were standing on the curb outside the airport with our bags at our feet.

"That one?"

I pointed to a beat-up truck heading our way. I half-expected a hound dog to be sitting in the back and a song about how the driver had been wronged by his woman to be playing on the radio.

"Yup."

Aaron waved and the truck pulled in and came to a stop in front of us. A large man with black hair and dark eyes hopped out and made his way to us. He pulled Aaron into a loose hug and then reached his hand out to me.

"Zach, this is my cousin, Steve."

"Hi, Zach. Nice to finally meet you. We were all starting to wonder if you were a figment of Aaron's imagination."

Steve winked, picked up our bags, and put them in the back of his truck.

"Aaron does have a great imagination, but I'm real. So which side of the family are you from, Steve? You two look nothing alike."

Steve and Aaron both laughed and spoke at the same time.

"Neighbor cousins."

I gave Aaron a "what does that mean" look. Steve tossed Aaron the keys and opened the door for me to slide into the middle seat. Then he got into the passenger seat and buckled up. Aaron walked around and got behind the wheel.

"Our dads were neighbors as kids, grew up next door to each other. The two families were super-close and that never changed. So all our family events growing up included the neighbor cousins just like our biological cousins. My dad says he has twelve brothers and sisters, but five of them are on the neighbor side."

Aaron stopped talking and a sad look passed over

his face. Steve reached across me and patted his shoulder.

"Four now, I guess. Aunt Bev passed away."

I didn't feel as sad when my mother died as Aaron and Steve looked when thinking of their aunt's death.

"Drop me back at the firehouse, Aaron. I've got another twenty-four on my shift, but I'll see you tomorrow for the barbeque and game."

Damn, I should've asked for more information about Aaron's family and our itinerary. I felt completely lost. Thankfully, Aaron was good about keeping me in the loop.

"Steve is a firefighter. They work in shifts, three days on, four days off. He took a break to pick us up and loan us his extra truck while we're here. And the barbeque is a family gathering. We eat, catch up, and then play Wiffle Ball. Family tradition at every gathering from the time we were kids."

Steve pointed at Aaron.

"Your man here is one of our star players. I'm going to see what I can do to get him on my team this time."

I wasn't sure what I expected from the truck driving bear of a man, but it was nice to feel acceptance. He seemed to have no issue with Aaron bringing home a male partner.

When we got to the firehouse, Steve surprised me by leaning down and giving me a hug.

"It's nice to meet you, guy. We've all been worried about Aaron since Michael died. We didn't know if he'd ever find anyone again, and we're so grateful he has you."

It was a sweet, but weird thing to say. If Aaron hadn't

told me about the "friendship" nature of his relationship with Michael, it might have made more sense. Although, thinking about how young Aaron's siblings were when they got married, I understood why his family might have thought heartbreak had been the thing holding him back. I suppose being closer to thirty than he was to twenty and still being single didn't make sense in a world where other people got married before leaving their teens.

That thought led me straight to another—the fact that Aaron had been holding himself back because he was waiting for true love like some sort of fairytale. And then my heart melted when I looked at him and remembered how he'd smiled at me that first day in Dean's kitchen, how he'd touched me that night in the bar, and how he'd begged me to let him love me the next night in bed. His beauty, kindness, and patience with me were staggering. Was that any different from a fairytale?

When Aaron pulled out and started driving, I unbuckled my seatbelt and inched toward him in the seat. He turned to me with a confused look on his face.

"What are you doing, babe?"

I let my fingers do the talking and ran them down his chest to his pants. I didn't bother with the belt, and went straight for the zipper.

"Zach!" Aaron's voice came out in a gasp.

I fished his hardening dick out through the opening in his briefs and through his fly, and then I bent my head into his lap and went to town. Aaron's musky sent, the heat of his skin, and the taste of his precum filled me so completely that I forgot where I was. I sucked and bobbed my head, moved my hand down his pants and cupped his balls through the fabric, and felt Aaron's hand on my head. Then Aaron exploded in my mouth, and I swallowed happily.

I nuzzled his dick and tucked it back into his briefs. I hadn't gotten his zipper up yet, when I heard a loud rapping sound. My head flew up to see a broad, tall man standing at the window. That was when I realized Aaron must have pulled over.

Damn, I just got caught with my head in Aaron's lap. My heart started racing with fear. Is that the kind of thing people get beaten for in this part of the country?

CHAPTER THIRTY-TWO

MY HEART raced and my palms were clammy. Did a redneck homophobe just catch me sucking cock?

Aaron patted my shoulder.

"Give me a minute, babe."

I sat up, and he zipped his pants, then opened his door and stepped out. I took my first good look at the man outside the truck. He wore boots, faded jeans, and a brown uniform shirt with a badge on the front. Police. Well, we might get arrested, but hopefully not attacked.

The officer stepped back from the truck, his side to me, and I took in his packed crotch and tight ass. His hair was a deep black and his eyes an incredible shade of green. His face had strong, masculine features and there was something almost frightening in his hard expression.

I've got to tell you that, even though I'd just been caught sucking dick on the side of a country road, my cock was seriously confused as to whether it should piss in my pants or come in them, because that police officer was hot as hell. Scary as shit, too, but damn, the man had a body that wouldn't quit and a face to match.

I looked away, afraid that staring at him would get us into more trouble. Then I heard the driver's side door open, and Aaron slid back into the truck with a smile on his face.

"Ready to meet my folks? Their house is just down the street."

He buckled his seatbelt and started the engine. I sat there with my jaw open, staring at him.

"That's it? We're not getting beaten or arrested?"

Aaron laughed and patted my knee.

"Nope. My cousin wants to meet you, but I told him he'll have to wait. I figured you weren't in the mood for introductions right about now."

I chuckled and reached for my seatbelt.

"That was another cousin? Damn, Aaron, that guy was—"

"Fucking hot."

I almost choked on my own saliva. Those words were so unexpected coming from Aaron's mouth. Then again, it was a perfect description of Officer Hard-On, so I couldn't be too surprised.

"Yeah, fucking hot about covers it, along with a pinch of fucking scary."

Aaron reached over and rubbed my arm.

"Nah, he's harmless. Well, that's not true. He's actually kind of violent. But not to family. Or at least not to me. Don't worry. You'll be fine."

Well, now. That did absolutely nothing to ease my concerns. Note to self: stay the fuck away from Officer Hard-On at the family gathering or risk getting beaten to a pulp if he catches me checking him out, which, frankly, was unavoidable. Like Aaron said, the man was fucking hot.

A short car ride later, and we pulled up to a green ranch house with black shutters. I was a little nervous. No past boyfriends meant no past meet-the-parents moments, and it wasn't like I had a good track record with my own parents. I didn't want to let Aaron down. Well, there was no choice in the matter. Besides, they raised Aaron; they had to be easy to get along with.

We got out of the truck, and I walked to the back to retrieve our bags.

"Those aren't coming in with us."

"Oh. This isn't home?"

"Nope. This is my parents' house. Home is with you."

"Awww. Now that is just about the sweetest and cheesiest thing I've heard all day. But why aren't we bringing in our bags?"

"Because we aren't staying here. There isn't room unless we want to sleep on the pull-out sofa in the den. Diana's old bedroom has been converted into a craft room, and the room Brad and I shared is loaded with bunk beds and cribs for the kids. We're going to stay at my cousin's house. We're just here for dinner and so you can meet everyone."

He leaned down and gave me a kiss. Then he held my hand, and we walked to the door.

"I CAN'T tell you how glad I am that you're finally here.

We've been asking Aaron to bring you home for months. Honestly, we raised him better than this. He sent pictures, of course, but that's not enough. Oh, and they didn't do you justice. You are such a handsome man. And an accomplished chef, from what I understand. I can't wait to learn some of your tricks. If only this trip wasn't so short. Two nights is not enough time. I know Aaron said you've got that new clinic opening, but—"

Okay, I know it's rude, but at some point, I stopped listening to Aaron's mother. I know, I know, but you have to believe me when I tell you that it wasn't intentional. My brain instinctively put up some sort of science-fiction-type force field after about thirty minutes of non-stop chattering. That wasn't the only mystical part of the situation. I wasn't sure Aaron's mother was human, because I hadn't seen her take a single pause to breathe. I'm also not sure she blinked, although I can't swear to that because there were moments when I looked away from her, trying to figure out if there was any way out of that living room.

"Are you doing okay?"

A new voice broke my trance.

"Huh?"

Deep laughter from the seat next to me. Oh, the other voice was blessedly quiet. I blinked a couple of times and turned to my right. Aaron's brother-in-law, Cliff, was sitting next to me on the couch.

"She went to check on dinner. I'd say we have about ten minutes before she comes back."

My brain tried to make its way back from the safe cave in which it was hiding. I eventually managed to get out a question.

"How long have we been sitting here?"

It felt like days. Not exaggerating here, people. Motherfucking days.

Cliff laughed.

"You've been here for at least an hour. No one should have to face Mimi on their own, so I came in to keep you company about forty minutes ago. Besides, I've been inoculated. I've known the Paulsons my whole life, and Diana and I have been dating since I was sixteen. After ten years of almost daily exposure, I'm happy to report that the first twenty-five minutes or so of Mimi's conversations are completely painless. I've even been known to enjoy listening to her now and then."

That was funny, right? I'm not being sarcastic here, I'm actually asking. You have to understand that my brain was numb, and I'd started to lose feeling in my legs. Why were my legs impacted when all I'd been doing was sitting on a couch, listening to Aaron's mother talk? I have no fucking idea.

"Where's Aaron?"

I left out the "How in the hell could he abandon me like this?" portion of the question. I'm pretty sure that was fucking implied.

"He's been helping Diana and Janie feed the kids their dinner and get them ready for bed. Come on, I'll show you where they are."

I got up on my wobbly legs and followed Cliff. As

we started walking down the hallway, he turned back to me and whispered, "Oh, and Zach, a piece of advice from the other guy lucky enough to marry into this family, don't say a word to Aaron or any of the Paulsons about what we just experienced."

"They don't know?"

I was incredulous. I've got to tell you, Aaron's mother was like a non-fucking-stop tape recorder. I've heard auctioneers who couldn't talk that long or that fast. How hadn't other people noticed that?

"Well, it's like they don't want to know. They think Mimi can do no wrong. I find it's easier to keep my mouth shut than to point out the fact that she can't. Trust me on this, I speak from personal experience. I've lived through two sex strikes, a half dozen nights on the couch, and any number of shouting matches when I've tried to lodge a complaint with Diana."

"Yeah, okay. Thanks."

Really, what could I say? I was still in shock, and Aaron had given me no indication of his mother's unholy powers, so maybe he couldn't see it.

We walked into a bedroom that had three sets of bunk beds lined up against the wall, with a crib at the foot of each one. There was barely any floor space left, and that small amount was occupied by Aaron, his sister, and his sister-in-law. The kids were all piled in the beds and cribs.

"There you are. I was wondering what was keeping you."

Aaron had a big smile on his innocent face, like he

honestly didn't know that his mother had the power to suck people into the torture chamber of her voice. I heard a snort and looked over at Janie, Aaron's sister-in-law. I could see that she was choking back laughter. She walked over to me and took my arm.

"Aaron, I need to show Zach some of the scrapbooks we've been working on. We'll be in the craft room. Will you please let us know when dinner's ready?"

"Sure thing, Jane. I'll help Di finish up here and then check with Mom."

Janie pulled me toward the door and Cliff spoke up.

"Oh, Jane, weren't you going to show me that..."

"Right. Of course. Come with us, Cliff."

The three of us walked down the hallway, past the bathroom, and into another bedroom that had been converted into what looked like a sewing room. There were boxes of fabric and colorful papers everywhere and two long tables flanked one of the walls. There was also a comfortable looking couch and that was where Cliff flopped down.

Janie looked over at me.

"Have a seat. We can hide out in here for a while."

Then she got onto her stomach on the ground, reached underneath the couch, and pulled out a flask. She sat on the couch, opened the lid, took a swig, and passed it to Cliff.

"Do you like vodka? It's odorless, so it's the only thing we can drink without being caught."

Thank fucking God. I joined my new favorite

people on the couch and waited my turn.

"Are you kidding me? It's the gay man's water. Pass it over."

Cliff handed me the flask.

"It's a good thing you drink. I know Aaron doesn't, so I wasn't sure. There's no way to survive more than three hours in this house without some sort of chemical assistance."

She was dead right. That house might not be in hell, but I could see it from there.

After a few swigs from the flask, I felt my body relax, and I started enjoying myself. Aaron's in-laws were funny, and we had a good time talking and trading stories. Then we heard a voice from the hallway.

"Cliff?"

"Shit! That's Di. I better get out there before they come in and take us all down. I'll try to buy you guys an extra few minutes."

Cliff got up and quickly walked to the door, slid out, and closed the door behind him. Then we heard his voice fade as he answered his wife.

Janie patted my knee and passed me the bottle.

"Here you go. Last sip for the new guy. I'll hide this in my purse and restock for tomorrow."

When I'd drained every last drop, I handed her the bottle. She stood up and straightened her skirt.

"I better show you a couple of pictures in case they ask questions."

She walked over to one of the boxes, pulled out a photo album and brought it back to the couch. I opened it and started flipping through the pages. There were pictures of the nieces and nephews, Mimi and Fred, Diana and Cliff, Janie and Brad, and some of Aaron.

"Okay, we better get out there. It goes without saying, but I'm going to say it anyway, because I don't believe in taking chances. No one finds out about this space, okay? It's like the bat cave. And I'm not being selfish here; it's self-preservation for you too. You can't give away our secrets without exposing Aaron to the nightmare that is his mother. Try that, and you'll suffer needlessly, because he'll never believe you. I risked talking to Brad about it after we'd been married for five years, and I'd given him two sons. He didn't talk to me for a week straight, and we didn't have sex for a month. It's a hopeless cause. Take my word for it. They're all blind. And that includes Fred."

My tension came back as we approached the door. I felt like I was about to face my executioner. For the first time in two weeks, I was grateful we'd had to do all the moving in such a short period of time because it meant the trip to Bryerville had been cut to two nights. I couldn't even begin to imagine the horror of being stuck with Aaron's mother for an entire week.

"What now? Dinner, right? All of us together?"

Janie nodded.

"Yeah, we're pretty safe. She's actually a decent cook, and she likes people to enjoy her food, so when we're at the dinner table, she's quiet, comparatively speaking."

Okay, so the dining room table was like Kryptonite. Got it. I trusted Janie. We hadn't known each other long, but nothing makes people bond faster than a common threat. In the case of me, Janie, and Cliff, that threat was a five foot six inch blonde with an unfortunate affection for Calico and a preternatural ability to talk about nothing and everything all at once but a tragically lacking ability to shut the fuck up.

As Janie and I were approaching the kitchen, I felt Aaron's strong arms wrap around me.

"We'll be there in a minute, Jane. I need to talk to Zach."

"Sure thing, Aaron. I'll let Mimi and Fred know."

Aaron turned around and Janie met my eyes and mouthed a silent, "*Be cool.*"

I know you're probably laughing about how silly all of that sneaking around sounds, but if you'd lived through a conversation with Mimi, you'd understand our pain. It was no laughing matter.

I followed Aaron into the scene of the crime, a.k.a. the living room. As soon as we were all the way in the room and out of sight of the hallway, he pulled me up against him and bent down for a long, deep kiss. His tongue swiped across my lips, then entered my mouth when I parted them for him. He moved through my mouth, then sucked my tongue into his. The whole time we were kissing, his hands were roaming over my body— shoulders, back, ass.

I instinctively started rubbing my hard cock against him. He felt so fucking good, tasted so fucking good, smelled so fucking good. Damn, the man turned me on like none other. I could come just from kissing him. And with that realization, I reluctantly pulled back.

"We've got to stop. I don't have clean clothes here, and I can't deal with walking into your parents' dining room with a huge wet spot on my pants."

Aaron groaned. He leaned his forehead down against mine and stroked my cheeks with his thumb.

"I don't want to stop, but I guess you're right. As soon as we get out of here, though, I'm going to taste your ass. I'll lick it, suck it, and then penetrate it with my tongue until you lose your mind. And when you're ready to come, I'm going to take you into my mouth and suck you dry, Zach. Not gonna spill a drop."

His voice was low and husky as he described his plans. And he was grinding his body against my cock with increasing pressure. By the time he finished his description, I was panting and barely hanging on by a thread. Then he flattened his tongue and ran it from the bottom of my jaw up to my ear. When he poked his tongue into my ear, I shuddered and cried out.

"Aaron, Aaron, can't...can't stop...gonna—"

The next thing I knew, my dick was plunged into warm, wet heat, and I came hard. I looked down and saw Aaron on his knees in front of me. My pants were pulled down below my balls and my cock was in his mouth.

I remembered where we were and looked around in a panic. We were still alone. I reached down and frantically pulled my pants up.

"Sorry, Zach. I lost control there. Don't know what I was thinking. I'm so attracted to you."

Okay, that was a stupid move, and it could've resulted in tremendous humiliation. But how could I get mad at him when I'd done the same thing in the truck? And besides, all's well that ends well, right? And that ended really fucking well.

"No worries, big guy. We need to get in there, because we're holding up dinner. But if your parents' dining room table is the right height, you can bend me over it and fuck me between courses."

A surprised cough from Aaron followed by a groan.

"No way am I going to be able to concentrate on dinner now. That visual is going to distract me throughout the meal."

I turned and waggled my eyebrows at him.

"The visual and my hand in your lap. You better hope for a long tablecloth."

CHAPTER THIRTY-THREE

DINNER WITH Aaron's family was actually fun. Janie was right, his mother was relatively normal in that setting. Other people were given an opportunity to exercise their vocal cords, and she had long stretches of silence while she ate or drank. Note that by "long stretches" I meant relative to her normal speech patterns, so forty-five seconds constituted long.

Anyway, the food was good. I sat with Aaron on one side and Cliff on the other. Janie was across the table, and when Mimi did something particularly insane, I'd feel a light kick on my ankle from across the way. That always made me look down, so I could swallow my laugh before someone started wondering what we were up to. I was half-worried Aaron would start asking about what was so fucking interesting on my plate that I kept examining it so closely, but thankfully, he was having such a nice time catching up with his family, he didn't notice.

After we finished eating, we helped clean up and then said our goodbyes. The nieces and nephews were staying the night, but the rest of us walked out front together. I was halfway to the truck when I heard a new voice.

"Goodnight, everyone. We'll see you tomorrow at the barbecue."

I stopped in my tracks when I realized that must have been Aaron's dad. Fucking hell. I hadn't heard the man say a single word in the three hours we'd been in that house. How was that possible? And was he so damn quiet because he was married to Mimi, or did he and Mimi fall for each other because together their speech averaged to an almost normal amount of words per second? Kind of like a chicken or egg conundrum. I'll let you keep chewing on that one; I've never figured it out.

"Is your cousin's place far?"

Aaron chuckled.

"Nothing is far. He's in Bryerville proper, not one of the neighboring towns. You'll like him. He's a real sweetheart of a guy. Incredibly kind and decent."

I reached over and rubbed my hand on Aaron's leg.

"Must run in the family."

He patted my hand, then lifted it to his mouth and kissed it.

By the time we got to his cousin's house, it was pretty late.

"I'm going to call his cell and let him know we're out here. If we knock on the door, we might wake his daughter."

I nodded, got out of the truck, and picked up our bags.

"Hey, we're out front. 'Kay. See you in a sec."

Aaron ended the call and took one of the bags from me. Then he put his arm around me and walked me to the door.

"How many kids does this cousin have?"

"One. Adorable, precocious little girl. She's four going on fourteen."

The front door opened, and Aaron's cousin came running out. His hair was a lighter shade of blond than Aaron's, his eyes a lighter shade of blue, his skin a lighter color, and his frame was, well, lighter. Not scrawny, but he didn't have Aaron's muscular build. The guy was cute, nothing more.

Aaron dropped his bag and the two of them shared a long, warm hug.

"Missed you so much, Air Bear. Glad you're here."

"I missed you too."

Aaron kissed his cousin's cheek, then turned to me.

"Zach, I want you to meet one of my lifelong role models. Nate, I want you to meet my life partner."

I held myself back from rolling my eyes or teasing Mister Schmaltzy.

"Wonderful to meet you, Zach."

Nate gave me a hug, took my bag, and walked us to the door.

"What can I get you to drink? I know alcohol is out, but we have tea, soda, milk, and juice."

"I'd love a glass of milk, Nate. But I'll get it myself. And Zach drinks."

Aaron turned to me.

"What can I get you, babe? They have a well-stocked fridge and liquor cabinet."

"Geez, Aaron, if you're trying to liquor me up so you can have your way with me I should tell you up front that I'm a sure thing."

The words came out of my mouth before I'd had a chance to think. Was that inappropriate? His cousin was our age, so I figured it was probably fine. Plus, if this cousin compared notes with Officer Hard-On at the family gathering, they'd come to the conclusion that, if nothing else, I was honest.

Aaron laughed at my comment, but waited for my real answer.

"Water is fine, big guy. Thanks."

"Nate?"

"A glass of water would be great for me too. Thanks, Air."

Nate and I sat on the couch while Aaron went into the kitchen to get our drinks. He absently turned his wedding band around his finger. It was an interesting shade of gold. From a distance the metal looked brushed, but up close I could see that it was actually worn—full of scratches and dings that gave it character and depth.

"How long?"

Nate looked up at me.

"Excuse me?"

I gestured toward his wedding ring.

"How long have you been together?"

I didn't actually give a shit. I was making conversation.

"We've always been together. From the beginning."

Before I could closely ponder what the fuck he

meant by that, Aaron came back with our drinks. Then the three of us sat on the couch and talked. Talking with Aaron's cousin was...fine. He was nice, asked questions, nodded his head at the right times, seemed to care about Aaron, and he was clearly smart. More than smart, probably sporting some genius IQ. But it was like he wasn't, I don't know, completely there. The whole picture—his appearance, the way he held himself, the way he spoke—the whole thing actually reminded me of a picture. A faded one. You know those old Polaroid cameras? The ones that printed those instant pictures? I remember finding one of those pictures in a drawer once. It had faded. I could still see the image, still know what was there, but it was all ...lighter, hazier.

That was what Aaron's cousin was like. Until he wasn't.

"Jake's home."

In the same moment he said those words, Nate's blue eyes sparkled, his fair skin glowed, his posture lifted and straightened, and a truly magnificent smile lit up his face. And just like that, Aaron's cousin went from being cute to being incredibly beautiful. The sudden metamorphosis made me gasp.

He got up and walked toward the kitchen. I wasn't sure why, because I hadn't heard anyone come in.

"What was that?"

Aaron smiled at me.

"That was Nate. The other guy we've been talking to was a placeholder."

I looked at him, waiting for him to explain what

the fuck that meant, but he didn't say anything else.

"Aaron? What kind of new age bullshit is that? What do you mean?"

He stroked my leg.

"New age bullshit, huh? You're saying you didn't see it? Everyone else does."

I did see it. Weirdest fucking thing I'd ever seen. It was like the guy transformed right before my eyes.

"Yeah, I saw it. What the fuck was it?"

"Do you believe in soul mates?"

Okay, seriously?

"Aaron, come on."

"Hey, I'm answering your question. Wait until you see them together, and you'll understand. Can't have one without the other, and when you do, neither is whole. I know it sounds strange, but trust me on this. My parents have been married for over thirty years, but Nate and Jake are the reason I believe in true love. I've never seen two people more committed to each other. It's inspiring. You'll see for yourself in a minute. Jake's home."

Nate and Jake? So Nate was the gay cousin. Huh. I hadn't realized that, but I'd been thrown off by the wedding ring and the kid. And was I the only one who hadn't seen or heard anyone else come into the house?

"I didn't hear him either."

"Huh?"

I looked at Aaron, wide-eyed.

"That's what you were wondering, right? I saw the confused look on your face. Each of them always knows when the other one is there. I didn't hear Jake come in, but I'd bet my last dollar that he's in the kitchen now. The two of them are probably saying their hellos, and then Jake will come meet you."

I needed to clear my head for a few minutes. That weird change in Nate's entire posture and appearance had thrown me. Plus, I didn't know what to make of the whole soul mates, sense-each-other's-presence thing. It was fucking strange as shit.

"Where's the bathroom, Aaron?"

"Down the hall, second door on the left."

I used the facilities, washed my hands, and splashed some water on my face. When I approached the living room, I heard a deep, rough voice.

"So you finally managed to make it out of the truck, Aaron? Looked pretty cozy in there."

I walked in and was surprised to see the owner of that voice. It was Officer Hard-On. Only he didn't look menacing anymore. His green eyes were softer and his stance more relaxed.

"Come on, Owens. We both know it's nothing you haven't seen before. I went camping with you two last year and our tents weren't that far apart, remember?"

Aaron reached his hand out to me when he saw me enter the room.

"Zach Johnson, this is my cousin, Jake Owens. He's actually a cousin twice over. Once on the neighbor cousin side and another because he's Nate's partner."

Jake walked over to me and held out his hand.

"Nice to meet you, Zach. Aaron's been talking and writing about you for months."

He looked into my eyes when he spoke. There was something about him that made me feel at ease. Wait, did Aaron say this guy was his cousin's partner? He was gay? I wondered what the return policy was on gaydar, because my shit had been on the fritz since the first day I'd met Aaron.

I shook Officer Hard-On's...Jake's hand. So Aaron had told them about me, but I knew nothing about them. I made a mental note to apologize for making him feel like I wasn't interested in this part of his life.

My brain barely began registering another person entering the room when Jake dropped my hand, reached behind himself instinctively, and pulled Nate up to his side. Then he twined his arm around Nate's waist and pulled him up against his chest.

"How's Billy?"

Jake kissed Nate's forehead and stroked the back of his neck. Nate melted into the embrace, nestling his face into the base of Jake's throat. It was an incredibly intimate and tender moment. Aaron was right; you could practically see the feelings between them rippling through the air.

"He's going to be fine."

Another kiss, this time on the top of Nate's head, and then Jake looked at us.

"One of the boys on my team. He lost his father a couple of months ago, and he's having a rough time."

Aaron pressed himself against my back and wrapped his arms around me, enveloping me in warmth.

"When he's not out keeping Bryerville safe from

crime, Jake coaches over at the high school."

I nodded and made an "umm-hmm" sound. Aaron gave a little chuckle.

"Okay, guys. I think we better hit the sack. Zach's practically asleep on his feet."

I'd have argued about that, insisted I was wide awake so Aaron could catch up with his cousins, but I thought the yawn escaping my mouth at that moment would've made my lack of sincerity painfully obvious.

"I'll show Zach the guest room and make sure you guys have clean towels and whatever else you need."

Jake walked over to the bags we had set down by the door.

"Just these?"

He raised his eyebrows in question.

"Yeah. We're only here for two nights."

He nodded, picked both bags up like they were made of feathers, and walked down the hall. I followed him and tried not to look at his ass. Truly, I wasn't interested in anyone other than Aaron, but I was only human, and that man had an ass made for jeans. When we got into the room, Jake set the bags down, walked into the attached bathroom, satisfied himself that we had everything we needed, and then joined me in the bedroom.

"So you had dinner with Mimi and the gang tonight?"

I nodded carefully and tried to read the amused look on Jake's face.

"Janie and Cliff still self-medicating in the craft room?"

Slight panic flooded my stomach. I'd been sworn to secrecy, so I didn't know what to say.

Jake laughed.

"I'm a detective, and those two aren't exactly great at hiding things. Don't worry; your secret is safe with me."

Well, this was silly. No reason to panic. The whole thing was actually kind of funny, now that I was safely out of range from Mimi's bionic voice.

"Thankfully, yes, they still keep the flask there. I don't think I'd have made it otherwise."

Jake nodded in understanding.

"Yeah, Mimi is a real piece of work. I don't really have in-laws. Nate and I had four parents growing up, even though biologically one set was his and the other mine. Still having his folks around is one of the things that gave me the strength to go on after my folks died. Of course the main reason I was able to survive was Nate, but what's new with that? He's always been the reason for everything. I don't exist without Nate."

Jesus! How was I supposed to respond to that? Thankfully, Jake didn't seem to expect a reply. He patted my shoulder.

"Get some sleep. You'll meet the whole clan tomorrow at the barbeque. That's going to take all your energy."

I said goodnight, took a fast shower, and crawled into bed as Aaron entered the room.

"Hey. Sorry it took me a while to get in here. I was chatting a little more with Nate."

I sat up in the bed and watched Aaron undress.

"I'm sorry."

He looked up and raised his eyebrows.

"Why are you sorry?"

"I'm sorry that I didn't think to ask about your family."

Aaron joined me on the bed and pulled me onto his lap. I settled my head on his shoulder and enjoyed the warm feeling of his hand caressing my back.

"Don't be sorry. It's okay. Besides, you're here now, and you'll meet them all. This way, when we get back home, and I tell you stories, you'll have faces to go with the names."

I sighed and relaxed against Aaron's hard body. Damn, he felt good. Warm, strong, safe. I must have drifted off because his whisper startled me.

"Zach?"

"Mmm hmm."

"I know it's soon and this is your first time meeting everyone, and that we live far away, so it'll take time, but I hope eventually you'll feel like they're your family too."

A million cousins, a maddening mother, a bunch of kids running around. I had to be out of my fucking mind in love with the guy, because instead of bolting, I kissed his neck and said, "Well, we can't open the clinic on weekends at all because of the zoning restriction, so let's try to get out here more often. No reason we can't find at least one weekend a month to come visit. That way I can get to know them better, and you can keep in closer touch with them."

Aaron clung to me and cleared his throat. His voice

was husky when he finally spoke.

"Thank you, Zach. I can't tell you what that means to me."

He didn't need to tell me. I already knew.

"I love you, Aaron."

CHAPTER THIRTY-FOUR

I DIDN'T know whether it was the feeling of a new bed or general restlessness from traveling, but I woke up in the middle of the night and couldn't get back to sleep. Insomnia advice for all of you—get off. A good orgasm always helps me fall asleep. Of course, thinking of my dick immediately made me think of Aaron.

I didn't want to wake him, honest. I just wanted to feel his skin against mine, smell him, maybe taste him a little. I think it was the last one that woke him. I was stroking myself and licking Aaron's nipple when he shifted and his breathing changed.

"Mmmm. Feels good, babe. What time is it?"

One more lick, and then a little suck.

"It's three in the morning. Didn't mean to wake you. Go back to sleep, big guy."

He must have felt my arm moving because he reached over, rested his hand on my shoulder, and then gently moved it down my upper arm, past my elbow and forearm, and rested it on top of my hand, joining my movement.

"This is so much better than sleep."

Oh well, can't argue with that logic. Might as well

blow him. What? That non sequitur doesn't make sense to you? Clearly, that's because you haven't seen Aaron's dick.

I ran my tongue down his chest, over his ribs, into his belly button, and then eventually made it over to his cock. I twirled my tongue around the crown, flicked the ridge, dipped into his slit, and then sucked on the head. The whole time I worked on his body with my mouth, Aaron ran his hand over my shoulders and back, then on my ass and up and down my crack.

I instinctively pushed back against his fingers and humped the mattress.

"Oh, Christ! Zach, come here."

He wrapped his arm around my waist and pulled me up against him, then over his body, so I was straddling him with my ass pointing at his face and my cock pressed against his chest. As you might imagine, that was like pouring kerosene on the humping fire, and I increased the pace of my hips along with the motion of my mouth bobbing up and down on his dick.

"Ugh, so good! Zach!"

I raised my mouth off Aaron's cock to give his crown another lick when I felt him grasp my hips and pull me backward. My ass slammed onto his chin, and he raised my body so that I was essentially sitting on his face. Then he opened his mouth and started licking and sucking my ass with an unmatched ferocity.

"Aaron... Aaron... What... Oh, damn!"

I moved my hand to my dick and stroked myself while I rode his face like a fucking horse. I briefly thought that maybe the whole thing was too much, that he couldn't possibly be enjoying my ass on his face like that. But Aaron was penetrating me with his tongue and making moaning and whimpering noises that clearly indicated pleasure. Oh, and I had a good view of his dick from that position, and it was leaking like a fucking faucet.

The sight of his hard dick, the head a dark purple, a string of precum connecting it to the puddle forming on his stomach, proved to be my undoing. I reluctantly removed my ass from Aaron's face, and licked my way down his chest to his stomach where I cleaned up his seed. When that was done, I swallowed his cock and sucked hard while I pumped my dick against his chest.

My ass was dripping with his saliva, so there was plenty of lubrication for Aaron's fingers, which promptly found their way to my opening. First one, then two, and finally three of his big fingers fucked my hole in time with the motion of my hips humping his chest.

My moans were muffled by his big dick in my mouth. So Aaron's cries of "Oh, God!" and "Yes, Zach!" were the main noises that filled the air as he pushed his fingers deep into my hole and thrust his hips up. I didn't know which one of us lost it first, but after a few minutes, my mouth flooded with his cum as I unleashed onto his chest and stomach.

I swallowed every drop, moaned in appreciation, and suckled his softening member. Eventually, I pulled off, turned around, and crawled up his body. I licked his throat and gnawed the base of his neck where it met his shoulder. He ran his hands up and down my back, whimpered quietly, and whispered loving words into my ear.

We must have both drifted off to sleep, because the next thing I remembered was the sun sneaking in through the shutters. I was lying on my side, and Aaron was spooned behind me, warm and strong, with his arm wrapped around my chest.

"Morning, beautiful. Thanks for last night."

His voice was rough with sleep, which I found sexy as hell. I wiggled my ass back against him to test the state of events. My guy passed that test with flying colors when I felt his hard dick twitch, and he pushed forward. Aaron ran his hand down the side of my body and rested it on my hip. He kissed the side of my neck and sighed.

"You feel so good, Zach."

I continued my wiggle and added a thrusting motion so that I was pushing back against his dick.

"Yeah? I bet I feel even better inside. Wanna check?"

His breath hitched, and I felt him nod against my chin. Then his warmth left my back, and I heard him ruffle through one of our bags, which was next to the bed. The sound of a cap snapping open preceded the cool lube that he rubbed into my pucker. Aaron slid his knee between my legs, and lined his lubed cock against me.

I pushed back as Aaron pushed forward, and he was in me balls deep, both of us moaning and grunting. He moved his slick hand to my cock and stroked me in time with his thrusts into my chute. His tongue worked the back of my neck, the area behind my ear, and eventually found its way into my ear.

"Mmmmm. You're so warm and tight. Love being in you. So good, Zach."

It was a slow, gentle fuck. Both of us still waking up, enjoying the warmth and feel of each other's bodies. Aaron tightened his grip on my cock as his thrusts into my channel became sporadic. As soon as I heard him gasp and felt him pulse inside me, I groaned and shot my load into his hand.

Aaron's moans turned into gentle sighs, and he nuzzled my neck and shoulders.

"I don't want to get out of bed. Don't want to get out of you, either."

His voice was muffled because he was talking into the back of my neck as he sucked on my skin.

I half-chuckled, half-whimpered.

"Well, we're at your cousin's house, so we have to get up. But next weekend we're back home. Don't make any plans, and we won't have to get out of bed for forty-eight hours. And you won't have to get out of my ass that whole time either."

Aaron groaned.

"If I get unfettered, uninterrupted access to your body for that long, I'm afraid you won't be able to walk."

"Promises, promises. Come on, big guy. Shower time."

FRENCH TOAST, eggs, and bacon were cooking in the kitchen when we walked in. Nate was standing at the stove, and Jake was feeding a beautiful blond-haired, blue-eyed little girl sitting in a booster chair.

"Good morning, guys."

I looked down at Jake to say hello, when I noticed his face and hair looked like they were covered with pink and lavender glitter. Aaron squeezed Jake's shoulder as he walked by the table and made his way to the coffee pot.

"Feeling extra gay this morning, Owens?"

Jake laughed and flipped Aaron off.

"Alexis wanted to look extra pretty, so we sprayed some glitter in her hair. That stuff tends to have a wide landing area."

Aaron turned back to the little girl, kissed the top of her head, and smiled warmly.

"You look beautiful, honey. I like your dress. I want you to meet someone very special."

He held his arm out to me. I walked over, sat in the chair next to Alexis, and reached my hand out to her.

"Hi there. I'm Zach. Can I shake your hand?"

She giggled and put her little hand in mine.

"Hi, Uncle Zach. Papa and Daddy told me you were coming. I've even seen you on the 'puter."

I looked at Jake with raised eyebrows. He mouthed the word "computer" at me. I guessed that Aaron had e-mailed pictures to his cousins.

"Yeah? Well, I'm much bigger in person."

Another giggle from the little girl, and then she

started telling me about her shoes. They were the plastic dress-up kind, and they must have been three sizes too big for her.

Nate put a plate of food in front of me and kissed his daughter's head.

"Grandma bought those for her. Jake and I were both only children, so she never had a little girl to spoil. She's having a ball. You wouldn't believe the amount of princess outfits, crowns, and plastic jewelry we have in this house."

That comment must have reminded Alexis of something because she started wiggling and begging to be released from her chair.

"The purple dress, Daddy! I need to show Uncle Zach the purple dress!"

Jake lifted her out the chair, set her on the ground, and she ran off in the direction of the bedrooms. Jake rolled his eyes.

"We're in for it now. One wardrobe change is never enough, so you should get ready for the fashion show."

And that was pretty much how the morning passed. We sat around, drank coffee, and helped Alexis with zippers, snaps, and buckles, only to have her ask to undo them all so she could put on yet another dress. In-between all of that, I got to know Aaron's cousins. They were great guys, and I knew that so long as we got to stay with them, the monthly visits I'd agreed to would be fun rather than tolerable.

"You guys are wonderful with her. Do you think you want more?"

Nate and Jake were wrapped around each other on the couch, and Aaron was looking between them when he asked the question. Jake turned to Nate, who shrugged.

"I never thought I'd get the chance for one kid, so I'm grateful for her and haven't thought about the rest of it."

The conversation was making me uncomfortable. At first I wasn't sure why. It wasn't about me. Why should I care whether those guys wanted another kid? And then I realized my anxiousness wasn't caused by the thought of what they wanted, but by the thought of what Aaron wanted. He was Mister Family Man, constantly helping his siblings and my brother with their kids. Was that what he saw in our future? I wanted to make Aaron happy more than anything, but I had no desire to be a father.

Aaron's voice broke into my thoughts.

"Want to go for a walk? I can show you my old school, the park where I learned to ride a bike, the first place I broke my arm...fun stuff."

"Yeah, sure. Sounds good."

We snagged a couple bottles of water from the fridge, put on our jackets, and headed out. Aaron took my hand in his and rubbed his thumb over the back of it.

"You okay?"

"I'm great. Why?"

"You drifted off in there. Seemed like you were deep in thought."

A shiver of happiness went through me at the reminder of how well he knew me, how tuned he was to my feelings and emotions. Damn, what a wonderful man.

I was so fucking lucky.

I reached my hand up and circled it behind his neck. Then I pulled him down to me. Our mouths met in a warm, soft kiss. His tongue ran along the crease of my lips, seeking entry. I opened to him and my tongue welcomed its mate.

Eventually we had to separate for air. I took the opportunity to answer Aaron's question.

"I was thinking about kids. When we were inside, I mean."

"What about them?"

"Whether you want to have them."

He didn't say anything, just started walking with his forehead creased. After a few minutes, I nudged him with my shoulder.

"Well?"

"Would you think I'm a horrible person if said no?"

Huh. Not the answer I was expecting—the "no" or the question.

"Of course I don't think you're horrible. But I am surprised. Kids seem like such a big part of everyone's life around here. And I know how much you like spending time with Dean's kids."

Aaron nodded.

"That's true. But I like spending time with you more. I'm pretty selfish, Zach."

If there was one thing Aaron wasn't, it was selfish. He was the most giving, generous person I knew. We'd managed to make our way over to the neighborhood park. I saw a bench underneath a tree, so I walked over and sat down. Aaron sat next to me, never letting go of my hand.

"There's nothing selfish about you, Aaron. What do you mean?"

"Oh, that's not true, at least not when it comes to you. I hate the thought of sharing you. And when you have kids, they have to come first." His voice lowered to a whisper. "I want to be first with you, Zach. I want to be the center of your attention."

His cheeks were red, and he was looking down as he spoke. I caressed his face, and he leaned into my touch.

"You are first with me, big guy. And you've been the center of my attention since the first day we met. You complete me, Aaron."

He sighed.

"I enjoy that so much, Zach. It makes me feel special and warm inside. I don't want to give it up, don't want to share you. I like having you all to myself at home at night. I like waking up with each other and nobody else to focus on. I like how much you take care of me, of us. Is that terrible? Are you disappointed?"

I'd spent more than half my childhood in a house where, on a good day, nobody wanted anything to do with me. So the idea that Aaron valued me so much that he not only wanted to spend time with me, but also wanted me all to himself, didn't disappoint me; it warmed me down to my core.

"I'm flattered and happy. I love that you feel that way about me, Aaron, that you want me that much. Besides, between all the kids here in Bryerville, and Dean's kids, we're like super-uncles or something. That's about as paternal as I can get."

I rested my head on Aaron's shoulder and brought his hand up to my mouth for a kiss.

"So it's you and me against the world, big guy?"

He nodded.

"I like the thought of that."

I SNUCK into the empty living room, sat on the couch, and picked at my plate of ambrosia salad. PS—that's not a fucking salad. Nor is it a fucking dessert. Hell, I don't know what the fuck it is, but I sure as shit wouldn't eat it. Every damn ingredient came from a can.

Are you wondering why I was hiding out in the living room when Aaron's entire family was in the kitchen and backyard enjoying the barbeque?

First, keep in mind that I wasn't jealous of Aaron's dead ex. But I have to tell you that my head was going to explode if one more fucking person told me a story about the poor man who'd been taken too young and how fucking devoted Aaron had been to him, how brokenhearted Aaron was when he'd died, and how they'd all thought Aaron'd live like a fucking monk the rest of his life in honor of his lost love. Now, to be fair, the stories always ended with an "it's so wonderful he found love again" and a "welcome to the family," but by the time we got to that point in the conversation, my skin was too itchy to hear it.

"They're wrong, you know. Losing Michael wasn't

the tragic end of a beautiful love story."

The couch dipped next to me and I looked up to see Jake's gorgeous face.

"I was living out of state when they were dating, but I'd met Michael, seen them together when I visited, heard Aaron talk about him. That wasn't love. The way he talks about you, looks at you, touches you whenever you're nearby, now that is love."

Okay, maybe I'd felt a little jealous, because hearing those words eased a knot in my stomach. Jake squeezed my shoulder.

"He called me the day he met you, said that you were the one. Then we talked again a few days later, and he told me you left, and tried to push him away and break things off. I asked him what he was going to do, and do you know what he told me?"

I shook my head.

"He said you were worth the wait and effort, that he'd waited twenty-seven years to find you and that no push was going to make him give you up."

Tears worked their way into my eyes as I thought about how patient and wonderful Aaron had been with me from the beginning. How he'd waited for me to catch up and own our relationship, even when I'd been a real ass.

"Welcome to the family, Zach. We're pleased as hell to have you."

And with those words, I truly felt like they were including me in their family, not only Jake, but all of them.

"There you are."

I looked up to see Aaron's warm, affectionate smile.

"I've been looking everywhere for you."

Jake got up and patted Aaron's back.

"He's all yours. I'm going to find Nate and Lexi. I think we've all had enough for one day. You ready to head back to our place?"

Aaron nodded.

"Yeah. Thanks, Jake."

Jake walked out of the room, and Aaron sat next to me on the couch. I set the plate of food (generous description on my part, considering the shit was inedible) on the floor, crawled onto his lap, wrapped my arms around his neck, and rested my head on his chest. He rubbed my back.

"Everything okay, babe?"

I nodded and mumbled an "ummhmm."

"I love you, Zach."

I moved my head off his chest and gazed into his eyes.

"Thank you for giving me this, Aaron."

"What's that, babe?"

"A family, a wonderful life, and a future with you."

Aaron kissed me and stroked my cheek.

"You gave me those same things, Zach."

THE END

(BUT WAIT…THERE'S MORE—BONUS CHAPTER AHEAD.)

BONUS CHAPTER

*When the U.S. Supreme Court released their histor-
ic marriage decision, I wanted to celebrate so I wrote
a bonus chapter with Zach and Aaron's reaction to
the wonderful news. I hope you enjoy it. —CC*

I'M NOT known for being particularly traditional or old-fashioned or nice or...fuck it, I'm a pervy, brash bastard. But if you've stuck with me long enough to be reading this, then you're just fucked-up enough to find me charming. Either that or you're a glutton for punishment.

My partner, Aaron, though, is everything I'm not. Case in point: marriage. Early on in our relationship, he told me that if we could get legally married, he'd pop the question. At the time, I nearly lost my shit. At twenty-seven and twenty-eight, I had felt like we were both too young to get married. Plus, marriage wasn't ever something I had wanted. Hell, dating a guy for longer than a few orgasms wasn't something I had wanted.

But my guy is übertraditional. Before we got together, he had been a virgin dreaming of finding "the one." No, really, that's the truth. An actual twenty-seven-year-old virgin. Those are so rare they're, like, collectors' items or something, right?

So Aaron was plugging along...well, not literally,

because he wouldn't plug anyone, if you know what I mean. Too much? Okay, I'll take it easy.

Aaron had this idea that he'd hold out for the perfect someone and then build a till-death-do-us-part life that resembled a Norman Rockwell painting. When we met, he decided I was the man he wanted next to him in that picture, and he put up with a whole truckful of my shit before I realized I wanted the same thing. Except with loads of butt-fucking.

Anyway, this is a long-winded way of explaining what I've known almost from the beginning: one day Aaron and I would be saying "I do." It was only a matter of time before all the work advocates like him put into the fight for marriage equality would pan out. The day the Supreme Court decided to take up the Defense of Marriage Act, Aaron was buzzing with excitement. And on that same day, I started planning a wedding.

Now, here's the tricky thing—I couldn't tell Aaron about any of my plans. When I say my guy is an old-fashioned dreamer type, I mean it. So even though he'd never come right out and said it, I knew he had an idea in his head of how his wedding would unfold, and it no doubt started with a proposal.

You might be wondering why I didn't just ask him and eliminate the need for covert operations, so I'll tell you. I figured Aaron had always dreamed of doing the whole down-on-one-knee traditional proposal thing, and I didn't want to take that away from him. So I planned and arranged in private while we waited for the court decision to come down, knowing it would impact whether

Aaron and I could make what we already had—a lifetime commitment—into something recognized under the law. And then the day finally came.

That morning started out like any other.

"What do you have going on today?" Aaron asked me over breakfast.

He was just finishing up his second bowl of cereal. He ate one bowl of Wheaties and one bowl of Special K, in that order, every single weekday morning. I stopped teasing him about it two years ago, which was probably about two years too soon, because, seriously, the same wholesome breakfast every motherfucking day? Who does that?

But I had to stop making fun of Aaron's breakfast of boring-as-dirt champions when I realized I had started doing the same thing, only with oatmeal. Of course, he never said a thing about my hypocrisy or teased me in retaliation, because he is the nicest person on earth. Thank fuck I was around to even things out. Between us, we were like an average person.

"I have a new dog biscuit recipe I want to try, and those jeweled, hand-stitched cat collars came in. I need to figure out the best way to display them." I managed an animal boutique and bakery adjacent to Aaron's veterinary clinic. Both of them were on the first level of our two-story house. "How about you?"

"I'm booked all the way through until six. I'm going to have to grab food in between appointments."

I grinned at him. "So pretty much like every other day, then, huh?"

He reached across the table and I put my hand in his. "It's going well, right? If we keep up this pace, I think I can hire another vet. I knew moving to EC West would increase business, but we're booking weeks out. I think we've got almost twice the number of new clients than I predicted." He furrowed his brow in thought, looking earnest and fuckable. I darted my eyes over to the clock, hoping there was enough time to get sweaty before work. There wasn't. "I don't know if I ran the numbers wrong or if I had bad data."

"Uh-huh." I was proud of myself for holding back my laughter.

"What?" he asked. "What's so funny?"

Apparently, my guy knew me well enough to discern amusement from my facial expression, even without an accompanying audio track.

"You do realize why we have such an influx of new customers, don't you?"

"What do you mean?" He looked honestly confused. "Why?"

I traced his plump lips with my finger. "Because they want to ogle the hot veterinarian."

Aaron blushed. "That's ridiculous, babe. Nobody except you wants to look at me."

I got up from my chair, walked over to him, squeezed in front of the table, and straddled his lap. "Every gay man and straight woman in this town wants to check you out, big guy." I circled my arms around his neck and dipped my face for a kiss. Aaron sighed and opened for me. He caressed my lower back as our lips connected and our tongues danced. When we separated, I gave him a cocky grin and said, "Sucks for them that you're already taken and there's only one man you're sucking." I waggled my eyebrows at that last part.

I saw Aaron glance at the clock and knew exactly what he had in mind. He had a serious oral fixation. I swear, if we were home alone for any length of time, he'd pounce and suck my cock down his throat or stick his tongue up my ass. Sometimes both. But not at the same time, obviously.

"No time, big guy," I told him sadly. I forced myself to get up, took his hand, and pulled him out of his chair. "We need to get dressed and get downstairs." I looked back at him over my shoulder. "People will be coming in soon, and you need to give them wank material for weeks to come."

His jaw dropped and the red started moving up his neck. I laughed my ass off.

AARON WAS changing into his work clothes while I ran some grooming clay through my hair. I had just finished getting everything into the perfect faux-hawk when I caught sight of him in the mirror and froze.

"Uh, Aaron?"

"Yes?"

I turned around slowly and leaned my ass against the counter. "What are you wearing?"

He looked down at his clothes. "Pants and a button-down shirt. It's what I always wear to work." He walked toward the door and said, "Are you ready?"

I crossed my arms over my chest and raised one eyebrow. "No, usually you wear clothes that fit. Those pants are two sizes too big. Where did you even find them? And are you going to tuck that shirt in?"

He tugged on the bottom of the shirt. "Uh, no. I think it looks good like this."

"Come here," I said gently.

He looked down, shuffled over to me, and wrapped his arms around me. I tucked my head under his chin.

"Are you mad at me?" he asked.

"Why would I be mad?"

"I don't know." He shrugged. "I wouldn't like it if guys were checking you out."

I tipped my head up and met his gaze. "Yeah, well, I'm just enough of an asshole to like the idea that everyone wants you but only I can have you."

"You do?"

That shy smile of his killed me every time. I swear to fuck, when he looked at me like that, all I wanted to do was drop my pants and bend over the nearest flat surface. I reminded myself once again that we had to go to work.

"Yes, I do," I said. "Now go change into your normal clothes."

"Okay."

Aaron walked back to the closet, and I called after him, "Hey, if you have a few minutes between appointments, let me know. We can make out in the waiting room so everyone can eat their hearts out."

He didn't say anything, but he stumbled a little and shook his head. I counted that as a victory.

UNFORTUNATELY, THERE was no time for semipublic make-out sessions. My poor guy was slammed all day. He was so busy, in fact, that I wondered whether he'd heard about the Supreme Court decision being published. It didn't take long for me to find out the answer to that question.

"Zach!" Aaron called my name just as the front door slammed open.

"I'm in the kitchen," I answered as I wiped my hands on a towel.

I'd finished work before him, so I'd gone upstairs, taken a shower, and started dinner. There was a white lasagna in the oven, and I had put together a lime vinaigrette. Just because I no longer cooked for humans in a professional capacity didn't mean my skills were now limited to those who got around on all fours. Come to think of it, I spent a decent amount of time on my hands and knees, so maybe that wasn't exactly true.

"I just finished up for the day and checked my e-mail." Aaron's face was flushed and he was a little breathless, as if he had run up the stairs at full speed. "Did you hear the news?"

"Yeah." I smiled at him. "Pretty great."

"Pretty great?" He marched over, circled his arms around my hips, cupped my ass, and then picked me right up and spun around in a circle. "It's amazing! You know what this means, right? We can get married! We can actually get married! There's nothing stopping us."

I tangled my hands in his hair and chuckled. "Well, there's one thing."

He stopped moving. "What?"

"Well"—I drew the word out slowly—"I think you have to ask me first."

It didn't even take a second before I was being deposited in a chair and Aaron was kneeling in front of me. "Zach," he said breathlessly. "Will you—"

After all that time waiting for what I thought would be Aaron's moment, I found myself just as excited. So much so that I answered before he finished asking the question.

"Yes," I said in a rush. "I'll marry you."

I don't think I'd ever seen him look so overjoyed. And I'm including the first time I went down on him. Do you have any idea how happy a guy is when his dick is being sucked for the first time ever? Yeah, exactly. And I'm no slouch in the sack, let me tell you. My blow jobs are legendary. So you can picture the level of happiness I'm describing here.

Aaron popped to his feet and scooped me into his arms, and then we were back to spinning and smiling and laughing. "I want to do it soon," he said. "We have to figure out where to go. One of the states where it's legal, of course. Maybe New York or—"

"I was thinking Massachusetts," I said. "There's a little inn in western Mass. The grounds are gorgeous, the chef is supposed to be amazing, and I have reservations the weekend of July nineteenth and an appointment with a justice of the peace on the twentieth."

The spinning stopped and Aaron locked his gorgeous blue eyes on my brown ones. "You have reservations? You mean, you—" He swallowed hard. "You planned this already?"

Suddenly I worried that I'd made a mistake, that I shouldn't have taken it upon myself to make choices we should have been making together. But then Aaron pushed me up against the wall, slammed his mouth on mine, and ground his hard dick against my hip, so I figured he wasn't pissed.

"Zach," he cried out when we separated for an oxygen break. "I love that you were thinking about this, about us getting married." He nibbled his way across my jaw, shoved his hand between our bodies, and groped my dick through my pants. "I need you, babe. Right now."

Then his mouth was back on mine, ferocious and desperate. He was making these needy whimper noises and grinding harder and faster. If he didn't let up a little, I was going to come in my pants. Fucking in the kitchen was fun—well, fucking anywhere was fun—but it wasn't what I wanted right then.

"Bed," I managed to choke out. "Aaron." He cupped my balls and squeezed them. "Ungh! Aaron, take me to bed."

He was rubbing my erection, sucking on my neck,

and rutting against me. "Okay," he huffed out. He thrust his hips forward and circled them. I groaned. "Okay," he said. "Bed."

My legs were shaky, but I managed to remain mostly upright when he set me down; then the two of us stumbled across the house, kissing and touching, bumping into furniture and walls, and somehow managed to remove our clothing along the way. By the time we got to the bedroom, we were both naked and breathless and so fucking hard it was crazy.

I fisted Aaron's thick cock and gave it a couple of strokes. "This won't take long, big guy. I am so damn hot for you right now. The second you shove this bad boy inside, I'm going to shoot hard enough to make myself go blind."

He laughed and kissed me, a bunch of pecks followed by a tug on my lower lip. I was so focused on his mouth against mine and his dick in my hand that I missed what he was doing with his hands until one was rolling my balls and the other was nudging into my crease.

"God, yes," I moaned. I walked backward toward the bed and held onto Aaron's dick, forcing him to come with me.

"It isn't a leash," he said with a chuckle.

"Bullshit," I answered. "I take hold of this bad boy and I can get you to follow me anywhere."

The back of my knees hit the bed then, so I toppled onto it and scooted backward, upside down crab-style. Aaron crawled up until he straddled me with his face above mine. "It isn't the hold you have on my dick that'd make me follow you to the ends of the earth, Zach. It's the one you have on my heart."

I know, I know. Mushy and fluffy and sugary sweet. Roll your eyes and laugh all you want, I fucking love it.

You know what else I love? Aaron's face buried in my ass. Which was exactly what happened next.

"Roll over, babe," he said, his voice deep and husky. "Wanna taste you." He licked his lips, and I had to squeeze the base of my dick to keep from shooting my load right that second.

I flipped onto my stomach, tucked my knees up and spread them out, then lowered my face onto the mattress. In that position, my ass was on full display.

"God, Zach." Aaron sounded awed. He ran a trembling hand down my back, into my channel, and then circled my pucker with one long finger. "You are so beautiful."

After a few seconds of him looking at me and barely touching, he made a strangled sound, grasped my ass and spread me open, and then lowered his face and started licking. He flattened his tongue and dragged it from just below my balls all the way up my cleft. When I was shaking and moaning, he changed approaches and started lapping at my hole.

"Aaron!" I cried out when I couldn't take any more teasing. "Need you inside."

I meant his dick, but he started with his tongue, pointing it and then pushing past the ring of muscle and into my body. He gripped my ass with both hands, leaving me completely exposed to his mouth and his tongue and his teeth as he licked and sucked and nipped and then started the whole process all over again.

Somewhere along the way, I lost all my mental faculties, and all I could do was feel and moan and cry Aaron's name out like a prayer. Then his big body blanketed my smaller one and he pushed his hands underneath my chest and held onto my shoulders as he pressed his swollen shaft to my sensitive entrance.

He slid in nice and slow at first, making both of us gasp when he bottomed out. Aaron kissed my nape. "Love you," he said; then he started thrusting in and out.

"Uh, uh, uh," I grunted and pushed back against his invasion, taking him in as deep as possible.

We moved together in a dance we'd perfected over the years. After a couple of minutes, Aaron pulled me up and leaned back on his haunches until I was practically in his lap, my back against his chest. Then he reached around, took my chin in his hand, and turned my head toward his. Our eyes met for a second before his mouth came down on mine, the kiss as powerful as his thrusts up into me.

I yanked my mouth away long enough to gasp, "Yes, Aaron, fuck me. Oh God, fuck me so hard!" And then I captured his lips and sucked on his tongue as I rocked my hips back, slamming against his groin and taking his dick in so fucking deep I could cry with how good it was.

If Aaron had so much as touched my dick, I would have gone off like a rocket, which he knew, so he kept his hands everywhere else—pinching my nipples, pulling my hair, caressing my face. But even without stimulation to that part of my body, I could only hold out for so long under his erotic assault.

"Gonna come, Aaron," I warned him. "Shit!" I whined and slammed back harder. "Now! Gonna come now, now, now!" I screamed the last word as the first shot left my dick, and I didn't stop shouting until I had painted the sheets with my release while Aaron pulsed deep inside me and cried out my name.

He sat back on his heels and held on to me, rubbing my belly as he kissed me, gently this time. "God, Zach," he said, his expression nothing short of adoring. "You're amazing."

I sucked on his bottom lip a little and caressed his hip. "We're amazing together," I reminded him.

Aaron beamed. "Well, then, it's a good thing we're getting married."

"Yup." I sighed contentedly and dropped my head back against his shoulder. "It really, really is."

THE END

OTHER BOOKS BY CARDENO C.

ABOUT THE AUTHOR

Cardeno C.—CC to friends—is a hopeless romantic who wants to add a lot of happiness and a few *awwws* into a reader's day. Writing is a nice break from real life as a corporate type and volunteer work with gay rights organizations. Cardeno's stories range from sweet to intense, contemporary to paranormal, long to short, but they always include strong relationships and walks into the happily-ever-after sunset.

Cardeno's *Home*, *Family*, and *Mates* series have received awards from Love Romances and More Golden Roses, Rainbow Awards, the Goodreads M/M Romance Group, and various reviewers. But even more special to CC are heartfelt reactions from readers, like, "You bring joy and love and make it part of the every day."

Email: cardenoc@gmail.com

Website: www.cardenoc.com

Twitter: @CardenoC

Facebook: http://www.facebook.com/CardenoC

Pinterest: http://www.pinterest.com/cardenoC

Blog: http://caferisque.blogspot.com

AVAILABLE NOW

He Completes Me
(2nd Edition)

Not even his mother's funeral can convince self-proclaimed party boy Zach Johnson to tone down his snark or think about settling down. He is who he is, and he refuses to change for anyone. When straight-laced, compassionate Aaron Paulson claims he's falling for him, Zach is certain Aaron sees him as another project, one more lost soul for the idealistic Aaron to save. But Zach doesn't need to be fixed and he refuses to be with someone who sees him as broken.

Patience is one of Aaron's many virtues. He has waited years for a man who can share his heart and complete his life and he insists Zach is the one. Pride, fear, and old hurts wither in the wake of Aaron's adoring loyalty, and as Zach reevaluates his perceptions of love and family, he finds himself tempted to believe in the impossible: a happily-ever-after.

Home Again
(2nd Edition)

Imposing, temperamental Noah Forman wakes up in a hospital and can't remember how he got there. He holds it together, taking comfort in the fact that the man he has loved since childhood is on the way. But when his one and only finally arrives, Noah is horrified to discover that he doesn't remember anything from the past three years.

Loyal, serious Clark Lehman built a life around the

person who insisted from their first meeting that they were meant to be together. Now, years later, two men whose love has never faltered must relive their most treasured and most painful moments in order to recover lost memories and secure their future.

Just What the Truth Is
(2nd Edition)

People-pleaser Ben Forman has been in the closet so long he has almost convinced himself he is straight, but his denial train gets derailed when hotshot lawyer Micah Trains walks into his life. Micah is brilliant, funny, driven... and he assumes Ben is gay and starts dating him. Finding himself truly happy for the first time, Ben doesn't have the willpower to resist Micah's affection.

When his relationship with Micah heats up, Ben realizes has a problem: his parents won't tolerate a gay son and self-confident Micah isn't the type to hide. If Ben wants to maintain his hold on his happiness, he'll have to decide what's important and own up to the truth of who he is. The trouble is figuring out just what that truth is.

Love at First Sight
(2nd Edition)

The moment naïve, optimistic Jonathan Doyle glimpses a gorgeous blue-eyed stranger from afar, he believes in love at first sight. Unfortunately, he loses sight of the man before they meet and then spends years desperately trying to find him. Just as he is about to give up, Jonathan gets a break and finally encounters David Miller face to face.

Successful, confident David turns Jonathan's previously lonely life into a fairy tale, giving him more than he ever imagined. But the years spent searching were hard on Jonathan, and he's terrified his young son and scandalous past will destroy his blossoming relationship. For David and Jonathan to build a future together, they'll both have to dig deep: David for the courage to share himself in a way he's never considered and Jonathan for the strength to tell the truth.

The One Who Saves Me
(2nd Edition)

At fourteen, Andrew Thompson and Caleb Lakes become best friends. As the years pass, they stand by each other through family trauma, school, and the start of their careers. They share their first sexual experiences, learning and experimenting, and they talk each other through countless dates and breakups.

Decades of trust and loyalty build a deep and abiding friendship, one that surpasses any relationship in their lives. But when the parameters of their unique friendship change, neither man knows how to break out of their established roles to build something new. After all, boyfriends come and go, but best friends are forever.

Walk With Me
(2nd Edition)

When Eli Block steps into his parents' living room and sees his childhood crush sitting on the couch, he starts a shameless campaign to seduce the young rabbi. Unfortunately, Seth Cohen barely remembers Eli and he resolutely shuts down all his advances. As a tenuous and then binding friendship forms between the two men, Eli must find a way to move past his unrequited love while still keeping his best friend in his life. Not an easy feat when the same person occupies both roles.

Professional, proper Seth is shocked by Eli's brashness, overt sexuality, and easy defiance of societal norms. But he's also drawn to the happy, funny, light-filled man. As their friendship deepens over the years, Seth watches Eli mature into a man he admires and respects. When Seth finds himself longing for what Eli had so easily offered, he has to decide whether he's willing to veer from his safe life-plan to build a future with Eli.

Made in the USA
Middletown, DE
07 February 2021